PHANTOM LIMB

PHANTOM LIMB
CHRIS KOHLER

Atlantic Books
London

First published in hardback in Great Britain in 2024 by Atlantic Books, an imprint of Atlantic Books Ltd.

1 2 3 4 5 6 7 8 9

A CIP catalogue record for this book is available from the British Library.

Hardback ISBN: 978 1 80546 081 7
EBook ISBN: 978 1 80546 082 4

Printed in Great Britain by CPI Group (UK) Ltd, Croydon CR0 4YY
Atlantic Books
An Imprint of Atlantic Books Ltd
Ormond House
26–27 Boswell Street
London
WC1N 3JZ

www.atlantic-books.co.uk

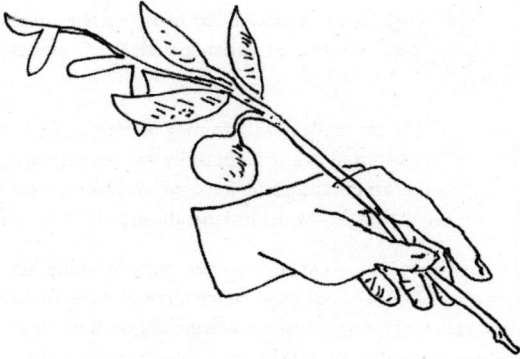

To be yersel's – and to mak' that worth bein',
Nae harder job to mortals has been gi'en.

Hugh MacDiarmid

For Kathryn

CHAPTER ONE

It was his eighth funeral of that week. Like a conductor clipping a ticket, the dead needed him to get them into the ground. Even a few months ago, it had been a job like any other, black shoes and jacket, iron your shirt, comb your hair. But it was beginning to weigh on him. The mourners kept calling him Father.

'That's the Catholics,' one said.

'What do you call the others then?'

'Just by their name.'

The men talked amongst themselves, then turned to stare at him. His first name had drifted away in the last years of primary school. Overtaken by several similarly named boys who had promised to share. He had to admit that everyone called him Gillis.

'What's that, Irish?'

'Thought you said you weren't Catholic?' The man jabbed his elbow into the minister as he passed over a glass of whisky.

'I knew a Gillis at school. Funny guy. Kept to himself, thought he was an athlete. . . Is that you? No? Can't be. . . you're a minister?'

Given the opportunity to explain himself, he didn't bother.

'The running didn't work out.'

His lungs had not been deep enough. His legs had not been long enough. His eyes watered in the cold. He went through a pair of trainers every couple of months.

'That's a shame. What happened?'

'Knees.' Gillis looked down at his suit trousers, and the men nodded.

'I mind you running at school,' the schoolmate pointed at him. 'Away round the football pitches. All on his own. Rain. Snow. Frost. No bother.'

Gillis smiled. 'I know.'

'Still get out?'

'Not with the knees. I can't.'

'A proper champion though, weren't you? Like UK wide. Got medals and all that?'

Gillis nodded. 'I ran in England.'

The men smiled. 'Oh, England.'

Newcastle, Leeds, Manchester, once in London, second and third places, a few finals and qualifiers, some participation medals. Then, the disaster that brought on the knees. After all that, a job in a printer's office, in a hotel, in a shop warehouse. The draught, and then the dregs. He had come back home a few years ago.

'What have you done to yourself?' his dad had asked. He had always been a happy boy. Now, too nervous to leave a room or start a conversation, let alone renounce a tradition, he had gone back to the old kirk, where his granny had taken him to Sunday school. He sat with her in the pews. Helped her make the teas and coffees. The minister, and the deacons, and all the old folk remembered him. They seemed to think his life was ahead of him. The minister was retiring – and dying, though he didn't know it yet. And the Lord asked, 'Whom shall I send?' The silence was deafening. Out of politeness, Gillis answered, 'Send me.'

'Listen.' The old minister had taken Gillis to one side. 'It's not a bad job. The wages aren't much, but you get the manse guaranteed, and a motor, and you'll have your mornings and evenings. Mostly it's just hospital, funeral, home by five.'

He was thirty-one. In a photograph on his granny's shelf, he held a degree in Divinity like a cudgel.

The mourners were bored. An old man had died. He loved the wife he'd left. And the children he'd disowned. He loved the hills he hadn't climbed in thirty years. And the football team whose players he couldn't name. They watched impatiently as tricky corners of cling film were picked from silver oblongs covered in sandwiches, and broad bowls of crisps were set down.

'Help yourselves, folks.'

With a sandwich, a sausage and a whisky all balanced in one hand, Gillis accepted a pint, and then another. He smiled though his mouth was full. People liked to get the minister a drink, and thank him for his lovely words. They looked at him as though he was a boy, new to the world, blushing and blinking, asking silly questions, wanting impossible answers.

There was a toast, and Gillis poured his whisky into a half-downed pint. His back was slapped and his hand was shaken.

'That's what I like to see,' they said.

The dead man's cousin stood on a chair at the back of the pub, his baldy head wavering close to a flickering light bulb. He raised his glass, and the chattering stopped.

'May we all go at life like Sandy did. He never asked what his duty was, to him it was simple. And as for his pleasures, they were simple too. He liked to have a drink, and he loved to smoke. So he smoked! And he didn't care who he was around. Whether it was bairns and babies, he smoked from the age of seven to the age of seventy-eight. For Sandy.'

The man pressed his glass into the crook of his elbow to free his fingers, pushed a cigarette between his lips and passed the packet down to a woman who was grappling at his legs, trying to hold him steady. He leant on her shoulder as he sparked the cigarette and repeated, 'For Sandy!' The mourners laughed, and the old men took out their lighters and fag packets as the barman ran around shouting, 'Not in here, not in here!'

'Leave us alone, ya bastard,' yelled the cousin, but as he tried to step down, his body ran the length of the woman holding him up and his belt buckle snagged at her necklace and collar. The old man unhooked himself, found his feet and griped about freedom. Can a grown man not smoke in peace? Can folk not mind their own business any more? What in hell was happening to this country? Then the cigarettes were blunted on tables or nipped and stored away, or taken out into the rain, and the dead man's cousin disappeared and when he returned he had tears on his face, and the barman had his arm around him. 'I know, I know,' he said.

A baby gurned in the darkest corner of the pub, bound into a car seat, surrounded by dozens of wet jackets and scarves. Between toothless gums, the mother's finger was being softly bitten. She was stretched over toward her friends, ignoring the baby, to laugh and sip from a glass of wine, until she glanced over and caught Gillis's eye. He had drunk enough not to react, and they held one another's gaze. The mother muttered and rolled her eyes, and her friends looked over. She lifted the car seat onto the table and dug her fingers into folds of white muslin to lift the baby out. Pushed her wine glass to the edge of the table and refused another.

'I shouldn't even be drinking, honestly.' She cut a scowling glance back at Gillis. But his eyes were away, wandering over the pub decoration, framed photos of men with collared horses, kneeling next to trophies, standing beside fishing boats, huddled in ancient uniforms.

Underneath, seated in a long line, the dads and granddads, some silent, others immobile, in wheelchairs and oversized black jackets, a regimental pin glinting from a buttonhole. Standing by them, ignoring them, the uncles and cousins shouted over one another, and when their conversations abruptly ended, they scratched at their stubble and jangled the change in their pockets. Running between their legs, kids were carrying cups of tea and coffee to their aunts and auld grannies, getting a pound or a mint, or a toffee from strangers who held them by the neck, or ran hands through their hair, or told jokes and riddles that made no sense. As his gaze completed a full circle, returning to the woman in the corner whose baby was now burping and retching into a napkin, Gillis imagined himself as a lighthouse, big light beaming from the middle of his forehead, cemented in place by the sugared remainder of spilt drink, warning passers-by to keep away from hidden depths and sudden shallows, from rocks that will sink you.

'You're looking lost.' By his elbow, a man's head exceeded reasonable limits. For its sheer scale, its breadth, its height, once its present occupant was finished with it, this skull would have to be cleaned, polished and preserved. Startled, Gillis had to step back to take in all of the features. Crow's feet, drinker's rosacea, cheeks pockmarked with acne scars, along with two eyes, and a nose, and a grinning mouth. The teeth. The parts reassembled when the man spoke. 'Can I shake your hand, Father? It's not an easy job you do.'

The man was almost bald, but closely cropped grey hairs speckled his head and the heights of his cheeks where he had missed shaving that morning. The broad hand which gripped Gillis's looked swollen, as though the gold watch which pinched the wrist was holding in an excess of blood.

'How do you know the deceased?' Gillis asked. The man was still holding him, and smiling. 'Are you related?'

The man laughed. 'No. Not related. I'm their boss. I'm Nichol.' He said his name with a note of false humility, as though it was a title, or a prize that had been won.

'Whose boss?'

'What?'

'I said whose boss are you?'

Nichol let go of his grip on the minister to point across the back wall, where the uncles and cousins, the dads and granddads looked up and raised their glasses, pursed their lips and lifted their eyebrows. 'All of them.'

'Fish.'

'Fish.'

'Aye, fish.'

Nichol had brought a few of the younger men over, and he pointed at each of them in passing – 'Fish farm, fishmonger, fisherman' – then outside, over their heads, beyond the low buildings and houses, to the coast. 'I own the big salmon farms and all they smokehouses, couple of boats, part share in the harbour, the hotel, the wee vans you see kicking about, all of that, and other wee bits and pieces. *Nichol!*' he repeated. 'Honestly, you'll have seen me about.'

Gillis had to shrug. He lived alone, the manse lay in the half-rural outskirts of the town. The fields were nothing but scrub and heather, a scrapyard, a tip, and the rusted rigging of abandoned coal mines. The false hills, partly green with moss, unstable mounds gouged from the earth some fifty, sixty years ago. The kirk which sidekicked the manse was a great heap of granite, topped with a crooked spire, off limits for structural reasons. A kitchen, an office and a great empty hall. The pews had been sold to a junk dealer last year, and the floorboards had been left to swell and split. Sanctuary of burrowing mice, nesting pigeons and in each corner and nook a different species of ant, slater and beetle. He had no congregation – the old folk and the Sunday school had died or drifted away as the previous minister passed on. Gillis had been given a rolling contract, to deliver funerals and visit the sick on a freelance basis. He logged his hours on a spreadsheet he didn't understand, courtesy of a whining laptop, and sent a weekly update to the Church offices in Edinburgh. He tried to keep costs down by eating scavenged dinners of sandwiches and sausage rolls, shortbread, tiffin and scones, collected from the funeral homes, working men's clubs and veterans' halls he spent most of his days in. All to say that his only contact with others was in the preparation and delivery of funerals, and the man's name had never come up.

'Right, I've got one question. . .' Nichol laid a broad hand on the minister's shoulder and looked around at his audience. More of his employees had assembled round, waiting with their smiles ready to go. 'D'you not like fucking?'

Gillis laughed along with the fishermen. He remembered to look up, arch his back and open his throat, smile not just with the mouth, but push the cheeks up to crinkle the eyes. Don't sip the pint too early, don't hide in the glass, don't nip the elbows in. Say, 'OK, take it easy.' He chose one of the men and said, 'Did you like that one?' To divert and laugh at the laughing. He held out for as long as he could until, by impulse, he sheltered in the pint glass. Eyes in a kaleidoscope of lager, their figures drowned in orange light, until he surfaced and shook his head, then stared at the floor.

'Sorry buddy, cheap shot,' said Nichol. 'I don't mean to be coarse, but honestly, what's a young guy like you, in the prime of your life, doing being a minister?'

'Oh. . . there's got to be someone. And. . . it's just a job.'

'Settle down, lads.' Nichol waved a hand over his acolytes. 'I'm just kidding, pal. Ignore me, and ignore all them.' He passed his credit card to one of the schoolboys running past and the boy was given a beer mat and a biro and a small crowd of the kids walked around tallying pints and whiskies and glasses of wine.

'No, I'll be honest.' Nichol gripped the minister by the bicep and leant in. 'You weren't to know. But see you taking the manse? That kind of fucked me up.' Nichol was prodded and pointed toward the barman, who was standing on a chair, waving the credit card. Nichol yelled his pin number across the crowded room, then returned to Gillis. 'We'll talk about it, doesn't have to be now. Enjoy yourself. Give the lad your order. It's on me. . .' Nichol's presence dissolved part by part, the swollen hand left the minister's back, and his heavy shoes depressed the floorboards further and further away, until only the eyes remained, watching Gillis between shoulders, through door frames and chasing his gaze from the back fire door to the broad mirror behind the bar.

Gillis downed the last of his pint. His mouth was full of peat, mud, silt and grass, he couldn't taste the alcohol any more, only the waters and grains, the tannins which backed it. He rolled his tongue about the inners of his mouth and pursed his lips. Then, a harsh acidic belch. Couldn't taste anything. Felt ill. His stomach grappled with his ribs, and he went outside.

'See you later on, Father.' Smokers huddled under a tattered awning shouted him over and shook his hand. Was he away? He was. He wasn't driving, was he? No, no, just looking for something in the back. He jangled his keys as he crossed the road. Checked his watch and his empty pockets, looked thoughtfully at his phone until they turned back to their conversation. Then got in the front seat and started the engine, warmed his hands at the heater, turned on the radio, rummaged through the glovebox and under the seats, filled his mouth with toffees to sober up a little. And when the smokers walked back inside, he drove away, very carefully and very slowly, squinting through the blemished windscreen. Took the back roads, and kept in close to the high hedges. Going thirty in a sixty, he pulled to one side to let a bus go by, and rolled down the window. He waited and waited. Was he going to sneeze? He retched into the gorse and hawthorn.

'You OK, mate?' A car had pulled up alongside his, the man had his window down, and his elbow out, hazards on. Gillis stuck two fingers up. The car left. Others beeped their horns. He was half on the road, half off to the side. He forced another couple of toffees into his mouth and carried on. Ditched the motor at the bottom of a hill and walked the last winding stretch up to the manse, taking deep breaths, pressing from his thighs as it started to rain. His ears were burning red, warm at the core, but chilled at every edge. From the crest of that hill, he could see back to his car, the red paint glowing beneath the last street lamp, a burning ember flit from a fire. All around him, in the darkness, his parishioners. Stone dykes, barbed wire and pylons, sheep and cows that would soon be low-grade mutton and beef, and the moon, his favourite congregant, and the rain, the black trees, the piles of leaves, the rabbits, the screeching foxes, the tarmac and tar, the cat's eyes, the dandelions, the rusted tin cans, and up there on top of the hill, the manse and the old kirk, whose dark cross could be seen, sitting squint, black against the heavy grey and blue of the sky.

He hardly recognized the kirk, or the manse. Up until a week ago, there had been a dark and rotten elm tree which stood between them, overbearing the manse and poisoning the harl, splitting the brickwork of the kirk, running a long crack that wound from the foundations through the hall and set the spire askew. The building was pinioned by scaffolding and metal cables tethered to heavy blocks of concrete. The tree had to go. Its stump now sat severed and heavy in the pit of its roots, pulled and abandoned, its great oxters exposed where the council workers had dug through and run ropes underneath, attached them to the towbar on their van and tried to haul the stump out of the ground, but failed. Like a desperate drunk who in self-disgust refuses to stand, the broad stump of the elm tree had only lifted a few feet, then dropped down and refused to shift from its excavations.

Gillis stepped carefully around the broad empty hole it had left, to the doorway of the manse. In the kitchen he drank two glasses of cold water, then ate the outsider from a loaf of bread, slicked with margarine. Held a cup of tea against his stomach and sipped it carefully. Rooted through his jacket for a cigarette. He had given up, of course, but still smoked one or two when he was alone, and threw the packets away three-quarters full, and bought one again an hour later, or the next morning, so in all the back and forth of chucking out and buying new, he paid for a habit he didn't really have. He walked out the back for some fresh air and sauntered about the house; carefully tiptoeing around the edge of the hole, he leant against the stump of the elm tree. Stared into the dark sky, looking for space junk and satellites.

He drew deeply from the cigarette and watched the smoke as it formed a strange shape that held in the air for a moment. It was the head and shoulders of a man, a little shorter than himself, whirling in the still air, an uncanny mirror.

'Leave me alone.' He reached into the smoke to break its shape, and the ghost was gone.

He let the cold settle on his body. The hands of his watch glowed in the dark. He forgot where he was standing, and with a melancholy sigh, walked blindly forward. His front foot fell into the hole before him and he dropped into darkness, tumbling forward, kneed himself on the chin and bit his tongue. The fall was over as soon as it started, but he had been thrown topsy-turvy, the trouser cuff of his trailing leg snagged in the roots overhead. He pressed his forehead and elbows into the muck, twisting until his legs suddenly dropped as the trousers tore. Folded in half, pinched at the neck, he scrounged on his back until he could turn and sit upright.

He started to cough and laugh, imagining a rose landing on his shirt front and a scatter of dirt across his face and a prayer and a hymn and a word or two from a man dressed just like himself. But stopped as soon as he felt something move. It was a rustle, or a scurry. An animal, a rat? Beneath him, or to his side? At his ankle? Disgusted, he kicked back and scrabbled away. He reached above his head, but the sides of the hole were slick with rainwater, so he dug his fingers and the points of his shoes into the soil and clambered upward. He had ruined his funeral suit. He rolled free of the hole and stared back into the empty depth. A primitive urge demanded that he stamp on and kill whatever animal had touched him. He found his phone in his pocket and shone the torchlight into the midden of black roots and dark mud. There was a spot of bright white. Torchlight reflected against pale skin and red blood. He peered closer. It was a severed hand. Four fingers and a thumb, a broken wrist and a bracelet of ragged flesh. He slid one leg down through the muck, reaching for it just as it began to move, and it turned slightly and curled as though pointing a single accusing finger at his forehead.

CHAPTER TWO

It was hard for Gillis to believe, but there was a whole world outside his house. Billions of people who were wandering around, buying and selling, sleeping and dying, all in ignorance of these moments, this room and this man. They couldn't see him, as he stood with a shovel in hand, dressed in funeral shoes, funeral trousers and funeral jacket, streaked with clay and mud. Half a bucket's worth of soil lay on the careful French polish of his dinner table, on top of an embroidered table runner, now stained beyond use. The fruit bowl had fallen on the floor. An apple had been crushed, and as the minutes passed, Gillis could see its pulp ageing already, beginning to brown. It was part of the world as it had always been. By rotting, it was playing by rules that had been set a million or more years ago, that no object had thus far dared to contradict. But alongside the apple lay a man's severed hand. A left hand. Its white skin, ragged nails, the raw, red portion of wrist, cut squint across the bone. It didn't bleed, but it was full of blood. The skin was painfully cracked. At first, it moved the knuckles only occasionally, as though it was settling or drying out. But as Gillis watched, it opened and closed, grasping for something that wasn't there. It moved around as though orientating itself, then turned toward him and again pointed the accusing finger.

He had seen hundreds of dead bodies. He had grown used to them. They were no longer people, they had become objects. But the hand that rocked back and forward on the table was somewhere between, like a bulb or a seed just planted, both dead and alive. Gillis needed to feel something solid behind him. He took two quiet steps to the side, away from the pointing finger. The severed hand seemed to notice, consider this, then crawl toward him. A streak of mud lay across the table in its trail. It moved to the edge and teetered there. Imagining that it might suddenly drop down and scrabble across the linoleum, Gillis backed toward the kitchen bunker, lifting his feet from the floor. His heart was beating in the wrong place, in his throat, in his head, in his ears. The hand felt the edge of the table, dropped a finger underneath and cannily retreated.

In the deepest kitchen drawer, Gillis had an old shortbread tin, printed with a castle suffering an ecstatic sunset. A coat of arms and an elaborately folded display of bright red tartan surrounded the castle. Inside, the tin was dazzling gold. He threw the plastic wrapping and the last broken remnants of shortbread into the sink, and tiptoed back to the table, holding the upturned tin. He pounced and captured the hand as though it was an enormous spider, and dragged the shortbread tin to the edge of the table, scoring the varnish as he went. The gold interior flashed as he pulled the tin to meet the lid, and flipped both parts at once, then rapped each corner with a closed fist and pressed down, buckling the lid and sealing it with all his strength.

He found an atlas, a dictionary and a great heavy stone, hauled from the garden. He stacked them on top of the lid, then rooted through his rucksack to find his Bible, opened it to the Psalms and laid it over the rock. Maybe God's word would seep from the ghostly thin pages and disinfect whatever demon inhabited that poor bit of humanity, squirming alone in darkness, in ground sugar and shortbread crumb.

Too scared to turn his back on the tin, Gillis ran out the back door, circled the manse and returned by the front. Once inside, he barricaded the kitchen with an armchair and a low bookcase. Trembling in his bed, he unfolded his penknife and slept with it clasped dangerously close to both his aorta and his jugular vein.

He had dreams of animals. A hawk on his arm. A dog's head. An insect with a lot of legs. He woke from each believing less and less in all that had occurred, until he folded the knife away, and laughed when his clock radio jostled and reinstated the ordinary world with a jingle for a carpet showroom. These things can't coexist. Sacred ground can't be upscaled or redecorated. As he sat up, he downgraded the severed hand from a miracle to a hallucination, and all of last night's fear began to shift from something out there, to something within. Was this the beginning of a terrible madness? He washed his face and shook his head as he pissed. He tried to pray, but he never knew how. Now that he was a minister, now that he served at the table, should he still have to beg for scraps? *Lord, keep me sane*, he said to the mirror, and the window, and the descending stairs.

The manse was scattered with last night's confusion. His jacket was thrown across the hallway floor, arms flung out in mimicry of his panic. The dirt from his shovel and boots had been trodden across the carpet. The furniture stacked against the kitchen door embarrassed him, testament to his silliness, so he quietly returned the bookcase and armchair to their places. Then carefully opened the kitchen door. The atlas, dictionary and Bible had fallen from the table, their pages overlapped and crushed together. As he swung the door wide, it struck the heavy rock which he had taken from the garden – it had pierced the linoleum in its fall. His stomach began to ache when he saw the shortbread tin lying open, completely empty. Then he saw the severed hand, pale and bloody as before, writhing up against the fridge. He almost said hello. Fear rose from his stomach, clambering up his body, soon saddling his head and shoulders, blinkering his eyes and pulling at his mouth. He was lost to it. At least God gives you a choice whether to believe in Him or not. Angels and devils discreetly hide themselves, polite enough to veil their faces with mountains, trees and rivers, but now, even the spirits had to shout and scream and force themselves in front of you like adverts for incredible bargains and once-in-a-lifetime deals. This disgusting hand. He stared at the mess it had made of his kitchen. What ill-bred miracle intrudes on a man outside working hours? In his own home? Outrage suddenly bottled, he blinked and squinted. Something was happening, a terrifying noise, a frantic rattle. His phone was on the floor. The number blaring from the screen looked kabbalic. He raised it to his ear, expecting a heavenly choir, the tambourines and trumpets of God's faithful.

'Am I speaking to the minister of Kirkmouth?' the voice asked. 'Did we have it wrong? We were expecting you.'

It was only another death. A fisherman, flung into the water. A thin, delicate woman answered the door. Grey hair clipped into a set of overlapping fringes, all tinted ashen blonde. Tears pushed to the edges of her face. She had dressed up to meet the minister. Pressed black trousers, shimmering blouse overlaid with a cardigan, handkerchief hidden in the sleeve.

'I'm sorry I'm late. I had a. . . thing.'

Gillis skulked toward the kitchen table while she made him a tea. He dissolved a biscuit between his tongue and the roof of his mouth as she showed him pictures. The dead man at work, on a boat, in his garden, with the wean on his knee.

'You're so young for a minister. . . you'd be ages with my son. Maybe you'd know him?'

He shook his head.

'Are you sure I can't take your coat?' This time Gillis relented, and unveiled a battered track jumper, emblazoned with colourful logos and sponsorship deals. Why had he worn that? He took it off; he had a black polo shirt underneath which had a collar at least. 'You don't look well,' she said. 'Are you feeling ill?'

'No, I'm fine thank you.' Only an hour ago he had been stalking a severed hand across his kitchen floor. Could the thing see? Of course it couldn't. Could it hear? No. Could it feel his footsteps? Maybe. He'd lunged, dropped the tin back over the hand, then slotted the lid beneath. Like a rugby player mid-scrum, he had pressed his neck and head into the fridge, rocking it back until there was just enough space to slide the tin underneath. Then he'd carefully laid the full weight of the fridge down on the shortbread tin, which bowed at its edges, but held.

'If you'd like to delay?'

'No!' He shuffled a set of documents that he needed to give to the family. 'No. I'm good, I'm grand, I'm good to go.' He cleared his throat and began his little spiel. 'Now, when we bury your husband. . .'

'My husband? I'm sixty-five! He was my son.'

Gillis hid in his papers, frowning through his collection of pamphlets. He started to read aloud the titles and keywords, passing them one by one to the grieving mother, until the focus drifted from himself to the grim finality of it all.

'Of course, a funeral is a time to honour the deceased.' Gillis knew this part by heart. 'But we must make time to think of ourselves. What do we want to say, that we might not get a chance to say again?'

She stared beyond the pamphlets, to the table, then turned to him, eyes misting over. 'Will my boy be in heaven?' It had always been hard for Gillis to stomach the clichés, the soothing visions of endless wheat fields and summer holidays, white robes and clouds, streets of gold, all your old cats and dogs, and a full cast reunion of your dead. But now he could answer with conviction, thinking of the severed hand.

'There's some kind of life after death, yes.'

'I know that's where he is. Waiting for me. . .' The woman tried to prompt the minister into his duties.

'Yes.' What if the hand had overturned the fridge and escaped? 'I wouldn't be surprised if he was.'

'I can just imagine him saying, *Mum, don't fuss over me, stop your silly crying. I won't be back for dinner, I'm up here in heaven.* That's the kind of thing he'd say.'

'That'd be nice, wouldn't it.' Maybe the severed hand belonged to someone he hadn't buried right, who had come back to strangle him in his sleep or poke his eyes out. *Try me,* he thought, *come for me and see what happens.*

The woman stood and walked to the window. 'Here she is now.'

'Who?'

'The wife.'

There was a rattle of keys before the door swung open. 'Look who it is,' the young woman said as she came in. 'Marathon Man.' She had brought in a draught of cold air, and there was rain speckled across her jacket. She held a few shopping bags and a folder full of paper under one arm. For a moment, Gillis was so startled that he forgot her name. It was weighted down with so many memories and associations that it required near on physical hauling and dredging through his skull to unearth.

'Rachel.' He managed it. They had known each other most of their lives. Sunday school, primary, secondary. Kissed her on a dare. Tormented one another for years, cheating and fighting through high school, renting a flat together, splitting the bills, settled into domesticity at twenty, abandoned for good at twenty-two. Her hair was naturally blonde, but she had dyed parts of it blonder. A small boy followed after, muzzled by the overlapping collars of his shirt, jumper and jacket. The older woman began to witter as she unzipped the boy's jacket and pulled at his wrists, while Rachel laid down all her burdens and unexpectedly, when she stood again, pulled Gillis close and kissed his cheek. His face and neck were cooled by the rain on her jacket. She still wore the same perfume. A decade ago, Gillis had strained his bank balance, gritted his teeth and sprung for the bigger bottle. Maybe she'd managed to eke it out, all these years, dilute it a little, but keep the essence. Or maybe she'd been smelling the same for years, through birthdays and boyfriends, bottle after bottle.

They lingered in an awkward silence until Gillis nodded at the boy and asked, 'What age is he?'

She hesitated. 'Si. . . Seven.'

'Oh, for goodness' sake.' Her mother-in-law looked disgusted. 'He turned eight in the summer. Didn't you?' She prodded the boy, but he didn't speak. 'Your mummy doesn't even know your age.'

A quick scan of the timeline worried him. Almost ten years since he had left Kirkmouth. Time enough for a pregnancy and a curtailed childhood.

'Anyway,' Rachel ignored her mother-in-law. 'You're a minister now?'

He quickly explained what she already knew. The running, the medals, the trip to England, the disaster, the knees, the physio, the attempts to start over, to try shorter distances and different disciplines. All that failure, and he wasn't going to admit to the job-seeking, the redundancy, the unfair dismissal, and the year or so spent living in his dad's front room, so he just said, 'I wanted to help people.' Though all he had done was bury them. He was a step away from walking through the streets and ringing a bell. *Bring out your dead.* His mouth hurt a little. He was gathering all the flesh of his face in tight points on either side of his head. It looked more or less like a smile.

'And you?' Gillis tried to divert attention. 'What have you been up to?'

'I've been grieving.'

Gillis was sorry, he couldn't imagine. He hadn't known she was married, he had never asked anyone about her. He had sort of assumed she was still waiting in her parents' kitchen, trying to get him on the phone.

'He always tried to call himself a fisherman, but he was an accountant really.' Rachel pursed her lips. 'He shouldn't have been anywhere near the water, I don't know why they had him out there. He didn't know what he was doing.'

'When was this?' Gillis asked.

'Two Tuesdays back. They gave up looking a week ago. They say with the currents, and the depth of the water, the body could be anywhere. We thought we may as well go ahead.'

'Closure,' the old woman called across the room.

Rachel nodded along. 'We're looking for closure.'

'And it's been a week? Sorry if you couldn't get in touch, I'm bad for not getting back to people.'

'It's not me that's seeing to it,' she leant a little closer and whispered. 'Mother-in-law's not letting me.' Jerked her eyes toward the older woman and tightened her face into a prim, stoic smile, then walked to the boy standing with jumper, jacket and scarf piled at his feet like autumnal leaves. 'Come on, I'll get your shoes off.' The boy sat on the sofa with legs sticking out. As she untied the laces, she said, 'We tried other places. But they were all busy.' She took a seat next to the boy and tangled her fingers into his hair. 'This is Jamie,' she said. 'He's named after his dad's dad. Aren't you? And your dad's dad's dad. There's generations of Jamies.'

Gillis waved, but the boy was sulking and staring at his knees.

'I don't think he understands what's happened. Or it hasn't hit him yet.'

'If only we could see the body. He could have said goodbye.' The older woman fussed at the table, refilling a little basket of biscuits, arranging them in a line. 'For me, seeing my mother at peace. . . it was a big help.'

They talked over the options. What the Church could do, what the funeral home would handle. Rachel let her mother-in-law decide on everything. 'Abide with Me', 'Amazing Grace', 'There is a Redeemer', a passage from the Bible of the minister's choosing.

'*In my Father's house there's many mansions, I go to prepare a place for you?*' Gillis quoted. The mother-in-law nodded. They'd have teas and coffees at the end.

'Can we have that in the church?'

'It's not in any shape for that. But the funeral home can organize something.'

'Mr Nicholson offered to help.' The mother-in-law raised her palms and shrugged her shoulders, surrendering slightly to Rachel's frustration.

'We spoke about that,' she said.

'The poor man feels responsible. Which I told him was ridiculous. Accidents are accidents. Fishing is a very dangerous profession.'

'He was an accountant.'

'An accountant for a fishery.'

Rachel rolled her eyes as her mother-in-law bustled from the room. 'I'm sorry about this,' she mouthed at Gillis as they followed.

'Here's what we have,' the mother-in-law led Gillis upstairs, trailed by Rachel and her son. On the floor of her bedroom, an empty suit was laid out next to an empty football uniform, as though two men had lain on the floor and evaporated. Shirt inside waistcoat, inside jacket. Black tie carefully knotted, trousers belted and zipped, spring of heather in the lapel, and a pair of good black shoes, freshly polished. Next to a bright red goalkeeper's jersey, grass-stained shorts, long socks and football boots, and two absurd goalkeeping gloves, palms open and expectant. 'We've agreed on the suit, haven't we?'

'Have we?' Rachel dragged the back of her hand across her forehead.

'We said it was more fitting. Now, will we need to weigh it down with something?' The mother-in-law turned to Gillis.

'Weigh what down?'

'The coffin.' She pointed to the side of her bed. 'Here's what we thought we might put in, but none of them are very heavy.' A couple of trophies, a games console, a watch, a stack of photographs. 'Those are the definitelys. That's the maybes over there.' A favourite jar of jam, a favourite tin of beer, a favourite film on DVD. To one side, a set of red and black barbells. 'Those might be too heavy?'

'I was dreading this.' Rachel walked him through the front door. 'Seeing you again. I didn't know if you'd know? How I got with Douglas after you left. Or that we were married and had Jamie. You're not on any of the social media. So. . . I didn't know.'

Now that her son and mother-in-law were hidden inside, watching cartoons and eating biscuits together, her movements relaxed a little.

'What is it you were studying again?' It was on the tip of his tongue. 'Total. . . Totality Management?'

'Hospitality. And Tourist Management.'

He nodded. That was it.

'All that did was qualify me for the job I already had. And when Jamie came along, Dougie's wages were enough for a while.'

'You're letting in the cold,' her mother-in-law yelled from the living room.

'In a minute,' Rachel called back. She stepped out, closed the front door behind her, folded her arms and leant against the door jamb, steadying herself against a shiver that rustled her shoulders. She let her eyes meet his. Although each of them had long prepared for the silence that followed, although they had both rehearsed airtight accounts of their actions, and memorized the chain of events which justified their own failings and cast the other's as pure, unjustifiable sadism, they both let the moment slip by. So in place of anger or recrimination or even forgiveness, they could only pass back and forth a polite, embarrassed smile.

'We think we'll burn him.' Rachel broke the silence. 'Feels silly to bury an empty coffin.'

'Seems sensible.'

'All they said is it wasn't suicide. Just an accident. You forget these things happen. What with all the technology.

You'd think it wouldn't. Maybe this kind of thing happens all the time?'

Gillis shrugged. Though he knew it didn't.

'Want to hear something funny?' Rachel asked. 'I prayed last night. Not prayed since I was a little kid. Want to know what I wanted? My shopping list?'

He nodded.

'I asked God to send him back to me. And if He couldn't manage that, just to send a bit of him. To know what happened. You feel like. . . maybe he just buggered off. Ran away from his responsibilities. From his debts.'

Gillis thought of the severed hand, and the severed arm that it once must have joined to, the severed torso and severed legs and severed head. For the first time, he wondered who was missing.

'Calms you down a little, doesn't it? Praying. It's like sucking your thumb.'

Gillis could only agree. 'But what's wrong with that?'

'Nothing wrong, nothing right.' She shook her head, and shivered again. Pulled her jumper sleeves over her fingers. 'Anyway, I've got the tea to cook, and the boy to bath. . . It was good to see you again.'

'You too.' As he turned from the front door, away from the words just spoken, he was surprised to have meant it. All those years avoiding her, all for that? His bad leg twitched and he thought again about the empty suit, laid across the floor. The shirtsleeves and the cufflinks looped around nothing. The severed hand must have been severed *from* something. He was struck by the obvious. He had pulled it from the ground without checking for an accompanying arm, or torso, or head. He hurried to his car, fussing in and out of the wrong gears as he rolled into the street, watching

as the lights in Rachel's house turned off, staring at the
empty windows as he passed by.

He drove recklessly. Parked and left his keys in the ignition,
headlights scalding the manse garden, the stump of the
great tree and the hole below. He ran across to the kirk and
ransacked a back cupboard. A jumble of mismatched tools
collected over half a century, scraps of piping and tiling and
two-by-four pine. An ancient pick with a rind of cement
encrusted along its edge.

Envisioning a shallow grave set into the roots, an unquiet
spirit, a victim calling for revenge, he dug at the edges of the
hole until the sun began to set. Striking root after root, the
blade began to slacken from the handle. His muscles warmed
as his skin froze and he began to emanate a haze of steam. He
gouged and scored away at the depths until his back trembled,
as though it might collapse in weakness. He drove the car
closer to the hole, but saw nothing. He wanted another hand,
or a foot, or a face. A corpse to reanimate. An ear to listen to
him, an eye to see him, a mouth to tell him what to do.

Hands prickling, fingernails full of dirt, he gave in and
warmed them under the kitchen tap. After a long period
of fearful countdowns – *ten, nine, eight, I'll do it, seven, six,
I won't, five, four, I will, and two, two, two, I will, one. . . and
zero, now, do it. Now* – he bowed and drove his shoulder into
the fridge, freeing the shortbread tin. Jumping back as he
pulled it free and popped the lid, he had expected the hand
to attack; instead it opened finger and thumb as though
shyly reaching for something. Scrolling through his phone,
he tried to find photos of Rachel and her husband online. He
found a profile picture, now the headstone of a memorial
page dedicated to the dead man. He zoomed in further and
further, examining the shape of the man's hand. The hair
that covered the knuckles. The blunt, stubby fingers. He held

the image close to the severed hand. From one angle, they looked similar. From another, completely different.

Late in the evening, it occurred to him that the hand might have something to say. To him, or to Rachel, or to pass on from the other life, wherever that was. He laid blank sheets of paper down like bedding for a dog, and used a wooden spoon to coax the hand from the shortbread tin and roll across the paper. Then he placed a pen between its forefinger and thumb. It seemed to sense that it was holding something, gripped and rolled the pen, scribbled a little, relaxed for a long moment and suddenly, in a tight squirrelling motion, drew a face that stared upwards, with a tiny little man striding across the eyeballs.

Hundreds of years ago, a dark, heavy cloud collected its water from the rivers and lakes of a dozen countries and condensed these waters high in the atmosphere, in a vast construction of towers and battlements. The cloud blocked the sun, and cast the following days into dreadful shadow, until the cracked earth and the weakened sinews of old rivers began to demand that the rain fall. When the cloud broke, water fell unevenly across the dozen countries, respecting no borders, punishing one corner while sparing another.

Beneath its anger lay a young man named Jan, an apprentice painter and a terrible swimmer. His clothes and his boots dragged against him as he struggled in the currents of the river he had been thrown into. Insults and laughter followed in the wake of the boat above him. A sailor shouted, 'And take your magic book!' From the railing of the boat which had carried him over the channel and up north, into the open mouth of this country, his book burst open in the wind like a frantic, flightless bird. With a heavy slap it landed on the water, divided through its middle. And the embossing on the cover rushed through with water, the leather blushed black and all the gilding, all the ivory and vermilion and verdigris, carnation and turquoise, the thousand colours which had been dutifully mixed by the apprentices and applied by the masters of the Guild of St Luke, rushed into the cold water and began to dissolve. Jan, the apprentice painter, struggled into the draw of the ship's passage to catch the last corner of the book as it sank, cold water sotted to the hilt of the binding. He hefted it from the river like the wheel of a cart sunk into boglands. As the water carried him away, contradicting the passage of the boat, the jeers and gobs of spit which arced from the deck receded and he lay on his back and allowed the river to carry him. He opened the book and laid it over his head like the roof of a tiny house, uprooted and loose in the terrible waters of a world-ending flood. A woven red ribbon, a bookmark sewn into the hilt, dropped across his face, and he held it in his teeth as he lay back in the coursing currents of the river.

Saltwater ceded to fresh, and the in-drawing tidal currents slowed. The wide sails of the boat carried it seaward. Too weak to swim, Jan lay on his back and concentrated on the sky. There was blue in its black. Ignoring the painful cold and the shore he couldn't see, he drew his knees up and clutched his hands tighter around the book. The river ran through a violent spot and the book dropped into the water again; at each dousing, it lost saints and angels overboard, and the tight script of Psalms and prayers unravelled into the water. As he entered the country, he left a thin golden tail of rippling paint, like a comet falling to earth, his passage unnoticed.

As he tired, his legs drooped, and his toes grazed over what could only have been an enormous fish, here to swallow him or grant his wishes in return for its freedom. Then close to his eyes passed a blade of grass, a brave flagpole, jutting from the course of water. Another, a spear or standard, a reed, a teasel, bent against his shoulder and buckled as it passed him. Then the fish returned to his toe, and transfigured into silt or sand, and he burrowed down and found he could stand, just barely. Sinking in muck, he steadied the book on his head and tasted the cascade of water and paint running from the illuminated pages. Gilt, rain, river water and gold leaf ran through his scant beard and cropped hair. Like bristling pins or paintbrushes, clumped reeds and blades of grass stuck out from the water. He grabbed a handful and pulled himself forward.

As the sun strained against the horizon, Jan witnessed the creation of land, a country of his own. The Lord separated light from darkness, then divided the water above from the water below. A blaspheming witness, he trudged back and forth on the bare tread of land that emerged in the middle of the wide river.

'God's blood, God's wound, God died,' he repeated. Through the dawning morning the water receded, down past his knees and ankles, to expose a long sandbar that split the river. He pressed an armful of reeds down over the slop of mud and tried to sleep, clasping the ruined book to his chest like the fastenings of a jacket, and muttering. *God bless these sandbars*, he thought. Miraculous little nations created anew every night, which have no religion, no walls or forts, that welcome every stranger and couldn't care what they believe or where they were born. Turning to one side, he crushed the left-hand pages of his book, and as he slept, the territory diminished.

CHAPTER THREE

The spine of Gillis's Bible was deeply scored in just a few places. Left to fall open in his hands, the pages collapsed to either side, revealing, one by one, his funeral verses.

'*The righteous perish, and no one takes it to heart.*' Though he had started with confidence, he could feel the spine of his Bible straining as he cut a new division into the glue. He had strayed, and didn't recognize the verse.

'*The devout are taken away and no one understands.*' Sitting before him, Rachel stared determinedly at the middle of the lectern, ignoring the words he read. Her son sat by her, watching the floral arrangement and the coffin it concealed. Beside the boy, gripping his shoulder, the dead man's mother grimaced at the minister, gritting her teeth through the words that Gillis spoke in a steadily slowing monotone. He was trying to make them so dull that they would be ignored.

'*The righteous are taken away to be spared evil.*' Behind the widow, the son and the mother, rows of black suits, with occasional dark grey or deep navy mixed throughout. Workmates and school pals, cousins and uncles, his mother's friends. In their laps, in their pockets, at their mouths, shrouded in sleeves or encased in gloves, rooting through bags, clutching handkerchiefs or folding orders of service, their hands lay in a hundred different expressions.

'*Those who walk uprightly enter into peace.*' Gillis was too distracted to notice the heads turning upward, smiling slightly, feeling the resolution of the Bible verse. He carried on. '*They find rest as they lie in death.*' Some faces flinched at that last word. '*But you – come here, you children of a. . .*' The next word was *sorceress*. The verses went on to cover adulterers and prostitutes. Rebels, offspring of liars, who sacrificed children in ravines, who placed pagan symbols on the walls and behind doorposts; Gillis flushed red as he scanned down the page, searching for a phrase to end on. The paragraph before the page break seemed, at first glance, suitable. Clean of any insults at least. *When you cry out for help, let your collection of idols save you. The wind will carry them off, a mere breath will carry them away.* He slowed, trying to find the sense of the paragraph, pronounced the last few words deliberately and underlined them with a religious expression and a soft thump of his hand against the Bible. '*But whoever takes refuge in me will inherit the land.*' He gripped the lectern and stared out at the collected mourners. They bowed their heads, they stared at their hands. Then he chanced his eyes toward Rachel. Her head was tilted upright, her expression was stern, her face was sallow and drawn as though she was biting the insides of her cheeks.

'If you'll please rise.' On command, all hundred and fifty of them stood, and sang. The organ played, and the coffin disappeared.

'Have you burned it yet?' Gillis stood over the coffin, massaging his right hand. It was aching from all the handshakes he had been subjected to, a tendon behind his thumb trembled. Men sought to leave an impression. They grabbed at the flesh, and tried to mould it into the shape of their own.

The funeral director solemnly shook his head. 'There's a backlog.' They were in the basement beneath the funeral home. 'We couldn't get the furnace hot enough this morning. . . It's only getting there now.' A convoy of black and brown coffins lay along the corridor, a patient traffic jam interrupted by several coffins that lay at an angle, cutting in line from recent funerals, eager to burn.

Gillis had his satchel gripped underarm. It had been hidden inside the lectern throughout the funeral. He had been standing on it while reading from the Bible. Inside, behind his papers, bound with several leather belts and a few pointless shoelaces, was the shortbread tin, within which the severed hand scratched and tapped.

'I always think the mechanism just leads straight into the fire!' Gillis shouted above a clatter of trolleys jostling over uneven concrete flooring.

'People worry they'll see flames!' the funeral director shouted back. 'They don't want to think about hell!' He had missed a few greying hairs from the base of his nose, and it looked as though he was growing a minuscule moustache. Gillis couldn't remember the man's name, even though he worked with him nearly every week.

'It was a good turnout,' the director said.

'It was. . . Are you actually going to burn it?'

The director looked puzzled.

'They never found the guy that died. It's just got clothes and a couple of CDs in it. I thought you might empty it out and use it again?'

He shook his head. 'They bought it. We burn it. That's the deal.'

At the end of the corridor, next to a line of three coffins, men in blue overalls were throwing spanners and screwdrivers into a toolbox. They rubbed their hands and laughed loudly as they explained why the furnace had been failing to ignite. It was something to do with clogged filters, a build-up of ash.

'Listen,' Gillis had been trying to build up his confidence to ask for something strange. 'You know the widow, Rachel? She wanted me to have a last look inside the coffin. Just to say a prayer. And chuck one last thing in there. Something she forgot.' He patted his satchel. 'Can I?' He tried to lift a corner of the lid.

'It's all bolted down. . .' The director looked up at a sudden grunt, then whine, from the conveyor belt, as the trolleys began to jostle forward now that the furnace was back up and burning again. 'I'd have to get permission. I'd have to check with the mother. She's paid for all of it, so it's more her decision.'

'Do you know,' Gillis contorted his face at the funeral director, trying out eye rolls and raised eyebrows, none of which broke through the man's cold exterior, 'I wouldn't bother. To be honest, she said it to me kind of offhand, I don't know if she expected anything. It was more like, *Maybe I should have done that?* And I wanted to say to her I'd tried.'

The director nodded. 'It's easy enough to call her?'

'No! I wouldn't. Not now, let's just get it moving. I've never seen it, you know, I've never seen it going in.' Gillis loosened the shortbread tin from his satchel, his hand veiled by the folds of his jacket. He hoped that a moment would appear – maybe the funeral director would turn his back – when he could throw the severed hand into the flames. Before or after, or on top of the coffin. Laying the whole thing to rest. Forgetting everything. He could sleep through the night again.

'I'm happy to tell her you added it in?' the director said. 'For all the difference it would make.'

'Don't tell her anything. I don't know if she expected it. It's one of those things, she was crying and she said something, and I made a promise, but did she mean it, did she not, it's that kind of thing. Y'know?'

The funeral director didn't know, and wouldn't know; he was drawn into a technical conversation with the boiler-suited cremators. They mentioned overheating elements, build-ups of splintered bone. As they talked, they moved the coffin from its trolley and onto spinning metal rolls which led into the furnace. It glinted evil and hot, the all-consuming fire, confined behind a little door. Gillis walked along with the coffin, waiting for his moment. But every inch of the process was monitored. Gillis pictured himself leaping between the workers and flinging the severed hand inside – he could almost smell the skin burning, almost hear a terrible scream, an echo down the corridor. As he daydreamt, the light and heat of the furnace burst into the room when the grate was opened and the coffin was suddenly pushed inside. The door was immediately closed, clamped and locked. The workers moved on to another task, and the director was shuffling notes in his hand for the next service, silently mouthing the loved one's name. Through the tiny window that looked into the furnace, Gillis had hoped to see the coffin burn away, but the flames were far too bright.

'Can I ask you one last question?' Gillis touched the funeral director at the elbow. The man looked irritated. 'Have a look at this drawing, tell me what you think it is?' He had been carrying the first doodle which the severed hand had made. He unfolded the slip of paper and laid it on the order of service which the funeral director was studying.

'I don't know, a desert island or something.' He quickly passed it back.

'An island?'

'Isn't it?'

'No, look again, it's a little man standing on a bigger man's eye.'

The funeral director frowned with impatience. Gillis met his expression with complete innocence, his eyes wide open and the rest of his face soft and relaxed.

'I'm too busy for this.' The director's shoes made clip-clopping noises as he escaped along the corridor to meet his next clients, another huddle of grieving relatives. Left alone, Gillis wandered toward the workers who monitored a few pressure gauges and thermometers, and shouted questions at them. How did they grind the bones down? Did anything ever explode? 'There's a machine for it,' they said. And pacemaker batteries sometimes popped, but that was all. Now that the flames had bitten into the coffin and died down a little, Gillis could see the brass handles and corner fittings, the only things which would remain.

'Guys, what do you think this is a drawing of?' he asked.

The men squinted at the paper.

'Your boss said it was a desert island?' Gillis suggested.

'Is it fuck.'

The back-room bar of the Nicholson Hotel had been dusted and hoovered, the red velvet chairs shrouded with white coverings, tucked into fold-away tables, and pressed tight into a border that surrounded the room. Plates of food were laid out and rounds of drinks were ordered in hushed voices.

'I won't say no,' the crowd of mourning men said.

'A pint, is it?'

'Go on, aye, a pint.' Solemnly, they toasted the dead man, toasted his trade, and toasted themselves by proxy. They remembered his kindness and gentleness, and after a while, they remembered his tight fists and his temper.

Rachel stood alongside the minister, pulled back and forth as the hands of various family members reached out to console her, and rescue one another from the awkward, stilted conversation. Below her, Jamie looked up at Gillis with wide, terrified eyes.

'I don't think he likes the black shirt,' she said.

'It'll be the dog collar.' Gillis pulled the silly white ticket from his throat and undid his top button.

As Gillis straightened his shirt, a hefty old man, related somehow, a great-uncle or a second cousin, pressed through the little crowd surrounding the widow. He took Jamie's face in his hand. 'You're the man of the house now,' he said. 'You'll have to look after your mother. Will you do that?'

Jamie nodded into the depth of the old man's eyes.

'That'sa boy.' The man stood slowly, one knee strained and cracked as he pulled Rachel close and whispered in her ear. Hoarse advice and consolation, his own wife had died, he had to learn how to cook his own dinner. Now look at him, he'd put on three stone, his cooking was that good. 'And she always used this washing powder that made me itch. Forty year she used it and I never knew why my neck was itching, or why my wrists and my ankles were coming out red. Now, I wash all my own clothes with that other one. Is it the bio or the non-bio? What's the one? The green bottle, the one that's got a blue swirl. You see it on the telly. What is it?'

Rachel didn't know. The old man asked the woman sitting next to him, and she asked her sister. The sister asked her husband, who scowled, ignored her and stared into space. The chain of questioners looked back at the man, who shrugged. Then he tousled Jamie's hair and grinned at Rachel as he repeated, 'You're the big man, the man of the house,' before leaving so as not to miss the good sandwiches. 'Better get myself in there before the gannets descend.' He moved through the crowd as though he was swimming.

Then Jamie was alone, below the sight of the adults who distracted his mother and pulled her toward an ancient relative and a poorly told tale of young love and early death. The boy was lost amid the old and middle-aged in a room he didn't know, that stank of alcohol and wet wool; held in the ill fit of his Sunday best, pinched at the neck and waist. A black jacket that scratched, and grey trousers that bunched at the back, bound by an elastic belt. His toes were pressed into a pair of shoes with a strange pattern cut into the leather. His mother had rubbed stinking black shoe polish into them that morning, but gave up halfway through rubbing it off again. They were mockit with excess polish.

Gillis leant down to the boy but Jamie ignored him, concentrating instead on holding his trouser legs, bunched at the knees, away from the dirty shoes. But the minister pushed the boy's chin up to unpick the black tie from his collar.

'Should we go get a drink of juice?' he asked. Guided by the back of the head, Jamie walked through the function room and into an empty corner of the hotel kitchen. Gillis closed the serving hatch and lifted the boy onto the metal counter, then he rolled the black tie and placed it in the boy's pocket.

Harried and exhausted, Rachel found the pair trying to watch cartoons on Gillis's phone. Her cheeks were deep red, flyaway curls of hair spiralled from the tight wind at her crown, and Gillis was shocked at the sight of her. Anger made her glow.

'We've been eating biscuits, haven't we?' he said, but the boy ignored them both and focused on the screen. The webpage was crashing, the audio played as the image froze. 'Well, we have been,' Gillis smiled.

She ignored him. 'I can't not know where he is. You can't just take him away.'

'He was needing a break.'

'I'm the one who decides what he needs. He needs to be with his family.'

'Just thought it was a bit much for him.'

'I know what's too much. I looked down and he wasn't there, so I've been going around asking where he was. And someone said he left with a man. Do you know what that could mean?'

Gillis laughed, 'But I just took him for a drink of juice.'

Rachel pulled the phone from Jamie's hand and pressed it into Gillis's chest, then lifted the boy from the counter and held him close. 'I've got enough hassle from all them, thinking what they think about me, about how I am, how I'm a mum and I'm not right, and I'm not good at it. Without losing him, without them thinking that I can't look after my own baby.' Her words caught in her throat, and her face gripped tight around her eyes. Jamie turned his face away from her sadness and squirmed until she put him down. He took a few steps away and turned his back on her. She stood on her own, pressing the back of her wrist into each eye, and flinched as Gillis tried a comforting hand on her shoulder.

He straightened his suit and ran a glass of water for each of them and soon they stood in a row with their lips wet, glasses now half-empty. Gillis sighed, and Jamie sighed in harmony, and Rachel dipped her fingers in the last cold dregs of the water and touched it to her eyes and cheeks before drying them on the sleeve of her black cardigan. She sipped the remainder and laid the glass gently in the steep trough of a wide metal sink. Then, as though her spine had suddenly snapped, she folded in half, and undid her long hair until it all hung straight and untangled. Upside down, she collected it all together and wound it through her hands, binding with a black bobble, so that as she stood slowly all her hair was contained and smoothed away from her face and shoulders. 'Back out, I suppose,' she lifted her child, returning to the cloying fold of gossip and commiseration.

'Where's your lovely tie?' he heard them ask Jamie, and he pulled it from his pocket.

'Come here, son, I'll give you a hand putting it back on.' His collar was buttoned and his shoelaces were double-knotted. They asked around for a comb, and parted his hair to one side. 'The spit of his father,' they said.

Gillis emptied his glass and saw, once more, behind his eyelids, Rachel inverting, collecting her hair and returning.

Prawns and kippers and smoked haddock, tuna and salmon sandwiches were stacked in odorous heaps. All your basic ham and cheese were gone.

'Sick of this shite.' The dead man's friends, all fishermen of some kind, picked through the crusts and flung anything from the sea to one side. 'Eat it day in day out.'

The jukebox began to play a run of three songs that would end in a jolt of silence, until the bar grew noisier, and trays of drinks were handed back through the crowd like wartime supplies.

'Minister. . . Minister Gillis, can I say what a good service we had there?' Nichol's broad, majestic head loomed toward him, flanked by a series of employees. But even as he spoke, one eye wandered over Gillis's shoulder, scanning the room, as an ear monitored a distant conversation. 'When we lose a friend, we need a way of saying goodbye. A way to underline what matters in the world, and for that, it's the Church, isn't it? The only option. I'd say, you just can't beat it.'

If the man had been at the funeral, Gillis hadn't seen him. But this was his hotel, his back room and his bar; he was standing drinks and welcoming stragglers as though the deceased had been his own son.

'Douglas was a good man, and a terrific father. But unfortunately, he wasn't much of a swimmer.' Nichol laughed at his own joke before realizing that no one was joining in. 'He wouldn't have minded me saying that. Remember the mouth he had on him? Sometimes it was a bit much. Even for me.'

Men that Gillis didn't recognize sulked in dark corners. 'He shouldn't have been near the water,' one said, listening in.

'Aye, you might be right there,' said Nichol with a tight smile, and then he excused himself to move around the room, chatting and joking but avoiding Rachel and the close family, drawing the attention and energy of the room in his wake. Gillis sought out his rain jacket and his satchel and explained to the barman, 'I'll have to be heading,' even as he accepted a pint and leant back against the bar. As he sipped, he could feel the severed hand scrabbling against the shortbread tin clamped under his arm. It almost tickled. If the room hadn't been so noisy, they all would have turned toward the metallic scribble and clink.

'Hold on a sec, listen, wait a minute.' Nichol was on the back foot, defending himself from a grizzled old man.

'I'm long retired, son, long retired.' A friend of the drowned man's father pointed tobacco-stained fingers. 'So I can say what I like about your lot.' He described the

Nicholsons. A grandfather who owned two fishing boats, a father who owned ten. And an ungrateful child who'd cashed in and sold up the boats and sacked the old fishermen. Dug ponds and farmed fish like they were wheat! Whoever heard of farming a fish? This drowning never would have happened under Nichol's father's watch. They respected the sea back then, the man said. They took what they needed. Arrogance, that's what had killed the boy. Greed. Ignorance. None of them could navigate. None of them could graft. Half the men couldn't even swim. They wore life jackets to splash in puddles. None of them had children. They were all still children themselves.

Nichol quickly agreed, seeing a chance to break away. 'The boat's covered with handrails and walkways and I give them all rubber boots. But if they don't wear them, what can I do? They're grown men, it's their own responsibility. He was just off shift from the office, and he was wearing his leather shoes. Simple as that. Accidents happen.'

'There's no fish out there,' the old man grinned. 'Is there?'

'Accidents happen.' Instead of replying, Nichol straightened his back and rose above the conversation, loomed over the room, examining dark shadows and distant faces.

'The only fish out there are the ones you flung there.'

'Accidents happen.' Nichol shook his head.

'Aye. You were chucking them back 'cause they're all rotten, aren't they?'

Nichol loomed close to the man's face, 'Have you met the minister?' And he grabbed at Gillis and pushed him toward the old man until their faces almost touched. Nichol used his momentum to shove by them, wind his way to the bar, out of any danger.

'He's no his father,' the old man said.

'Nobody is,' Gillis replied.

The night repeated as so many had. They wanted to get the minister a drink. And the minister couldn't say no.

'Let me ask you a question, Father, how do you think Rachel's coping?' asked an anonymous face that blurted from the collar of a bleached white shirt.

'She's been through a lot.' Gillis steadied himself against a pillar, satchel and shortbread tin hidden behind his back.

'She has.'

'But she's a strong woman.' He could see the back of her head; nodding, pretending to laugh, then being forced into a long embrace and a pep talk.

'She is that. Putting up with Dougie. God bless him, he wasn't an easy man to be around.'

The jukebox had been stuffed with a glut of pound coins, and the lights had been lowered. The mourners assured themselves, it's what Douglas would have wanted. A few women were dancing together, moving in the orbit of black-suited men who were too scared to dance in front of their pals, so defended themselves with leering comments and pointed to their wedding rings. What they'd do if they were ten years younger. What they'd do if they were free. A picture of the dead man sat on the bar surrounded by lilies and knots of lifeless grass.

Gillis's gaze washed across the ceiling, onto the walls and all around the room. As his thoughts returned to his stomach where the hand lay encased in tin, and as he straightened his jacket, adjusted the satchel and resolved to leave, he started to worry that the hand might burrow into his body. Grab parts of him and start chucking them out. A liver? Who needs it? Out it goes! A lung, whack! Planked on the table, dripping blood onto the carpet. Intestines wrapped about his arms, heart dropped down between his ankles, still beating. He clattered his glass down on the bar and made for the door.

'Gillis!' Nichol snagged his arm as he pushed through the crowd. 'Kind of a weird question here, and maybe now's not the time, but if you have a minute, I'd like your help, if I can?'

The minister tried to refuse and push through the crowd.

'It really won't take long. . . Ah, there's Dougie's dad and step-mum, or his step-mum and step-dad or something. Pair of snooty pricks. Hang on.' Nichol gurned at the old couple as they left. 'Such a tragedy, such a terrible mistake.' They ignored his outstretched hand, holding their noses in the air as they passed by.

Gillis took the opportunity to escape by the propped fire exit, into the dark, wet air. He leant against the brickwork and breathed carefully. In through the nose, and out through the mouth. Where had he parked his car?

'Thought I'd lost you.' Nichol appeared next to him. 'Off to the car park? I'll walk with you.'

They started off up the drive, away from the noise and light, Nichol shouting illegible banter at the smokers under the awning, while Gillis focused on breathing deeply and trying to slow his spinning vision.

'You'll know about the plans I have. For the kirk?' Nichol turned his attention to the minister. 'Well, listen, it came up in a property sale for a very good price. This was two year ago. I was flash with the cash back then. Now, when the deeds came through, I got a real shock. Didn't know I got all the graves as well. And my plan had been, sell the manse, get a bit of quick cash, use it to cut the kirk into flats, sell them off one by one. But who wants to look out on a graveyard every morning, know what I mean? Now, I've went around reading the dates on those graves and there's not one before nineteen hundred and who gives a fuck, so what I'm thinking is, dig them up, drop them somewhere else. But see, trying to find out how to do that. . .' He rolled his eyes. The bloody red tape. 'So here I am, I own this lump of granite I can't use for anything, and my money's all tied up, turns out the place is listed, can't knock it down. And then we pull out that big tree and cracks start appearing all over the walls, right up into the spire. We put up all the scaffolding and now what? It's a money pit. I thought, lawsuit. Get them on false pretences, because I didn't know I'd end up owning and having to upkeep two hundred graves. But then I wondered if you could sound out your bosses, have a word and see if they'd be up for taking the bodies and gravestones out? Consolidating sites or something. There's piles of room in that other one. I'd be happy to help with it. Maybe you could sound them out? Get the ball rolling and all that— Watch yourself now!'

Nichol's monologue was cut short as Gillis suddenly pitched forward, hands on knees.

'You OK there, minister?'

'Fine, fine,' Gillis muttered. He'd had too much to drink, and tripped on a loose slab or a stray root or worse, on his own feet. He groped for the stone dyke that separated the car park from the scrap ground and leant against it, refocusing on Nichol.

'I want to do right by you, Gillis, because I appreciate what you're doing for the people here. For Rachel and Dougie, God rest him, and for the family and the wee lad too. Those beautiful words you had back there, what was it? Trust in God and you'll inherit land? That makes you think, doesn't it. Lot of wisdom these old timers had.'

Gillis hadn't followed the conversation. He wanted home, he wanted to sit in his house and eat toast until he felt better. He could have a sit-down and a long think. What to do? How to be? How to go about doing what he should do, and being how he should be?

'Have a look at that.' Gillis searched his jacket and pulled the little drawing which the severed hand had made from his top pocket. Nichol stared at the image. 'What do you think it's meant to be?' the minister asked.

'I don't know, is it a ship?'

'Can you not see a face?'

'I'd need my specs.' Nichol moved to hold the drawing beneath the orange streetlight, while Gillis tried to imagine a pair of glasses which could span the breadth of Nichol's head. 'What's it meant to be?'

'I don't know,' Gillis said. 'That's how I'm asking.'

Nichol found his glasses. They looked handmade. Ovular lenses bolted to a wonky length of wire, they folded around his face and sat squint on the tip of his nose.

Nichol shifted the drawing back and forward in his focal range. 'Who's this meant to be?' He stepped close. 'Are you on the wind-up? After a good pal of mine dies. And I charge nothing for all this. They still can't stop gossiping, can they? Is it meant to be a joke? A man's dead, and they draw cartoons?'

Gillis didn't understand. Nichol seemed to grow, feeding on his own anger. Suddenly, Gillis was holding the drawing again – Nichol had pushed it into his chest, forcing him to let go his grip on the satchel. As he stepped backward, his knees and ankles were suddenly betrayed, and he watched his feet tumble overhead, tripped by the low stone dyke behind him, into a tangle of nettles and dandelion heads.

As he fell, his arms opened wide and his head cracked against a heap of stones, spilt from the wall's construction. His satchel flung open as his arms flailed and the shortbread tin shot loose and burst on the scattered stones, and the severed hand lay exposed, framed by the bright gold interior. Nichol followed him over the wall, and bent low to cradle the minister's head in one hand.

'Easy, buddy, you all right? Didn't mean to scare you. . .'
But he stopped short as he squinted through his glasses at
the golden light emanating above them. Passing headlights
ricocheted against the tin, and Nichol stepped beyond Gillis
to lean down and touch the severed hand. He prodded the
gory red end of the wrist bone, and all colour bled from his
face. His eyes divided starkly into sharp white outlines and
tiny spots of black, and he turned to Gillis with a fearful,
questioning look. Nearby, the smokers, having jeered or
clapped at Gillis's fall, began to gather.

'Don't!' one woman cried out, assuming that Nichol was
about to attack the minister. As they collected, rumours
passed among the little assembly. Was he hit? Why was he hit?
And who was he? They saw nothing in the tin but maybe a
pulped fruit or a weird toy, a contorted doll, something from
a joke shop. But as they approached, Gillis rolled through the
weeds and reassembled the tin, the pain in his head following
in slow-motion pulses of weighted blood. Clutching the tin
tight to his body, he forced it back into his satchel.

'What was that?' Nichol asked as Gillis stumbled over the
wall, holding the back of his head. It was bleeding, and a
weird lump was beginning to develop.

'It's nothing.' The minister's feet zigzagged with indeci-
sion, then took him toward his car.

'Where did you get that?' Nichol held on to Gillis's jacket,
and the onlookers began to call for a truce, or a proper square
go at least. Gillis spat into the thistles. Nichol pulled at his
jacket, grabbed his arm, asked his question again, but was
pulled and held back by the mourners.

'It's not worth it, mate! It's not worth it!' they shouted.

'Leave it, Nichol, leave it,' they said as he pushed back.

'Kill him!' someone shouted from the developing huddle
– hushed by disapproving voices but goaded by laughter,

the joke kept on. 'Kill the cunt, Nichol, pull his head off!'

But Nichol's friends and employees held him by the shoulders. He pressed against them, and they generated strength as they tangled, Nichol trying to force his way toward Gillis, who was fumbling in his pockets for his car keys. They held Nichol back until he turned on them, shoving one into the other. They protested, they were only trying to help! You can't go battering a minister, can you? As they argued amongst themselves, Gillis limped to his car, cradling his head in his hands, until a spell of dizziness unseated him and he fell backward, sitting down in the full beams of a slowing car. He carefully lifted his head to see Rachel staring down at him from the car above, as though her body was made of two swirling circles of golden light.

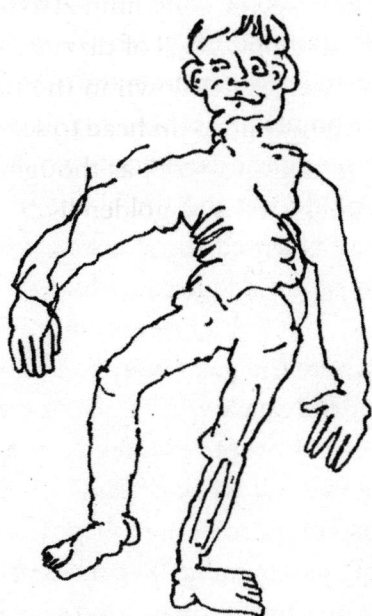

A bell rang. Faintly, from the church tower, or bright and close, from a horse's bridle, or the point of a jester's shoe, calling the faithful to prayer, or the workers to work, or the lords and ladies to laugh. Wrapped in what could have become his shroud, Jan, the lowland painter, clamped his teeth about the flesh of his cheeks and shivered against the painful itch of chilblains emerging on the points of his fingers and toes. Steam rose from him, from his clothes and boots which lay over-close to a fire, they would scald and smell, but Jan was too weak to care. They had warmed some beer for him, and cut it with ginger and onion. He held it close to his chest. The bell kept ringing, moving closer, and Jan stirred to look out a window where the glass warped the dawn light into patches of brass and shadow. The street was all mud and puddle. Cart tracks wavered like reeds in a river. The bell drew closer. He needn't work or laugh. It was an ageing, doddering monk cut loose in the villages, stepping in time with his handbell, proclaiming. 'Repent, repent, you sinners!' An old refrain. 'A new time is on us. God's house is in disarray. A shame on you. On you, sir. On you too. A shame on me. Repent!' The bell stopped as the monk passed by the window. Jan gripped and tightened his blankets.

'Have a drink, Brother Malcolm. Malcolm! You'll have a drink?'

'Aye, come in, monk, and see something we found. A weird fish we pulled from the river. A big white eel that speaks!'

'Come see his golden book.'

Brother Malcolm came inside, smirking, 'Repent, you daft sinner. You long-haired liar. You shrew. And you there, with no shoes. This is holy ground! Wrap your legs in the words of God and walk in His light. And repent, you sinners!' His words were drowned in a froth of bitter ale, and his bell shivered as he set it down beside him on the ageing planks of a long bench. In the middle of the bare room, Jan's golden book lay open, spilling saints and angels. The monk parted the crowded company who stared at the book, whose arms were wet to the elbows, who still held short wooden paddles and lengths of rope, who had only just now returned from the fading continent, the sandbars which appeared nightly, mid-river, which had shipwrecked Jan as he had floated backward into this country, a selkie too ugly to seduce.

Quiet words and a pointing finger flit to accuse Jan. 'A shame on you, sir, a real shame, you'll repent for this, you'll repent. And I'll repent too.' The monk shook his head in dismay, set his beer on the floor and carefully pried the pages apart. 'Oh, they're here, all the saints are here, and you've killed and tortured them all over again. Was fire not enough, did they have to drown too? Oh, God will punish you.'

The monk looked down with disgust. Bright green and yellow pigment were smudged across his thumb and forefinger. What had been the yellow feather of seraphim wings, and the long grass it descended to, he pressed and printed against the rough scrim of his jacket.

'Oh, you will suffer,' Brother Malcolm repeated. 'Thieves get the gibbet.'

Backed into a corner, Jan searched through his pockets for his papers, trying to reassure the monk and the fishermen that the golden book belonged to him. He unearthed pieces of flint, handspans of kindling and pulls of sheep's wool, and a little bag where he kept a handful of seeds and nuts, now mulched into a cold porridge. He shook the jacket in despair, imagining his papers lying in the silted bottom of the river he had just been pulled from. He upturned his satchel, unfurled a roll of leather which held his pig's hair brushes, and his knife, and a binder's awl, and a wind of thick thread streaked with beeswax, and three small sheets of gold leaf, now as fragmented as moth's wings. And in the remote corners of his satchel, softened, stodgy briquettes of pigment, for touch-ups and repairs.

'How would I have any of this if I was a thief?'

The monk and the fishermen were on their feet. 'You could have stole all that too!'

'But I didn't!'

'But you might have.'

Then, in one last desperate unfolding of his jacket, he found, bright white against his black coat, the identifying papers which held the wax seal of the Guild of St Luke. The paper was wet, and the heavy stodge of wax was tearing it to pieces.

'Look, it says here that I'm a messenger, and that I carry a delivery for a Laird of Hamilton, which is a Book of Hours and Prayers made as a gift to his wife. Commissioned, now delivered. And I'm to receive the payment and bring that back to my employers.'

The fishermen looked to Brother Malcolm, who leant over the papers. 'I'm not so conversant with writing,' the monk said. 'But the words look about right.'

Jan nodded and took his papers back, and relaxed some as the fishermen lost interest. The barman's wife was bringing over bowls of broth.

The monk folded the book and pushed it to one side. 'Ask God to hide you,' he said, lowering his voice. 'And dull these paints, and cloud your mind and break your fingers. There's an illness in this country. You'll see its symptoms soon enough.'

CHAPTER FOUR

'You should all be ashamed of yourselves,' Rachel muttered as she pushed through the little crowd and stooped to examine the slick notch in the back of Gillis's head. The blood that was spilling down the back of his ear and over the collar of his shirt. 'Come on, this'll need cleaning.' She pulled him to his feet and spotted Nichol backing away through the assembled mourners and employees. 'This anything to do with you?'

Nichol shook his head, amazed at the allegation. 'He fell.'

'Everyone's falling, aren't they?'

Nichol bit his tongue and opened his arms in exasperation, then turned to complain to his subordinates.

She led Gillis through the back courts and bins to the kitchen fire exit, propped with a half-brick, allowing the stifling sweat of a hundred dinners to dissipate. 'Go sit on the counter,' she pointed him in the right direction. His eyes were watering, but he wasn't crying or anything. It's automatic when you get a jolt to the head, or even in the cold air, he explained. Used to happen on his winter runs.

Rachel knew the chef and the two kitchen porters who were hunched over the washing-up, scrubbing pots and heaving grey plastic trays in and out of the steam washer. A deep steel sink choked through the last gulps of oily black water, while in the one next door, steel pots and iron pans stained beyond recovery lay in a soft cloud of lemony soapsuds.

'Watch that floor, it's just been washed,' they called to her in unison.

Rachel walked flat-footed, steadying herself across the whirling brushstrokes of water, then opened a crypt-like chest freezer and leant over the edge, forcing her arm deep into overlapping packets of frozen vegetables. Even half-blinded by the knock to his head, Gillis couldn't help staring at her body. Her skirt rose beyond the knee, her legs were taut, overlapping, she writhed a little as she returned, pulling free a packet of crinkle-cut carrots. Her shoe had slipped sideways and she danced it around until her heel was straight again. Gillis pretended he hadn't been looking as she bundled the carrots in a dishtowel and held it to his head.

'He's got some punch on him, that Nichol,' the chef was wringing his hands through a dishrag. 'I had him knocking lumps out of me once and I thought, fuck, this is me, man, I'm dead.' He laughed and threw the rag onto the drying racks. Rachel brought Gillis a glass of water and they all watched as he drank. The chef examined the cut and patted Gillis on the back. Diagnosed him with wounded pride. Gillis agreed, it was nothing, just a fright.

'You don't want the hospital?'

He'd be all right, he claimed. Carefully, he released his satchel from a desperate underarm grip, and shyly poked around the edges of the shortbread tin, searching for his car keys. Half-expecting his wrist to be grabbed and twisted behind his back by the severed hand contained inside, he pulled the jangling keys loose with a weird, relieved smile. The chef laughed.

'You're not driving,' Rachel said. 'For one, you've been drinking all night. Don't think we didn't see you. And for two, you can't shift gears and keep that icepack in place.'

He'd get a cab, he said. He'd pay extra to bleed on the seats. Maybe they could put a bag over his head, or wind a scarf around his neck. But Rachel refused – she was the only one sober. She thanked the chef for his help and started toward the fire exit.

'On you come.' She prodded Gillis in the back. 'Bring your carrots.'

She was driving too fast. Gillis reeled from the bucking of the car, from the flickering lights ahead. His head felt like it was expanding, ballooning out to fill the car. His shirt was spattered with blood.

'Are you sure I can't take you to the hospital?'

He slowly shook his head, careful not to rattle the brain, didn't want any more of it spilling out. 'They'll just wipe up the blood and send me home.' The words came out shorn of their consonants. All those sharp ascenders and descenders might do him some damage. He nuzzled closer to the cold glass of the passenger window, avoiding the critical gaze of his own reflection.

'You shouldn't be trying to keep up with those boys.' Rachel gripped the steering wheel at its apex. 'They're fishermen, they couldn't throw up if they tried.'

Gillis recognized nothing in the darkened streets they were passing through. Bare metal fencing and harled houses, trees like a crone's hand, and each approaching set of headlights was followed by an after-image of the oncoming driver, faces set in stern, unrelenting judgement.

'What is it with men and fighting? They can go ten years, twenty, no bother with anyone. They can be dads and granddads, but after a certain point, something just clicks and they'll be back at it like wee boys. With Dougie, Christ, he'd try and say he fell over at work. He'd have all these scabs on his knuckles.'

'We weren't fighting,' Gillis explained. 'I just got a fright and fell over.'

She looked over, sceptically. 'Well. . . I wouldn't worry about the guys laughing at you. They'll just be glad it wasn't them.' They weren't a bad lot, she said. And most of them had been in the same position, upended into ditches and thrown over walls, dooked in the sea, flung into streams and rivers. Nichol ran Kirkmouth like he owned it. And he did own it. Just about anything you could look at, there he was, him and his father and his grandfather. A petty empire sprung from a few fishing boats.

'Just up here.' A winding black road snaked uphill and ended with the kirk and the manse on either side. It had never felt like home, too weighed down with the previous occupants, whose fittings and furniture, clothes, ornaments and books had been left behind, passing into the common ownership of the Church. Gillis had a suitcase worth of objects scattered around, claiming little territories for himself. Toothbrush and shower gel, razor and toenail clippers. A stack of trainers and boots by the front door. A clothes horse covered in black and dark grey trousers. He looked over his shoulder at the empty back seat.

'Where's the wee man?' He imagined Jamie alone, abandoned in the hotel bar.

Rachel laughed. 'It's one in the morning. He's at his granny's.'

They rounded the last corner of the narrow road. Tarmac gave way to gravel and compacted mud as they passed by the front door, to the gap between the looming kirk and the manse.

'Watch that tree stump,' Gillis said.

'I'm watching.' But the car suddenly lurched and dropped downward. Rachel gasped as they pitched recklessly to the left and were flung sideways. Gillis's arms flailed and he gripped at the glovebox, which popped open as the fall abruptly stopped, spilling toys, sunglasses and unopened bills into his lap. A front wheel spun uselessly; the car had shifted and disappeared into a space below Gillis, as though the earth had opened and attempted to swallow them. Rachel stamped on the accelerator, but the wheels were braced tight at one side, and loose at the other, and the car only rocked slightly as it settled and in frustration, she honked the horn. 'Fuck,' she hissed.

They climbed free of the car. The wheel on the passenger side was completely hidden, buried underground. The car lay thrown to one side, pointing its headlights into the upper storeys of the manse. Rachel walked around in dismay. 'You *dug* this hole?'

'No, I widened and deepened it.'

'Why?'

'Why. . .? I was trying to dig up the roots. See the stump.' He pointed to the black mound which terminated the driveway. The dead elm under which the severed hand had appeared. In that week since the hand's discovery, between hospital visits and funerals, Gillis had been watching the uncanny movements of the severed hand, and straining to interpret the idiotic drawings which the hand continued to make, observing coldly as waves of fear rose and broke over him. He had begun digging further and deeper underneath the tree, scraping at the thick clay soil, both dreading and hoping to find further body parts beyond the next spadeful. Then, following a vague intuition, he had struck out to the middle of the driveway and cut a fresh hole, dug until he lost the feeling in his fingers, and worn himself out in the process. Having worked so hard, he had slept through a full night, with no dreams of severed arms strangling him in his sleep, or pulling out his tongue, or cutting off his dick. Of course, he couldn't dig a hole in the ground every night. But the temptation lay there, and after work, alone, the sound of the TV lost his interest and the shovel beckoned. He shared none of these reasons with Rachel; instead, he described how the winding of a tree's roots, as she probably knew, could undermine the foundations of a house. She looked unconvinced. He told her that the kirk had a terrible crack running through its brickwork, which was true, and that the tree had been pulled down to save the building. Also true. She trod carefully about his handiwork. Three waist-deep holes lay in the ground, all leading toward the elm tree. Four, including the one that her car had fallen into. She looked over at him, down into the hole, back to him, up and down his body. Part of him wanted to shout, *I've found a mysterious body part and I don't know what to do! It seems like God is sending me a message that's getting scrambled in the transmission!* But the runner in him, the rod of self-discipline which he had been able to wield over himself, forcing his legs and lungs from strength into weakness, wringing the last drop of energy and strength from his body, urged silence and patience. *Wait,* it said, *pace yourself. There's a medal here, there's a trophy in this.*

Inside the manse, two, going on three in the morning, after Gillis had stumbled around, pushed at the front and back bumper, after he had sat on the bonnet as Rachel stamped the accelerator, trying to give the spinning wheels some purchase on the dirt, after they had raked the garden for broken branches and gravel to pack the wheels with, after he had retched into the empty flower bed, and reminded her that his head was still bleeding, and the sweat across his forehead and down his back had chilled him until he shivered in a way that looked a little fake, but honestly wasn't, they sat at the bare dinner table with cups of red, milkless tea scalding their fingers and tongues. They had given up.

In the middle of the table, the packet of crinkle-cut carrots melted in an ignoble heap. 'It was good for me, I think,' Rachel said, a fragment of a hidden monologue. Gillis looked over in surprise. 'In the end. When you went away to try out your running. I was really angry, then I was sad. Then, just bored. I wanted to have something I wanted that badly. I did my degree, but that wasn't it. Not sure I ever found it.' The last of the tea was bitter; she picked loose leaves from the tip of her tongue. 'After a race, you'd have this faraway look, like you'd been somewhere. Like you didn't recognize me, you didn't know where you were. And I thought when you went down to England, that was it, you were off into the history books. How could you be that committed, and not have it come to something? I thought the next time I saw you, you'd be on TV.'

'So did I.' Gillis empathized with himself. 'But I had the knees.' He squinted in mock-pain, pointing at his leg.

'The knees.' She nodded. 'I forgot you had those knees.'

When the tea was finished, he locked himself in the bathroom and washed his head, handling his skull like some newly uncovered artefact. He still had the satchel hanging tight under one arm.

'Are you all right in there?' Rachel called through the door.

'Fine.' He pushed the satchel into the corner below the cistern and opened the door. She had two white pills and a glass of water.

'They're good ones,' she said. 'They'll knock you out.' As he swallowed them, she touched his neck and ear, steadying him, to examine the little gouge etched into his head.

It was strange to have someone inside. She was the first guest to see what he had done with the place. Next to nothing. He had taken most of the furniture and stacked it in the shed. But the kitchen was very clean, and the grouting of the bathroom tiles had been scrubbed so well that it had crumbled and fallen out in loose squarish grounds. It was a new thing, this tidiness, provoked by his discovery. Because when he wasn't burying or burning, or digging holes outside, or scrubbing the walls and mopping the floors, his mind inevitably turned to the severed hand.

'You're welcome to stay here,' Gillis told her.

'I'll have to, won't I?'

'We could get you a taxi?'

'That's another hour. Them coming out here, me getting taken back. I'm better off sleeping. Head in the morning.'

'You'll take the bed. I'll take the couch,' he said with a note of chivalry.

She noticed that he wanted a response, 'I know I will. After all that?'

'Just a minute.' He held his head together as he walked up to his bedroom. The mattress lay upended against the wall. He had been scrubbing the wooden slats and frame, he had washed his sheets and pillowcases at boiling point. Unfortunately a blue biro had been caught up in the tangled cotton, and the greying sheets hung from the curtain pole, with expressionistic splotches of ink spread across them. He reassembled the bed, and stretched the stained bedsheet tight across the mattress. Smoothed wrinkles from the covers, and sprayed deodorant into the stale air. 'OK,' he called over the banister and Rachel began to climb the stairs.

'They're not dirty or anything, but the bedsheets look a bit funny.' He flung the covers back as though revealing a painting. 'It's kind of beautiful in a way?' He waved his hand over the tie-dyed sheet. 'Looks like a ship there. Or a sheep actually. Or a cow? Head there. Horn. Legs. Missing a leg there. Like it's turned toward you?' Gillis traced the outline of the animal with his finger, but Rachel ignored him and threw her jacket on the bed, blinkering the cow.

'It'll do fine.'

'I'll be downstairs.' He took a jumper and joggers from his chest of drawers and left her to it. She didn't respond when he shouted up, 'Take anything you need!'

After the upstairs lights clicked off, and her footsteps returned to the bed, Gillis waited a full ten minutes, watching the clock hands creep acutely from one number to the next, before he retrieved his satchel from the bathroom and examined his shortbread tin. Its lid was sitting wonky and bent now that he had fallen on it. He checked over his shoulder for intruders. The hand was still in there, still moving, still making gestures as though expressing an uninterrupted conversation, conducted by a distant brain and a whispering mouth. Maybe still encased in mud beneath his feet. It curled and uncurled its fingers, then turned to find him and pointed ominously. The sharp fingernail seemed to be accusing him of something. He covered the tin and pushed it underneath the sofa cushions. Wrapped himself in blankets and lay awake in darkness, shifting around the sharp corners of the tin that dug into his back, wondering, *What did I do?*

It didn't take long for answers to trickle in. Everyone has a past. Maybe that was it, maybe the hand wanted him to atone for something. He could start with Rachel, an honest apology, beginning with a promise not to drink again. And to avoid arguments with local businessmen. He would promise to help her and her son in any way he could, starting by waiving his fee for the funeral service. From there, he would range bravely across his many failures, as a man, as a minister, and in the distant past, as a boyfriend. Beginning with primary school, pigtail-pulling, rumour-mongering. He had told the class she still believed in Santa, and that her dad had lost his job, and was growing a beard. He had stolen money from her schoolbag, and burst her nose in a badly timed tackle. He had accused another boy, and been believed. In high school, he would confess, he told the boys she had let him finger her beneath the railway arches. He would tell her they wanted to smell his fingers, and he had let them. He had described her body to strangers. Ranked and compared her to other girls.

After leaving school, he persuaded her to stay at home, and stay with him despite their arguments and breakups. They had been given a caution by the police, for shouting at each other in the street. A vengeful text message, a tearful weekend. He had worn holes in the knees of his trousers, begging for forgiveness. They got back together. Saved their money and rented a flat. Then he fucked off to England and stayed for years. Left without a real explanation, a panicked last bid at success which came to nothing. Stopped returning calls and hid out at his mum's place, never came back except for Christmas and his dad's birthday. Year after year, skulked through the bus station with his hood up, for fear of seeing her in passing. Why was the severed hand interested in any of this? Some of it, he probably wouldn't confess to, but just keep things on an abstract level. Describe how he had kept her at a distance, flinched away from her warmth, but been angered by her coldness, receded and blamed her for the distance created. If Rachel needed an apology, surely one overarching *sorry* could cover everything? As long as he was thinking about all the specifics as he said it. The severed hand would know what he meant.

A pressure grew in his chest, as though his bones were calcifying. Was there any escape? Any excuse? How could he account for himself? Well, to start with, he hadn't had it easy growing up. What kind of example had his parents set? They could have made him kinder and friendlier, stronger and more confident. It was probably, actually, all *their* fault. They should have forced him to practise smiling, until it came naturally. Everyone likes to see some teeth. He only smiled on sports day. Envied as *The Fastest in the Class*, he walked around gloating, giving condescending advice to his schoolmates. Try taking bigger strides. Try standing a little taller. Try putting one foot in front of the other a little quicker, that'll make a big difference. He became *The Fastest in Scotland* for a year or two, once he had found his niche. In the mud-spattered countryside, grazed knees, sodden trainers, lanes of the course barely distinguished from a slurry of mud and sleet, but what had that come to? Nothing! He had run away to England to train and run in the big races, but it came down to the knees. The bastard knees!

People had known his name, and shouted it from the sidelines. It was etched into trophies and medals, written down for ever in magazines and newspapers. He still had them saved, a mouldering bundle in a back cupboard, the corner of his page folded down. He had expected his name to be shouted and screamed and used to describe a method, a style, a whole philosophy. Both of running and of living, squinting into the sun, folding his socks just so, tying his laces twice, turning his eyes away from the other runners, celebrating nothing and shaking no hands, ducking underneath the white tape and mingling with the spectators, like a king incognito among the common folk. Taking the bus home, still stinking and spattered with mud.

All leading upwards, into silver and gold, until he lost his temper and fucked it all up. A nice woman in physio broke the news. Ligaments banjaxed. And he limped around for a year and still had to hobble and stretch the leg every night and every morning. And didn't have the humility to come back home, after bragging and burning his bridges, so had stayed away and ignored the long texts and emails Rachel sent and when she phoned he let it ring out, too scared to even hang up and let that petty brutality tell her that he wasn't coming home. But what else could he have done?

He lay on the sofa, relitigating old arguments with his fists tight, stared out the living room window into a rectangle of inky black, stirred by currents outside, branches, winds and somewhere far beyond, a poor shivering herd of sheep. He should run out and join them. Eat grass and live among the animals. He was only fit for a riverbed or a sharp rock or a razor and a cold bath full of blood.

But then she wasn't perfect either. So to defend himself against the severed hand, he listed Rachel's faults. Her coldness and her distance, by which method he slowly absolved himself, and chipped away at the block of stone in his chest until not only himself and Rachel, but everyone in his life, however tangential and fleeting an appearance they made, seemed to be stricken with the same debilitating condition. The running clubs, the football teams, the schools and colleges, the shops and petrol stations, the hospitals, the Kirk, the judicial system, the aviation industry, the oil and gas board, the retail sector, all tourism and foreign trade, and every charity for every kind of affliction and deficiency, all in terminal decline, all steeped in conspiracy against his ambitions. How deep had this sickness set into the world? It was immeasurable, the scale of it, he dwarfed himself and his faults in the overwhelming shadow of history and geopolitics. Wasn't he living through a worldwide recession half his life? And wasn't the system rigged against the common man? Wasn't it impossible to live an honest life in a dishonest world? Soothed by the threat of apocalypse, he turned onto his side and fell asleep.

In his dreams, a dark corridor, a hole in the ground, a river, a set of golden letters, a crowd, a fire, a building collapsing. Then a vision of Rachel, haloed by the hall light. Wearing only her underwear and one of his T-shirts, a black funeral jacket draped over her shoulders. She didn't speak, but walked over, lay down next to him and slept in his arms. Again and again in the night, he woke to find her still there, sometimes asleep and lightly snoring, and sometimes awake. He could see the tips of her eyelashes, blinking as she stared into the darkness of the room.

Morning light illuminated the curtains, and framed Rachel's silhouette as she rose from beside him and left the room, returning fully dressed. She sighed, and searched the floor for her purse, phone and keys, brushed her palms over the crinkles in her blouse, and scraped a fingernail across spots of blood that pockmarked the front. Gillis watched her through cross-hatched eyelashes, afraid to break this brief moment of peace. He knew that an inch above him, a crushing headache waited; four or five inches above that, as he sat up straight, the pain would slip from his forehead and spill down his neck, into his stomach, as the alcohol shifted and the wound in his head thumped with each heartbeat. Once he sat up completely, he knew that Rachel would turn around and the pain would keep shifting. Regret would flicker across her face, but she would politely hide it. They would be strangers again. He pushed his head further back into the cushions and pretended to sleep. She worked her hair through her fingers and tied it all tightly at her crown. Her shadow passed over him. In the kitchen, she spoke to a local garage – did they have a good tow truck? One that could take a bit of punishment?

The minister sat up slowly, battling through blotches of colour.

'I didn't want to wake you,' she spoke from the hallway. She was hidden by the frantic speckling of his retinas and he shielded his eyes inside his elbow. When he looked again, she was gone. He rose with the blankets. She was standing in the hallway, looking out at her car.

He prodded the back of his head. A bird's nest of dried blood and hair covered a painful cut.

'Come here,' she said. 'Let me see.'

He bent to one knee. She moved his head back and forth, staring into the wound. Could she see through the little hole, into his thoughts being formed?

'You'll survive.' She patted his shoulder and walked back to the window. Staring at the tilted car.

In the bathroom, last night's shirt lay draped across the radiator. He arranged a shaving mirror to clash with the mirrored glass bolted to the tiles, so he could stare at himself in miniature. Prod at the cut. Could *he* see what he was thinking? He imagined his hair parting to reveal a little stage, and a set of tiny actors, who would replay the night before. If he could look at himself objectively, analyse the situations he found himself in, maybe he'd know how to act right. He scrubbed his face with soap, tasted the flowery suds, filled the cool ceramic sink with freezing water, and dipped his head. Opened his eyes and stared at the black rubber plug.

'Can I ask you a question?' Gillis dried the backs of his neck and ears, ruining a good towel, as he walked through to the kitchen. Rachel stared at an incoming phone call until it stopped.

'Sure.'

'Was he a good man?'

'Who?'

'Your husband. Douglas.'

'Oh. He was OK.'

'Only OK?'

'He was good with kids. Close with his parents. Had a lot of friends. He was good enough.' She flinched as she spoke. 'You don't have any bread, do you?'

Gillis pointed at a plastic packet. 'And your husband. . . did he have anything on his hands? Like a mark or a freckle or a mole or anything like that?'

She stuffed the thick end slices into the toaster. Found margarine and jam, shook her head along the way, in part-answer to his question. 'He didn't really have anything in particular. He was good-looking though. And he had really clear skin. I know what you're doing.' The toast popped and she scrubbed margarine into the black crust and crumb.

'What am I doing?' Gillis asked.

'You want to make me look more like a widow. That's what they all want. I don't know why, but I can't be a widow. I don't have it.'

'I don't want you to cry.' *Actually*, he thought, *you've no idea why I'm asking.*

'They're going to need to know where I am.' She stared at her phone again, as it jittered silently in her hand. Another call was coming through.

'Was your husband religious?'

'He was a lovely man, what do you want to know? He walked on light.' She ate her toast as a tow truck reeled up the driveway and blared its horn.

'I don't want to be a pain, but could I see a photo? I've seen his picture, but I'd like to get a better look at him.' He followed as she collected her bag and clothes together.

'Where's my coat?' It was on the back of a chair.

'Maybe just send me something? Or if there's some online, I'll look there.'

'Where's my bag?' It was in the hallway.

As she reached the door, she turned back and pointed. 'OK, this is the story. . . you got hurt and I brought you here. Then I went back and stayed with a friend, that's all you know. I'll get the car pulled free and get it seen to, and no one needs to know I was here last night.' She opened the door and the driver of the truck, who was walking across to meet her, flung his arms out in frustration, pointing at the holes in the kirk garden.

'Why are these not fenced off? I could have drove the truck right into one.'

Rachel reacted, said it wasn't her driveway and they weren't her responsibility.

The man circled the stranded car, swearing and shaking his head. Gillis watched from the doorway, caught between the warm air of the house and the deep chill of the morning. The man attached a big hook to the bumper of Rachel's car, and there was creaking, clanking, and a few unhealthy knocks and scrapes when the car dropped down to four wheels and was dragged back from the hole. The man unhooked it and waited for payment. They argued. Rachel forced him to check the car. To find out what that creak and clank had been. The man tried the ignition and the engine turned over but didn't catch. Rachel swore.

'Listen,' Gillis shouted over. 'I'm happy to go halfers on however much it'll cost.'

She gripped her arms to her body as the car was coupled to the truck. The driver began to explain what would happen next, ignoring Rachel and shouting out the cab window to Gillis. The minister nodded along and retained nothing. The mechanic revved his engine, ready to leave. He opened the passenger door and shouted out to Rachel. She turned to go and the pause as they looked at one another could have been filled with a kiss or a hug or a promise to meet again soon, but it wasn't. Instead, he felt around in his pocket and found a little drawing which the severed hand had made.

'Was your husband any good at drawing?'

'I don't know,' she said. 'No.'

He unfolded the paper and held it in front of her, 'What do you think that looks like?'

'I don't have time for any psychological shit.' She pulled away, and Gillis followed her toward the truck. She climbed up into the seat.

'I know, but what do you see?' He held the drawing up to the cab window, stood in the way of the door closing, even as she leant out and held the handle. The mechanic shouted and Rachel shouted back, then looked down at the drawing for a second or two.

'I don't know what it is.' She squinted closer. 'A baby smoking a cigarette.'

The truck's engine revved, and as Gillis stepped back to look at the drawing she took the opportunity to slam the door closed. They stared at one another through the glass. Face severe, black clothes tight to her body, hair wound tightly to her head. She lost her name for a moment, lost her personality. She looked like any passenger, any bystander, any randomly selected member of the electoral roll. The truck backed out of the kirkyard and down the circular driveway with a high-pitched beeping, and a whirling orange light on the roof of its cab. Gillis turned the paper sideways, and right enough, from that angle, the drawing began to look like a baby smoking a broken roll-up.

The first page of the golden book was marbled. Its bright patterning lay like new white roots burrowing into fermented vegetables, flashes of yellow seated in whirls of green and blue. Jan, apprentice painter, held the book open before the fishermen who had saved him. They stared. Their eyes separated from their bodies, and wandered into that maze of colour. They had never seen so many horizons.

Jan could remember the whole process. Above a reeking steel tray, a mixture of water, oil and coloured ink was stirred with feathers and combs. Finely produced vellum – calfskin – was held by its corners and lowered to the clutching ink, the sheet gripped the surface, and when it was lifted free, clean water dripped from the bottom edge. Swirls of oil and ink grappled across the vellum, which bowed as it dried, then relaxed as the ink tired and lost its argument. He wondered whether he would ever use that knowledge again.

The fishermen didn't trust that page, they wanted their eyes back where they belonged. They wanted to see that first saint again. Who held up a thumb and two fingers as he burned. St Somebody, patron of Something; the identifying description and accompanying prayer had been washed away. They crossed themselves anyway.

The tavern owner offered Jan a bed in the corner of the room, and in the days that followed, his nose dripped between his thumb and forefingers and he coughed up gobbets of catarrh that he spat into the fire. He shivered and blushed red when he sat too close to the flames, but he burned and his skin turned blue when he sat too far away. In dreams, he imagined his piled blankets were the turf that would lie on his grave. He heard mourners above him, fellow apprentices of the Guild; spots of pigment fell from their palette knives into the earth, into the tangled ball of bedsheets that lay on his chest. In the first few nights, he had been watched over, soothed and tended to, the fever slowly drawn from him. Now, he was finding the limits of charity. His portions were ladled smaller, and his fire often smouldered and died.

By the low light of a candle and a dithering sunrise, he attempted to clean his golden book with the point of his knife. He trimmed the ruined edges and cut the worst pages away entirely. Threw them in the fire. With rags, he cleaned mud and silt from the cover and spine, and as he heard his hosts waking, he quickly wrapped the book in winds of sacking, packed it to the bottom of his satchel and tiptoed away from the tavern. He stifled a racking cough, provoked by a chill in the air, and walked to the street. Footprints and cart tracks showed each person's passage as a thread that ran from scattered piers and berthings by the shore, and wove inland into a complicated pattern on the grounds of the empty market. Through which Jan's passage was an errant thread, unspooled from the general design, suitable for the nip of a weaver's scissors.

'Away to your sin?' To one side of the woven road, Brother Malcolm sat, just as loose, a brass bell cradled in his arms.

'Away with my book, to get my price for it.'

The monk smiled. 'Know which way you're going?'

'Avoiding the sea. Going north, over there.' He pointed beyond the last of the cottages, to a hill which sheltered a craggy battlement, like a severed jaw turning away to stifle a gap-toothed grin.

'Running out on your debt?' The monk stifled the clapper of his bell as he rose and walked with the apprentice painter.

'I left them offcuts of my book. The pieces I couldn't use. There's gold leaf in there. And in one you can see St Mark, with a lion on his lap, pointing at a book.'

'Compared to how many eggs you ate? And how many cups of broth, and porridge, and I saw you with a carrot or two. And all the fish – they might have too many of those at times, but it wasn't you that dredged them from the sea. Good haddock they gave you, good cod. Pulled you out the river, back from your death. And you ruined their blankets and took up their front room. They turned away a cousin for you. So come on, cut out a full-size saint for them. A full page. It must be worth it? Bless the people that tried to help you.'

Jan laughed and walked faster; the old monk's legs weren't long enough to keep stride with him. 'This book I'm holding. . . don't you know what it costs? More than that forest and all the wood in it. And more than the stinking river and all the fish in it too. Do you know why? Because men like me made it. Men who go home from their work with gold leaf under their fingernails. Who have to scrape it off their skin, and pick it from their nose, and spit it out.'

'It's a very golden book,' the monk admitted. Out of breath, he fell behind as they left the empty marketplace. He stood with his legs wide, and began to ring his bell, breaching the silent morning, welcoming the late autumn sun. He shouted, 'But it used to be golder!'

CHAPTER FIVE

A vast box telly spoke to the furniture while Gillis stared at his coffee table, daring himself to uncover the shortbread tin and lift the severed hand free, place it on some paper and coax it to draw or write again. Skiing championships proceeded on screen, drawing his eye every now and again. The snow had been stained with adverts, logos and slogans, the air was full of cow bells and shouts, the noise of the crowd had been overlaid with frantic commentary. Underneath it all, the damaged mountain, scarred by the racecourse, the crowd and cameras, seemed to lean slightly forward. A giant that had been worshipped and feared lay pinned in place by a thousand fenceposts and slalom poles.

Maybe the hand had been cut off by the whirring motor of a fishing boat? The body might have been in an ambulance, and the hand might have fallen out. Somehow still alive, the hand might have journeyed through Kirkmouth, all the way uphill to the kirk, and fallen into the hole left by the elm's uprooting. Sustained by an unfolding miracle, the severed hand must have been preserved in order to send a message to the people of central Scotland. Were the lines of communication between heaven and earth so badly damaged? Were they having to improvise? Had the hand been preserved and assigned a task, only to forget the message it was to pass on?

By the looks of photos online, Rachel's husband was only five-five or five-six, half-bald, and owned two suits, one chequered grey and one blue, which he alternated for the weddings and work nights out he had been photographed attending. Gillis didn't see anything about the man worth preserving. In one image, his hand was raised in celebration of something, and Gillis could see that the fingers were thick and stubby, that the nails were broad and curved, and he had to admit that the crooked, emaciated fingers of the severed hand didn't seem to match. The hand could belong to almost anyone in the graveyard, however long dead. Maybe it had scratched its way free from a coffin and dug upward, through the mud, following tree roots, until it reached the light. Was Gillis meant to help it on its way? Take it somewhere? Show it to someone? He turned the TV off as a klaxon peeled across the mountain, and with a fish slice and a wooden spoon, held through gardening gloves, Gillis moved the hand onto the coffee table, covered in sheets of white paper, and pressed a pen between its thumb and forefinger. He turned on the heating and waited.

Seemingly distracted, the hand barely gripped the pen and made some indifferent scribbles on the page. The minister paced around the table, trying to interpret the marks as letters or numbers. When the hand rested and let go of the pen, he tried to work out if it was a diagram of something or a map to somewhere? It wasn't.

'Say what you need to say. Now. Say it now.' His words echoed and sounded ridiculous. Maybe the hand had nothing to say. A little man standing on a bigger man's face. A fish wrapped around a human figure. A whorl of scribbles, stirred by a feather. How much time passed in the waiting? The whole day. It was gloomy outside, and dark in the room. Gillis left the hand on its own as he paced through to the kitchen, the gyp of his knee forcing him to hobble until the muscles slackened and the joint cracked.

The doorbell rang, the door was knocked, the letterbox was rattled, and the window was tapped. Gillis was hiding, slumped low along the sofa, trying to pull papers from the table and hide them in the shortbread tin.

'I can see you in there.' Nichol had his hands cupped to his eyes and was shouting through the windowpane. His breath was clouding the glass. 'I can see you moving!'

But surely he could only see the back of Gillis's head? And maybe the movement of his shoulders? Probably couldn't see the severed hand? Or the drawings? Gillis wormed his legs beneath the table and dropped to the floor. The windowpanes trembled as Nichol knocked again. In one movement, Gillis pulled the severed hand and all of its papers clattering into the tin. Maybe one day, these items would be venerated. He replaced the lid quietly, and pushed it all beneath the sofa.

'I can see your chair moving! I'm here to apologize, you fucking—' Nichol stopped short, he was trying to control his temper. Footsteps on the gravel outside left the window and returned to the door. The handle jittered and the letterbox danced.

'I'm not going anywhere!'

Gillis crawled across the living room and stood in the open door frame. He planned to tiptoe past the front door and hide upstairs. Put his headphones on and drown Nichol's complaints with an hour or two of aggressive guitar. But a set of eyes peeped from the letterbox. Nichol spoke hoarsely. 'I can see you.' Like two snooker balls suddenly pocketed, the eyes disappeared and the door chapped twice as though they had fallen to the floor through holes in the netting.

'Calm down, I'm coming.' As he opened the door, Gillis pretended to have been sleeping. He rubbed an eye and mouthed an empty yawn. 'I dropped off.'

'So you did.' Nichol steadied himself in the doorway as he rose to his full height. It had been raining, and he was heavy with the smell of a sour wax jacket and a dog-hair jumper. 'Am I coming in?' he asked. But as soon as Gillis stepped to the side, he changed his mind. 'No, wait, I need you to come out.' He tramped down the driveway, back into the dark evening. Then called from its clutches. 'Follow me.'

They stood on either side of an ancient gravestone, each letter of the inscription reduced to a pockmark in the sandstone.

'Someone'll pay good money for that.' Nichol had been waggling the block back and forward, demonstrating how easy it would be to rip each one of them out. Cut them down the middle, good solid stone. Sit them this way and that, with all the interesting details facing out. 'Could clad a house with it, or make a memorial wall kind of thing.' He'd sold old fishing nets and knackered buoys for hundreds of pounds. He'd sold his granddad's boat just last year. Some architect type had used the timber to refit his kitchen. 'Takes all sorts,' Nichol shrugged. He'd had a good couple of years, rooting through the back sheds, selling battered oilskins and life jackets, outdated charts and rusted compasses, broken plotters and set squares. There was a market for all that junk. As long as you could tell them that it had been somewhere or done something. 'Folk like to think they came from a proper place. Where people did real, proper things. And that there's a bit of that left in them. What's got more of that than this?' He slapped the gravestone.

Gillis wasn't convinced.

'Trust me.' Nichol hauled at the gravestone, as though he might be able to lift it, but made no impression. 'We'll get a wee digger.' He patted the stone as though reassuring it.

'But what about the bodies?' Gillis dug his toe into the soil.

'Dig them out, stack them up? Over here, or there.' His pointing finger drifted across the kirkyard to the crooked spire that loomed over them. 'And then there's that thing.'

'The kirk?'

The kirk was historical, the foundations were medieval. These things sell. 'Especially if we can cover it with a nice, modern finish. But I'm stalled here until we can see about desanctication? Or desancafation? What the fuck's it called?'

'Desanctification.'

Nichol nodded. 'Desanctification these graves so we can dig them up. Build some decent flats for the people here. Time's ticking, but the market's good. Prices are high. There'll be money going around and proper, good, old-fashioned jobs. I know you can't discriminate but I'll be taking local people first, believe me. There's too many out of work here, just chucking their lives away. I know you agree.'

He walked to the edge of the kirkyard and looked over the back wall, down to the wastelands. Empty fields cordoned by rusting fences, spotted by an occasional dark patch, a bath full of stale water for the cows and sheep. 'I've been emailing Americans. Big investment money, hidden assets, that kind of thing. They all think they've got ancestors back here and I've been buttering them up, saying, *oh aye, I know a guy with that name, maybe he's your cousin, maybe he's your granddad, you should come out and meet him.* We'll do a big reception, we'll all be in kilts, there'll be a pipe band and a ceilidh and we'll put swords on the walls an all that shite. Some of these guys are convinced the world's cracking up, and they don't want to be in America when it happens. So I've been laying it on thick about how *yer Highland ancestors battled off invaders from these hills for centuries.* The world's changing. A good businessman tries to get ahead of that. Make moves, think one step ahead of the competition.'

He turned back to the minister. 'You're used to telling folk bad news. That's a handy skill.' Nichol's tongue flit across the gaps in his teeth as he pointed to the corners of the graveyard. 'You'll have to find a way of not saying *mass grave*, but call it. . . like a *community resting place*? Something like that. . . You can't just expect the world to wait for ever, know what I mean? Like, what are they waiting for?' He threw his arm across the dark graves. It was a bit selfish to take up all this room, Nichol thought. When there was things needing done. When you're dead you're dead. Was he right or was he right?

'First – or second, I suppose – I just wanted to apologize. For my behaviour.' Nichol laid his jacket over the back of a chair in the kitchen. He asked for a tea and settled down at the table. Grimaced as he swept his hand across the broken surface. 'You've went and wrecked this polish. This is good wood. It's not mahogany, is it? What a waste. This is a good old-fashioned table, you'll have to get that stripped back.' He was down at the table legs, thumbnail notched in the dovetails, examining nicks and scrapes inflicted over the near hundred years since the table had been expressly made for the manse. 'What a shame. Listen, I know a guy who'd give you a good deal on this. He'll scrub it back and repair the damage. Won't be cheap, mind, but in the long run, a good table's something you can hand down the generations. See the old minister, he would have had a couple of tablecloths on there, keeping it all protected.'

Gillis set a cup of tea on an untouched spot of varnish. Nichol yelped and lifted it quickly, but the heat and the wet mug had already scalded a white crescent, so the man tutted and ran his hand back and forward over the mark as it dulled. Gillis sat down opposite and pressed the base of his own mug into a patch of dark, untouched varnish. Nichol looked dumbfounded by the minister's stupidity.

'You were apologizing?' Gillis lifted his mug proudly from the full circle of white scalding it had left behind.

'I was. . .' Nichol described a few hard years. An errant son, a wayward daughter, a death or two in the family and an illness of some kind. Let alone the business side of things. Combined, surely these were a hefty downpayment against his behaviour? 'I guess I thought your wee drawing was some kind of provocation. And I'll be honest, I didn't know what it meant, but it seemed cheeky. And I thought, is he taking the piss? I know some of the boys have been saying that I shouldn't have had Douglas out on the old boat. How he was just an office monkey. Which is only sort of true. His dad was a trawlerman. But when I saw the drawing, the little guy standing on the other guy, I thought it was you saying. . . that the big guy drowning was him? And how I was the little one standing on him. But anyway, you tripped, and I didn't hit you. So. . . I don't have a lot to apologize for. But I shouldn't have gotten angry. And everything's OK anyway, isn't it?'

'Sure,' Gillis agreed.

'And you got home all right, didn't you?'

Gillis nodded.

'Rachel, she brought you back?'

He nodded again.

'And she had some bother with her car here?'

Gillis shrugged and sipped at his mug.

'No, it's just my pal that runs the garage, he said he came to pick her up from here. In the morning.'

Gillis shook his head.

'Doesn't matter, I'm just being nosey. And here, she's a widow. Timing wise, is it nice? Does it look good? Who's to say. But is it illegal? No. I'd say, all in all, fire in.' The two men held a moment of uncomfortable silence. 'Others might not. I'll leave it at that.' They nodded back and forth, and focused on little sips of the tea. 'But I had a couple more things though, items on the agenda kind of thing. Just that drawing set me off. Got me all wound up. I'm apologizing. Trying to make a habit of it. Wife's been a blessing. And getting off the drink, they tell you to say sorry. I used to be worse, I promise you. I used to be much worse.'

Gillis patted his pockets, looked around and sought his jacket. Laid the drawing on the table and explained. 'Just came across it. And I thought I'd ask around and see what it was.'

Nichol leant in to examine closer. 'It's a lot of nonsense is what it is. Some of these pricks that work for me have got it into their heads that it's all my fault? Like I can be everywhere at once. Or like I haven't told them a million times, don't get lazy, don't get overtired, wear the rubber boots. Wear the big jacket. But they want to wear their trainers and their hoodies, they're like weans at school. They tell me the jacket and the boots aren't trendy, they don't look nice.' Nichol switched to falsetto and primped an imaginary haircut with one hand. *'Ooooh, the colour clashes with my eyes.'*

The joke fell to the table and rolled over, dead.

'But you don't know, do you?' Nichol coughed the lingering falsetto from his throat. 'Who might have done it?'

'Done what? Done in Douglas?'

'The drawing. Who was it sitting by you in the bar? You would know some of them, wouldn't you? Was it a tall guy, blond hair? Or a wee stumpy guy, patchy beard? Or like a big guy, broad shoulders, no chin?'

Gillis shook his head. 'I got it before the funeral. Found it in here. In the house.'

'Someone post it through the letterbox?'

'Nothing like that. Just found it. Found it outside.'

'Was it a kid? No, you don't know. Fair play.' Nichol stared into his tea, in its bland depth his thoughts resolved, and the matter of the drawing was set aside. When he raised his head, he was on to the next item of business. The empty sea. The challenging economic climate. Market volatility. Competition with larger firms.

'You'd think what with having the fish on land you'd be golden, seeing as you don't have to chase them any more. But they still live in water and the water needs filtering and now it's you that has to feed them.' He described the stinking concrete circles he kept them in. 'You can see them from up here. And you'll have smelt them too.' His father had been dead for twenty years, and under Nichol's watch the last of the boats had been called in, and the fish farms had flourished, but now, unfortunately, struggled to prop up the rest of the business. The hotel? Well, who was coming out here to stay? And the chip shop? Well, how much can you charge for a fish supper?

'And that's why you want to sell the kirk? You need the money.'

'I wouldn't say *need*. I'd say I. . . Or aye, actually I would just say need. I'd say I need it. The money.' As that last word left his mouth he sighed and shook that frustrated desire from his mind, then scratched at his face with an open palm, from cheek to temple and back again, before clearing his throat and beginning to flush with embarrassment. 'Look, I've got an item three. Or four or wherever we are. On my agenda.'

His eyes shied from Gillis as he wriggled his left hand into
the cuff of his jumper. Then he stood and pulled the sleeve
overhead in a rainbow motion; the jumper swallowed him
and spat him back out. He was wearing a ratty blue polo
shirt, but not for long; he undid the buttons, tucked his chin
and whisked it overhead. Sucked in his gut and flinched his
biceps. One arm was pale white, with a cinch of red skin at
the elbow, and the other was covered in a constellation of
painful blotches that merged past the wrist into bumps and
sores that faintly glistened.

'I know it's not nice to look at.' Nichol turned the pale
arm over, front to back, then stretched his arms out like a
bloated Christ. He turned around to show Gillis his back,
where the skin faded from white into deep purple and pink.
'That thing that fell out your bag the other night. I mean, I
might be wrong, but it looked to me like a person's hand.
The blood got on me. I don't know what to say. But look
what it did to me.'

'Did it burn you?' Gillis asked in horror, staring at the
rough arm.

'No, it did this.' Nichol shook the pale arm. 'This one's
me normally.' He turned the red arm over. 'Yesterday, both
of them were bright red, fingertip to fingertip. Have been for
years. It's a skin thing. They tell me it's all to do with getting het
up and anxious, and what's funny is that I actually feel much
more anxious and worried since I saw that thing. Can't sleep,
can't think about anything else. But all the symptoms are away.
It spread upwards, from the finger that touched the hand.'

Against the minister's silence, Nichol lowered his arms
and sat back down, picked up his bundled polo and tried to
find the collar.

'Carol, my wife, she's Catholic. It's been twenty-five
years. . . twenty-six in June. . .' Nichol held up his wedding

ring for Gillis to admire. 'I said to her how you had this thing that fell out your bag. That it looked like a hand that had been cut off. She said sometimes churches chop up a saint who's died, and share out the bits. She was in Rome with all her pals, and said she'd seen this shinbone, but it was all rotten. I told her this one wasn't rotten. Well, she said, this shinbone in Italy was in a gold box with rubies and emeralds and silver carvings all stuck to it. And I said, the one you had was in a golden box with these patterns and different colours all over the outside. And she called it a relic. She's lapsed. A lapsed Catholic, but she said she didn't think Protestants had anything like that. But maybe they keep it secret? Like, just for people in the know. Like a club, or an exclusive thing, just for the minister and some close pals. Like a, or not like a bowling club, but you know what I mean.'

Gillis nodded along.

Nichol dropped his polo shirt into his lap. 'So, I'm sort of saying, what am I meant to do? Is there a way to join? I'd like to touch it again. With my other hand this time.' He held up his left hand where the skin was raw. 'I thought if this one got healed, the two might meet in the middle, and that'd be me cured.' He began to put on his shirt.

Gillis attempted to deny everything. He tried to explain the healing properties of certain plants. They could be found in any old strip of grass. Dock leaves and so on. He couldn't name another. Aloe vera, that kind of thing. And it was dark, and they'd had a drink. People see all kinds of things.

As Gillis spoke, Nichol shrouded his head in his polo, arms wavering around him as he searched for the sleeves, and then he was suddenly birthed through the collar. He cleared his throat, and his eyes narrowed. 'Stop being silly.' The room grew heavy with the smell of his wet clothes as he pulled on his jumper. 'I'd like to see it now. I want to know what I'm dealing with.'

'I can't let you.' Gillis pushed his chair back and stood as Nichol put on his jacket and one arm swung wide, casting a haymaker shadow across the room. 'And I don't know what you're talking about.'

'Then we have a problem,' Nichol said, as he began to search the house.

'Where is the Lord?' Jan asked a bypasser, who scowled at the odd accent.

'In heaven, you dirty pagan.'

'Of the big house, I mean.' The apprentice painter stood at the gates of a grand manor house, whose Laird's name was inscribed in the front page of the golden book which lay under his arm, the topmost branch of a family tree whose downmost root was Adam, pictured basking naked beneath its leaves.

'I've got a gold book,' Jan shouted through to the gatekeeper. The man's returning stare made the eyes seem painted on. 'From the Lowlands. It took me eight weeks to get here. Once the Laird comes and sees that I've been kept waiting, you'll be sorry.'

As the day passed, the gate creaked, letting single persons through, masons and carpenters, meek petitioners there for table scraps. And the gate yawed wide for carts and carriages, horses trotting prettily on new shoes, cattle dragged through to the back fields. And at each opening, Jan attempted to walk alongside or hide in shadow until discovered and set back to wait outside. He watched as starlings and finches flitted between the bars of the gate, then up to the trees, then out to the fields, passing from commons to Laird's land and back again.

'Bring me out some of that.' Jan tore a tiny sliver from the back pages of his book and promised that painted leg and painted complex of grass to a beggar in exchange for a portion of scraps from the manor kitchens. Once the deal was made, he sat in a cold sod of fallen leaves as he ate bread steeped in peas and thin gravy.

Just before dark, the sky was like a paint palette being washed, colours mixed together into mute greyish blue that thrilled for a second as a spot of dried pigment suddenly broke and spilt a pure colour, before disappearing into the volume and movement of water. Riders came, circled by a pack of hunting dogs, following the same route which Jan had walked. The foremost two held torches. Eight more followed, clustered tightly around a central figure. They held a standard which Jan couldn't see. The dogs wove between the arched legs of the horses, hooves nipped at paws, and teeth nipped at ankles. They hobbled as they ran, tongues loose and pink, their breath clouding the air. In the midst of the riders, head shrouded in a patterned scarf, crested with a velvet hat, was it the Laird? It was a shadow, an empty space that passed by. From the puddle he stood in, Jan shouted, and one of the Laird's mounted men extended a boot to push the painter back. The gate shrieked as the keeper scrambled to open it, and in the slowing of the horses, a heavy stink of blood became apparent, dripping from the carcasses of hares and foxes and a young stag, all thrown like loose coats over the hindquarters of two unsaddled horses that trailed the hunting party.

Jan tried to call to the group, but his voice was lost in the noise of their passing, so in desperation he reached into his bag and hurled his golden book into the air. As it soared before them and reflected the last light of the sun, and the fires being kindled at the gatehouse, and the torches which the riders carried, the golden book seemed to burst into flames, then die as though extinguished by two enormous fingers that had been licked to pinch the wick. It fell among the horses, and the gold terrified them. The riders tangled and fell, and the Laird's face was suddenly visible as his scarf unfurled and fell to one side. The features were bloated, his cheeks were as pockmarked and pale as the surface of the moon. As the horses reared and kicked, the riders fought with their reins, and the dogs leapt. But peacefully, almost idiotically, the Laird leant down to look at the golden book, his features waned from sight and only his aristocratic profile could be seen. A cudgel nose above wet lips and a scant beard, he squinted at the dirt and ignored the panic of his riders. After they had battled and kicked their horses into submission, one turned to Jan and struck him across the face. Then their hands were in his armpits and at his belt and he was lifted up and carried. He hadn't known he was so light.

He shouted, 'Honourable Lord! I came from over the sea! To deliver, here, the book you wanted. A gift for your wife! Her blessed name is written in the front and so's yours. The last root of a family tree that stretches back to Adam. That's your book there, lying open on a page I painted, those curtains which St Sebastian is being tortured in front of, I arranged and ruffled them and painted their shadows! I've been sent here by the masters of the Guild of St Luke, here to deliver this book and collect payment!' He stopped speaking when the Laird signalled for the book to be picked from the dirt and brought to him. Torches were lifted high and one of the riders whispered in his ear, 'Look at this tattered vellum. The paint has dripped. And look at the edges – they've torn. He must be a thief.'

'The first page,' Jan shouted up to the Laird. 'Look at the tree that's painted there, it's an elm, it has Adam and Eve at the bottom in Eden, and then Cain, Abel, up to David, and then it rises through peoples of this kingdom and arrives at you. I was there when they made it, in my bag I have papers.' He was allowed to rummage, but the papers which held the seal of his guild were ignored. They were torn and muddy too.

The crescent profile of the Laird waxed full as he turned to smile at Jan. The features were blank, and behind his eyes there was nothing, as though the Laird was sleep-walking, overseeing another world in his mind. He extended his hand and returned the book. Nodding and smiling as he wiped the inks and softened paints from his fingers into the mane of his horse. Still peacefully grinning, the Laird patted his horse's neck as it trotted through the gate and his companions followed one by one, then the hounds, giddy in their exhaustion. The last of the company, who marched alongside his trembling horse, passed by Jan's blind side and struck him across the socket of his eye. Then grabbed the golden book and pushed Jan to the ground, standing on his belly as he tried to rise. Jan struggled up as the man left and gripped a folio of pages, tearing them from the book. Binding thread tangled between them as the rider kicked the loose folio free from the spine and carried off the bulk of the painted book. One last thread joined Jan to the rider, and when the gate closed, moved zigzag, back and forth in the eyelets of the folded section he had saved. Until it whipped from the last eyelet and jounced along the ground for a second before leaping through the gate. Jan lay back in his pain and held the pages he had saved to his chest, then scrambled away from the gatehouse into darkness, hugging his pages and cursing both God and His representatives on earth.

CHAPTER SIX

mpty cupboards, empty cutlery drawers, empty fridge and freezer. 'I'm getting quite a picture of you,' Nichol said as he worked his way around the house, searching for the severed hand. 'But wouldn't it be easier if you just told me where it is?'

Gillis refused. He followed Nichol, denying the severed hand's existence as he went. An upturned drawer rattled loose a few broken candles, frozen peas and fish fingers were pulled from the freezer and scattered across the countertop, an old cordless phone lay in a cupboard next to an ironing board, scalded in a half-dozen places. A cork board made of wine tops, dense with pins, a calendar tangled beside it, with nothing in its days except funerals. Nichol stomped flat-footed up the stairs, forced his arms deep into cupboards, routing towels and old soaps, stacks of hymnbooks and sheet music, all of this a remnant of the old minister. Gillis watched his shirts and trousers come tumbling down the stairs.

'If you tell me where it is, I'll stop!'

When Nichol returned downstairs, Gillis barred the living room door. 'You don't have a right,' he began, but was pushed aside and Nichol ranged, wide-legged, into the room to throw books back and forward on the bookcase, then run his hands underneath the TV cabinet and coffee table. He crawled to the sofa and lifted one end, walking his hands along the bottom until it stood upright, almost touching the

ceiling, an absurd monument that held its shape for a second
or two before the blankets and loose cushions collapsed into
a heap on the floor. The shortbread tin lay exposed.

'Is that it?' Nichol asked.

His suspicions were confirmed by the way Gillis said *no*.
He dropped to his knees and lifted the tin to the coffee table.

'Is there anything I should do? Any words I have to say?'

Gillis trembled at the reckless attitude Nichol showed
toward the hand. Who knows how it might react. The lid
was popped off, and Nichol sighed when he saw the severed
hand again. 'I knew it. I knew what I saw.' He rolled up the
sleeve of his sore arm and with his forefinger, prodded the
raw end of the relic. A spot of blood printed onto the pad of
his finger, and the severed hand reacted slowly, turning and
curling a little. Nichol laughed in loud disbelief as the hand
shifted and made a gesture toward them.

'Did you see that?' Nichol's eyes were wide open. The
minister returned his look with a terrified stare.

'It points,' Gillis said. 'It accuses. It does the same to me.
It knows something.'

'What d'you mean? It gave me a thumbs-up.' Nichol
smeared the spot of blood from his forefinger onto his
thumb, then looked at his sore arm, willing the healing power
of the relic to move upwards. 'How long does it normally
take? With this arm it was about twenty-four hours. Is that
normal?'

Gillis waited for Nichol's sacrilege to be punished. 'You
shouldn't have done that,' he warned.

'It gave me a thumbs-up. It's happy with me.'

'It was pointing. It was warning you. You have to be
careful. It knows things.'

Nichol turned his arm back and forward, trying to spot
the changes which the miraculous hand was making. 'It'll

take a bit of time, won't it?' He placed the lid back on the tin. Then pulled the upended sofa back down to rest on the floor, keeping his own hand elevated the whole while. He sat down in the cushionless middle. 'There we go. Was that so hard?' He looked at the blood drying on his fingers, and made a quick sign of the cross. Spectacles, testicles, wallet and watch.

'That's a Catholic thing,' Gillis said.

Nichol shrugged. 'Does it make a difference?'

As Nichol returned to his car, arching his hands back and forth, watching for the beginnings of a miracle, Gillis was left alone, with an empty house and an empty evening in front of him. So he continued the wreckage and ransacking of the manse. He pulled the possessions of the old minister free from the cupboards. Rolled books and cutlery, candlesticks and ornaments into bedsheets and duvet covers, carried these unwieldy bundles outside and stuffed them into the kirk's bins. As he walked back and forward to the manse, he felt as though a strange sediment was settling around his heart. The previous hour repeated on him. His passivity disgusted him. He should have stood firm at the doorway. Refused to discuss any sale of the kirk, or ransacking of the graves. And as soon as the bastard took off his polo shirt, he should have slapped the raw skin and taken the severed hand underarm and run out the house, away downhill into town. *What gives you the right?* That's what Gillis should have said. *Who gave you the nerve to come here? Don't you know what's happening to me? Don't you know what I'm becoming? Don't you know what I have?* Nichol would have walked backward in fear as Gillis picked up the shortbread tin and held it above his head. And the hand would have raised itself, and pointed at Nichol.

The kitchen light would have reflected in the interior of the shortbread tin, and sent dazzling lines of gold and bronze radiating around the room. *Ask me what I am*, Gillis should have demanded.

What are you? Nichol would say weakly, as he cowered and backed down the hallway to the front door. He would have tripped as he left, panicking he would begin to ask, *What are you? What are you?* And Gillis would be holding the severed hand above his head as it pointed its finger in accusation at the world below the kirkyard. Gillis would know exactly what he was and what he had become. And Nichol would know too and soon they all would, every one of them.

But the self-deception turned in his stomach like rich food. He knew he would be the last person the hand chose to do God's work. Gillis had been lying all along. Never believed in God, or heaven, or anything. Just needed the work and wanted a house and a decent car. He knew heaven was empty, so who would it hurt? He looked toward the sky, the yellow clouds, the bestiary of constellations, beyond, into the path of meteors and satellites, planets made of gravel and gas. *Hello?* Gillis sent a silent radio signal from his front cortex, out into the deep black silence. *Can anyone hear me? I'm calling to complain about your customer service.* He wanted a ray of light or a whisper in the ear to clarify things. Deliver a job description, or a mission statement, or a ten-point plan. Nothing came. He limped indoors – the old gammy knee had frozen up in the cold.

Back in brogues and a black belt. Back in a dog collar and a grey-flecked suit. A woman buried in the morning, a man burned before lunch. Gillis had scalded two knuckles while he ironed his trousers, and he fussed at the burns as he waited in the kirk vestibule. Even though the congregation had deserted the church, and the last sermon had been preached there three years previous, the empty hall was brightened once a week by a scatter of gaudy plastic. A mound of cuddly toys and a miniature shopping trolley full of plastic fruit and vegetables, plastic beef and ham and roast chicken, every bit of which squeaked when squeezed. A Mums and Tots group alternated with a checkerboard of blue and pink yoga mats, laid out for an evening class. There was a janitor to open the hall, who kept the place tidy and fought the heavy smell of damp by opening the windows and letting in more rain. Gillis was there to steal some pens and a sheaf of paper from the children. He wanted to lay it across his kitchen floor, and leave the severed hand loose to send its final message. With some combination of drawing and writing, he expected it to tell him what he was meant to do, what his life had been leading to.

An urn's worth of tea, an arm's length of biscuits, and a motley collection of sipping cups full of diluting juice were laid out on the kitchen hatch, and two old ladies said hello as Gillis passed, then turned back to their preparations. The Mums and Tots were coming through from their closing singalong, and Gillis pushed by with a rictus smile intended to look friendly. He opened the cupboard and raided the church's stationery stash, which was held in three big ice-cream tubs, their insides speckled blue, red, black and green by the uncapped pens. Each one advertising an American mission, or a Bible translation network or embossed with an inspirational verse in gold lettering. These were the unwon Sunday school prizes from his early childhood, washed up here in the late nineties, paraphernalia of the church's former success. He filled his pockets and found a stack of loose printer paper, then searched for a rubber band to secure it all.

'Excuse me sir.' A finger tapped his shoulder. 'Will you be paying for those?'

Gillis expected his scowl and dog collar to frighten off some busybody, but was met instead by Rachel, smiling. She held a huge bundle of pink cotton, out of which a baby's hand poked. Jamie was standing behind her, staring beyond them both to the empty back wall.

'Just getting these pens,' Gillis mumbled. 'For a friend of mine, he's wanting them for his kids. Poor guy's skint. Do you want some? There's loads.'

'I'm good for pens, thanks. How's the head?'

'The head?' Gillis had almost forgotten, but the little cut was still there. 'It's a bit sore,' he realized.

'Well, that's to be expected.' She jogged the baby up and down, and the little hand bounced. 'Are you not saying hello?' She turned to Jamie and held her arm out. 'He's still not really speaking,' she whispered to the minister, waiting for the boy to answer. He didn't.

'Not speaking at all?'

The double doors opened, and the kirk's janitor, a man named Jim Macintyre, clattered through with a mop in one hand and a sloshing bucket in the other. His Christian name and surname had been permanently welded together, in order to distinguish him from three or four other Jims of the same age, build and occupation. Despite their subsequent deaths, emigrations and conversions to Catholicism, Jim Macintyre had kept every syllable of his name. Still light on his feet, he stepped carefully through a guddle of toys toward an ancient, knackered football.

'Here we go, wee man, here!' he called out to Jamie and chipped the ball over the spilt toys. It landed and rolled in a strange curve to slouch at Jamie's feet, as though the boy had summoned it with his mind. He swung his

leg and toe-bashed the ball into a distant corner of the
church.

'I'll get it, pal, I'll get it.' Jim Macintyre tilted his mop
against the wall and ran across, keys and coins jangling in
his pocket. He had known Gillis's grandparents and parents,
and had watched Gillis grow up, happy to look after the
boy for a few minutes, happy to skelp him across the ear or
crown of the head for drinking from the baptismal waters,
or swinging off the old coat racks. A tattoo on his arm
had lost all of its intended meaning, as the ink blurred and
the lines smudged; now it was only a vague leaf shape, a
regimental insignia, or a coat of arms. He slicked his hair
back in grey furrows that still held firmly in the track of
that morning's combing. His face blushed red as the ball
pattered back and forth. Between gasps, he bragged to the
little boy, loud enough for the adults to overhear, in the
eighties, he had played for Kilmarnock.

'D'you want to be a footballer when you grow up?' he
asked.

The boy nodded.

'Will you make a lot of money?'

He nodded again.

'That's a good idea, you can get your mummy a nice big
house and a new car, can't you?'

Jamie nodded along as the janitor described the wages,
the flash cars, the fans, the trophies, the sponsorship deals.
The women.

'I'm happy I ran into you.' Rachel nudged Gillis with her
shoulder. 'If anyone asks – they probably won't, but could
you tell them I slept in my car? They won't ask. But if they
do. There's a bit of gossip going around.'

Jamie stayed put as the old man chased the ball around the
waxed floorboards. 'I know nothing happened, and we didn't

do anything,' Rachel whispered as she jogged the bundle of baby clothes up and down. 'But in the morning, it was like, I couldn't be a wife. And couldn't be a widow either. Not even for a night. And I was so angry when I woke up. He doesn't even have a grave for me to visit. I wanted him to get a headstone that I could leave flowers by, but his mum thought it was better to cremate. She said his soul was away anyway. Do you believe that?'

'The soul?' A few dozen easy answers came to mind, some clichés and obscuring metaphors that normally served to carry the conversation beyond these tricky areas. Rachel deserved better. 'Maybe it stays on for a while. Maybe it still needs to say something. Maybe a grave's a good place to listen?'

'Like a ghost.'

He supposed so. Millions of people must have seen something.

'Witches? Vampires?' She was teasing him. 'Fairy folk?'

'Well, what do you believe in?' He moved his hand like a sliding scale. On the one end, a world overflowing with gods and angels and demons, on the other, just you, on your own.

'Centaurs?' she said. 'Selkies?'

He grinned.

'UFOs?'

'You're the one that asked.'

The baby jolted awake and began to cry. She jogged it up and down. 'I can never get them to calm down.' She strained her neck toward the doors. 'I'll need to get her back to her mum, sorry. I'm going to get the pram. Is Jamie OK here?' She turned her head away from Gillis and called across to the janitor. 'Is he all right with you for a sec?'

'We'll be fine, pal, don't worry.' The janitor waved to her, and when Jamie returned the ball, he stood on it for a second and shouted across the room, 'There's the man there. He might not look it now, but your minister there used to be an excellent footballer. Didn't you?'

Gillis smiled when Jamie turned to him.

'You could learn a lot from him. He even played in the big leagues down in England. Imagine that!'

'It was only trials,' Gillis said very quietly, happy for the janitor to confuse his botched efforts in athletics for a botched attempt at the Premier League. The janitor described the stadiums, the stands, the songs and the money these footballers get! Then suddenly chipped the ball waist high across the room. Gillis reacted by instinct, turned and drew power from his dipped shoulder, pulling strength from his whole body that whipped through to the old muscle memory embedded in his legs. His bad knee erupted in pain as he clipped the ball. It curled and spun, and thumped hard across Jamie's cheek, scattering the boy to the floor. The ball skittered under the chairs and the men ran toward the boy, who slowly sat himself back up, looking as though he had been expecting something like this for the whole of his short life. A scarlet mark blushed across his face. Gillis gritted his teeth and muttered, 'Christ, Christ,' as he helped the boy to his feet. They feared the waterworks, but though tears came into his eyes they fell with no sobbing or screaming. Jamie stared into space.

'Was that a sore one? That daft minister can't kick a ball, can he?' The janitor wiped the boy's cheek carefully with his thumb. There was a slight graze there. The boy didn't react. The janitor shook him a little and repeated, 'Was it sore?' But Jamie ignored him.

'You're not in shock, are you? Give us a smile? Do you want a biscuit? Do you want a hug? No? Well, I'm in the dark here. Am I getting the silent treatment? Is that it?' He looked up at Gillis and rolled his eyes. 'Well, it wasn't me that hit you, it was this big lump, not me.' He paused, kind of

joking, kind of not. 'All right, suit yourself, son.' He shook his
head. 'You want your mummy?' he said as an afterthought,
and without hearing a reply, he lifted the boy and walked
him from the room, like a grandfather clock carried out at
a flitting.

'Maybe you'll be a boxer, not a footballer, eh, wee man? You
canny half take a battering!' Jim Macintyre knelt in front
of Rachel. She had her boy captured between her legs and
she was comforting him as Jim pulled at the boy's arms,
forcing him to punch the air. After a jab, then an uppercut,
he collected his mop and bucket, and pretended not to listen
as Gillis apologized. Rachel didn't seem to mind.

'He's not in shock. It's just he's not been speaking. Not since
the funeral. Maybe earlier.' Her eyes were dark green, with
blue notches cut through them. Two gold hoops jostled from
her left ear, only one in the right. The left had been pierced
again, midway up. Gillis had forgotten about that second
piercing. She had regretted it, and wanted it to heal over. But
he had liked it, and when they kissed, he used to hold on to
the top earring. She hugged Jamie close to her, and spoke over
the top of his head. 'They're saying it's psychological.'

'Who's saying that?' Gillis balked at the idea. All this
meddling and fussing, analysing and diagnosing of every
word and gesture. A nation of hypochondriacs and neurotics,
whose petty weaknesses were endorsed by a culture keen
to sell soothing titbits and sugary serums, balms and oils,
apps and lifestyle plans draped with stock images of skeletal
sunbathers baring their teeth.

'The doctor said it.'

'Well, a doctor would say that. It's like me saying people
should go to church and read their Bible. Kind of convenient.'

She nodded noncommittally. 'I always thought convenience was a good thing.' She kissed the top of her boy's head and tilted her own to look at the minister. 'You seem tired, Gillis. Are you feeling OK?'

'Fine, honestly fine,' he muttered and they turned away to watch as the other Mums and Tots packed up and left in small groups. The pink bundle, and the baby that was hidden within it, left last, bug eyes squinting over the mother's shoulder.

'I like them like that,' Rachel said. 'Feed them or change them or hold them and they're happy. Not like this one.' She patted Jamie's head.

'He'll get over it.' Gillis was confident. Everything inside you ends. Even the sternest convictions, the worst memories, the toughest kernels of guilt.

'I hope so.'

'If there's anything I can do. . .' Gillis filled the silence with an empty gesture.

'No, I'll be OK. I've been talking to Nichol about getting my old job back. The woman that took it, years ago, she's not keeping well. So I might get to take over again. We'll see. I'm going to need more money now that Dougie's wage is away.'

'I thought you hated him? Nichol, I mean.'

'I need the work. And it's the least he can do.'

'Didn't you think he had something to do with—'

'I can't afford to think. And I can't afford to be principled either.' She widened her eyes as though cautioning Gillis, as though he had accused her of hypocrisy. 'And aren't the pair of you best pals now anyway? Now you're rubbing his belly.' She laughed as Gillis nodded.

'He told me, he showed me his tummy too. He's been telling everyone you'd made this big exception just for him. How there was bits in the Bible, where Jesus or God or

whoever brings people back to life or brings them to heaven
without them having to die? And how you'd cracked some
kind of code or found some kind of amazing secret potion
or whatever.' She was smiling and teasing him. 'You know
how he talks. But since he said that, I keep having these
dreams. He's there. Douglas, I mean. Sitting downstairs.
He's just there, and it's him, and he's normal. He won't
explain where he's been. He smells of sex. Sometimes. Or
of fire. He's been dead, he's been in heaven, and I'm on
at him about it. How dare he? I've got a kid to raise. I'm
thirty-one. Can't fuck around like that, going off, shagging
some tart from the town, dying for a few days. He'll just
say, *Well, I'm back now.*'

Gillis shook his head. 'I don't know what he's been saying,
but it doesn't work like that.'

'It wouldn't, would it? Too easy. Douglas wasn't a good
man anyway. Why would they send him back? But people
liked him.' She suddenly looked overwhelmed. Gillis knew
all the tactics, a hand on the shoulder, a kind word, a truism,
a verse from the Bible, a chorus of a hymn, a prayer, an
anecdote from his own life, and if any of those failed, he
would use one of the stories he kept to hand. An ornate
grotesquery of suffering and death, used to one-up or pale
their grief, force them to count their blessings, distract them
with a little blood and gore. If someone can suffer like *this*,
he implied, then you can struggle through. He liked to wrap
up these emotional moments with a reminder that the dead
will always be with us. In our hearts and memories, in our
children, in the thousands of products they had no doubt
accumulated over their lifetimes. In the property we stood
to inherit. In a loophole of some pension scheme that might
pay out. He could normally get from hysterical sobbing to
grim stoicism in under twenty minutes.

But he didn't want to lie to her and he knew she was wise to all the cheap tricks and easy answers. Back when they were together, whenever she was down, he'd press the flat of his thumb into the centre of her forehead and she'd frown and sigh. Started as a joke. Read about it in a magazine. Pressure points, chakras, that kind of thing. But it had stuck, and sometimes she would lie across his lap, and he would press from her forehead, down the line of her nose or across the arch of her eyebrows and imagine that any frustration or envy or sadness or guilt were all just movements of blood on the brain. He almost reached out, almost pressed his thumb soft against the wrinkles on her brow, but stopped himself. Collected his hands behind his back instead.

She gathered her bag and jacket, and Jamie's little rucksack. 'I suppose I'll see you around.' She paused in the doorway.

'I can show you something,' Gillis called after her. 'What Nichol's been on about. If you're interested?'

The last sixteen pages of the golden book were twisted into a tight, sturdy rod and jammed down the sleeve of Jan's coat, preventing his arm from bending. He slept on his left shoulder, cooried into the bark of a felled oak tree, with piles of rotten leaves underneath him. He had crooked a few branches of pine against the log, and crawled into the space created there. In the morning there was no sun, only grey cloud, and Jan began to walk deeper into the woods, searching for mushrooms, which he didn't find, or lime leaves, which he chewed into a cud.

He came on a team of woodcutters brewing porridge in the awning of a small shed, its walls barely upright, the nails rusting themselves loose. The men watched cautiously as Jan sat himself on a stump and waited for their Christian conscience to find him. They brought him a cup that he pressed against his chest, hoping to warm his blood. They had given him a rind of burnt oats, scraped from the bottom of their pot and diluted with water, and he ate with his fingertips. As he finished, they pointed him on the path which led into the Laird's villages, and soon he could see twists of smoke rising over the trees, the valley below the Laird's castle busy with incoming and outgoing traffic. Geese herded by a mangy sheepdog, carts full of silage and hay, salted and pickled herring, salmon and eels. In amongst them, Brother Malcolm rang his bell, calling for chastity and repentance to a crowd bent against both. 'Oh, it's the thief!' he yelled, sighting Jan. 'The painter and sinner! Did the Laird pay you for his ruined book?'

Jan ignored the monk, who clattered his bell after him.
'Seek treasures in heaven!' Brother Malcolm shouted. 'A clean
body is a fine emerald ring, glittering to the eye. And a clean
mouth is a lovely bracelet made of gold and studded with
rubies. A clean mind, another necklace, silver and pearl. And
it shines! All the way to heaven!'

In the thick of the market, Jan sat on a low wall next to a
stall selling smoked fish. To one side, a woman cut portions
of the meat and scalded them in a broad, shallow pan, kept
warm by a brazier underneath. He could taste the coked flesh
on his indrawn breath. Obscured by the steam and smoke,
Jan let the smell settle on his clothes and skin as he watched
the fish sellers clean and gut their catch. With curved knifes
they halved each fish and flung the innards into a bucket
sordid with flies, nipped at by the wild cats who lived in the
alleys between buildings. He rooted in his satchel, through
the useless brushes and damp, crumbling bricks of pigment,
small pots of colour mostly dead and dry, until his finger
pricked against the blade of his knife. He asked the fish sellers
if he could use a corner of their table, and they refused. Just
a corner? Just a flat surface, he would clean it himself! They
refused again and raised their knuckles, spangled with fish
guts and shards of pale bone.

With his back turned from any onlookers, Jan took the
sixteen pages from the sleeve of his jacket and one by one,
he carefully cut a thin sliver from the edge of each page.
Soon, he had sixteen lengths of the calfskin parchment,
spotted from end to end with a hundred colours. Corners
of green and blue, which had been sky and grass, or flower
stem and headdress, pale umber and bright red of a burning,
all-consuming fire, yellow, grey and black, the architecture
of heaven, the clouds from which angels descended, singing
and playing strange music. He tied a knot in one end of each

strand and cut a slit in the middle of the other, so that, like a daisy chain, he could join one to the other. He cleared his throat and spat, draped the strips of vellum over his arm and buried the maimed pages in his satchel.

'A gift for a sweetheart!' he shouted. 'For a wife, for a good daughter!' And as the day began to end, he tied these strips of coloured vellum around the wrists of merchants' wives and the necks of young girls. The last few, left unsold, he bundled in his pocket beside the money he had earned. Only a few coppers, but enough that he needn't sleep outside again.

The clouds had cleared and the sky was still bright in the last of the sun's reign, and the monk still clattered his bell in the market square and spoke of a different kind of jewellery. The iron chains, the weights tied to the ankle and head, the stocks and gallows.

'Brothers and sisters! A time of great trial comes! Our cousin country turns its back on the Lord! Our own Lairds read evil books in secret! The Pope cannot sleep at night! He turns back and forward, his stomach is sore, his teeth are aching, his feet are covered in corns, he thinks of us, he thinks of the Scottish people!'

A sod of turf was thrown from the edge of the market. A crowd of boys laughed. The monk rang his bell and cursed them. He said that the Pope dreamt a terrible dream. Of an Antichrist rising in the north. Another clump of dirt came, and crashed across his mouth. He shouted louder, his bell ringing constantly, piercing every conversation, drawing the attention of the dispersing crowd. Stones were thrown, old fish heads and offcuts of wood, but stopped abruptly as two men walked across the market square. They were dressed all in black, and the monk fell silent when he saw them. They were wearing wide-brimmed hats with folded pieces of paper tucked into the brim, fluttering in the evening air

like feathers. One spoke quietly to the monk, while the other
took the bell from him and wrenched the clapper loose. He
dropped the bell to the ground, where it rang for the last
time as the black-jacketed man raised his boot and flattened
it with a final bright note, then stepped back and kicked the
muted bell; it clanked and scratched across the cobbles like
any old piece of metal. The other man finished his quiet talk
with the monk, then patted him in a friendly way across the
shoulder. As they walked away, the young boys seated on the
market wall started to cheer. Some of the crowd laughed
and applauded, while many just ignored it all and walked on,
bought and sold their last items and returned home, almost
oblivious to the presence of the two black-jacketed men.
Jan, the apprentice painter, had seen them before. Not those
exact men, or that exact shade of black, but more or less. He
collected his satchel, made sure his pages were still there, and
disappeared among the crowd.

CHAPTER SEVEN

For three days, Gillis had phoned in sick, pretending to have some kind of catching bug. He had lowered his voice and talked very carefully on the call to his superiors, as though the disease might leap through the phone lines.

'I want to be sure I'm a hundred per cent.' He wrapped himself in a blanket, and monitored the progress of the severed hand. It had managed to produce another two drawings. One was a man with a beard, with a few leaves growing out of his forehead. The other was just a scribble, though at a stretch you could see a cloud with a foot coming down from it. The Kirk had sent someone down from the Highlands to cover his shifts. Apparently, the man had been getting on very well. That morning, as Gillis prepared his altered voice, summoning a relapse, his phone rang pre-emptively, and the boss on the other end of the line attempted to twist his arm. Surely he was better by now?

Under duress, Gillis left the manse to meet with a widower and his young children, and was now huddled in their front room, going through flower options and hymn selections. It felt like he was coming off the substitution bench, stretching his legs in the last few minutes of a game that had already been lost. Trying out his weight on the old shaky knee.

'That guy who was here yesterday, he won't be taking the funeral?' the widower asked.

'He's away back north.'

The man looked disappointed. 'It's just. . . we went over all this already.'

'He didn't leave me his notes.'

The widower wasn't keen to cry again. He flatly repeated the facts of his wife's short life. School, college, work, marriage, baby, illness, death. Gillis's notes became vague as the man described her good qualities. He could normally guess at those, they were always the same. Patience and kindness, etc. The woman had gone to the same school as Gillis, years before he'd even been born, when the old gym hall was brand new, the locker rooms less mouldy and the varnish not yet peeling from the benches.

The school football team hadn't suited him. Although he had been a good player, he was too shy for the changing room and the team bus, and he had no goal celebration except an embarrassed look down and a quick jog out of reach of his own side. The other boys jumped on each other's shoulders and held one another, touched foreheads and whispered things. They gloated at the opposite side, or grimaced at the huddled parents sheltered under golf brollies, drinking from steaming flasks of tea. Even now, Gillis couldn't watch a game on telly without thinking, *that could have been me*, but how could it? Sacked it in at sixteen. His dad had been very disappointed.

But then the running. He thought about the glory days of his youth, sore legs, grazed shins, cold showers, constantly washing and drying his shorts and socks. Blinding headaches, poor exam results, early nights and strict diets. Worth it for the feeling. Empty lungs, dead legs, ticker tape broken across his waist. The trophies and medals, collected like fridge magnets or tea towels from hidden fields and Scout huts and clubhouses. Places he had never returned to. He had been praised for his humility and his sportsmanship and his indifference to defeat, while inside he boiled with ambition and pride. *If they made the football pitch longer,* Gillis thought, *I'd have got on better.* If they made it so there were huge spaces between the players. They should have to run miles to meet one another, coax the ball over bogs, up hills and through woodlands, orienteering as they go. They should need a map and compass, waiting like snipers for movements of the opposite side. Instead, at fourteen, he had permanently slipped onto the subs bench. His voice had cracked when he quit the team, and the coach had laughed. He joined an athletics club. Ran circuits around the playing fields before school, and during lunch, sometimes suspecting that he might have accidentally broken the world record. He entered competitions and tournaments and began to collect a few trophies. His dad was proud again. Despite the blissful loneliness of the run, on the finishing line strangers still wanted to shake his hand. He took to running a little further than necessary. Beyond the ticker tape, he would find a tree to lean on and wait until his name was called. He climbed the podiums, and collected the medals. When his knees betrayed him, and the physio failed, all of his certainties – the gold and silver, the sponsorships and endorsements, his eventual retirement at thirty-five, relaxing into a life of sportsman's dinners and anecdotes of the old days, all flags and podiums and laurel leaves – all of it was suddenly shown to be nothing but vapour seeping from a softened brain. And the knees just wouldn't heal and although he had once hoped that Rachel would follow him – down into England and from England into Europe and from there, out into the world, the actual world where proper things happened to real people – he now had nothing to offer. No gold and no silver. He began to hope for a suicide mission. Or a heroic gesture. Maybe he would have the opportunity to throw himself in front of traffic as he pushed a child to safety. Or be provoked to violence by someone who deserved it. The battle would leave a picturesque scar on his face, which he would reluctantly explain to gathering crowds in pubs and restaurants. They would remember the story. *That was you?* they would say. Women's faces would flush. He would avoid photographers and give no interviews, but the enigmatic statements he made in passing would be printed in bold letters on the cover of several newspapers, and why not? Written down in history. Football had fucked up and running went to shit. Hiding away from ambition, he had taken the most practical and sensible route into responsible adulthood. Despite not believing in God, he had sucked it up, taken it on the chin, and pretended to for money. Plenty of people did worse.

'And how much do you cost?' The widower looked up from the brochures.

'Nothing,' Gillis answered, the imagery of his past disappearing.

'Nothing at all? What's the catch?'

'No catch.'

The widower turned his brochures back and forward, looking for the small print. 'But who pays you?'

'I'll get my reward in heaven, I suppose.'

The man smiled in pity.

A strange noise intervened. A beep or a whistle came from Gillis's jacket. It was only his phone, had it always made that noise? 'You'll have to. . .' Gillis's thought trailed off as he pulled out his phone. A message from Rachel read, *Could do tonight?*

He assumed, at first, that she had meant to contact someone else. So thumbed a solitary question mark in response. '. . .Excuse me.' His thought was recovered until the phone whistled again.

Thought I'd call in and see what all the fuss was. If you want.

He smiled as he pressed his phone back into his jacket and the widower carried on with his questions, but soon Gillis tuned out again, feeling the onrush of time passing. He had run so many races, overtaken so many runners. Each season, he rose in the rankings until he plateaued, muddled along, then fell spectacularly out of everything. The fucking knees. Bastard fucking knees. He stared at the traitors. But now, with the severed hand, he had a chance to set everything right again. Start over, work away on the quiet, build something up. Something he could be proud of. Just had to figure out how these things worked. Miracles and all that.

As he burled around the narrowing driveway that led to the manse, a looming patch of light and colour forced him to stamp the brake, throwing his chest tight to the steering wheel, before he dropped back into his seat. Rachel had parked on the blind corner. He could see her silhouette moving inside the car.

They both got out at the same time and met at the front door, Rachel pointedly walking around one of the holes in the drive to get there. She looked a little confused.

'I fell asleep for a second there, while I was waiting. I'm supposed to start my shift at the hotel in an hour. But here I am, I'm intrigued. . .' She checked her watch while he fumbled for the key and led her into the kitchen.

'Isn't it a bit soon to be going back to work?' Gillis asked, filling the kettle.

'Well, I need to pick up shifts while they're going. That woman's off for cancer treatment, Nichol's sidekick supposedly. Fingers crossed she'll be in hospital for a few months. And then, if she gets time off for stress, or for more treatment, it could go on for a wee while.'

'That's good.'

'Couldn't come at a better time.' She described her days. Lunch and break times filled with phone calls to banks and loan companies. All of her husband's debts were now transferring to her. A motorbike covered in dust. Sound systems and TVs she didn't know how to use. One remote control seemed to cancel out the other.

'How do you take it?' Gillis asked.

She shrugged. 'It isn't easy. But I've got to keep at it, for Jamie at least.'

'The milk, I meant. The tea.'

'Oh, that – I just take it as it is. You don't remember?'

'I thought you might have changed.' He passed the tea across with no milk and no sugar.

'Wouldn't know how.' She pressed the ceramic to her blouse and scalded her chest. There was a moment of weighted silence which Rachel dismissed with a sudden, 'Who's been dying? Anyone interesting?'

'Just the usual.'

'Anyone deserve it?'

'Every last one of them.'

She laughed at that, and he noticed himself relaxing in her company. He rocked his chair back and fumbled through a kitchen drawer, retrieved a crushed pack of cigarettes. Her eyes widened in surprise. 'You used to be a real militant anti-smoker.'

He nodded. 'I wanted to keep the lungs good. But I'm not really using them now, so thought I may as well.'

'Just when everyone's stopping, you decide to start?'

He pulled one free and jammed it in his mouth, pointed the pack at the door, and they walked out, to stand and stare at the unkempt garden and the pale ghost of the kirk.

'I don't get a chance to do this much,' she said, as he leant across to offer her a light.

'What's that? Smoke?'

'No, this.' She swirled the cigarette in the air between them. 'It's just nice to be out the house.' They began by turning away and blowing the smoke over their shoulders, but soon their conversation and a second cigarette was all contributing to a cloud of smoke that lingered between them and a scatter of ash that accumulated around their feet.

'Do you remember. . .' Rachel began to tell a long story, their old flat, how the window wouldn't open, the landlord was refusing to fix it, then came over in a temper just to prove it opened fine, just needed a bit of force. How he tried and tried and then it gave and he almost fell out and they'd had to grab at his feet. She couldn't get through a sentence without laughing. 'And then— How he was like— *See?*'

Then they remembered the leaking pipe, the broken boiler, the strange smell that rose from the sink. The intervening years seemed to have gilded all of these moments. So they could miss their boredom and loneliness and petty dissatisfaction which, in hindsight, had accumulated into a sort of happiness.

She said that her nights were empty. She said it was hard to look at Jamie. His face was an encrypted version of his father's. The boy kept quiet, as if he knew a secret. 'Dougie had good friends,' she said. They were protecting him, even now. They wouldn't tell her what had happened. If he had been drinking again. No one knew why he was working that night. She needed his passwords. She wanted to get into his phone and his email account and his social media. She had tried her name, the date they met, their son's name, the date he was born, nothing matched. She turned, expecting something from Gillis, a gesture, or an embrace. But his eyes were distant until the weight of her gaze forced him to jolt his head round to meet hers. She snorted a bitter laugh. 'Sorry for complaining.'

He promised he'd been listening, and hoped she wouldn't quiz him on the particulars.

'Let's go then,' she flicked a fag end into what had once been a flower bed. 'I'm here for whatever I'm here for.'

'Keep complaining,' he insisted; he wanted to hear it. But she ushered him back through the kitchen with sweeping movements of her arms, checking her watch as she went.

'It's fine, Gillis. It doesn't do me any good to dwell on it anyway.'

Since Nichol had searched the manse and discovered the severed hand, Gillis had put a little more effort into hiding the shortbread tin. He led Rachel upstairs, and paced toward the boiler cupboard like a priest approaching the tabernacle, barefoot, bowed and hatless.

'I'm not here for that.' She stared through at his bed.

'I know.'

'I'm just saying so you know.'

He opened the cupboard and threw a few towels and blankets to one side, uncovering a broken breeze block. Underneath, the shortbread tin, scratched and dented by the great weight of it. He pulled the tin free and paused for a moment. She was trembling slightly, and her anxiety was infectious. Gillis opened the tin. He waited for her reaction.

'Oh, OK.' She leant on his shoulder. 'I don't know what I was expecting.'

'Do you see it?'

'Feel like all that's crawling with spiders.' She stared into the corners of the boiler cupboard. 'Is that stuff yours?' A plastic Christmas tree, bound in a black bin bag, bent around the top of the boiler. Draped tinsel and loose baubles spilt onto the floor. Hymnals and Bibles were stacked next to bedsheets and spare soap.

'Don't you see that?' Gillis pointed at his shortbread tin. 'Can you see what it is?'

'It's a hand, I know.'

'But it's real.'

'And what is it? About a hundred or two hundred years old or something?'

'I don't know. Why do you think that?'

'They wouldn't keep it otherwise, would they? Everything gets valuable if enough time passes.' She looked at her watch. 'That's the thing Nichol wanted me to see?'

Gillis thought she have might screamed, or fallen to her knees and begun to worship the thing.

'Did you find it in the church?' she asked.

'Don't you see it moving?'

'I don't think so.' Her lips were curled in mild disgust as she watched the corners of the cupboard for spiders. The hand could have leapt in the air and stuck up its middle finger and she wouldn't have noticed.

'You can't see that?' The hand was making minor twitches and adjustments, a tapping finger, a glitch in the thumb.

'Maybe. Do you remember when we did *animal electricity*?' She said the words slowly, as if she would be corrected. 'In fourth year chemistry? You were there. We got a volt reading out a piece of meat. You can get a frog's leg to twitch if you attach it to a battery.' She swirled her hand in vague circles. 'Maybe the tin is conducting electricity. Or like, it's the rotting? The fermentation? It could make an electric build-up? Static electricity. Something like that?'

Gillis looked sceptical.

'Well, I don't know. What else could it be?'

He didn't want to say *miracle*. 'And it doesn't look familiar to you?'

'Should it?' She stared at the ragged fingernails, and the dark hairs that sprouted from the knuckles. She pressed a finger into its side. 'What are you meant to do, pray to it?'

'Don't touch it.' Gillis pulled her backward by a pinch of her jacket. 'You're not bothered by that?'

'You'd think it'd be all decomposed. They must have embalmed it with something, but I guess they'd have methods we don't know about.'

'Who would?'

'The old. . . Celtic people? When was that? St Patrick, when was he? That kind of time. Or St Andrew, he's the Scottish one, isn't he? What time was he around?'

Gillis didn't care. And he also didn't know. 'You definitely don't recognize it?'

'All this fuss between you and Nichol, just for an old church thing. What would I know?'

'Look at this.' Gillis pulled out his phone and scrolled through his saved images, stopped and lifted one to Rachel. She looked offended. In the image, Douglas had pulled up his shirt and was trying to lick his own nipple. It wasn't very flattering, but it showed the back of the man's hand perfectly. Black hairs on the knuckles, fingernails chewed and turning inward. 'Do you think it might be his?'

She pushed the phone down and flinched. 'Whose? Dougie's? How would it get there. . .?' Her eyes widened. 'Did you have something to do with it?'

'No. . . Wait a minute.' He struggled to explain as Rachel stood, blood draining from her face.

'Did you know?' she asked.

'Know what?'

The colour returned to her face in deep purple blossoms across her cheeks and neck as she clutched her jacket and gripped her car keys. Her footsteps met the stairs and struck out in a tremendous drumroll, the crescendo and cymbal crash given to Gillis. He shouted downstairs, 'It's nothing, it's just a joke!' but she was already out the door.

On reflection, he thought to himself the following morning, it all could have gone better. Gillis was big enough to acknowledge that. Though he had never sincerely apologized to man, woman or beast, he often found himself explaining away his actions to a crowd of imaginary interrogators. Vague individuals he could summon at any time. One part father, one part school teacher, one part political and societal expectation, with a small pinch of religion, a strong enough flavour to override almost every other part. He had wanted to be honest, but the honest answers were ridiculous, and they frightened him. He didn't believe that the severed hand belonged to Rachel's husband, but who else was unaccounted for? The whole body could be scattered across the town. A lower jaw, lying kerbside, picked at by crows. A femur and a knee bone, still clinging to one another, attempting to lift themselves and run from the terrible fate already dealt to them. Anything could be happening. What could Gillis exclude? Now that the severed hand was amongst us, he found it hard to deny there could be life after death. Or death within life, or life within death.

Shouldn't you think that anyway? said this concocted interrogator. *Aren't you claiming to be a man of God? Haven't you been telling every widow who will listen that you've clipped the man's ticket, stamped his passport and ushered him into a life of bliss?*

'Leave me alone,' Gillis whispered to his empty living room. Isn't it just nice to be nice? Gillis would like to watch these interrogators, whoever they were, confront a woman in tears and tell her, *No, your man's not even in hell. There's nowhere to go, he's only in the ground, not even waiting, not even expecting you to join him.*

What about the men? The widowers? these interrogators asked.

Some of them are right pricks, Gillis thought. *So I don't really say much to them.*

The interrogators shook a collective head. *Those poor men, lost and looking for comfort, turn to the oldest institution available, a repository of ancient wisdom, and what does it offer? Nothing but a cold shoulder.*

Worse than that, Gillis admitted. *An active shrug.*

His interrogation was interrupted by furious knocking at the front door. Gillis straightened his collar and readied himself to face Rachel with a barrage of explanations, all refined by his self-examination. But as he cautiously opened the door and made to speak, Nichol's face prodded through the gap, his progress stopped by the locking chain. 'Isn't it Sunday?'

Behind him, a dozen bodies shuffled, and among them, a pleading grimace. 'They're putting holes in the vestry walls.' Jim Macintyre, janitor of the kirk, placed himself in the sliver of daylight. 'They're pulling out the wiring.'

'We're working, and we're wanting to see the hand,' Nichol explained.

'And they're trampling plaster into the carpets,' Jim spoke over them.

'It's eleven o'clock on Sunday.' Nichol jostled against the janitor, pressing for the gap in the door. 'How's there no service?'

As Gillis unlatched and opened the door, he tried to explain. The congregation had either died or lost interest, moved away, or driven thirty miles to another church that had a lot of AV equipment. Nichol couldn't hear him. 'Hurry up, bud, it's freezing out here.'

'Fish.'
  'Fish.'
  'Yeah, mate, fish too.'
  The men were all Nichol's employees, following Gillis in a procession as he led them to the kirk.
  'We were getting things ready for the deconsecrator, and I was telling them how nothing shifts this sore skin, how I've tried every cream, potion, pill, you name it, until I touched that relic, the miracle you have here.'
  The visitors smirked.
  'And these bastards don't fucking believe me.' Nichol gripped the youngest of them by the head and noogied him until he yelped, squirmed until his head was loose and fell over. When the boy picked himself up, he grinned and trotted after them, like a dog happy to be hit.
  'Go get the hand and we'll do a service.' Nichol reacted jubilantly to his own idea, announced as Jim Macintyre opened the great oak door of the kirk and waved them all through. 'How many d'you need for it? I can get more. There's two working in the back of the smokehouse. I can pull someone out the hotel too, and the cleaners will be finishing up at half-past. Will that be enough? Get the hand and we'll do it.'
  Gillis managed to distract them from the severed hand by climbing to the pulpit, as his visitors set out a semicircle of chairs below. One joker sat on the back of a plastic tractor,

left over from the Mums and Tots group. He pushed the wheels back and forward as Gillis read from the Bible, until Nichol slapped him on the back of the head. He hunched over the little steering wheel and pretended to listen. Gillis pushed his thumb into the middle of the Bible and read the first thing he saw. *'When I came, was there no man? When I called was there none to answer?'* The visitors looked puzzled. *'At my rebuke I dry up the sea, I make rivers a wilderness: their fish stink, because there is no water, and die for thirst.'*

'Bring out the hand,' Nichol called from his seat. 'Show the boys what it does.' A silly squeaking noise followed. The man on the plastic tractor had found the horn.

Gillis ignored them and began to read through a brief sermon, the notes of which were stuffed into the back of his Bible. They were dated from three years back.

'Just show them the hand,' Nichol interrupted again.

'We could try a hymn.' Gillis climbed down the two steps of the pulpit and rushed to the corner of the kirk, where a Hammond organ lay unused, shrouded in heavy black material. Its keyboards were shuttered and locked, and the key had been lost years ago. He pried at the corner of the casing, and managed to wedge a finger inside. The keys made no noise. Gillis turned, knowing what Nichol would ask.

Nichol had climbed up into the pulpit and looked down from its slight elevation at the shallows of the hall. He splayed his arms and cupped his hands like a great orator. 'You could do a lot with this.' He stared back and forward at an imaginary crowd, taking in silent applause.

'Speech, speech, speech, speech.' His employees clapped their hands and stamped their boots on the floor.

Nichol laughed and opened his mouth to speak, but nothing came to him. He turned to the minister. 'Where's this hand then? Come on!'

'I'm getting a phone call.' Gillis footered in his pocket and fled to the doorway, pretending to look for privacy there. Into the dead phone screen, he spoke to an imaginary parishioner. 'Is that right?' he said. 'That's terrible,' and 'Yes, I'll be there as soon as I can.' He returned to the group shaking his head in disbelief, still trying to decide if there had been a car crash or a house fire.

'There's a man chucked himself off a bridge. And I'll need to go and see if he's OK.'

Nichol was exasperated. 'What about us? What have we been waiting for?'

'I know, I know.'

'Do *you* know where it is?' Nichol rounded on the janitor, who took a step back and began to make his own excuses.

'I've got my lunch to get. See with the time, it's a roast so she'll be setting the table now. I'll have to lock up and drive back. I should get going.'

'Thanks for coming though, lads.' Gillis swung his arms like a farmer herding cattle. But the visitors didn't move. They barely raised their heads from their phone screens.

'Just bring the hand in here, pal, and we'll lock the place ourselves.' Nichol smiled warmly. 'I've been meaning to get a set of keys cut anyway. So I could just take these, couldn't I?' His fingers clamped around the keyring in Jim Macintyre's hand, and the janitor looked to Gillis for help. 'I know the Church still has the lease, but I own the place, and we have a lot of work to do. So. . .' He looked toward the exit.

'Right. Yeah.' Gillis walked a couple of paces, not sure where he was going to go.

'The hand though.' Nichol's body seemed to change. Were the shoulders broader? Were his arms thicker? Was he gaining height?

'Sooner we get it, sooner you can go.' Nichol's employees began to stand and look around, bored and eager to help.

'I don't know. I put it down in here and it got tidied away.' Nichol looked to the janitor.

'I've not seen anything. Listen, my wife, she'll want to be eating by one. She's got roast beef and tatties,' he pleaded. 'She's got peas and carrots to make. And I always make the gravy. I'll have to get going now, I'm sorry, Gillis.' Jim Macintyre surrendered his keys, and his pockets no longer jangled as he walked, dejected, from the church hall.

'Will it take you two hours to make gravy?' Nichol called across the echoing floorboards.

The janitor laughed nervously. 'She needs me to cut the meat.'

The assembled employees all smirked, then laughed as the man left.

'He does it for free,' Gillis said. 'Jim there, he does it all for free.'

'Free?' Nichol's eyebrows leapt up and his front teeth struggled against the word.

'He's here most nights. Checking in. And he keeps the place clean. Fixes things that needs fixing.'

Nichol pretended to be impressed. 'I'll need to get him down to the fishery.'

'He wouldn't do that.'

'Why not?' Nichol seemed a little offended.

'He's here because he believes in it.'

'In what?'

'In all of it.'

Nichol rolled his eyes, then pointed with his confiscated keys to the cupboards and the back rooms. 'Is it somewhere in here?'

Gillis nodded.

'Sure it's not in your house?'

Gillis's nerves betrayed him. His head ticked toward the manse.

'We'll get on better if we're honest with each other. Won't we?'

As the minister led Nichol back across the kirkyard, into the manse and up the stairs, he had to continually modify the escape plans he envisioned. *I'll run ahead*, he thought, knowing he wouldn't. *I'll grab the hand and run out the back door.* He climbed the stairs. *I'll leap over the banister and jump in the car.* He opened the boiler cupboard door and passed the shortbread tin to Nichol.

'You going to that emergency?'

'Yes.' Gillis walked slowly down the stairs, through the knot of men collected in his doorway, out to his car.

'We can lock the place up.' Nichol followed him out. 'I'll get a good look at what I've got here. Maybe we should start thinking what we can do with it?'

After the tumult of two market days, the Laird's villages lay in purgatorial time. A Sabbath marked by heavy rain, so that steam rose from the mass-goers' felted clothes as they knelt, huddled together in the back half of the chapel, penned away from the pews by an ornate wooden barrier. Their knees ground against the cold flagstones, but their shoulders were warmed as they leant into one another. They were peasants and labourers, some of them were fishermen. Their eyes were either keen for the exit, or wandering around the vaults of the chapel, examining the ornate glass, the paintings of saints in sorrowful torture, the beaming light of God's presence which pierced them like a bower of colourful arrows. Latin glossolalia intertwined with curls of incense smoke and rose to the ceiling. The priest and his adjuncts spoke and sang, young boys draped in white smocks, their heads tilted back, necks straining, mouths as open and hungry as baby birds.

The eyes of the faithful, penned like cattle at the back of the chapel, followed two figures as they entered and sat alone in the ranks of empty pews. The Laird and Lady of Kirkmouth delicately stooped and pressed their knees into soft cushions before the altar. They took communion and returned to their seat. Only a year back, the pews had bowed and creaked like an overloaded barge, straining beneath the weight of the good families, presenting themselves to the priest and populace. Now, the families claimed to worship at home, amongst friends. The priest created a silence for the Laird and Lady to rise and cross themselves, then leave

by a side door as the peasants bent lower and turned away
from the bulbous head and empty expression of the Laird,
and the sunken, exhausted eyes of the Lady. As the nobles
left the chapel, a farting sound, belched from the huddle of
peasants, a quiet laugh. Was it a mouth or an arsehole that
made the noise? No one knew. Some smiled, some frowned,
some did both. It wasn't Jan, but he blushed anyway. He tried
to move backward through the crowd, but was held in place
by a broad hand on his shoulder.

'Sinner. Why only half-repent?' Brother Malcolm whispered down his neck.

The priest sighed loudly as he walked the length of the
chapel, to the rail before which the meek bowed. An altar
boy held a broad tray scattered with bread, and the priest
murmured his ritual and fed these children of God with a
little jump of his fingers, away from the colourful tongues
and cracked teeth that snatched at it. Why did communion
bread taste so different to their own? Was the flour more
refined? Was it salted? Was honey dripped into the dough, or
a tiny sprig of dill? Then came the silver cup. Wine, diluted
down. They sipped and their saliva was wiped away with a
rag.

'Where's your bell?' Jan hissed over his shoulder to the
monk who still held him in place. There was no reply, and
as the priest came to him, Jan stuck out his tongue, took the
bread and thin wine and that was that.

As the last of the peasants left, the young altar boys took
off their white robes and threw a bucket of rainwater across
the stinking mud which the crowd had tracked in. They
sluiced the excess out the chapel doors with two brooms,
pushing from the far corners into a tight conflict for the
narrowing exit.

That morning, Jan had hoped to follow the Laird and Lady and hold his remaining pages out for their consideration. After dazzling them with gold, he would offer to repair the book using these, his paintbrushes and pigments, and this, his wind of binding thread. Scuppered, he watched them recede uphill through the distant gatehouse, back to their vast estate. The peasants returned to their fields and cottages, shielding their faces from a gang of men in black jackets who shouted anti-papist slogans and threw stones at the chapel.

'Is your stomach not churning in rebellion against the meat of Jesus?' The idiot monk, Brother Malcolm, had followed him outside, clapping his hands instead of ringing his bell. 'Sinner! Straggler! You there, staring, repent your sins! God's judgement comes quickly, and treacherously!' He fell silent and bowed his head as they passed another huddle of men, black-jacketed and stern. They held cudgels and switches of green wood.

Jan tried to lose the monk, but he was trailed to the guesthouse, denying him the peace of the bench he had hired, the two wooden boards and blankets. He longed to lie down, roll one blanket beneath his head, and wind the other tight about his body. Hide from the landlord and his unravelling tab.

'Will you not have a drink, monk?' Two fishermen shouted from the doorway, chewing dandelion leaves and spitting into the runnel of water which raced past the guesthouse door. Their empty mugs lay in the mire. They had not been at mass. The monk shook their hands and agreed that he would, and followed Jan into the front room; lowered his broad hands from the threat of another clap and placed them on the long table as though downing a hammer and pick. Hidden from sight of the faithful, they pursued the Sabbath boredom with cards and dice. A pause for cheese, black bread, more beer. Dice again. A dozen candles were lit, and men began to crowd the tables, laugh too loudly, drink indiscreetly. The landlord took men by their necks and sobered them in the mud outside. Laid a bolt across the jambs of the door as they left. A half-dozen men stayed back, to sing and drink until morning when they were carried away to wring their bodies out with work in the fields. The monk was permitted to stay. He was gambling with the flattened bronze of his bell, which – if he lost possession of it – would be made into a knife, or a set of glittering fish hooks.

'Well then, Jan.' The landlord surveyed the scattered cards and dice. 'You'll have to pay your bill.' All that Jan had earned from the offcuts of his book was long gone in trades and penny bets. He pushed his hand across the table to clear a space and took the tightly wound baton of vellum from his sleeve, unrolled it and asked, 'Who would you like?' He turned from page to page, and settled on St James. Took a hooked knife from his pocket and as the last of the red ale soured in his mouth, he carefully etched the vellum, outlining and severing this saint from his fellow apostles, evicting him from heaven. He passed the painted figure to the landlord. The fragile wisp of vellum lay across the man's hand and was carried to the fireplace, pierced through the temple, pinned to the alehouse wall. The drunks crossed themselves.

'And for me, Jan, for pulling you out the water?' It was half a question and half a demand. Another page buckled and warped as Jan's knife removed the apostle Paul from the Damascus road, before his revelation could appear. The fisherman blessed himself, folded the apostle and pushed it inside his jacket. As the last hours of the Sabbath passed, the saints gradually descended, one and all, from heaven, to sit in the pockets of men, lie on their hands, and in moments of impiety, sit behind their ears or pounce, suddenly, from their closed mouths.

They were laughing too loudly, and retching too brazenly. As midnight drifted past unnoticed, the alehouse was surrounded by men in black jackets, incomers, drifting over from the hills and the nearest little township, partly reduced to charcoal, partly elevated to heaven. The men collected behind their leader, an advocate from the south, who knocked the door and demanded that the sinners inside show themselves.

CHAPTER EIGHT

If there had been a pulpit, or a high horse, or a soapbox, conveniently placed at the doors of the Nicholson Hotel, Gillis would have been standing tall and exclaiming from it. In its absence, he made do with the slight elevation that the back step and his good boots gave him, to rage and thunder against the sins of man, and one in particular. The waiters, the chefs, the kitchen porters and cleaners listened politely as he condemned them all to hell. Damnation patter came easy, all he had to do was turn the internal monologue outward, and dress it in religious garb.

'Where's Nichol? Where is he, the bastard?' None of them knew.

After Gillis had been pushed from his own home, after he'd rushed to save the imaginary suicide, he had driven back to the manse, and noticed with relief that Nichol's van had long since left the driveway. But the kirk doors had been firmly sealed, a large silver padlock hung from a new latch, and though he had tried his shoulder at the hinges, and even attempted to jam a screwdriver behind the hasp, the door held fast.

Now, he pushed his way through the hotel staff and found himself swaggering bow-legged through the small rooms and corridors, asking after the boss until finally a poor kitchen porter pointed to an empty office and said, 'Didn't I tell you?' With his long hair and beard partially bagged in loose blue hairnets, he looked like his features had been hastily tidied away from polite company. Hands concealed in bright blue gloves, he gestured at the door with a potato peeler. He was joined by a crowd of co-workers that Gillis began to berate. They served at the table of a thief. A thief and a murderer! The last insult felt reckless, but he wouldn't take it back. His blood congealed and set in his cheeks and ears.

'Customers can't be back here,' the kitchen porter said kindly.

'I'm not a customer,' Gillis stuttered. 'I'm a man of God.'

'Sure you are.'

Gillis strode from the kitchens and went back the way he'd come, pacing down the corridor, toward the loading bays. 'What's that smell?' He held his wrist over his nose as he approached a huddle of men, crowded around the exit. Nichol was in there, hidden within the oil slick of a black rain jacket. He had a fistful of crumpled paperwork and a biro, and was checking boxes as they were unpacked from a refrigerated van.

'Is it all of them?' he shouted through to his employees. They were plunging their hands into crushed ice and poly-styrene, guddling dozens of salmon from blue bags, and flinging them aside into plastic crates.

'Aye, they're all just as bad, boss.' Inside the van, an employee turned a fish back and forth in his hands. 'You wanting to see?'

The man bent double and read from the barcode stickers on the side of each box, slapping them as he went. 'Tuesday, Wednesday, Monday. Tuesday. That one's last week.'

When one of the plastic crates had been filled with putrid fish and tangled packaging, Nichol cursed viciously and screamed into the van. The rest would have to go out.

'Out?' The men looked suspicious. 'Like, out to the customers?'

'Sort through them. Take the best and send them out.'

'To the customers?' They looked at one another, wide-eyed. 'Are you sure?'

'Out! Out to the customers!'

'People'll get sick. . .'

Nichol pulled the inventory from his employee's hands and ticked his way through twenty-odd boxes, then signed his name at the bottom. 'Print new tickets, get new boxes and keep them cold, for Christ's sake.' Then he gripped the plastic crate and heaved it to chest height, turned, caught sight of the minister and startled. 'What a fright you gave me. I'm sorry, pal, but I'm a bit busy now.' He made to push past Gillis. But the minister pulled the crate from him and stood in his way.

'That's good of you, mate, I appreciate the help.' Nichol bowed to collect another half-filled crate and held his nose to one side as he faced the minister, still stuck in place since the reeking salmon had been forced into his hands. 'Chop-chop, just drop it in the kitchen door down there and the boys'll get it.' Nichol jostled him, and Gillis found himself turning and obediently carrying the crate back down the sloping corridor, into the kitchen again, staring at the contents the whole time. What once writhed now lay frozen in its writhing; a half-dozen eyes stared, lidless and cold. Guilty. Strangely petrol-coloured, almost green. On their skins, what looked like frozen flies. As he dropped the crate, several of the fish bounced loose onto the floor.

'I hear you've been hassling my staff?' Nichol lumped his own crate down on top of the other and knelt to retrieve the frozen salmon. As he stood, he grinned, teeth all crooked. 'I wouldn't worry, mate, I do it all the time. It's good to be a bit like that, a bit mental.' Nichol stepped close to him and waved his arms toward the door. 'Because you're a timid guy. But you need a bit of anger, a bit of force to get by in the world. You need to be able to say what's what. . . Most people manage that before they're thirty-odd, but I wouldn't worry. What comes to you comes at its own pace, doesn't it?'

Gillis was reminded of his mission, to confront and rebuke that devil, and reclaim the kirk and the severed hand all to himself. 'You locked me out! You had no right!' he hissed.

'Well, technically I do, pal. It belongs to me.'

'No, it's mine!' Gillis yelled and struck the door with his fist. It was a burst of purified anger, entirely separate from himself, fallen as if from heaven, bypassing his consciousness to inhabit his body. The hilt of his hand ached, and the two men stared at one another.

'Well. . . what d'you mean by that?'

The door danced again as Gillis's fist smacked the central panel and the signage. This one was weaker. Divine inspiration had dwindled, it was only a quotation of the previous action. Seeing the difference, Nichol forced himself into the gap. 'Well. . . if you'd been around, we would have given you a key.'

'It's mine, I found it.' Though it felt a little silly, Gillis invoked the ancient moral order of the world, the instinctive ethical language of mankind: 'Finders keepers.'

Unable to argue against that principle, Nichol paused, long enough for the moral feeling to swell, crest and crash down to nothing. Then he asserted the other playground strategy. Threat of force. 'We can argue all day over who's right and who's wrong. But we both know that if you hide that relic away again, I'll just go and get it. I can stand here and promise you I won't. But you'd know I was lying, if I need it again I'll go and take it. But if we leave it there, in the kirk, we can both have the use of it. We could work together. Isn't that more Christian?'

They waited in that stalemate until Gillis folded. 'Do I have a choice?'

'I'd say no.' Nichol rooted through his pocket and pulled out a couple of silver keys, jangled them over the table, then pushed his thumbnail into the keyring and separated the two keys. He passed one across, but pulled it back as soon as Gillis reached for it. 'We have to trust one another.'

Gillis reached for the key again, and they held either end. 'Do we?'

Gillis pulled back on the key, twisting it from the other man's grip.

'Very good.' Nichol grinned. 'You're learning.' He tried to coax the minister into smiling back, but Gillis ignored him and pressed himself against the wall as a couple of lads from the fishery marched down the corridor with arms full of chipped polystyrene and tangled cellophane. 'Wait. . .' Nichol grabbed at one of them.

'How you feeling?' He pulled the lad's hand back and forth, showing that the skin on his knuckles was cracked, and the fingernails were bitten down to half their normal size.

'Fine.'

'Hands still stinging?'

The man nodded.

'How about that anxiety and depression?'

The man shrugged.

'Early to tell, maybe by tomorrow.' He patted his employee on the back, and with his last touch, pushed him back to his work. 'He'll be all right. We had the severed hand sitting on him all afternoon. Spoke about all this to my Carol, the wife, and she said look at Lourdes, all the tourists who visit that place, all the miracles and everything. Imagine, we've found this relic and so we set up a little shrine to St Someone of Somewhere and everyone and their granny wants to come see it, see the site it was found at and pray, *Oh Jesus, help my heart keep ticking, help my back stop aching, help my weans, help my husband, please, please, help me keep my job.'* Nichol was simpering, hands clasped together in supplication, in imitation of a crowd of imaginary old folk, down on their knees, begging to be allowed a little elbow room in the time and space allotted to them. 'Obviously you can't just say, *Fuck the hospital, I'll heal you.* You'd have to see it as like self-help, or alternative wisdom. What's the one with the stones on your back? Or the needles they stick in you? It'd be like. . . ancient medicine. Wisdom of our ancestors, you'd have to talk like that. You wouldn't even be lying, not really. There's already millions of these things all around the world,' Nichol continued. 'Some churches have dozens of them. Heads and eyes and tongues and teeth. Some places even have a whole body, pickled like a big onion. Nothing's changed on these things in a hundred years. It's a mystery to science.'

Gillis wasn't listening. He was turning the key over in his hand, eyes closed, appealing to heaven. *Get that hand back to me. Tell me why I'm here, tell me what to do, or leave me alone. Whittle me into a spear, or throw me on a compost heap. Give me money and good holidays and stock options and all that kind of thing. Or destroy me completely. Make money fall from the sky, straight into my pockets. Or forget all of that and give me back the hand. What you've pushed on me, I'll accept. Don't let anyone else speak to you, make them go through me!*

'Honestly, it could be really serious money, and it could be good for the town.' Nichol didn't need another person to carry on a conversation, he could skip from one topic to another all on his own. 'It was plenty good for me. They were flying special creams out from America. Expensive, steroid stuff. You can get addicted to this kind of thing, it's a serious, heavy-duty cream, not for everyone. You've got to be careful. Pregnant women, wee kids can't be near it. And the smell of it. . .' His mouth soured. 'It's this thick, cloudy kind of smell. Like glue, but how glue used to be, back when they made it out of horses. Sometimes, when I'm really sore, I put on a double dose, and I have to say to Carol, *Stay away, hen*, 'cause if she gets too much of it rubbed into her skin, and it goes into her bloodstream, I don't know, it could be. . . not good. For hormones and. . . vitamins and what have you. So I don't take chances. Not with family. That's a principle I have.'

He paused a second, running his hand unconsciously over his arms and down his chest, circling his belly. 'Bedsheets get all greasy with it. You've got to wash them at a really high heat, to kind of melt the stuff down so it can wash away. Fucking hell, if I'm rid of that, you know. . . Thank Christ. I'm not a religious man, but if those are the kind of results you get. . . Might be money in it,' he concluded. 'I've told you and I tell everyone the same thing. I've got big plans for this town. And OK, a lot of them have come to fuck all, but that's how it works, isn't it? You fail and you fail and you fail, and then you succeed.'

Gillis opened his eyes, concluded his prayer. 'Or you fail, fail and fail, and someone else succeeds. Or fails too. They fail, and then fail and fail and fail all over again.'

Nichol squinted through the confusing repetition, but started to lose sight of that vague, golden future he had envisioned. Where fish leapt into the net, and money bred in the pocket. Brought back from his dream to the stinking salmon, Nichol replied grouchily, 'Well, I'm not going to be lectured on money matters by a priest.'

'Minister, not priest.'

'Dogs and cats, what's the difference?'

Gillis squeezed himself between the van and the last reeking crates of fish, and Nichol followed, stooping to collect the frozen spillage, calling out, 'You're not taking offence, are you? Where are you going?'

'The kirk, to get. . . to make sure that thing's OK.' As Gillis left he stared into the sky where dozens of seagulls circled and screamed in despair, desperate to approach the van.

'Don't take offence!' Nichol arched his good arm back and launched the rotten, melting fish into the air, laughing as the seagulls lunged and battled across the pavement to scrounge in the gravel at his feet.

The key turned easily, and broke the silver padlock which fell into his hands. The great oak door creaked and yawned onto the cold black corridor. The lights flickered. The church was silent save for spattering rain on the windows high overhead. Muddy boot prints surrounded the pulpit, and a jumper had been left behind. It looked as though a man had exhausted himself running in circles, before dissolving into the air. The heavy black Bible had been ousted from the pulpit, and in its place, the shortbread tin lay open, exposing the severed hand to the cold air. It writhed and slowly turned toward Gillis. It pointed its finger. But no secret was revealed. No clue had been left. No single step was advanced. Yet it pointed, and insisted on pointing at Gillis. 'I know, I'm back,' he reassured the thing. As he shifted from one side of the pulpit to the other, the hand adjusted and met his eyeline with a crooked fingernail. 'I know,' he said again, but felt a dimming of his guilt as he examined the insistent index finger. Its movements seemed a little different. A thought occurred. Maybe the pointed finger wasn't accusing. Maybe it was choosing him? Selecting him for something? For what, he didn't know, but as the weather strained the windowpanes and the floorboards creaked, Gillis felt the enormity of the empty space overhead, and its emptiness transformed into a sort of presence. 'I'll do it,' he spoke to the open room. 'I will. I'll do it.'

That evening, and the following day, he waited, telling the kitchen wall, the bathroom mirror and the kirk spire that he was ready. But ready for what? He half-expected revelation, divine commands, but nothing came. So he devoted himself to training. Preparing body and mind for whatever was necessary. He pulled the plug from his TV and began fasting, stemming his hunger with another cigarette. He flicked through the Bible, reading sentences at random, hoping that a message might come. He stared at the hand's scribblings, and when he had run out of patience, he did a few press-ups and sit-ups and squats. All to feel active.

Nichol arrived a couple of days later, suggesting a trip out, a flex of the muscles, in the grand spirit of their new collaboration. They should be out healing folk. Drumming up business. Getting the rumour mill turning. The best publicity is word of mouth.

'Hold on,' Gillis tried to argue. 'I didn't say we'd collaborate.'

'You said it was more Christian. To share.'

'You said that.'

Nichol squinted. 'It sounds more like something you would say.' He had him there. 'Look, minister. We've got. . . this amazing opportunity, and I want to use it to make a little profit. What's wrong with that? What do you want to use it for?'

Gillis was silent. He side-eyed the severed hand, idiotically doodling on the kitchen table. It gave him nothing. 'God's work,' he answered lamely.

'Well, that was exactly what I had in mind! Come along with me today and see how you feel about it. If you don't like it, we can go our own ways. Deal?'

There was a long pause while Gillis tried to figure out how to get out of it without seeming petty, but he couldn't think of anything. 'OK, but I want to carry it,' was all he could think to contribute.

They drove out to the big hospital two towns over. The passenger seat of Nichol's four-by-four was rigged with springs and it bounced up and down across the winding back roads. Gillis slunk toward the window as they passed through the long, empty valleys beyond Kirkmouth. He watched the windscreen wipers battle the incoming rain and justified his weakness. The only way to control Nichol would be to go along with everything, to run in the bigger man's slipstream, and in the last hundred metres, pounce and overtake and sprint for the finish.

He was led from the car park through waxen corridors, layers of bleach collected underfoot as he followed Nichol through to Oncology. Nichol seemed to know the doctors and nurses; they smiled and welcomed him as he beelined for a delicate women dwarfed by a thin duvet.

'Is this your wife?' Gillis whispered, readying his professional sympathies.

Nichol circled the bed, pulling the curtains and isolating them in artificial privacy. He stopped to sneer, 'You think *she's* my wife? She's a secretary. Did you hear that, Helen? He thinks we're married.'

The woman stirred and tried to raise herself, pressing her head back into the pillows. Her hair had been dyed in a thick red colour, but a mohawk of grey roots lay across the parting; given a month or two it would resemble a tonsure. After that, it would all fall out. She thanked Nichol for coming along.

Not many employers would be so kind. And the chemo was going well. She didn't feel as bad as yesterday.

'Look.' Nichol had been rifling through his phone, and he held a picture of a beautiful woman under Gillis's nose. Strictured cleavage, waist held sideways, leg stepping forward to prop out her arse. Wine glass raised in celebration of herself. '*That's* my wife.' He turned to the bed. 'Helen, he thought you and me. . .'

Helen smiled. A saline drip was attached to her arm, and a purple helium balloon bobbed over a collection of flowers and cards and a bowl full of oranges, all disturbed or toppled as Gillis pulled his rucksack across her cabinet. He laid the shortbread tin on the hospital bedsheets.

'Mind what I was saying?' Nichol asked the woman in baby talk. 'About miracles and my arm, and my pal's depression?'

Without a thought, Nichol reached across the bed for the severed hand, but stopped himself halfway and pointed at Gillis. 'Why don't you have a shot? That's right, yep, just there.' He supervised as the minister lifted the severed hand and laid it between her breasts. Helen barely reacted, only slowly turning her face in disgust. She said it smelled strange. Gillis wanted to rescue the hand, wanted to apologize to the woman, and run from the hospital and hide the hand from sight. But then what? He couldn't think.

'What's the point in winning if you have to look like that?' Nichol nodded at the TV screen. Men in skin-tight costumery threw themselves down a frozen track. 'No one sees your face, no one understands or respects the sport.' They waited, focusing on the telly and barely mentioning the severed hand's progress until Nichol's phone alarm, set for precisely thirty minutes, told them that Helen's time was up.

Whether the miraculous process had worked or not, Helen thanked them, and promised to get better. Though she wasn't one for religion, she said she felt a certain peace.

'Meds kicking in,' Gillis tried to joke as he took the severed hand from her chest.

'No, no,' she insisted, she was perfectly lucid. Then began to describe all the pills she took.

Nichol quickly interrupted. 'This isn't religion. Tell your pals in the ward. This is something different.'

Visiting hours over, Nichol ushered Gillis through the door. 'Here,' he held his hand out for the tin. Gillis reluctantly passed it over. 'Can you feel it?' Nichol weighed the tin in his hand, generating strength.

Gillis was biting the inside of his mouth. He felt guilty. Should he steal a scalpel from a nurses' station, hold it to Nichol's throat and force him to hand over the severed hand? Run to the top of the building and demand that God show himself?

'Seven, eight, nine, twelve guys in that ward. Ten in the other,' Nichol counted along. 'Think about it. No overheads. The hand doesn't even need feeding, doesn't need a wage, doesn't need a pension. Fuck me, we're in the money.'

Nichol promised to drive him home, but instead, they stopped off at several houses along the way. Chapped doors and let themselves in, filtered through hallways stacked with boxes. A divorcing couple, the man lay with a broken leg. Walked into traffic. Insisted it was a mistake. The severed hand lay across his shin, and Nichol kept winking. 'You'll be all right, mate,' he promised. 'Things are looking up.'

Next, a young woman whose kitchen floor was covered in small black droppings. The carpets were chewed and the walls were scratched. Cats lived among house rabbits in a precarious ceasefire that would last as long as the food kept coming. Her coffee table was covered in scrunched tissues and sachets of flu medicine. Her curtain rail held several dreamcatchers and wind chimes, there was a series of pink crystals along the sill. Her TV showed a computer game paused mid-battle; an elven-eared woman was being bitten by a wolf.

'Which one are you?' Gillis asked, nodding to the screen.

She rolled her eyes and refused to touch the severed hand. She informed Nichol that any pressure to return to work was illegal.

Back in the car, Nichol called the woman a hoor, then apologized for his language. On their way back to the kirk, they stopped in one of Nichol's chip shops, and Nichol took him through to the kitchen. They avoided the fish and battered a couple of smoked sausages instead, helping themselves to chips straight from the fryer. They sipped from cans of juice in the kirk car park, and as the very last dregs of small talk ran dry, they placed the shortbread tin back on the pulpit, checked all of the exits, locked up and shook hands in the darkness. 'We're getting there,' Nichol insisted. 'We're working it out.' Gillis nodded passively. 'Come on, you were there, you saw what we did. . . Didn't we do a good job?' Nichol punched his arm. 'We're on our way!' Then he held him by both biceps and shook the minister until a reluctant smile appeared at the silliness of it all. And then Nichol slapped his back and gripped him by the neck and repeated, 'You're some boy, Gillis, you're some boy.'

Black jackets, black hats, a sprig of white paper in the band. 'We've already spoken about this.' Two men stared through the landlord, into the guest room where the makings of a day and a night's drinking and dice had been hurriedly thrown beneath blankets and clothes, and the occupants were pretending to sleep, pretending to wake innocently from their dreams, hiding their faces in their pillows.

'You men have wives and children, mothers and fathers, but you've spent the Sabbath in the company of strangers and travellers? You have to be strong in order to work in the morning, but you've spent the evening weakening your body?' The more sheepish of the men stood and left. Used to scolding and moralizing, they were surprised to see that the black jackets were backed up this time by men holding clubs, who lined them up against the outside wall.

'And who's this?' The ghostly figure of St Ann appeared, a handspan high, kneeling in holy piety from the armpit of a drunk. King David, still a shepherd boy, stuck in the beard of an even vaster Goliath, failing to conquer. The prophet Jonah, swimming in a glass of beer, where no great fish would ever swallow and save him. Doubting Thomas, reaching out his finger to prod into Christ's side, met nothing but a table's edge, steady and unmiraculous. Abraham, outfitting Isaac in a jacket of kindling, scalded by a candle flame, wet with dripping wax, with no angel and no voice to halt the sacrifice. The black-jacketed men collected the cuttings of Jan's book from pockets and satchels, twisted, crumpled and folded, and scowled as each one appeared, and was laid on the outstretched palm of their leader, a tall, unbearded man in magistrate's clothing.

'Where did you find these?' the magistrate asked.

'Nowhere.'

'Can't remember.'

'Don't know.'

'Him there! Him there in the corner, the foreign lad.'

Jan was picked out and brought back inside the alehouse. The black jackets washed a mug in the rain barrel and brought it over, brimming with water strained from the roof thatch.

'Come on, sober up, where did you get these?'

Using words that slurred between his languages, Jan spoke about the Guild of St Luke, the Lowlands, his escape, his book, his passage to England, then to Scotland, his quarrelling with the sailors over religious matters, the interpretation of certain words, silly stuff, his drenching in the river, and the good people who pulled him out. He told about the Laird's hunting party who had knocked him to the ground and stolen the book created especially for the Laird and his wife. Commissioned some years ago, completed, and now delivered. Never paid for. And Jan, poor apprentice painter, had to make money however he could.

'So you charged for these?' The magistrate pointed at the paper dollies.

'I did. But I won't from now on.'

'For what purpose?'

Jan shrugged, and pointed around the room; the painted figures were hidden underneath pint pots, they were twisted through a handful of weeds that had been cut and arranged to scent the house, some bowed before others, some were arranged in scenes of blasphemous copulation. Fucking like dogs, end to end. The black jackets saw these dioramas and didn't smile.

'No one prayed to these?'

'Prayed to what?'

These black jackets were slight men with bowed heads, weak necks, thin arms, fingers refined and cold. Their foreheads had frown lines so deep they looked like hatchet wounds. They turned the vellum dollies back and forward in their hands. 'How did you make these?' They examined the paintwork. From underneath a pile of tangled bedding, Jan pulled the offcut folio, the sixteen pages he saved from the Laird's man. It had been dissected and depopulated, the pages now looked like tangled fishing nets, large holes bled imagery and text from one surface to another. Openings to Nazareth, Rome, Bethlehem, Jerusalem, heaven and hell yawned wide as he held it by the corner and the pages fell. A man could crawl through it. Two black jackets took a corner each and flicked through the pages; they were horrified by the waste, and thrilled by it too.

'And who bought this?'

'The Laird, the one on the hill, he sent a commission years ago and here I am, fulfilling it.'

They gathered the routed saints and angels and rolled them into the folio. They thanked Jan and led him outside to stand with the others. The drinkers were groaning, their heads and shoulders were bare, gleaming in the trembling light of two burning torches. They were being forced to duck themselves in the water barrel.

'Come on, you silly buggers.' They were led like geese, tapped at the shoulder or hip with switches of willow, led to the market square where their hands were tied and they were bent in half and fastened into stocks to face the last of the moon, greet the first of the sun and the first passers-by, going to their fields, or to the castle, to their boats and nets. Some ignored the collection of sorrowful drunks, some stared, some said hello to men they knew. Some spat. Some collected in groups to gather courage, then searched the ground and the polluted burn that ran through the centre of the village until they found a pail's worth of slops, rotten fish, mushroom and mould, cabbage rind and turned fruit. They threw it at the drunks, who cursed and cowered, or bared their teeth and hissed. As a rotten apple cracked across his forehead, Jan tried to lick the pulp from the heights of his cheeks, but failed and pressed the cold skin of his back into the middle of the huddled men, warming himself at their expense, for only a moment before they pushed him away.

CHAPTER NINE

Gillis spent all morning waiting with his trainers on. Knees bent, arms planted on the coffee table in front of him. Waiting for the starting pistol. A word from the severed hand. Each minute felt as though it needed to be carried from one side of the room to the other. He pushed all of his scheduled meetings until later in the afternoon, knowing that when the afternoon came, he would push them until tomorrow. He turned the whole pile of drawings back and forth, but no new message appeared.

'Better get to it,' he spoke to the empty room. But sat still for another ten minutes. Without Nichol to follow, he wasn't sure how to start. Could go back to the hospital? He knew he wouldn't. And when he turned the drawings back and forward, it wasn't obvious that the severed hand was asking him to intervene in anything. A bracelet of ducks, a wilted crucifixion, a man consuming his own stomach. 'Better just get on with it though,' he agreed with himself, but as soon as he made to stand, he couldn't figure out what room to walk into or what he should get on with when he got there. But he knew work was important. For its own sake. He had to show willing. Show initiative. Stick-to-it-ness. He watched the clock. When the minute hand hit the six, he would stand up, put on his rain jacket, find his wellies, grab the pick and shovel and carry on digging the kirk garden.

That would be something. He could find out, once and for all, if there was anything else buried down there. He owed that much to Rachel. What did she think of him? Right now. He remembered her face when she thought it was Dougie's hand in the tin. She probably thought he was a sadist or some kind of pervert. Or at least, a poor comedian. He should get up and dig. Confirm for her. *Your man's definitely not here.* It was something to do. It's important to keep busy, even if there was nothing to be busy doing. The minute hand passed the seven, the eight, the nine; he waited for the next six.

Before starting his work, Gillis had consulted the severed hand. He'd retrieved it from the kirk and now, holding it like a trembling compass, he tried to encourage it to point. Maybe he had misinterpreted the signs, but he was now beyond waist deep in the ground, with nothing to show for it except a half-dozen ring pulls, a pound coin and a bundle of ancient plastic bags. The rain had been steadily increasing so his joggers clung to the front of his legs and his hair was raked backward, streaked with mud. The shortbread tin lay open, and Gillis called across, 'Are we done with this?' But the severed hand slipped around in a slight pool of water, refusing any advice. He encountered a rock whose edges he hadn't been able to find, so he was hunkered down in the hole, gouging fingers into the dirt, trying to find a corner which he could jimmy the pick under. When his name was called, he almost believed that a very polite and understated angel might be behind him, ready to convey a message, so he turned slowly, leaning back on the blurred edge of his excavation. His eyes struggled to frame all the relevant information. Standing over him, a tall, thin man in a grey suit; behind him, an older woman sheltering beneath an umbrella; beyond them both, a fluorescent police car.

'I'm not interested, thanks.' Gillis tried to turn back to his digging, but the young man leant over and dangled an identification badge that swung from a tartan lanyard.

Gillis squinted back at them and held his hands open, mutely apologizing for the black dirt that was engrained across his skin.

'I'm Detective Cormack.' The tall one pointed to himself. 'And that's Detective Raeburn. We're here to ask a few questions?' The detective's eyelids suddenly flinched; rainwater was running down his forehead, tracking hair gel across the surface of his eyes. He wiped them with the inside of his wrist, combed his hair with his fingernails and held a sticky hand out to one side. 'You don't dig the graves yourself, do you?' the man asked.

'Good for my health.' Gillis stood squint, a pain in his spine clipping his breath. 'I sit down a lot at work, it's bad for the back. So I need to get a few hours out here, stretching it the other way.' He pushed himself out of the hole, straining the bad knee. The police officers didn't look convinced. 'Cheaper than the gym.' He dragged his pick and spade clear of the hole, but pushed and scraped at the heap of dirt on the other side, so it spilt into and concealed the shortbread tin. He dropped his tools on top of the mound and started to pick at the dirt under his fingernails, ushering the detectives toward the house.

'And did you find anything down there?'

Gillis pointed to his pile of tin cans, obstinate rocks, fractured pieces of wood. 'Nothing interesting.'

Cormack nodded. All of his pre-planned questioning had been pushed to the side by the effort it took to clamp his left eye completely closed and tilt his head in such a way that the rain fell across his right eyebrow. 'Sorry, this rain's putting me off. . .'

As they filed into the manse, Raeburn held back to explain where Cormack had gone wrong. First. He hadn't introduced them properly. Second. He didn't have any tactic. You can be nice, she explained. Tell the guy what the accusation is, see how he responds. Or go all in, boots on, you know why we're here, tell us what's happening.

'Right, yeah, OK.' Cormack's head bounced ahead of her words. 'So which should I go with?'

'It's up to you. . .' She was exasperated. 'You said you wanted to take the lead, so take the lead.'

Gillis directed them to the living room.

'Sorry, he's new.' Raeburn took an isolated armchair in the corner of the room and Cormack took the seat next to Gillis. His eye looked very pink.

'We've had several complaints,' Detective Cormack explained. That connected with some ongoing investigations. The line of questioning circled Douglas. His missing body. His widow, his child.

What was Gillis's relation to Rachel?

The minister struggled to answer, but settled on something that felt like a denial. 'She's a friend.'

The detective scribbled in his notebook.

'And to Douglas?'

That one was easier. 'Nothing.'

'But you buried him?'

'We cremated an empty coffin.'

There were rumours going round, tall tales, Cormack said, but wouldn't elaborate. It would be better for Gillis if he could clear them up.

'What's your connection to Mr Nicholson?'

'Friend.' The word felt false again. They were more like associates. Or disciples. Or comrades. What they were was changing. He couldn't say this. 'Just a friend.'

'Another friend,' Cormack repeated and scribbled the word once more. 'Do you have a lot of friends?'

'The usual amount,' he lied. Cormack turned his booklet back and forth and looked over to his colleague for help.

Raeburn forced herself to sit forward. 'Where do you look for all these friends? Where do you find them?'

Before Gillis could answer, she continued, 'Do you look in the hospital? Do you go around chapping doors?'

He denied it.

'When we spoke to your friend, the widow, she mentioned having been brought here. And shown something. Can you tell me what that was? What you were showing a young woman?'

Gillis kept his face strictly impassive, straining against the impulse to nod along. He would admit nothing. If the hand was given over to the police, it would be like winning gold for his country; the achievement would be immediately pulled from him and ascribed to a legion of bureaucrats. From there it could only fall into the grip of journalists, politicians and policy makers. Scientists and statesmen. He would be sidelined, and although it still embarrassed him to admit it, he knew that God was in the process of choosing him, and changing him into someone worth choosing.

'No offence,' Raeburn was saying. 'But a minister is exactly the kind of person we would normally look for in one of these cases. Your ears prick up when you hear *minister*, or *truck driver. . . school teacher. . .*' She turned to Cormack, who was busy scribbling. 'Maybe this guy sees things a bit differently? Maybe he's angry that people are out there happily sinning while he's stuck in here.' She held a cautioning, apologizing hand up to Gillis as she said, 'This is just an example. But say he hates drink or sex or something, he's tried to stop it, he's preaching about it all the time, it brings up some of the childhood stuff, he's out here, it's isolated. He thinks, *I'll chop them up.* Maybe he's angry, maybe he's shy, maybe he can't connect to people. Maybe it's a perversion.' She glanced again at Gillis. 'No offence.'

Gillis nodded. 'That's OK.'

'Or maybe he's not right with himself, might be a bit wandered, might have fixed ideas about the world. People like this need to explain what's wrong inside them. They go to radical politics, weird religions, anything to stop looking inside. They think it's the government's fault. Or the school system. Maybe he's angry, bullied as a kid, can't process it. Or rejected by women, can't even get a cuddle or a kiss. Parents don't like him, siblings are sick of him, his teachers said he was useless, and maybe he is? Can't find work, he's got no savings and no prospects and time's ticking on. Wasn't he meant to be a dad by now? Or own a house or have a missus.' She looked over at Gillis again. 'These are all just examples.'

The minister nodded.

'Now, you're legally allowed to believe anything you want. And you're legally allowed to practise that and even try to convert other people. But obviously, if you're using a body part to do it, that's where the law has to be involved. Doesn't it?'

Gillis kept his face completely impassive, trying not to agree.

'Especially when we have a body missing. A man who's linked to you. Linked to several of your friends.'

The detective waited for a moment in silence. 'If our suspect refuses to speak, what would we do?' She turned to her pupil.

Cormack jogged his knee up and down as he searched his memories.

'Would you search the house?' he asked.

'Exactly, we'd look in all those holes outside. And what then? And don't you say anything to help him. . .' She pointed at Gillis and left her hand up, fingers pinched as though sealing his lips.

Cormack grimaced, he didn't know.

'Question him! How many times do I have to tell you this? We'd take him down to the station, and what would we ask him?'

The detective nervously shook his head.

She counted on her fingers: 'Who, What, Where, Why.' The thumb came last. 'How!'

Cormack blushed and asked, 'Is that in the guidebook?'

'What use is a book? It's all very simple, you just need common sense. It's always the guy you think it is.' Her work phone began to shiver. 'Excuse me.' She walked from the room to answer it, then reappeared to yell, 'Question him then!'

The young detective's voice faltered as he began, 'Sorry. . . just a minute. . . where were you last night?'

Seeing the man's weakness, Gillis refused to answer any more questions.

Cormack looked over his shoulder, through the living room window. Out in the rain, his superior was bellowing instructions into her phone.

'Can you not just say something?'

Gillis didn't respond.

'I'll have to put down *refusing to cooperate*.'

'That's OK, that's what I'm doing.' Gillis oversaw the calming of the room's atmosphere. He acted the way he did with a grieving family, projecting patience and peace, authority over death. He didn't know how it worked, but if he held himself in a certain way, from the innermost core of his body, sometimes the world aligned. From there, he could open the conversation with a simple question like, 'Is it tough going, all your training?'

Cormack seemed a little suspicious of the question, but longed to answer it. 'The thing is, I can't mess it up this time. I've been through it twice already. But see, the exams, they're hard going. And my wife isn't very well, so we're a salary down until she gets better. It's a lot of pressure. We've got this mortgage.' He shook his head. 'We've got a couple of weans too. All their wee pals have got all the designer gear, all the tablets and phones and laptops. Can I not get you to say something? Before she comes back?'

Gillis scratched at the bristles on his cheek. 'Would you answer? If you were me?'

'Fair enough, we'll see what she says.'

Gillis nodded and tried to deepen and extend his projected patience, his grieving routine. He leant forward and listened to the texture of the room. He felt its parameters. He rested his elbows on his knees, and stared into the blank TV in front of them, where their reflections, darkly shadowed, stared back. He knew that Cormack could feel his gaze, and the detective responded by matching his body language. From there, Gillis lowered his head, and a moment of churchly quiet gathered in the room, a stillness between them, enhanced by a clock on the bookshelves ticking and a distant seagull's complaint and a silent complicity and understanding between the two men. They receded inward, to their own thoughts. Their bodies warmed their wet clothes. Their indrawn and outgoing breaths began to align. Their eyelids began to close.

'Are yous praying?' Raeburn stood in the open doorway, forcing her phone into the tight pocket of her trousers.

Cormack quickly unclasped his hands and sat straight. 'No, no!' He turned to Gillis and looked betrayed. 'I was asking questions. But he stopped answering.' His brow darkened. 'It's like I was too close. That's what it felt like.'

She rolled her eyes and stabbed a finger in Gillis's direction. 'Right, you, on your feet and show us where you've got this thing. We're going to have to take it and see what it is.'

Gillis stood. A faint mist, almost invisible, was rising from his body as his rain-soaked clothes began to dry. In his dizziness, the world outside his head seemed false and malleable. He lingered for a moment as the room was overlaid, a kind of double vision, or déjà vu. The situation was so familiar. It was as though he was in a film. 'Shouldn't you have a warrant?' That's what they said in this kind of scene.

Raeburn hesitated, and her face fell in disappointment. Just like the detectives did on the screen.

'I'll have to ask you to leave.' Gillis knew his lines, they had been relayed to him a hundred times, and he ushered them out as Raeburn tried to reason with him.

'You know what your current attitude makes me think?' she retorted. 'It makes me think I have to trust my gut. Know what my gut's telling me? That there's something funny about you. I don't want to think that, but you're making me.'

Gillis tried to laugh, but it came out more like a sheep's bleat.

'A prophet –' he could already feel a rush of crimson to his cheeks – 'isn't recognized in his own country.'

The furniture cringed, the lamplight shivered, the walls held back laughter. Gillis climbed the stairs and peered from his bedroom window, to watch a toy-sized police car turn onto the main road and merge into the tightly packed afternoon traffic. He waited, staring into the fields and woods around the manse – maybe they concealed camera equipment? Maybe they had sent these detectives to rattle him, have him panicked, leading them to the severed hand. If that was the plan, it worked. He zipped himself into a black rain jacket and pulled a black tammy over his head. Escaped through the back door and skirted the building, doubled over, running zigzag, ready to drop and roll if met with sniper fire. He sifted through the mound of dirt and unearthed the shortbread tin. Carefully scooped up the severed hand and pressed through the hedges, passed across the graves, tramping down the bones. He fumbled in his pockets for the silver key, but the kirk door lay ajar. He slipped through, and paused as he turned the light on, surprised by the coat racks, where empty fluorescent jackets and hard hats hung huddled together, as though clinging to one another in grief. Footsteps echoed down from an odd corner overhead, plastic safety tape lay tousled underfoot and paper signage, warning of falling timber, falling brick, danger of death, all lay crumpled to one side. An unfamiliar door opening where it shouldn't. It led into the kirk's condemned spire, a half-hearted attempt to pierce heaven, open for the first time since the great crack had set it askew.

Scratching noises echoed from the heights of the spire, and curiosity led Gillis up into the dark. The spire only rose one storey above the peaked roof of the hall, and was empty, with no bell and no clock, existing only to hold up its own sharp roof, now crowned with scaffolding from the guttering up to the hefty metal cross at the top. The staircase threaded up the spire until it began to reveal light, and more light, and then a bolt of pure white that blanched his eyes. He expected an angel to appear, a harried commuter, urging him to keep to the right, a queue of angry seraphim behind him. Instead, the light spoke.

'You gave me some fright there.' Cowering behind a Maglite, Nichol held a hand to his chest. 'My heart's racing.'

'Guilty conscience?'

'Couldn't feel guilty if I tried.' The curling staircase ended abruptly, severed by a small platform with nothing in it, and a cross-hatched window on each wall, occasional panes cracked or broken through. A small bench, inlaid to the wall, held a little bottle of whisky, with the crushed cap lying next to it. A cloud of cigarette smoke lingered there.

'You all right up here?' Gillis asked.

'Just surveying my kingdom. Didn't know you could see so far.' He pointed to the distance, where the lights of Kirkmouth fizzled into the sea. 'Beautiful, isn't it?' He hadn't meant to ask a question, but as they looked over the collected lights of the town, they both wondered. Was it beautiful, or is that just something people say? A flat horizon, a skelf of moon. 'How much would you pay for that view? Four hundred a month?' Nichol looked around the little platform. 'Bed here. Bedside cabinet. Little desk. Shower cubicle off on the side of the stairs. Would be a shame to waste all this space.' He shone his torch over Gillis, and spotted the mud-covered shortbread tin. 'What happened to our friend?' He jostled the light over the severed hand.

Gillis didn't reply.

'I think we need to be more careful, don't you?'

They left the whisky where it was, and walked down the staircase counter-clockwise, loosening the screw.

'What did those polis want?' Nichol kicked the door closed, grunting as he bent to pick up the strands of safety tape.

'They don't know what they want.'

'They didn't talk about us, did they. . .?' Nichol trailed off as they competed to hold the doors open, to find the light switch, to notice potential trip hazards and point them out. Each one guarding his inner life from the other, conscious that it might be visible. In the eyes, on the breath. 'They didn't mention our thing we have here?' Nichol led Gillis through the hall, to the vestry office. He had a new lock burrowed into the frame. Dozens of keys jangled like a broken tambourine in Nichol's hand.

'That's the chip shop, hotel safe, hotel room key, offices, burger van, lockup, house key, back door, garage, other garage – is it this one?'

It wasn't. They tried several more before the door gave, and admitted them to a sleek little sanctuary of tasteful grey and muted blue. Fresh plasterwork, fresh paint, new floors, imitation wood, a framed black-and-white photograph of an empty sand dune blotted by a set of footprints. In one corner, a bed. In the other, a basin.

'We thought we'd finish one of the little studio apartments. Help buyers see the vision.' Nichol threw his jacket onto a brand-new desk, its surface so smooth that the jacket streaked across and fell to the floor. He held out his hand and Gillis obediently passed him the shortbread tin. Nichol ran the tap and began to clean mud from both the tin and the severed hand. 'They weren't asking about anything important?'

Gillis shook his head.

'Nothing about our plans? About the boat? About Douglas?' Nichol kept trying little statements, all in passing as he tidied the corners of the room. 'Nothing about the fishery? Or about me? Or your dolly-bird?'

Though he knew he shouldn't, Gillis completed Nichol's thought. He said Rachel's name, and Nichol turned and stared. 'They mentioned something about her mentioning something. To them.'

'Oh, she did?'

'Just briefly. I'd showed her the hand. And she got the wrong end of the stick.'

Now Nichol nodded, turning away.

'Where's all the stuff?' Gillis tried to change the conversation. The room had once been packed with ornaments, furniture, catering equipment, broken speakers and mike stands. Nichol pointed vaguely out of the building. 'Do you think I tell my wife everything I do?' He began to pull his arm out of his jumper. 'Women sometimes. . .' He didn't finish the thought. 'Have a look at this.' He freed his arm from the jumper and turned it back and forward. 'I've not been that well moisturized since I was a teenager. And that's just a week. Me touching the severed hand once a night. And believe me, I'm up to high doh, stressed out, canny sleep, canny eat. . . got a million things to do, and they all need done yesterday. But I'm not scratching, not itching, no flaky bits falling off me. Honestly, it's a real miracle. I feel great. Well, my arms feel great anyway. I feel fucking rotten.' He was distracted by sounds outside the kirk – car doors, gravel and laughter.

'That's us here, boss.' A young lad knocked on the vestry door.

'Here, this is what I was telling you about.' Nichol displayed the arm, and his employee looked along the well-moisturized flesh and nodded. 'You didn't see it before, but see a week ago? Honestly, it was like a butcher's cutting block, wasn't it?'

Gillis nodded.

'The guys are wanting to know what's happening?'

'Tell them just sit down and keep quiet, we'll be along in a minute.'

His employee left, and Nichol covered his arm again, shivered a little in the cold.

'I'm a sponsor,' Nichol explained. 'For the alcoholics. Try to give back a wee bit. Used to be bad with it, years ago. You know these guys need a higher power? They tell them, doesn't have to be God, could be anything, could be your dad's ghost, could be your fridge-freezer. I said to them, I can do you one better than that.'

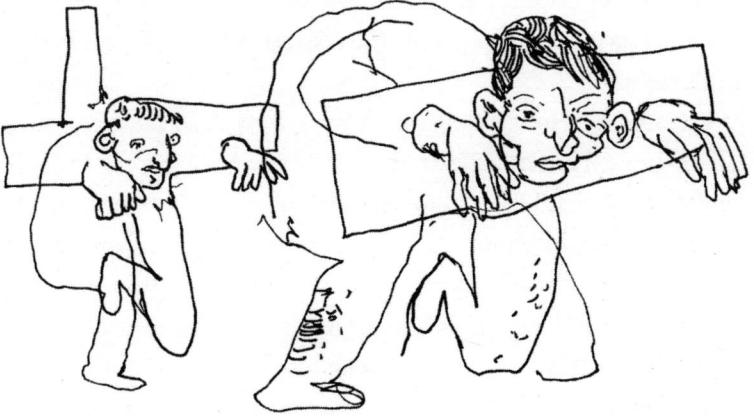

Jan's drinking companions had been lined up in front of the courthouse all day, their necks held in stocks, feet splashed by their own vomit, hands encrusted with mud and a settling of frost across their shoulders. Heavy petals of snow drifted through the air, caught one another and dissolved on contact with the earth. As Jan emerged from the courthouse, a free man, they shouted to him, how had he done it?

He stood before them like a king or a cardinal, standing tall as they all bowed. They strained their necks to angle their heads sideways. He explained. The black jackets had taken his painted figures, and carried them through the courthouse to a back room whose walls were tarnished by the smoke of dozens of candles and oil lamps that hung from brass chains, burning above an enormous desk like the rigging of a ship. All captained by a broad, heavy man with a long beard, who also wore the sombre black jacket and broad-brimmed hat, with a leaflet pressed into the band. Except in his case the leaflet had been carefully arranged in a fanlike fold, and the hat had been carefully brushed, and the jacket was made of black calfskin, the hems were double-stitched, the collars were long and impractically pointed, and the buttons shone and had been carefully etched with the image of a boar's head. As Jan was brought into the room, and stood before a tangle of his painted pages, his mouth began to water, salivating at the smell of the jacket, as though it was made of freshly cut and stitched veal. It creaked at the elbows and waist as the man stood and smoothed pale hands down his front, forcing its folds to conceal the shape of his body. His head protruded from the shirt as though it had been severed and displayed. When the man spoke, his words were so well decorated with elongated vowels that Jan struggled to understand. The words had to linger in his mind long enough for the floral embellishments to wither and expose the root meaning. The man introduced himself as Proctor Kelvin, and said something about cavorting and gambolling, about nuisance animals that steal crops in the night.

'Hares and rabbits, concealed in darkness, run through the rows and nibble at the crops, don't they? And the farmer prays for shoots to appear, little knowing that night after night, these seedlings are being eaten.'

The Proctor pressed his finger into the heap of painted figures. Some the size of a thumbnail, some as tall as a forearm; the Proctor began to pull them apart and arrange them side by side. Smiling, he held one to the light, pulled another loose and ran his thumb across the belly of St Agnes, up to her shoulders, exposed in her torture, before laying her back among the bundled dead and dying. The Proctor's eyes glinted, almost tearful as he swept his hands across the table, rolled the painted crowd into a bundle and cast them into the smouldering coals of the fireplace.

Sighing, he walked back to his desk. His own papers held no colour and no decoration, only tight lines of printed black letter. He sorted through until he found a blank white page. 'On this empty stage, our beloved cast of twenty-six actors mime and sing, whisper and point, mimic the world beyond, and often they lie, or cheat us. But look at their stature.' The Proctor pointed across the pages loose on his desk, the posters, letters and pamphlets. 'Which is the tallest letter? Which one is the most important?'

'The first one?' Jan tried.

'They're all the same size, aren't they? None makes any sense without the other. No single letter can stand alone.'

'*A* is a word on its own. Or *I*.'

The Proctor began to coax his papers into stacks, and the desk, like an untidy plot of land, was organized and divided, parts were overused, and parts cleared to lie fallow, replenished for new use.

As the hour passed, the blank paper took on rows of letters, sown like seeds, while the Proctor took notes, asking questions about the Laird, rolling vowels around his mouth like savoured lumps of sugar. And this book? And the time it was ordered? And in what year and for whom and how it was addressed? When did they meet? What words had the Laird used? Had he cursed? Had he struck Jan?

'These aren't the right questions,' Jan said. 'You need to ask about the book itself.'

The Proctor looked to the ashes in the fireplace.

Before he would explain himself, Jan asked for a proper meal and a bed for the night, but settled for lukewarm porridge and a pocketful of carrots to take away with him. He spooned oatmeal as he explained.

'Our business was to create painted books for rich men. A Scottish Laird wrote to us, asking for a book of holy saints in dedication to his wife. As an apprentice, my own part is very small, and normally I wouldn't know what made one book different from another. Most lords' requests are vague and a book can be assembled from the offcuts of another. Except that our orders for this book were disturbing. Along with his letters and descriptions, and the initial payments for the book, this Laird sent a half-dozen young calves which had long, deep red hair and curled horns, which were to be kept on a special diet known only to my masters. Now, you'll know what a book's pages are made of, won't you?'

'Vellum?' the Proctor said.

'Correct, calfskin. Prepared to special measures. You'll know what the measures are?'

'Shit.'

'Scrubbed with shit and piss. To remove any hair and thin the vellum. The shit's usually dog's, and the piss is collected by. . .?'

'Monks.'

'Correct, the good brothers collect their water in a barrel and send it out to scrub the vellum so it softens like paper, but lasts a long time.' His bowl of porridge soured with the memory of stinking tanneries, and sheets of vellum arriving to be painted, still unwashed. 'You'll have guessed that your Laird wanted these calves skinned and turned into the pages we just watched burn. Maybe you won't believe he went further. That the colours you saw in those saints were not created by any normal paint? The Laird demanded that the paints be mixed according to recipes he supplied himself. Us apprentice boys were confused. We were familiar with the short, bright life of blood, and how it blackens or browns after it is spilt. Imagine our fear, when the first cut was made. Deep into the throat, the blood ran red as it should, but when our master made the next cut, and burrowed into the stomach of the calf, the liquid running across his hand was mossy green, and when he found the liver and split it, the bile was bright yellow, and the brain, which had to be removed and wrung out like a rag, was royal blue, and these colours didn't seem to fade, even when we mixed them with the usual oils and resins we prepare our paints with.'

Jan ran his thumb around the edge of his bowl and sucked the starch from the back of his spoon. When it was clean, he laid it down and leant back. The black jackets who stood at the door looked bored. But the Proctor was enthused.

'And you made this calfskin into the pages of your book?'
he asked.

'We did.'

The Proctor looked into the fire, where the last of the
vellum figures coiled as though writhing from the pain
inflicted by the flames. He took a poker which hung to one
side and tried to pull the figure from the coals, but the poker
only chased the flame closer, and the figure, whether it was
a tortured saint, or a blissful angel, or a grinning peasant,
disappeared.

'The rest of the book is still in his house. One of his men
took it from me. Refused to pay because the book had been
damaged, and waterlogged.'

'And did they *worship* the book?'

Jan shrugged. 'They might have.'

'Did you see them worshipping it?'

'Like I said, they took it from me at the gate.'

'Maybe you saw them from far away?'

'I could have. When I think about it. Maybe they did?'

'Often they'll dance and sing around a book.'

'They might have, when I think about it.'

Another bowl of porridge appeared, this one hot and
sweetened with honey, and a mug of spiced beer, and a bowl
to wash his hands and face with.

As he washed, drank and ate, his account was noted down
in seedling letters, that began to grow and wind into an
unruly crop ripening for future harvest. The Proctor copied
from these notes, cutting and pruning the script, placing
careful letters onto a fresh piece of paper, each one tall and
straight, sharp at both ends. As the Proctor finished, and read
the account back, Jan blushed. Everything was a lie, or an
exaggeration, or a silly story repeated among the apprentices
to pass their time. But they had put so much effort in, and

his belly was full, so he signed, and with a pocket stuffed full of carrots, he was kicked up the arse and told to stay near, in case his testimony was ever needed. Leaning close to the men still confined to the stocks, he advised them.

'Make up some story about the Laird, about magic or religion, say you saw him blaspheming or fucking an animal. Look what they gave me.' The carrots were all cracked and dry, a day away from rot. As he walked away from the courthouse, he heard his drinking pals calling out to the black-jacketed men who guarded them, claiming to have information, demanding to speak to the magistrate, and to this man, Proctor Kelvin.

CHAPTER TEN

A week or two passed Gillis by, skipping and rescheduling appointments, shifting the blame and calling in sick, the bulk of his time lost to Nichol's experiments. Focus groups pulled from the Kirkmouth populace. AA meetings and bowling club AGMs derailed and decamped, out to the old kirk, assembled and exposed to the sight of the severed hand. Lacking any clear plans of his own, he thought he could run in Nichol's wake, allowing the big man to make all the mistakes, clipping at his heels until the end was in sight, when the minister would bolt from his shadow and race for the prize.

A ritual developed. If Gillis was quick enough, he could see the kirk's lights coming on, and could run across to help out, or sit at the back, hoping to deliver an ancient sermon, stink the room out with religion, chase the canny and sceptical out the door. Encourage them to either laugh everything off, or politely ask where the toilet was before running to their cars, or traipsing downhill to the bus stop. Failing that, he hoped that those remaining would be too embarrassed to have been inside a church to speak about what they saw.

'Why don't we keep the severed hand in the back office?' Gillis had managed to convince Nichol. 'We need to divide goats from sheep, that's in the Bible. *Many are called, few are chosen.* That's in there too.'

Despite Nichol's enthusiasm, they normally managed to whittle each meeting down to one or two of the shyest or laziest, poor souls with nothing else to do, and no one to go home to. They brought these victims through to the back office and revealed the severed limb. Nichol would sometimes take off his shirt, show his chest and arms, well on their way to recovery. As they approached Sunday, he began to insist that they hold a church service, something small, to consolidate their progress.

'Why?'

'Why? Captive audience.'

So Gillis opened the kirk doors at ten, and waited in the pulpit as Nichol delved through his contacts, calling out the faithful with electronic bells, and as people began to drift into the kirk, Jim Macintyre wheeled the old electric organ closer to the assembled seats. It was shrouded in black suede, like a sturdy old cow set for milking; he unzipped the moth-eaten cover, then produced a key, unlocked and pricked and goaded the machine into a preset function that automatically played 'Amazing Grace'. He handed out a set of hymnals and had the half-dozen congregants muttering and whistling shyly along by the second verse. The janitor tried to carry them by singing louder and deeper, his resonant baritone echoing from another age, pre-rock and roll, pre-swing, pre-amplification. But the preset ended and soon he was singing the obscurer verses alone. When he'd finished, he opened his eyes and slapped a hand down on the haunches of the organ, as though it would take fright and run back to its pen.

'What a disaster.' Nichol laughed from the back. The assembled alcoholics and overeager employees checked their watches. Their shift was starting soon. Jim Macintyre ran a hand over his chest, feeling the warmth of his voice die back into his lungs.

'What a pleasure it is to sing,' he said.

The eyes of the room circled toward the pulpit as Gillis opened his Bible and tried to read; his eyes skipped across the passage. *'The hand of the Lord was upon me, and carried me out. . . and set me down in the midst of a valley which was full of bones. . . And he said to me, Son of Man, can these bones live?'*

A stottering couple arrived at the doorway, derailed from the dregs of a house party at Nichol's invitation. They stared in horror at the minister's robotic voice, his strange words.

'Thus said the Lord God to these bones; Behold, I will cause breath to enter into you, and you shall live. . . And I will lay sinews on you, and will bring flesh upon you and cover you with skin.'

They tried to turn back, but Nichol leapt to catch them, and grabbing the woman by the arm, he leant backward as though straining against the weight of a fishing line.

'Then he said to me, Prophesy to the wind, and say. . . O breath, breathe upon these slain, that they may live.'

Mouths agape, heads reeling over the backs of their chairs, the couple foundered in their seats, and fidgeted uncomfortably, as though the stale air of the hall was poisoning them.

'So I prophesied as he commanded me, and the breath came into them, and they lived, and stood up upon their feet, an exceeding great army.'

Gillis grew pale as he read – was the book talking to him? If he wanted to, how would he go about prophesying to the wind? He looked back to the top of the page and tried to read through it in silence. The hall grew deeply quiet. As he raised his face from the Bible, the small assembly looked into his eyes. Red and sore for lack of sleep. Pupils splashed with spots of light. His hoarse whisper cut through the weighted air: *'I will open your graves, and cause you to come out of your graves. . . and place you in your own land.'*

As the service came to an end, Nichol dashed to the back of the hall and encouraged the slight congregation to file past the shortbread tin, improvise whatever bows and curtsies felt correct and touch the open palm with their fingers. Nichol nodded to each person as they left and insisted, 'Same time next week? Same time next week?' The partying couple were the last to leave; their trainers squeaked across the waxen floor as they clutched at their guts and asked for coffee, or a bit of bread, something to line the stomach.

Nichol held the shortbread tin instead.

'Can't look at that.' They covered their eyes and walked blindfolded out to the cold kirkyard air, and they braced themselves against the gravestones and spat on the chilled ground.

Nichol chased them across the graves, laughing and insisting that he could cure the pressure in their skulls and the sour taste in their mouths, and more, every compulsion and every weakness and every poor idea. Everything had the one cure.

Gillis was soon the only person in the kirk, looking back through the verses he had stumbled across. He had struggled to read any further and in place of a sermon, Nichol had improvised a testimonial which ended with a quick display of his arms and belly. The revelatory verses – Gillis read them again – could only be interpreted as a coincidence, or else God laying out His intention to raise an army of the dead and take Scotland by military force.

He read through the verses again and again and felt a rising compulsion to act. To do something! But what? He shuffled to his feet and, hearing movement in the back vestibule, followed the noises – only to find himself already there. Back turned, stomach bloated, hair shorn close to the head, but the same black shirt, black trousers and shoes, and little white

ticket at the throat. His doppelgänger turned, hearing the
door as it swung back and closed with a respectful hiss of
the hinges, and then grinned. 'Are they selling us in batches?'

The Edinburgh offices had asked this minister here –
Fowler, he called himself – to cover for the next few days, he
didn't know why. He had an order of service in his hand. The
dead man's name and picture displayed above the tagline,
Beloved Father, Husband and Brother.

'Did they not call you up?' Fowler returned to his task,
rooting about in the back cupboards. 'Isn't that typical? I'm
looking for the hymnals?' He kicked the cupboard closed and
ripped at some cardboard boxes he had found.

Gillis unearthed his phone, which had been turned off
since the detectives' visit. *That's how they get you*, he had
thought. Meaning the police and the judge and jury. But also
meaning Rachel; in the pit of his stomach he knew he had
done something wrong. As he booted up the phone, unread
messages began piling up, green and blue notifications, long
complaints about missed appointments, carefully worded
warnings from his superiors. He had been having nightmares
about a phone ringing, a letter coming through the door,
a headline on the evening news, a van full of doctors and
policemen coming to grab him. He deleted and ignored until
he stopped at Rachel's name, where he scanned through a
pulse of messages, all sent back to back. She was angry. He
would read them later. She'd misspelt the word *relic*. She
wanted to know what she'd done to deserve that kind of
treatment. Without reading her messages properly, he began
to tap out a reply but long before he could find the correct
balance of humility and humour, the battery symbol flashed
empty and the screen lapsed to pure black.

'Everything OK?' His double had found an armful of
hymnals and was beginning to walk toward the exit.

'Fine. There's obviously been a mix-up, that's all. I'll
need to try and get on to the Church offices and see what's
happening.' Gillis pointed at the base of his phone. 'Once
I'm back up and running.'

'Christ, that's an old one. You not due an update?'

'Here, it's coming back on.' The screen flickered and the
battery danced from one per cent to a hundred, then back
down to ten, once it had a moment to properly assess its
capabilities.

Fowler had passed forty a few years back, and grey
hairs speckled the side of his face where his beard drifted
northward to become eyebrow and haircut. 'This is a good
patch you have here. Nice population density. You must get
what, three or four funerals a week?'

'Sometimes it dips and I only get one or two.'

'Still, the winter'll keep you busy, won't it?'

Gillis nodded. 'A bit too busy sometimes.'

'I'm further north most of the time, and honestly, mate, the
folk up there canny half cling on. Some of them have got to be
lying about their age. They look a hundred years old. Living
on their own, soldiering on. I'm driving east to west, away up
north, getting ferries out to the islands – it's killing me, mate,
honestly. Can't get any time in the house – soon as I'm in, I'm
fast asleep. . . You don't get your fuel paid for, do you?'

'No.'

'Fair enough, it's the policy, but I'm driving all over
Scotland, burying and burning as I go. You'd think they could
fork out for the fuel costs, specially seeing as how some of
the boys in Glasgow hardly have to leave their side of the
city.'

As Gillis texted the Kirk secretary, Fowler talked about a
business scheme he had in mind. The Biblical Businessman.
Six-week course. Forty pound a session.

'We're going about the Church all wrong. If someone said to you, *I've got a life-changing scheme here*, and it costs nothing, what would you think? *They're at it*, right? Believe me, if we start charging, they'll be coming out the woodwork, begging to get in.'

Gillis's phone began to dance as another set of delayed notifications arrived.

'I know what you're thinking. What about poor people, jobseekers and all that, but there's plenty of folk already looking after them. We'll focus on your businessmen, your lawyers and teachers and doctors and so on. Everything's downhill from those types anyway.'

Emails and calendar notifications flickered like a pack of cards spilt in their shuffling.

'I'll be back in the week, you'll need a hand clearing that lot.' Fowler nodded to the chaos unfolding in Gillis's palm, then left, asking him to think over the business idea, cautioning as he walked off to meet the grieving family, that he had a lot of interested parties, and this was the kind of idea you'd want to be in on the ground floor for. Think back five years ago – where were your delivery apps and your social medias back then?

As Fowler left for his funeral, Gillis laid his work diary on the floor of the kirk, and tallied every notification against the cancelled funeral it applied to. The next four weeks were all gone. Had there been a lot of miracles? Resurrections? Ascensions to heaven? A call to the Edinburgh offices, bypassed through the seminary and the kirk session, eventually put Gillis on the line with a man who had some answers, though he refused to just spit them out.

'It shouldn't have been done this way,' the Church elder said.

'What shouldn't have been done what way?'

'Exactly. . . exactly. Give me a few hours, OK? I'll drive up. We'll do that. It'll be better in person. What's the weather like up your way?'

Gillis described the drizzle, the patina of the cloud, the threat of sunlight.

'What are you wearing?' the elder asked.

'Rain jacket and jumper.'

'Scarf?' the man asked.

'I'd bring it and you can put it in your pocket if you don't need it.'

'Hat?'

The elder wanted to meet at the kirk for a walk around the *beautiful surroundings*. He must have had somewhere else in mind. Gillis had panicked and rushed to tidy the place. Sweep the dirt. Straighten the furniture. Knuckle down, pay attention, defend himself, stand tall and strong, shoulders back, swallow his pride, get his head in the game, face facts and soldier on. Push on through, grin and bear it, remember why he was there, let his feet do the talking. He'd trained for this; even though conditions weren't ideal, he needed to get back out there and do what he did best. Reassure the fans, the bosses even. Get back to basics, eulogy, hymn, consoling shoulder. Repeat it all, say he needed another chance, say it'd been a hard time, say with time to reflect, he was ready to start over.

He paced back and forth, smoothing a freshly ironed shirt, tucking himself in, chin smarting from the razor, stinking of deodorant and toothpaste; his footsteps echoed through the building, with nothing but fluttering pigeon's wings in the rafters to respond. As though creating an alibi, covering up a crime, he arranged an untidy circle of chairs, with used coffee cups underneath and Bibles discarded on the seat, opened to random passages. His sleeves were rolled up, and though it had cost his comb a half-dozen prongs, he had a careful parting in his hair. Rumbling gravel in the car park became a set of stamping feet in the front entrance, a dark shadow on the rippled glass resolved into a tall silhouette. A boss he had never met. Gillis quickly turned his back and held his phone tight to his face as he collected Bibles underarm.

'It's not a problem. It's what I'm here for,' he said to an imaginary parishioner. 'Honestly. If you were in my shoes, I'm sure you would. . . Any time. . . Any time. . .' His voice sickly sweet. 'You know where we are.' The boss pushed through the hall doors, and called in broken syllables, 'He-llooo? He-llooo?' Gillis turned as though surprised and held up a finger. The boss nodded and Gillis fought through the lavish praise of his imaginary parishioner. He reminded the caller that although, yes, he had gone beyond his duty, and yes, it had strained all expectation, and yes, his actions bordered on saintly self-sacrifice, but come on, wasn't that the job?

'Sorry to keep you waiting.' Gillis collected the last of his Bibles and dropped them in a pile by the back cupboards. 'The place is a bit of a mess, we had a big study group in. Some challenging questions, some amazing testimonies, but it's heartening to see that hunger for the word!'

These lies seemed to carry beyond his boss into the space behind him, like radio waves resonating beyond the earth. Something was missing, as though the man had never been fitted with the necessary equipment to pick up on certain signals. He just extended a hand. 'Gillis, I presume?' He was extremely gaunt and long-legged. His collar bones pitched a loose shirt over the hollow space where his stomach should have been. As they shook hands, the man's eyes began to disappear, circled by a grey fog that condensed on the cold lenses of his glasses. Through a gap at the bottom of this gathering cloud, he squinted down at Gillis, like a jeweller examining for flaws.

'Alastair the elder,' the man said. His glasses were now completely fogged over, and he made no attempt to clear them. 'Ally, or Al, is fine too. Is it all right to call you Gill? What do your mates call you? Or do I not want to know?' The elder took off his jacket and laid it on a stack of chairs. 'I'll be honest, Gill, I've not been through the seminary, I'm not a minister, I didn't study the Bible. I came up through the private sector, worked with a lot of different companies, some of them big international firms, household brands, you'd know them. Certain cleaning products. Certain soaps. But nowadays I work for myself, I come in for a look at places that might need a bit of restructuring, a bit of tightening up. Because no matter who you are, if you've been looking at the same thing for a few decades, you'll lose focus. Let alone what, five hundred years? D'you know what I mean? The Church, it's trying so hard to limp along, it doesn't stop and think, *Is this the best way? Are we doing OK? Are we going in the right direction?* Does that chime with you?'

Gillis picked at his forefinger. By pressing his thumbnail into the soft flesh at the knuckle, he was creating a stable point of pain, from which he could anchor himself. 'Sure.'

Alastair lifted a couple of chairs from the stack and laid them across from each other. 'I'll be honest with you, we've had a couple of worrying, wouldn't say complaints, more like *notices of concern.*'

Alastair the elder leant back to oversee the raising of one elongated leg over the other, lifted slowly from the hip and across like the steady arm of a crane. Satisfied with the outcome, he spread an arm over the back of a neighbouring chair, and tilted his head back, so that he could look at Gillis through the demisted half of his glasses. Though the individual words he spoke meant almost nothing, they were conveyed in such clear waves of rising, then settling, emotion that Gillis felt pacified despite himself. A professional was at work here, someone who clearly had everyone's best interests at heart. If only Gillis could see things from this elevated perspective, everything would be OK. 'Sometimes it takes a stranger to say, *Hey, you look like you're struggling?* And believe me, we've had those strangers. Punters, mourners, coming to us and saying Gill did a great job. He did. But we've also had some of the same people tell us Gill didn't do a good job. In fact, he did a bad job. And actually, he was seen talking to himself. Maybe he even tried to get inside a coffin at some point? Maybe he got into a fight at a funeral? Listen, I'm not a minister, I'm a man of the world, who am I to say what's normal? You know? Who's to judge? I talk to myself all the time! I'll say, *Ally, you're getting a bit long-winded, you need to get to the point.* But the big thing is, I choose to not let anyone see that. Some people think, *Let it all hang out, man, do what you want, dude, be yourself,* they're great sentiments, they're really nice, and I actually even agree with them. But you have to do what you like and be who you want to be at home. Not at work.' Now that the mist had completely cleared from his glasses, Alastair took them off and wiped the lenses with the loose fabric of his shirt.

'I don't like doing this, but I'm here for a difficult talk. The Church has been declining for years, you'll know that. So our major focus this year is targeted action. Focusing our energies. We know you've not had a congregation up here for the last year or two. We've let that slide. But how many businesses can employ a worker to only do half a job?

Funerals are great, they're good for the community and good for the Church, but what was it Jesus said? *Let the dead bury their dead.* Going forward, we need to be looking at expansion. Growth. It's been my job to look at everything, pull out the weeds, pare back the branches, it isn't easy. But the Lord said, *I haven't come to bring peace, but to bring the sword.* So I'll just ask you outright, how do you feel about your employment here, in the Church?'

Gillis stood, interrupting the elder mid-sentence, who began to narrate his movements.

'You're leaving the conversation! You're leaving the hall, you're going into the corridor? You've left the conversation!' Alone, the elder's voice echoed. 'Are you coming back? Gill? Are you coming back? You are. You are coming back. Here you are, you're back in the room. OK. . . thank you.' As Gillis sat himself down again, the elder searched the rafters for his train of thought.

The minister was out of breath, he had almost run from the room, and now sat with his hands shaking, gripping the shortbread tin. He wanted to crack it across the elder's smug mouth, press his face into the flesh of the severed limb and demand an explanation, whisper, *You have seen me and believed, blessed are they who believe without seeing.* Demand answers. What was the procedure for this? Was it covered by health and safety legislation? What did it say in his contract about direct manifestations of power over death? Surely these kinds of things should be expected in his line of work? Gillis offered the shortbread tin to the elder.

'I'm OK for now, thank you.'

'Open it.' Gillis pressed the tin closer.

'I'm reducing my sugar intake. The wife wants rid of this.' Alastair the elder tried to pat his belly, but met only the empty fabric of his shirt. Did she want rid of him entirely?

Trembling, Gillis opened the tin and laid it on the floor between them. He felt as though cold water was being poured down his neck. Maybe the elder would take the severed hand away? To a secret committee at the Church headquarters? Maybe parts of this saint were scattered around the country? Maybe they were trying to assemble him and let him speak? Prophesy to the wind. *Breathe upon these slain, that they may live.* Lead the people out of death, toward paradise. These were stupid thoughts. He would enjoy thinking about simple things again. When Gillis looked at the elder, the man smirked and Gillis was wrong-footed. 'Can you see it?' he had to say.

'Honestly, I'd rather not.'

'You need to look properly.' Gillis kicked the shortbread tin closer.

Between the minister and the Church elder, the severed hand began to move. Curling one finger, it tilted on its heel and leant on the bloodied stump as it faced Gillis and pointed. The finger was demanding a response.

'Is this how you're spending your time?' Alastair the elder asked.

'Can't you see it pointing?'

'I can see it fine. I'm bracketing that. For now, I want to talk about *you*. How are *you* feeling?'

The hand pointed between the minister's eyes. 'It doesn't matter how I feel.'

'Now we're getting to the problem.' The elder made a little steeple with his fingers that he held before his eyes to avoid looking into the shortbread tin. 'Why would you think your feelings don't matter?'

'They're calling it a holy relic.' Gillis found that his saliva had thickened. He searched the empty hall for his bag, and pulled free a bundle of the hand's latest scribblings. A little man stood on a bigger man's eye socket. A bearded head, broken open, released a blossoming flower.

'I'm glad I came up.' Alastair glanced through the drawings before setting them aside. 'I'm not an expert but I did take a course. . . from the complaints, descriptions of your behaviour, my guess would be. . . well. . . probably shouldn't start diagnosing anything. Back in the olden days I'm sure we'd have been worried you had some sort of demon possessing you. But now we know a bit more about mania. About grand visions. About mental health. As an organization, we're obligated to encourage you to look at getting help.' The elder reached out to touch Gillis's knee.

'I don't need that kind of help.'

The elder pulled his hand back and pretended to swagger in his seat. '"I'm a big, strong man and I don't need anyone."' He laughed. 'It's not the nineteen-fifties. You don't need to act tough. Listen, back last year, we had our dog die on us. Me and my wife, we were crying and crying and crying. All for a silly wee dog we ended up replacing. I cry all the time, Gillis, it's natural. I cried this morning. Couldn't even have told you why.'

Gillis rolled his eyes. 'I'm not going to do that.'

'Oh, you should. You should. It's so necessary,' the elder implored, but on looking into the blank shadow of Gillis's eyes, he grew nervous and shuffled his papers. 'Speak to a doctor. When I was having some bowel issues, well, colon, bowel and colon issues—'

'What if it's God?' Gillis whispered – he didn't want the hall to echo and amplify his voice, he didn't want anyone overhearing him. 'What if He's speaking to me?'

'Well, I wouldn't be surprised, I think He speaks to us all the time! But we're so wrapped up in ourselves, aren't we? With our phones and our internet and our TV. You can fill your whole day with silliness. Pornography. . . Gambling. . . Shopping.'

'I don't do any of that.'

Gillis was ignored.

'When was the last time you just sat still and did nothing? What I do is take baths. A shower, you're in and out. A bath you can take a bit of time. You can lie back and say, *Jesus! Speak to me.* And it's good for your muscles and skin too. Some of the ministers are a bit squeamish about meditation, but I think it's a wonderful thing. I have this great app. . .' He pulled his phone from his pocket and with the movements of one finger, he manipulated some celestial music. 'Look at the visuals. It's like you're zooming into space.' He stared at geometric forms that whirled around his fingernail. 'This thing has me trained. Two minutes looking at it and I'm ready to sleep.' His eyes glazed over, and the music grew more melancholic, and the geometric forms thinned into a fragmented arrow, rushing through a dark landscape, crossing hundreds of miles of deep space beyond the screen. The elder's head listed and his expression dulled, until Gillis shifted in his seat and cleared his throat.

'You're dribbling.' Gillis pointed to the man's glimmering mouth.

'I'm not.' He touched his lips and the music suddenly died, as though the harp strings had been savagely cut, and the angelic trumpets had been stuffed with rags. He pushed his phone into the pocket of his rain jacket. 'I'll be honest. I can't have you deciding there's holy relics lying around. I can't have you not showing up to your appointments. I can't have you going off piste and improvising little parables. And I can't have you bringing widows back to the manse overnight.'

'How did you hear about that?'

The elder tried to stifle a grin. 'You're a guy, I'm a guy. . . between us? Fair play to you, I know when an opportunity comes up, who's going to say no? But come on. Not after a funeral. You know what I mean, don't you?'

Gillis tried to think who had grassed. Couldn't have been Rachel. Must have been Nichol, or the mother-in-law? Or maybe the police had been asking around.

Finally, Alastair the elder looked down into the shortbread tin, and pointed to the severed hand. 'And I *definitely* can't have this. What even is it?'

'It's like a holy, sacred relic kind of thing. Body part of a saint or something?'

'But what is it *really*? What's going on with *you* that you need this to distract yourself. . . don't you see what I mean? Everything *means* something, doesn't it? Everything we do, there's a purpose behind it. Do you understand? It's all inside.'

'My thing's nothing like that.' Gillis sternly denied. 'My thing's real. It's in the world. You're meant to say, that's a relic, or that's not a relic, it's holy or it's just normal and not holy. You're the boss, you're meant to make the call. That's a ghost or an angel or a demon or whatever. You need to go and ask around in Edinburgh and look me out an old book from a hundred years ago that talks about this kind of thing. There has to be something. Will you ask around? I'm begging you, I actually am.'

The elder looked upward as though outflanked by an aerial attack from the heavens. 'If this thing *is* a relic – which, by the way, as a member of a *Protestant Church*, you shouldn't believe in. But if it is one, and it was found in the ground or in the kirk, then officially it belongs to Mr Nicholson or to his company that bought the grounds. And if I were you I'd hand it over to him, and he can get it put

on display somewhere. Some historical, university types
will want it. I'd do that.'

'God sent it to me.'

'No, he didn't.'

'He did.'

There was a glint of pity and superiority in the elder's
eyes. Gillis gripped the shortbread tin and imagined cracking
it across the man's forehead. Breaking his glasses, breaking
his nose, breaking his cheekbone, fracturing his skull. But
it was an image taken from a film, a therapeutic burst of
imagined violence.

The elder ploughed on. 'What I can see here, maybe
others can't, but I see frustration. Tell me if I'm wrong?
Maybe you joined the Church and expected more. . . maybe
not excitement, but why not? Maybe you expected a bit of
excitement? The guys in the seminary aren't happy, they want
me to come back with your dog collar and your Bible, they
want me to say, *He's gone, he's out the manse, we can finalize
the sale and get the money.* That's what they want. I'm looking
here at my spreadsheets and I see an area where there's only
a funeral every couple of days. That's what? Three hours'
work you're doing. My goal is to get you guys burying at
least four, five people every day. And for sermons, probably
doubling that too. In your area, that means cutting twelve
ministers down to three. No joke. The other guys on the
board, they look at your recent record. No congregation,
acting out, giving us a bad look, a bad name. It's an easy cut.
Lucky for you, there's employment laws, even for ministers. I
have to put you under review. Suspend you from the funerals.
Come back in two weeks and assess things. So this is a formal
warning. I can write *stress* on these forms. And when I come
back, if things have changed. . . I'd hate to get rid of a young
guy. We're not exactly flush with them. I want to push out

the older ones, if I'm honest. But I need you to be on board. Deal with this. . .' He pointed at the shortbread tin. 'Fling it in a river. Why not? Chuck it in the bin. Forget about it. Think about what you really want, go for a wee holiday, use these two weeks to relax, calm down, set your head straight.' He clapped his knees with his last few words.

Gillis nodded. 'I didn't know I was under review.'

'And listen. . . there's no shame in finding the funerals tough going. Speak to a doctor. Get a real check-up, get him to really root around in there. Get in touch with yourself. And listen, if you don't, I'll be on your case, OK? Is that a yes? Two weeks then? I'll come back and reassess.'

Gillis nodded, still gripping the shortbread tin, and they walked from the hall into the front entrance.

'We'll get you back at it in no time.'

Outside, a Nicholson Fisheries van was parked crookedly across the car park, and a ladder was being unclipped from the roof. An apprentice in a boiler suit was swinging a hammer around and making kung-fu noises, while Nichol was struggling with a large sheet of heavy canvas, coated with a scramble of coloured letters.

'Hoi! Prick! Give us a hand with this,' Nichol shouted at the apprentice.

'Friends of yours?' the elder smiled.

'He's the one that owns the place.'

The elder settled in his car, lowered his window and asked directions to some beauty spot Gillis had never heard of. Behind them, Nichol sent his apprentice up the ladder with one corner of the canvas and a mouthful of nails. They shifted to the other side and the canvas opened.

FISHERS OF MEN

The elder looked confused, but couldn't seem to process the poster, the passive smiling minister standing before it, the argument in progress between the boss and the apprentice on the ladder. 'I'll be off then,' he announced cheerily, then drove away slowly, looking over his shoulder.

'What was he wanting?' Nichol asked as Gillis walked backward and waved.

'He was here to give me the sack. But he decided just to give me a disciplinary.'

'Did he, aye? Next time he comes by, you bring me along, OK?'

'I'm meant to see him in two weeks for a review.'

'Is that right?' Nichol suddenly lunged forward and jostled the ladder, shouting up at the apprentice. 'The whole thing's sitting squint, pull that side up!' He walked back and stuck out his tongue. 'Noising the wee bastard up,' he explained. 'Worst-case scenario. They give you the boot? I'll hire you back on. Actually, what d'you make?'

Gillis told him his salary.

Nichol laughed. 'Aye, I think we can manage that.'

Jan cheerfully ate his carrots as he walked away from the courthouse, ears pink, body still aglow from the warmth instilled by the vast fireplaces inside. He waved back at his drinking companions as they called for their keepers, to tell rumours and lies about the Laird for their freedom.

'What'll happen to them?' Jan spat fragments of carrot as he spoke to the black jacket who had followed him out of the court.

'The Proctor'll pray for guidance and then they'll be whipped.' On the man's head, a soft black hat held a protestor's tract stuffed into the band; pages grey and worn, it moved in the wind like the last tuft of hair on a bald man's head. He held a long club which he tapped against his leg as they walked. 'Down this way.' The black jacket motioned left.

With the blunt and bitten end of his carrot, Jan pointed out of the little town, to the hills and forests. 'Thought I'd head that way, see if I can go south.'

The black jacket raised his club and touched Jan's shoulder with a slight tap, the way a man might guide a docile cow or calf. Twenty or thirty paces back, another black jacket came into sight and stopped. Stared at them, lifted his own club and held it ready. Jan turned left. They circled the market, where a half-dozen meetings of black-jacketed men were beginning to merge, to make a crowd, or a mob. They sat on bundled blankets, starting little fires, joined by more, filtering through the houses, walking in twos and threes.

'Companions of yours?' Jan was ignored and escorted between pillarbox houses, round the back of the courthouse.

The front of the building was covered in ornate carvings, statues of the Apostles and of Justice, dramatically blinded, bound and gagged. Round the back, nothing but stern blocks of coarse unfinished stone, stacked on a thin foundation of sleekit mud.

'The Proctor had instructions.' The man behind him apologized.

They took him through the stable yards and locked him in a cell.

A small girl, elfin-eared and buck-toothed, sat quietly in the cell next to his. He tried to whisper, ask her what was happening. He was shushed, so he curled in a corner to sleep. Next morning, he was led into a room where a dozen men stood bollock naked, several of the drinkers among them. Waiting on cold flagstones as buckets of steaming water were prepared. Soon, their heads were haloed in soap. Blood and blacksmithing washed away. Jan drank the floral water as he received the same treatment. Two elderly women from the town combed and cut his hair, cropped the boyish fuzz that collected on his upper lip and chin. A white cotton shirt was thrown over his bruises. It itched. The drawstring was pulled and tied. They brought trousers and shoes and a jacket made of stained black leather, whose buttons were made of bone.

Beneath a heavy oak ceiling, sitting in a circle, the Proctor was duplicated half a dozen times. Men with long beards streaked grey and white sat straight-backed and prim; they pursed their mouths and sorted through stacks of loose paper, annotating and scribbling like tallying merchants. Behind them, penned like a herd in for milking, a tightly packed crowd of black-jacketed men. Above, in a gallery, staring down, the local folk. They whispered amongst themselves when the ceremonies began.

'Tell the tribunal what you told me.' The elfin girl went first. She muttered and her words were echoed by a court clerk. Interference on a quiet hill. The landlord of the drinking den spoke next. Sighting of the Laird and his Lady drawing symbols in the earth and dancing a complicated jig, intended to summon the Devil. Other accusers spoke about taxes and rents, but embellished these with shameful stories, servants asked to assist at wild orgies. Coupling of man, woman and beast, glimpsed through steamy windows.

Jan approached the witness box. As he climbed the brief stairs to the stand, he saw the Laird. Tucked away in a corner with an empty desk before him, flanked by an advisor. Jan described the book he had been commissioned to deliver. Its contents, its expense. Cross-hatched sunlight illuminated the Laird's head, as though melted bronze for a casting had been poured over his skull. Jan told his story about the red calves, the skin they used for the book, and the paints derived from sediment found in their body parts.

'And they worshipped using this book?'

'Yes. And they never paid me for it either.' Pointed back to his seat, Jan spent the remainder of the tribunal enjoying the rustling of his new clothes. Fresh white linen against his skin, scrubbed for the first time in months.

The tribunal lasted all day, as witnesses of the Laird's sins and blasphemies appeared in the form of young children and drunks, followed by reputable tenant farmers and merchants, then the blacksmith, then a tax collector and finally, casting the last vote of condemnation, two local nobles who owned vast tracts of land on either side of the Laird. These men, although blessed with hundreds of miles of cold granite, useless heather and moss, felt that the fishing port and marketplace could be better managed, and although they had never witnessed any of the corrupting acts which had been described throughout the morning and afternoon, couldn't, what with God looking down at them and the people looking up to them, refuse to act; their hands were tied, the die was cast, and so on. So they had drawn up a plan between them which would divide the Laird's properties and lands in such a way that all might prosper.

'*Beggars before priests.*' The noble lord pronounced this slogan delicately, and adjusted the ill-fitting black jacket he had commissioned especially for his appearance at the court.

'Yes, *beggars before priests,*' the second noble said. 'Please place that on the record.'

The court's decision was hurried along as the sun was setting and the courthouse was running low on candles. The day's evidence was quickly summarized and a verdict delayed until an inspection could be carried out. Rumours of Papistry, idolatry and witchcraft needed careful investigation. So, cheerfully released from their wooden pews, the crowds stumbled from the court and paced into darkness. Shaking pins and needles from their feet, digging knuckles into aching spines and throbbing temples, rubbing hands across empty bellies, cracking their stooped backs and rolling their shoulders, one and all, peasant, yeoman and lord of the land, united in a great moaning, as, like a herd of weary cattle, they paced uphill, led by the Laird and Lady, whose hands were tied together.

A busy troupe of children danced and ran ahead of the severe phalanx of black jackets. They had been waiting outside the courts as their parents and elder siblings watched the gossiping trial. Now, in a night-time alive with light and anger, they could barely contain their happiness. They ran through the crowd, torturing dogs, pinching one another, then desperately seeking their mothers, in tears suddenly stemmed by another opportunity to fight, tease or spit. Old folk hobbled at the back of the crowd, asking for their arms to be held, but the young people pulled their elbows free and ran on ahead, or lingered back in deserted streets to walk into empty houses, touch things, steal blankets, set animals loose, taste tomorrow's bread, winch in secret the one they should have married, but didn't, or couldn't, or look for them in the crowd and stare. Was anything possible? Now that the great Laird was to be punished.

The castle gatehouse had been locked, and though the Laird's hunting party had either scattered or joined the accusing witnesses, a small group of servants and loyal guards were standing with pikes and daggers before and behind the gate. The black jackets only carried torches and clubs, but their ranks were full of soldiers chased out of France. A mix of Englishmen, Lowland and Highland Scots, faces still sunburnt from fights on the Continent. They filtered through the crowd and scaled the fences, flanked the guards and servants and soon the gates were open. Servants ran from the castle into the surrounding woodland, throwing uniforms and weapons to the ground. The crowds chanted and sang, the last of the day's light disappearing like a closing eyelid. One of the magistrates knocked at the door, and it was opened. Black jackets entered flat-footed and close-fisted, and the crowd were disappointed when two gallous souls stepped forward and tried to follow the Proctor and magistrates inside, but their way was barred. Some drifted downhill muttering that nothing would happen, nothing ever happened, but ran back when they heard the crowd cheering. Black jackets began flinging armfuls of expensive robes and garlands and daft hats, statues and icons and communion wine, down from high windows into the courtyard. All was swept and collected in a great heap, stacked on a cross-hatch of ash planks and switches of dried pine, then burned.

Beyond the heat and noise, a man was preaching, pointing to a vernacular Bible. He talked about a new world, and a new chosen people, beggars before priests, and Scotland as a new Jerusalem. Routed from a cubbyhole hidden in the walls, the Laird's priest appeared, slapped across the baldy head and pushed down the stairs. They jeered as he tripped, and fell at the feet of his Laird and Lady, who pulled their toes from his reach. As he watched the looting of his castle, the Laird bared his teeth and strained against the rope which bound him at his middle. His eyes were white puncture marks in the folded flesh of his head, as he called for the dignity, respect and cordiality due to a man in his position. But they took the three prisoners to a carriage waiting nearby, and the crowds surged about them.

The people were loyal to everything at once, feeling sorrow for the bloated, diseased Laird who had extorted them all their lives by rent and taxes, who banned them from the woodland, and the quiet, slow-running bend of the river, where shady trees and good swimming lay, but the poor bugger always sat tall on his horse and wore colourful clothes as he passed by the fields. So some of the stones, clumps of grass and clods of dirt which flew overhead and struck the carriage were intended for the Laird, but some were intended for the captors, and both sides of the crowd seemed to think they were in the majority, confusing one another's indignation for encouragement, so when a half-brick struck and near killed a black jacket, the cheer that rose from the crowd could have been factional in either direction, but might also have been a pre-factional cheering for the violence, happy to see that something was finally happening.

Now that the first blood had been spilt, more bricks and stones were thrown until the crowd had to retreat from itself, as the advance guard turned on the stone-throwers, and in the confusion, Jan dragged his fellow witnesses by the rope that bound them together toward the bundles of burning clothes and books and held their binding to the scaling coals of that fire. The rope burnt through, and now separated, Jan and his fellow prisoners all scattered and disappeared into the crowd or ran toward the house; blacking their faces with ash, turning their jackets inside out, they blended into the chaos. As the Laird, Lady and priest were driven away, the crowd turned toward the empty castle and the black jackets began to swing their clubs to defend the doors, but the crowd brought out their fish knives and sickles and fought for the cause they thought they knew best, the old or the new religion, motivated by hatred of anyone who held a club, or hatred of anyone with such little sense as to get hit with one. In the confusion, Jan receded from the fire and stood in shadow, watching as the crowd overwhelmed the black jackets and forced their way inside the great castle.

CHAPTER ELEVEN

A heavy morning frost misted the gravestones, and the kirk doors and the silver padlock that sealed them. Gillis's skin stuck to the cold metal as he made his way inside and knelt before the severed hand, struggling to ignore his surroundings. Muzzle the doubt fostered by MDF and chipboard furniture, formica and tastefully dull decoration. Without his work to wake up for, without even the avoidance of his work to arrange, Gillis was stuck waiting for something to happen. The TV seemed to be repeating itself, declaring a war which had been lost a decade ago, annotating an election whose results were already in. The severed hand was up already, scribbling nonsense figures, men standing on their heads, animals confused with plants, wheels contorting into boats, long straight lines and curves and nondescript stippling. Eventually, Gillis took the pen away from the hand and tried to pray. But his armpits no longer warmed his hands, and his feet had gone to sleep. He didn't know how to pray or what to pray for.

'Oh, you're here,' Nichol interrupted, dumping two great sealed buckets of white paint in a corner of the room. 'Want to give us a hand?'

A large white van had been strenuously reversed from the car park, along the grass verge and over a long-suffering rose bush, to press its rear bumper against the entrance of the kirk.

'Have you met the wife?' Hidden in his shadow, a very short woman, dressed with the severe practicality of a horse owner. She wore long leather boots, leggings and a thick body warmer, hair thoroughly brushed and laid to one side, in imitation of a stallion's mane. She had her hand on Nichol's sleeve as if she might grasp it at any moment, drive her boot into his pocket, straddle his shoulders and take him cantering around the graveyard. 'Carol's been helping out with decorating.'

'And the business side too.' Pale white fingers stretched from the door frame into Gillis's hand and he felt an ancient impulse to bow. She released him and led her husband into the shadows of the kirk. Her metallic heels clip-clopped across the floorboards, and the lights began to flicker as they warmed, strip bulbs chiming like tin bells.

'What's all this *Fishing Men* stuff?' Gillis asked. The heavy canvas which had been proudly tacked over the kirk entrance now lay crumpled beneath the coat racks. The rough drawing of a severed hand could still be seen, raised in greeting.

'Oh, don't get her started,' Nichol shouted over his shoulder, before disappearing into the hall.

'I wouldn't have called it that.' Carol looked disdainfully at the vulgar colours and typefaces.

'That was the only one on the list you highlighted!' Nichol's voice echoed.

'Gillis, if you saw a list of names and one had a *red line* through it. Would you think, that one's out, or that's the one we're going with?'

Gillis didn't answer.

'Come on, what does a red line mean? In school?'

Nichol reappeared, propping the inner doors to the main hall with triangular wooden offcuts stashed in his jacket pocket. 'Two hundred quid wasted,' he flung the unused props on top of the poster.

'You did the usual,' Carol spoke through Gillis's skull to Nichol who stood just beyond, ignoring her. 'You wanted my help, then you lost patience with me, then you talked to some daft pal of yours and went with a silly name you made up.'

'I told you before, we found it in the Bible.'

'Well. It's not what I would have called it.'

'She wouldn't get it, it's a guy thing. Doesn't it sound good?' He jostled Gillis with his elbow.

'Don't get him involved.'

'If it's good enough for Jesus, it's good enough for Kirkmouth.' Nichol gripped Gillis by the bicep. 'You needing a workout?' The Nicholson Fisheries van that sat by the entrance contained a great jumble of timber, plasterboard and blue tarpaulin, with reels of overlapping cables and pipes strewn by the sides. Nichol clambered inside, knocking dents and cracking corners of the plasterboard as he went; forcing himself into a tiny space behind the pallets, he began to drag the top third of the pile in one chunk and as Gillis walked backward, he took more and more of the overwhelming weight.

'She reckons. . . it's a dead loss. . . competing with the NHS,' Nichol explained between grunts and gasps, as he scrambled from the van and took his half of the weight. 'And we. . . should focus. . . on the fish.'

'You can't undercut zero, can you?' Carol walked ahead of them, holding back doors that had already been propped. She held out her thumb and added a finger to it with each point she made. 'One, you don't know what you're doing. Two, you *might* heal people, but you might make them worse. Three, you might get sued. Four, even if you succeed, do you really want to start a religion?'

Nichol dutifully nodded. 'Well, we're not starting it. We're carrying it on.'

As they walked the piled plasterboards through the first double doors, Carol stood on her tiptoes and held her head back, thinning herself by a millimetre or so as they struggled through. 'I've been trying to tell him religion's out. Therapy's in. Do you remember Reiki? Or Acupuncture? Hypnosis? They all had their moment in the sun. Some folk would've made millions. Us girls were out getting a tarot reading last week. You don't have to promise as much. It's not eternity in heaven, it's pep in your step. It's about feeling good.'

The two men struggled step by step, through the entrance and into the hall.

'But he won't listen!' Carol called from the hallway. Nichol waited until he could rest the boards down and arch his back, before he gritted his teeth and ran a thumb across his throat, pantomiming his own death. He searched Gillis's face for some acknowledgement of his joke. Tried until Gillis reacted with a minimal smile.

'Oh,' Nichol said as they made to lift again. 'I set Rachel straight.'

'Set her straight?' Gillis dropped his half.

'She had herself all worked up thinking the hand was Dougie's! She was all for speaking to the polis. I told her about what we'd been up to.'

'Silly cow,' Carol called from behind them. 'Just as well we're rid of her.'

'What do you mean, rid of her?'

'Our Helen's back. Good as new,' Nichol said. 'Cancer's away, after our wee intervention. You can't explain that, can you?' He goaded his wife.

She wasn't convinced. She said the mind was the most powerful organ, it's all to do with self-belief, self-respect even.

Some people just didn't have the willpower, they more or less gave in, let the illness win. Whereas Helen, God bless her, was clearly made of sterner stuff. You wouldn't think it to look at her.

Nichol spoke over her. 'We had to let Rachel go. Just isn't the shifts for her.'

'But she needs that job, she's got her kid.'

Nichol grimaced and sighed. 'I feel sorry for her and all that, what with the widowing, but at the end of the day, I don't believe in charity.'

'And with all her little comments and insinuations,' muttered Carol darkly.

'She's just all mixed up because of the grief. Doesn't know what she's saying. Anyway, what are we doing here?' He suddenly lifted the boards and began to rush across the room.

'Wait! Slowly,' Gillis tried to caution and staggered backward until his heel snagged on a jutting nail in the floorboards and he twisted, and the great weight swung to one arm, and pressed further against his weak knee. As he felt his fingers slipping he leapt backward and dropped his end, provoking a great clap of thunder as the pile fell. He limped and clutched at the bad leg. The empty hall boomed once more, as Nichol stumbled and dropped the other end.

'Careful!' he demanded. 'D'you know how much these cost?'

Although Carol recommended a pressure bandage and an aspirin, Nichol was much more practical – why not use the severed hand? He had it right there.

'You'll be eating your words,' he pointed to Carol, and silenced Gillis with a quick question. 'Do you want to be in pain?' And marched through to search the back vestry, opened the shortbread tin and dumped the holy relic onto Gillis's leg without any preamble or preparation.

'Give it a few minutes. I don't know if your trousers will interfere with whatever it does.'

Gillis tried to hold Nichol back, ignore both the pain in his knee and his disgust at the touch of the severed hand. 'Did you really have to let Rachel go? She's got the boy. She's got a lot of debt. She needs the money.'

'Ach, hard times call for hard decisions, mate. And anyway,' he was suddenly furious, 'she grassed! What do you care? And we healed Helen! Am I the only one who. . . She's back working ten-hour days, no problem. That's all down to us, that is. Now roll these up,' Nichol grabbed at the hem of Gillis's trousers and tried to pull them upwards, but the minister scrambled away from both miracle and miracle-giver. The severed hand fell from his knee and lay sprawled like a seagull downed mid-flight.

'Would you behave yourself?' Nichol gripped the leg and the relic and brought the two back together, then husband and wife left the room to struggle with the next load of plasterboard. From the silent hall, Gillis could hear Nichol insisting he could take all the weight himself, as Carol said she was just as strong, if not stronger than him, through there. The truth lay somewhere in the middle.

'You'll give yourself a heart attack,' Carol slapped at Nichol's arms as he pulled the boards from the van. She took one end and strained herself shuffling it forward a metre or so. She laid her end on the ground, stepped back, out of breath; if she could just get a good grip on the edge, she insisted, she'd be able to lift it fine. The severed hand wearily extended an accusatory forefinger, pointing between Gillis's eyes, and the minister nodded. 'I know.' He polished the floorboards with the seat of his trousers as he squirmed around, trying to stretch the calf, the shin and the weak lateral muscles of his knee.

'Is it that bad?' Carol abandoned her struggle with the heaped plasterboard as a few employees arrived and pushed her aside in mock chivalry. A sheen of sweat battled through a clotted coating of foundation and concealer.

'It's this old injury, I'm always buckling in the same bit.'

Nichol shouted for help. Carol drew a long breath to calm herself and shouted back, 'I'm seeing to the minister!'

The van rattled and the hallway boomed as he turned to his wife, 'Are you wanting to help or not?'

'Not if you're being like that!' She jutted her chin at the empty doorway and the receding footsteps.

'Used to be a runner.' Gillis tried to make small talk. 'Tried football. Didn't stick.' Preferred being alone. Liked the long-distance, cross-country events. Where the track almost disappeared, and time passed like spells of depression and recovery. Devious things happened in hidden corners of the race, sharp elbows, little kicks.

Carol excused herself impeccably, drifting almost unnoticed from his side, back to berate her husband. The small talk became smaller and quieter, he was muttering on his own. Rachel used to stand shivering at the finish line. She wore his medals. And didn't mind the taste of salt on his neck, kissing congratulations through the sweat running off his hair. He was good enough to end up in trials. Trials in England. The trainers and coaches acted like priests routing out sin. Something wrong in him could be remedied by running faster and escaping their notice. Too slow? Time waster, dawdler, skiver. Too fast? Try hard, glory hunter. Despite all the effort, other boys trained less and ran better. *Many are called, few are chosen.*

Who shall I send? God had asked.

Gillis eagerly kept his hand up, but God couldn't see him. *Nobody?*

Gillis stared at the bastard leg, and twisted his ankle back and forth, balancing the severed hand. He remembered his dad's confusion, 'England? What if you make it through? Would you stay down there? You could stay with your mum, I suppose. . .'

She had moved into a little flat after the divorce. To a little harbour town just across the spectral border. It was just like Kirkmouth. But little things were out. The money looked odd and the papers had different headlines and the houses looked like slices of fruit cake with their harling stripped away.

'I'll be back soon,' he'd promised Rachel. 'But if I get it, everything'll change.' He could picture it. New tracksuits. New shorts. Money. Free trainers. Sponsors. Ad campaigns. 'We might have to move.' They'd grinned at one another.

Running trials lasted all weekend. His mum made him enormous plates of watery pasta – his dad had always been the better cook. The furniture was simple, and the flat bare, 'I'm still getting things set up,' she said. The kitchen counter was empty save for a poly bag full of bananas. 'For your running.'

The first day had gone well. Made decent times. But that night, when he called Rachel, he lied. Dropped a few seconds from his times.

'Almost a PB,' she sounded excited.

'Almost.'

Met another Scottish boy and clung to him. Late Sunday, in the last race, did a boy trip him? Or snag his laces? Or clip his heel? In big unstable steps, Gillis fell out of the top five and struggled to make the time back. In the locker rooms, they were making fun of him.

'What age are you?' the boy said. 'You're a grown man.'
They were all sixteen, eighteen, nineteen at most. What
was he? Surely not twenty-three? He didn't remember his
birthdays, could hardly remember leaving school, how had
he passed the time? Their faces were flushed in childish red
blotches, they had bare, feathery moustaches and sideburns.

'Give it up, you fat fucker, it's not happening.' The boy
was probably right. Was it possible to run one last, good race?
Even if all the others had been mediocre?

As the boy taunted him, Gillis did what any man of pride
and standing would do. He waited until the little prick turned
his back and booted him up the arse while he was footering
with his shoelaces. Pitched suddenly forward, the boy's head
cracked a tile on the locker room wall, and the crowd of
runners shouted in joy at the outbreaking fight. Some had
tried to grab at Gillis, holding him back as the boy's friends
helped him to his feet. There was blood smeared across his
forehead and he began to shout insults as it dripped into his
eyes. Gillis couldn't put his foot down properly, it was as if
one of the tendons in his knee had slipped right across the
kneecap. He couldn't straighten the leg. He pushed backward,
into the boys that held him, searching for the benches amid a
cloud of deodorant and foot powder. He pushed aside a knot
of sweat-stained shorts and vests, tangled and stinking like
a clump of seaweed. The boy threw his head back to squint
through the blood that dripped on either side of his nose
and into his mouth. 'Psycho,' he spat, and his friends rallied.

Gillis looked around in panic for the other Scottish boy, as
if they could stand back to back, in Jacobite formation, and
fight their way through the auld enemy. Lead the English into
close confines and fight them one by one. Gillis made for the
showers, but history refused to repeat. Whatever damage
had been done to the tendons doubled as Gillis fell to the

floor, knee bent awkwardly back on itself. Though they stuck
the boot in a few times, they didn't have the stomach for a
proper kicking. A minute or two more, then the coaches
came in and broke it all up. The boy needed stitches and
fucked off to hospital, and the physio looked over Gillis's
leg. The man refused to listen to excuses or explanations,
leaving Gillis ice-packed and tension-strapped, propped on
a bench, alone in the dark locker room, in foreign territory
with nothing but his thoughts for company.

But in a corner of the room, Gillis noticed a spider whose
web kept breaking in the draught coming through a cracked
window. Each time that the cobweb broke, the brave little
creature swung across and repaired the damage, and each
time he tried and failed, the web strengthened, until finally,
it held against the draughty window. Gillis stared at the web
and the brave, resolute spider and knew it didn't matter what
he decided or how much grit and determination and stern
Scottish resolve and Protestant work ethic and sublimated
sexual desire he applied, it was over, and there was no point
in trying any more. But still, he waited around and took a
telling-off from a tracksuited solicitor, and an ex-Olympian
with a gold tooth and hair gel that hadn't dried yet, who had
no time for this kind of nonsense. Was Gillis's treatment
evidence of an anti-Celtic streak in British sport? Could
be. Was it part of society's veneration of the young at the
expense of those who were twenty-three or twenty-four and
couldn't remember their birthdays? Maybe. Gillis tried to
defend himself, but was given a six-month ban. 'With your
knee like that, you'll struggle to walk, let alone run,' the
physio chipped in.

He had been too sore to move from the sofa. Then too
embarrassed to leave the house. Then too delusional to
leave England. He applied for the next year's trials, he spoke

to administrators and coaches on the phone. He joined an athletics club and sat on the sideline.

'Is this it then?' Rachel sounded stoic on the phone. In response to his silence, she arranged to send all of his stuff round to his dad's.

He had limped around England for a few years. Moved back when it looked like independence might happen. Took up the old room in his dad's place. Hobbled door to door with a clipboard and a jacket covered in badges. Pleading with people. Say Yes. Got to know his local councillor, and a band of high-school students, pensioners and stay-at-home mums who flew plastic Saltires from the aerials on their car roofs, and said a quick *slàinte* before every sip of diluting orange. Caught up in the rallies and meetings, the chattering online, Gillis thought his big chance might come with Scotland 2.0. He could get himself a haircut and a good suit, get himself a career in advertising, sell the state to the people, sell the state assets to rich people. Even if things went pear-shaped, they would need more policemen to stop the rioting, and more firemen to stop the fires, and more nurses and ambulance drivers to tend to the coshed and chibbed masses, more teachers to tell the children to tell their parents to calm down. And if things went really bad, he'd still be in the age range to be drafted into the army. If things went well, all the better.

He knew where Rachel was, but didn't contact her. He knew where all her pals drank, but avoided them. Until, in the supermarket with his dad, leaning all his weight on the trolley, he had almost knocked over her cousin.

'That you back, is it?' she stared at the sugary cereal in his hand.

He nodded.

'Not famous no?'

He wasn't.

'You voting Yes?' She nodded at the pin on his jacket.

'Yeah. You?'

She wasn't.

All the campaigners watched the vote coming in from the kirk hall. They hadn't sold the pews yet. Still had a little congregation. The old minister, pre-stroke and pre-heart attack, spat feathers and denounced this country full of cowards, and before midnight, his astonished 'I don't believe it' had soured and deepened, though the words remained the same.

'I do not believe,' he said, 'that the British state would let us *vote* our way out.' He spoke about a secret oilfield, discovered a week before the vote, a real gamechanger. All kept quiet, of course. That night, Gillis helped the old minister back to the manse. They sat in the living room and drank through the dregs of a bottle of sherry, and eventually, though they felt bad about it, desperate circumstances and all that, they began to drink the communion wine.

'Will you be all right for work tomorrow?' Gillis had asked the minister. Who laughed and described a career in decline. A people gone Godless, who only looked to the Kirk to get married or buried. 'They used to be like jackals.' The minister pointed to the kirk. 'Any weakness they spotted, they pulled at it with their teeth. Spat it out in front of you, so you'd be forced to stare at it. I used to spend all week biting my nails till they bled. Look at me now.' He held out his hand, each fingernail was long and white. 'I'd score everything in my sermon out, start over, examine every sentence for contradiction, ambiguity, sharpening it up all week. Then I'd go to the pulpit and speak, and at the end, after the hymns, I'd stand at the back and wait for them. Practically blindfolded and bound. Waiting for reviews coming in. And the *looks* I'd get, they'd trip over themselves finding deviance from scripture, I'd get anonymous letters full of theories about how I was drifting into heresy. Leading my flock into mortal sins, things which even Christ would struggle to forgive. Used to hate them. Their handwriting. Every word looked like a Celtic knot. Every letter joined up perfectly to the next. They're all dead now, of course. And now, whenever I have to write a sermon, I don't even bother checking my spelling. I'm practically gnostic these days, you won't know what that means, I'm Manichean. The punters don't notice. I could say anything. We're just biding time in there.'

When the morning dawned, the big vote fully counted, announced, drifting into history, Gillis walked back to his dad's place and felt God calling him to a job with a decent salary, and a free house and car. And people who probably wouldn't notice that he didn't really believe in anything, and might even be glad of it. A year of training, and three years of work, and here he was, under review. What would he do if they kicked him out? Limp around an office, limp around a warehouse? Limp around the back of a restaurant?

His thoughts were interrupted by husband and wife, carrying smaller piles of plasterboard to the back wall of the kirk. Arguing the merits of three backbreaking trips versus thirty easygoing. Nichol soon stood beside the whole pile, veering precariously to one side. He was staring at the ceiling and walls, spanning the floor with his measuring tape.

'How's the knee?' Nichol pointed with a carpenter's pencil.

Like a dog winding down to sleep, the severed hand crawled in a circle and settled, fingers splayed across the old injury.

'It doesn't hurt,' Gillis realized.

'What's it been? Half an hour? You'll be good with that. In my experience but, you'd want to top it up every day or two. You've got a key, sit in the back room, there's a little telly. . .' He chipped the hand into the shortbread tin and laid it to one side with roughly the same amount of care that an expensive power drill or a complicated socket set receives. Can't be thrown loose into a toolbag like a hammer, couldn't be kept in a cabinet like an antique gun. Gillis shifted to one side, testing the leg, one hand pressed at his waist; it must have looked like he was going for his wallet, because Nichol demurred.

'Like I said, miracles are free.'

As another van arrived, and the workers searched for Nichol in the back reaches of the building, a terrible smell followed them. It seemed to coat the driver's hair and clothes and contaminate everything he stood beside.

Gillis tried to ignore it as he pressed into the floorboards with his heel and toe. He strained one side and another, stood, pressed his full weight on the old injury and could feel nothing. No pain, no frailty, no sensation at all.

'You're not answering your phone,' the driver shouted back as their boss berated them.

'Didn't I say I'd deal with it tomorrow?' Nichol pushed through from the vestibule to the van, flung open the doors and reeled back from the smell. He hid in his elbow.

'Where are we meant to put it? It can't stay in the van, I keep it in my driveway. The whole street's fucking stinking. Next door's threatening to call the council.' To enforce his point, the workers threw open the other door and a dozen salmon tumbled out, their bodies breaking apart and recombining on the ground. Flies and lice scattered the air around them.

'Well, we can't keep chucking it. . .' Nichol checked over his shoulder. 'We can't keep flinging it in the water either.'

'I can't,' Carol muzzled her nose into her elbow and shook her head, fleeing for the cover of her car as Nichol looked around himself. Suddenly interested again in the miracle, he pointed at the minister's knee as he tried to escape the smell, walking out to the fresh air across the kirk garden.

'Didn't I tell you?' he bellowed.

Gillis couldn't speak, for fear that the smell would spill into his mouth. He pulled the collar of his shirt up and breathed through the fabric.

Carol had fled to her car, an enormous German paper-weight, silvery black, tinted windows and leather seats. She sealed the air vents and blasted the air con. She rifled through her bag for a bottle of perfume, and misted herself in a cloud of alcoholic flowers.

'What did I say?' Nichol bellowed at the oncoming windscreen, pointing at Gillis's leg as her car rounded the gravel.

She lowered her window as she passed and looked up and down the backtracking minister. 'Well, if he's half as daft as you!' It didn't make much sense, but she revved her engine and raced to the exit, covering the banality of her speech with a slick display of the finest European engineering.

Alone in the manse, Gillis took lunging steps, jumps, hops along the hallway and up the stairs. He took off his trousers and draped them over his shoulder as he examined the knee. If only it was translucent, if only he could see how the miracle had been wrought. Had the torn tendons been rethreaded? Transplanted? He stood on one leg, no pain. Jogged on the spot for a good few minutes, no pain. Felt a rising joy fill his body with strength, put his trousers and trainers back on, and walked around and around the manse garden, turning hard corners, testing his capabilities. Stood on one leg and swung the other until he was throwing it away up, almost touching his face, swinging back, scything thistles from the borders of the grass. Up, losing balance, back, he jumped to one side, up, the gravel underneath him slipped and he fell back; landing on his spine he lay and watched the early evening appear, laid the bad leg over the good and stretched it back and forth until the cold encroached on him. He thanked the severed hand, he bowed before the empty kirk. Blasphemously perhaps, but he couldn't care. What a blessing.

In the warm air of the house, he pulled the bad leg behind him and strained his hamstring, burying his heel in the flesh of his arse. His phone lay on the kitchen table, and as soon as he saw it, he noticed it ringing. An unknown number.

A woman's voice was thickly clotted with mucus. 'Is she there?'

'Is who here?'

'Rachel. Is she there?' She apologized to him as he denied it. It was just. You heard rumours. And now she needed help. Another funeral, how did it work? She didn't know. Could Gillis see to it? Could he help? He tried to calm her and explain that he had been suspended, but she spoke over him. She'd had to go and look at the body. She had to speak to Rachel.

'Wait, who is this? Who's passed away?'

He asked her to repeat the words she slurred with grief. He heard her cough and swallow away from the phone. 'It's Douglas, my boy.'

'Wait. Calm down,' he tried to reason with her. 'We already cremated him, weeks ago. That's all over.' He scanned the kitchen for his calendar – he was right, wasn't he?

No, she explained. Douglas's body had washed on shore. Tangled in seaweed, folded in a nook of rock. Stuck at the foot of the cliffs. Discovered by a dog walker. They had asked her to identify the body. Although the face was bloated beyond recognition, he was wearing his wedding ring and wristwatch. She wished she had refused.

Jan hid within distant long grasses, watching the great house like a paper theatre, and the grand bonfire raging before it, just a little candle. Tiny cut-out characters fought one another, and occasionally, one or two ran from the little theatre, into the woodlands, or back downhill toward the town. Over undulating marshland, trenches laid like numbered seats, a woman outlined in gold ran with her arms full of embroidered lace, spilling ghostly fishing nets as she went, cast across a cold and fishless landscape. Animals groaned, disturbed by the noise. Broken furniture, smashed glass.

'Sinners! Repent!' a voice called from the middle distance. Lowing cattle a stone's throw in front of him. 'Thieves! Sin no more!'

Jan rocked from foot to foot, fingers growing cold, toes growing numb. Kept from his full escape by the call of his beautiful book. The voice from within the cattle shouted again. 'Strengthen your arms! Weaken your legs! Train your toes to grab and pinch! Stub your fingers into stumps! You will use them as feet in the world as it turns upside down! Children of God! Repent!'

The cows began to move, drawing closer to the grand house; Jan could see a man hidden with them, leaning on their flanks, coaxing them toward the fire. The man bowed low and began to shout through the udders. 'Repent! You miserable hoor! Reaping a false harvest! The grain is still green! You are crows grown used to the scarecrow, but the tenant and his strapping sons stand in the doorway

of their barn! Armed with nets. And slingshots! Sinners,
repent!'

'Away home, Brother Malcolm! Get some rest, you'll be
next!' Clots of earth were thrown by those making their way
home from the crowd, and the monk hidden within the cattle
laughed despite himself. Though he was being trampled in
their irritation, he seemed to be enjoying his evening. Jan
skirted by him, walking against the flow of people till he
reached where black jackets and panicking townspeople
jostled for control of the house. Peasants who had trodden
mud and horse shit into the halls and upper corridors of
the Laird's house were being thrown down the front steps,
holding jugs full of milk, waxed paper packages full of
butter, pockets stuffed with vegetables. They were slapped
and searched for the valuables they had looted. Necklaces
and bangles were pulled from their necks, wrists and ankles.

'I came in with that apple!' one woman screamed, as her
pockets were turned out and revealed a stash of cutlery
and a shank of bacon, dripping grease down her leg. A man
dashed past her, a wooden bowl clasped to his heart, only
for a soldier to grab and struggle with the man and break his
nose with a metallic head butt.

A conference of horse riders who had accompanied the crowd
began to break apart, moving into loose formation. A line that
advanced on the people. These were the adjacent landowners
and their men, raising long pikes into the air. They waited
for the black jackets to force the last of the peasants from
the house, then seal the doors with timber planks and long
nails. How would they divide the estate among themselves
if it was reduced to nothing? The horsemen lowered their
pikes and continued to move. Most of the peasants laughed

and scattered, amazed at their luck, how far they had got in such little time. Some left with nothing but a mouthful of chestnut bread or pigeon pie, stolen from the kitchen. Some carried a torn piece of tapestry, useless but beautiful. One couple stumbled and fell into wet ditches, fattened by a dozen tablecloths and a set of curtains, stuffed into their jackets and up their skirts. They wandered back into the woods and fields and shouted curses at the house, the riders and the black jackets.

The bonfire's light dimmed, and the house seceded, once again, from the world around it.

'Friends!' Brother Malcolm huddled beneath his cows. 'You tried to storm heaven and have taken a wrong turning. You have hit purgatory! And been denied permission to wait there. You've been sent back to earth!' He stood up, and shouted across the cows' backs, between the horns. The crowd passed around him, ignoring the speech. 'You've seen it now! The purgatory where they wait. The empty rooms, the quiet! Inhabited by the pale-skinned, the fat and clean-fingernailed! Refined and burnished, skin polished to a sheen by soft fabrics, soft bedclothes, soft curtains and cushions. They do nothing but wait in there, wait to be admitted to another place. And while they wait, they stay clean, they keep the world at bay by scrubbing and sweeping and dusting and polishing. Stem the stinking mud, the weeds and thorns, midges, ticks and worms, crows and pigeons! And also the bonny pink bullfinch that strikes the window it cannot see and dies! And the rutting, screeching fox that eats poison intended for the rats and dies! And the cow that is cleaned by the stripping of its head and skeleton, and all semblance and smell of any animal, fit to enter the spiritless purgatory via the dinner plate! Friends, reject purgatory and find heaven! For heaven is here among you, it is in the cow shit and the uncut meat! Inside that empty house they hide the last taste of good blood with gravy, sweet lamb and veal for their table, and they smother it with salt and pepper! You are a lowing herd of cattle that has climbed the stairs and been somewhere you do not belong! Find the place you belong! The heaven of grass and cattle, the heaven of grain, the heaven of hatred!'

Closer now to the flames, Jan pushed his way through the crowd of onlookers. The bonfire was collapsing, having chewed through crosses, altarpieces, transoms and icons, the remaining timber fell into heaps of soft ash and dulling ember. Jackets lay abandoned in the heat, as men in their shirtsleeves tried to stoke the coals and loosed thick plumes of ash into one another's path. Their faces were blanched bright grey, with pink circles round the eyes and red lips that circled open, choking mouths. As the wind changed and a man retched at the scalding smoke, Jan ran forward and took the long pike from his hand. The man thanked him as he retreated to cough in clean air. 'Good man, good man.' He drank from a stoppered pig bladder, then leant back and baptized himself, rubbed his eyes and combed his hair with trembling hands. Jan stabbed and slashed at the dying fire until the grey skin broke and exposed the raw embers. There, among them, the golden book. Half-taken, half-surrendered. He threw the pike to one side and ran into the fire, grabbed at the book and threw it overhead, into wet grass, then danced through the flames, jumping from brick to unburnt plank, he batted aside the long staffs and burning pikes that rose to stab at him, and leapt into the long grasses. He lunged for the burning book and ran, sparks trailing after him, flames reborn in the wind. Stokers chased him into the grass until he fell and smothered the book with his body, tamping the flames with his shirt and jacket. Flames now dead, he ran in darkness, passing dozens of men and women fleeing and losing their takings, stealing from one another as they stumbled. He made it to the treeline and ran on until the thin birches gave way to thick pine, and their branches clawed at his sleeves and hips, scratched at his eyes and eventually, struck his head. Falling down, he pushed his back against the tree that had felled him and opened the book; the pages still glowed, still burned in obscure corners.

CHAPTER TWELVE

'Thing is,' Rachel said, 'we burned his good suit.'

Gillis stood in her bedroom, taking notes on his phone, helping to plan a second funeral.

'If you hadn't been so keen to get shot of his things,' the mother-in-law turned to the hallway to voice her criticisms. They stood before a rack of cupboards that contained nothing but furls of dust and hair. At their feet, a kilt, a Jacobite shirt with the lace missing, and a pair of sand-coloured boots, with a plastic sgian-dubh laid across their toes. 'That's just a cheapy kilt he bought for a stag do.'

'Well, it's either that or we buy something new.' Rachel had already had this argument, but she dutifully replayed her part in it. 'And we don't really know what size he is now. . . with the body all bloated. But I can ask the undertakers?' They faced the cupboards, and spoke not toward one another's bodies and faces, but toward their reflections, caught in a full-length mirror. 'And I can go buy a suit.' Rachel's eyes bored through the glass. 'Would that make you happy?'

The mother-in-law turned on her heel and left the room.

'She's doing this deliberately,' Rachel whispered as she sat down on the edge of her bed. Stared at the cheap kilt. 'She takes over the first funeral. Then she complains that I did nothing. So I take over the second one. And she complains that I haven't consulted her.'

Gillis took a seat beside her, and noticed for the first time that Jamie was sitting behind them. Cradled in a heap of pillows, he sat hunched over a stack of paper laid across his knees. He was carefully scribbling.

'God's got some sense of humour, hasn't He? I ask for him back. And that's what I get?' She folded the kilt and shirt into each other and draped them over a coat hanger. Kicked the boots and the plastic knife into a corner.

'When I called his pals, they all started telling me that Douglas was already dead. Like I didn't know.' She smiled. 'They were saying, *Listen, sweetheart, we had him cremated weeks ago.* Had to tell them that the coffin we cremated was empty. Some of them didn't know. What a waste of wood. Could have just waited. Know how much they cost?'

She wanted to have the service in the church. Nichol called her and offered to help, said he was a big believer in charity. 'I think the fucker just feels guilty,' she said. 'Wants to make amends.'

'For your husband? Or for the job?'

She narrowed her eyes. 'Both.'

'I'm sorry about that,' said Gillis. 'That he fired you.'

'Well, if only Helen had kept her cancer, we'd have been fine. Quite an amazing recovery, she was stage four.'

Gillis avoided meeting her eye.

'Anyway. I should apologize too.'

'For what?'

'For grassing, for speaking to the police. I thought the hand was. . . I don't know, I got confused.'

'OK. And anyway,' Gillis cringed a little, knowing she might take offence at what he wanted to ask. 'It was all there?' He held back another sentence. The body. And both hands.

She looked a little shocked. 'Yes. It was all there.'

'Sorry,' he quickly nodded the question away, but she had taken it as a rebuke.

'Shouldn't have jumped to conclusions,' she acknowledged. 'Should have made sure. I can only say I'm sorry.'

'Well, I'm sorry for not calling. Or replying. Or explaining myself.'

'We can stop all that now.'

'All what?'

'The sorry, sorry, sorry. Let's just get this done.' It had been a long morning. A long afternoon. She'd find something. She'd land on her feet. Couldn't really not. What with the wee man to look after.

'OK, what about flowers then?' Gillis asked.

She shook her head. Nichol had promised to take care of that. To redecorate the kirk. To send him off in style. 'He's trying to keep me sweet. Now the body's with the police. He doesn't want me saying anything silly.'

'What would you say?' Gillis tried to sound casual.

She shrugged. 'I'm to get a plot in the kirkyard, he says. Big enough that I can go in next to Douglas. If I want to.'

'Generous of him.'

'It is and it isn't.'

'I thought he was digging it up, getting rid of all the graves.'

'He said he'd free up some space,' Rachel said.

'By chucking someone else out?'

Rachel shrugged again, 'You can't expect to take up space for ever.'

Gratitude kept Gillis awake. Gratitude and hip flexers. Squats and lunges, yoga poses, mountain climbers, burpees, warriors one and two. The severed hand seemed to have completely healed his knee. He searched the Bible, but could find no precedent. The words seemed irrelevant. God was no longer contained in the book. When he finally slept, legs and sheets tangled, clammy with sweat, he dreamt of athletic success. A kind of decathlon, whose stages entailed running, climbing, sermonizing, tree felling, irrigation, stone clearing, architectural planning, flag planting and nation building. The dream ended in vague premonitions, fires and floods, acts of God.

When he woke, the clock was pointing shyly to the early hours. He felt like he'd been asleep for years. His cupboards and fridge were empty. He took that as a sign he should fast. He wouldn't eat until he found an answer. Wouldn't smoke either. He crushed up the packets and poured water over them, knowing that in an hour or two he would have been tempted to rake through the bin.

When his alarm clock finally sounded, its shrill cry echoed uselessly around the manse. Waking nothing but the dormant rooms, the empty hall, the open door. Gillis was already awake, brooding in the back vestibule of the kirk, not exactly bowing before the hand, just kneeling, lowering his head and gripping his hands together. Admittedly, his eyes were closed, but the saltwater surrounding them was just a natural by-product of the cold air. And the words he was whispering weren't any kind of prayer, more like a story he was telling himself. Asking questions of both the hand and the God that lingered somewhere around it. Should he take the severed hand to the authorities? To the police? To the library? Or down to the capital, hand it to the government? Or the Royal Family? Hand it over for their use, or use it to skelp their faces, shame and punish them, grab the state's rudder and course correct? The destination would reveal itself; like St Brendan setting out in a reeling coracle, he could find himself another America and start everything over. Or grab the maces and swords, the golden instruments of power and crown himself? Or break the crown? Bend the mace beyond use, or swing it around his head? In contradictory images, he passed the hours, kneeling on a painless knee, until a shadow paced from the threshold of the church, down the corridor, to stop in the doorway of the vestibule. 'Here, big man, is Nichol about?'

Although the old gammy leg moved with childlike agility, the rest of Gillis's body had seized up around it. His vertebrae crunched as he twisted and his bones cracked as he stood.

'It's just I've got this heifer here. Last night Nichol was on to us about his arm and his belly and that relic thingwy he had, we had a fiver bet on it, but he's went and forgotten, hasn't he?' The shadow walked away from Gillis, leading him from the church.

Once outside, the shadow became a gangly twenty-something with a bright green tammy barely gripping the top of his head. Tufts of ginger hair outlined a pair of jutting lugs, awkwardly folded on either side.

He strode toward a van and livestock trailer that was jackknifed across the car park, continuing a conversation that didn't seem to stop. '. . .aye and my old man says I was to say to Nichol that finding Jesus all of a sudden was a sign of senility. I said to him Nichol said it wasn't religion but he wasn't having it. *Why not try it?* I said this morning. Anything that'll help, but the old man said Nichol wouldny show and right enough. . .' He opened the van door and lifted his welly boot to the cabin, but paused and held out his hand.

'Billy,' he took the minister by the hand.

'Gillis.'

Billy was only wearing a T-shirt and his skin was beginning to prickle and scald red in the cold. 'You couldn't do it, could you?'

He took the silence for assent and hopped back out the cab, shepherding Gillis to the trailer.

'. . .I said to my da we have to try something. See vets? They're fucking scam artists, man, swear to God. They come over like this,' Billy pulled on his bristling forearms as through rolling up sleeves. 'Pure dying to stick their fingers up the cow's arse. I could say, *Eh, she's just got a problem with her teeth*, and the vet'll be like, *Aye, I know, I'm going in the long way.*' He enjoyed his joke as he jostled the trailer, kicked a latch and dropped the ramp down. Great metallic bangs and clatters rocked the trailer until Billy pushed himself inside and returned leading a cow by a rope tied around its neck. 'Canny have calves, can you?' He clapped her back. 'Keep dying on us, don't they?' He folded the cow's ear beneath his palm.

Gillis stared into the blank water of the cow's eye. Her mouth bristled with little sores, and her skin was mangy in patches. The udders looked wrinkled and chapped. But Gillis hadn't been this close to a cow since he was a boy. Maybe they all looked like this.

'Lost one last week, didn't you? Won't milk any more, will you?'

'Hang on,' Gillis muttered, and jogged back to the kirk, returning with the shortbread tin tucked under his arm. He pulled back the lid and stood for a moment as rain began to speckle the golden inners, and with forefinger and thumb he picked the relic up by the palm, then laid it with its fingers splayed across the cow's spine. He closed his eyes and began to pray.

'Don't I know you?' Billy bumped Gillis with his elbow, interrupting the silent prayer. 'You drink in Speedie's? No? In the Bull? Or the Nichy Hotel? Where do I know you? Play fives? No? Sevens? No, I know you, where is it?' They ticked off snooker and pool, women he hadn't dated and men he didn't know, clubs and gyms he had never heard of, a go-kart track he had never seen, and a driving range that had closed down.

'Maybe I *don't* know you. . .' Billy scowled at that remote possibility. 'Were you at the high school or the academy? What year?'

Gillis ignored the interrogation, clasped his hands and paced toward the cow, bowing his head to his knuckles. The colours behind his eyelids became shadows, hidden places, hillsides and fields. Maybe hope lay in the farmers. The cow before him groaned, and he imagined the severed hand grappling into the hair on the animal's head. Gillis throwing his bad leg over her back and lumbering beyond the manse, into the patchwork of fields and ditches beyond. The Scottish church belongs outdoors. He imagined his manifesto. In fields, in pulpits made of stone. The hand would draw a new covenant, binding God to the people, and the people to God. He would be hidden from the authorities by sympathetic farming folk. Up at five to serve him porridge and receive God's blessing. Abundant crops, milk and honey. He would hide among the livestock as policemen scoured the countryside. He would be given an ancient musket. Here Gillis's history failed him. But it would be the personal weapon of some Jacobite or Covenantor, saved for generations. A rusted mechanism which would only fire when a true prophet appeared. He would travel down to Edinburgh on the back of his cow, climbing Arthur's Seat and declaring it a commons. From those heights he would pass the rifle scope over the comings and goings of the parliament and palace. The temples and foreheads of politicians and judges, big-time oil men and arms manufacturers, journalists and TV personalities. He would lay the severed hand's forefinger on the trigger, and

allow it to make divine decisions. Place the last full stop on a
new covenant. Up there, he would found a new parliament,
a round table. Did Arthur's Seat mean King Arthur? Gillis
had no idea.

With a wet slap, the severed hand fell from the cow's back
and landed in the mud; the cow turned from the men and
lumbered toward a patch of thistle.

'Is that you done now?' Billy followed her, reaching
underneath to the chapped udders. He twisted at the teat
until a thin jet of milk dripped across his fingers and onto the
wet gravel. He stood and licked his palm. 'Maybe,' he wiped
saliva and milk across the front of his T-shirt.

'Yeah?'

'Maybe,' he tried again. Milk spurted forcefully into the
stones.

Gillis sat, huddled in the blankets of his bed, thinking about
the puddled milk, how it wound in the gravel and seeped
through the mud until it ran translucent at its edges and
the rain began to pockmark and dissolve the miraculous.
He thought about the cow, and the cancerous woman, and
the knee folded under him, and wondered at the limit of
its power. Healing humans, now animals, and what else?
He imagined the hand's power radiating out to the houses
beyond the manse, the densely stacked flats, the bus queues,
the petrol station, the snooker hall and the Nicholson Hotel.
He would probably never hear about all the sudden recoveries
of God's creatures, the fractured ankles fixed, the kennel
cough gone, the clotted arteries cleared, the ticks and fleas
exiled, the overstrained eyes, recurring migraines and colds
that just couldn't be shifted, all suddenly gone. He would
only hear of the miraculous and strange.

A man, only just now knifed, whose stomach pushes the blade back out and leaves no scar. A dead cat whose trampled ribcage restores as it crawls beyond the car tyre that killed it. A mother who drops a newborn baby straight on its forehead and up it bounces back into her arms. She blinks, she can't believe it. She looks through her curtains and sees a figure looking benignly down at her house, surrounded by a halo of mist. Who is it? She can't make him out. But it's the young minister, his sad eyes and slight smile illuminated flatteringly by the moonlight; next to him, his miraculous severed hand. Thank God, a beacon of light still shines in the darkness of this world.

And beyond Kirkmouth, Gillis knew, he would wander through the smaller places, knots of farmland tethered to a postbox and a corner shop, touching the very edge of a vast tract of grass and heather, marsh, peat bog and cragged unclaimed rock. Tempted, all of a sudden, to retreat to that wilderness and dare God to show Himself. He scrolled through the contacts on his phone, unsure if he was looking for help, or wanting to spread the good news. Most of the numbers he had never used. Some names he couldn't place, old colleagues, or old clients, someone's next of kin. A few names he ignored, and stifled the slight leap of his heart, the guilty gulp of his throat, a first name with no surname, women he'd never really known, an old boss, a school pal. He stabbed the screen at random and the number pulsed until it rang out. The next, his younger cousin, answered fine, but wouldn't let Gillis speak a single word. Just ranted about the hour. Didn't he know it was nine at night? Just got the kids in bed, wife in her jammies and he had half an hour for a shot on the console before he needs to get to his bed. So no, couldn't talk and didn't want to. Had work in the morning, fuck sake.

He pulled his trailing blankets down through the cold of the house and stood at the open living room window, trying to find the stars in case one of them was twinkling in a suggestive manner, but couldn't make them out, what with the light pollution and the cloud cover. He opened the door and tried to listen to the whispering wind but it said nothing. He walked to the kitchen and laid his phone alongside the severed hand and waited as its fingers found the screen and etched a nail over the cold surface. The hand tapped and smudged the rolling index of names. The phone screen jerked up and down, but the hand didn't have the necessary lightness of touch. Gillis helped a little, swiping down through the contacts, pausing near the bottom. Q, R, S. The hand made cross-hatching gestures, prods and pokes that barely registered on the screen. Gillis refined the scroll to R. A familiar pattern of letters. He looked away, and jostled the shortbread tin. Nothing happened, jostled again, until the hand nudged Rachel's name, and it doubled in size and eradicated all other names and images. A circular picture of her, smiling, way back in what? Twenty-ten? And he had the briefest glimpse of something visible amongst the confusion and fear of the past weeks, as though the relic had been patiently teaching him something all along. He couldn't see any larger design or plot any route but the step from hand to cow to Rachel implied a kind of arc, and he only had to put one foot in front of the other. For once, he knew what to do.

He found a pair of shorts, a little jacket, a cap. And at the bottom of his cupboard, an old kitbag. A good pair of running trainers, treads of the soles still thick with English mud which crumbled into the carpet as Gillis stretched his legs. The plastic uppers creaked as he pulled at the laces, still stiff with decade-old sweat. He took lunging steps, jumps, hops along the hallway and up the stairs. He walked through the open doors, to breathe the cold air and pace around the manse garden, turning hard corners, testing his capabilities. Butt kicks, high knees. Maybe, after this, he could get back out in the mornings. Build his strength and stamina, take stretching seriously, maybe see a physio, make some connections, join a club, find a training partner. Kick his bad habits, expand his lungs, maybe enter a couple of competitions. See how he got on. Men's under forty. Try a middle distance at first, see how it felt.

He pushed the shortbread tin into his kitbag and fastened it tight across his shoulder. Retied his laces, folded his socks back on themselves and jogged through the graveyard and off downhill. His breath projected before him in great ghosts of air. He struggled to find a good breathing pattern and quickly lapsed into hoarse, open-mouthed panting, tongue prodding out, tasting the mist, but he kept on, clutching his lungs and spitting phlegm into the nettles. In fits and spurts, both walking and running, he made his way through the cold hinterland, the fields whose only inhabitants were the shadows of sheep and cows, standing in sinister huddles, like prisoners plotting an escape. The bastard knee held up, excelled even, as he leapt a drystone wall, connected the dots from landmark to landmark, until he passed through the struts of the bespoke metal signage, which marked the entrance to Nicholson Fisheries. Looming overhead like the sponsor of a race, all lettering was rusted beyond legibility, leaving only the image of a leaping salmon. He slowed and staggered loose-legged across the semicircle of one-storey buildings that surrounded the car park. Their architect must have been going through a depressive phase: a black tar roof lay heavily on the walls, as though to prevent another storey even being contemplated. Guttering leaked down the brickwork, and the far windows were tinted yellow by a thin patina of moss.

As his breathing steadied, he began to feel the taste of rotting fish, cloying from his mouth, up the back of his nose. He struggled to control his stomach. Breathing through the collar of his T-shirt, pulled across his mouth. He held the severed hand close to his body and skirted the black windows of locked-up offices, round to the back of the site. Everyone had gone home. He tested fences and walls, found a fire exit and leant his shoulder against it, testing the give. With a sudden jut of aggression, a little kick, it popped open.

He tracked kirkyard moss and gravel across the carpeting, wandered between rows of blank computer screens and tucked-in chairs. A large office – presumably Nichol's – was the only room in the building which had been made over. Plush leather chairs and a great mahogany desk riddled with compartments and drawers, all empty. Gillis wandered to a set of framed photos on the wall. Nichol's father and grandfather and great-grandfather and great-great-grandfather. Each ancestor leaner than the last, and more suspicious of the camera, until the very oldest, a skull-like smudge with grubby marks for eyes. From the back window, he could see outside to the great concrete basins, full of churning waters, cut with nets and sluice gates, arched by steel lattice bridges and scaffold guardrails, signs of danger of death, danger of drowning, danger of electrocution and of nesting birds.

'We'll have a look,' he spoke to the shortbread tin in his hands, found the access door and pressed through. The smell deepened, cloying across his skin. To one side of the concrete pools, a deep black bucket held the remains of hundreds of fish. Their skin peeling and their bodies broken, the air above was ridden with flies. Around the edges of the pool, fish tails and sloughs of skin turned to mould and as he approached the waters he could see the fish passing over and under one another, mottled and sore, plagued by the fleas and ticks that danced across the water's surface.

On the wall, a circular blue net with an extruding handle. He pulled it free and walked to the gangways that skirted the artificial ponds. He took the severed hand and placed it in the net, then lowered it over the water. A deep gloom hung over the buildings, Gillis examined the sky, the clouds, the broiling water, the fire exits and the overhead lights, the heaped ropework and canvas, the trees on the hills above them.

He lowered the relic into the waters, extended the aluminium handle and began to walk in circles as though stirring a great pot. He imagined the fish nipping and biting the severed hand down to nothing, he imagined them fleeing in fear, he imagined them ignoring it altogether. Then tried to push all doubt from his mind and believe, for once, completely believe and exist now and press all of his heart if he had one, or soul if he had one, into this moment, this one passing now. Stirring the pond, he gained speed and completed a full circle, then walked the length of the gangway that spanned the ponds, pressed the middle of the aluminium bar into the safety rails and attempted to raise it from the water.

Was it an arcing light, or a broken bulb, or an archangel flit from heaven, stooping to touch the waters? A great flash of light broke the gloom, and when Gillis opened his eyes, there was nothing but a confusion of purple and yellow, pulsing with his heartbeat. His retinas had been scalded and he staggered back as they healed, and suddenly every bluebottle, tick and flea that circled the water and tormented these fish took fright and rushed toward the minister, who turned his face away from the swarm that fled against their nature in direct, straight lines, across his body and away into the sky, and what couldn't fly, jumped and crawled about his legs and feet so that the concrete speckled black as though a shadow was passing across the earth. Into the weeds and chucky stones, into the guttering and mud, the insects escaped and all that remained of the angel or the arcing electricity was a solitary circling gull, bright white against the black cloud above. Gillis still held onto his netting, and the severed hand was still somewhere amongst the salmon. He pulled at the handle, but the weight had doubled, and continued to increase as he hauled it along the gangway and back to the siding of the pond. He couldn't haul it free, so dragged and scraped the pole along the ground until he could wrench the net clear of the water. As the netting broke the surface, it overflowed with salmon that leapt from either side, some to the safety of the water and some to the pain and fear of concrete and gravel. The pole clattered as the salmon slapped and panicked. Then Gillis was among them, tangled in the net, pressing one body and another to the side until he could see the severed hand, pale and red as ever, lying on its knuckles, open palm facing the sky as though it was gasping for air. The fish arced and bowed in great confusion, attempting to leap and throw themselves back in the waters. Gillis stood to his full height and cradled the severed hand in the folds of his shirt and carefully turned on the spot, fish chancing across his trainers and slapping at his ankles, he leapt to one side and stared out at the waters, imagining he could part them into columns or walk right across their surface. He lifted his severed hand in the air in triumph, facing the moon, the sky, the whirling seagull. Now the waters would part and the people would flee from captivity, led by himself, a column of smoke, a column of fire.

A voice called from the very back of the compound, a wooden shed now spilling light, a gang hut rigged with a heater and a set of TV screens. The figure was pulling on a thick jacket, howling across the pools and gangways, making wild gestures and contradictory moves, unsure which direction to chase Gillis in. The minister shouted nonsense back across the water, about miracles, about plagues.

'You're on video!' the worker pointed to a flagpole that loomed over the whole complex, crowned with a series of cameras, angled in all directions.

Walking backward, Gillis stared into the lens, pushing the severed hand back into his kitbag; covertly stretching his calves and ankles, he broke into a run. As he rounded the last of the water, he glimpsed the fish sliding over one another, their skins supple and thick, and he knew there had been a true miracle. He battered back through the offices, leaping over chairs and tables, and knew that a despoiling curse had been lifted, that without him would have festered for ever. He broke from the fire exit, across the car park and back beneath the broken signage. Having spent so much of his life waiting, he felt that a gun had been fired, and it was his duty to run.

By pinprick light of small, tallow candles, shielded from the wind and sight of soldiers by mounds of dirt, half a dozen monks were digging down into the thick, near frozen forest floor. Jan, apprentice painter, sat a short distance away, an uneasy truce established by shy glances and cautious nods. Across his lap, the golden book lay, still steaming and hissing from the bonfire, its paints and glues dripping across his fingers, and the edges of its pages still occasionally bursting from a faint smoulder into a little flame, extinguished by the sodden hem of Jan's sleeve. At sight of him, these monks, many of whom had not spoken a single word in over a decade, having sworn themselves to pious silence, broke their vows and a few commandments in the next few moments as they struggled to defend themselves from what they had assumed was a black jacket, or a magistrate, or a soldier. Sinning not really in deed, mostly in word and thought, as they shouted, swore and grabbed impiously at holy relics, golden boxes containing the fingernails, locks of hair and occasional severed limbs of local saints, and used them as shields or clubs. Jan took a few knocks to the head before tripping over his legs and scattering loose pages from the book as he fell. Once seated, babbling in a mixture of Lowland Dutch, English and Scots, the monks quickly realized that Jan was no threat, cursed him again, and went on with their digging. Jan stayed put, pressed his back into the trunk of a young elm tree, and eventually laid his book down next to him and rested his head on the soft vellum pages. He fell asleep, and confused the distant noise of the crowd still tussling at the castle, with the intimate gasps, complaints and whispers of the monks. He dreamt of a giant whose enormous legs and feet were steeped in a muddy hillside, whose body was made of brick and stone slab, whose ribcage was an arched vault of wood, whose mouth was sealed with an iron gate. Tapestries and paintings lined the inside of the giant's head, the beautiful images concealed row after row of teeth.

Towering above him, in a thick grey robe bound at the middle with a cord of rope, a monk stared down at Jan, and kicked his shoulder. He asked, 'Should your book go in the hole too?' Pointing over his shoulder to the crowd of monks who stood in faint dawning light, faces shining with sweat, their bared torsos, like cattle, giving steam to the cold air.

'No,' Jan tried to stand, but the golden book beneath his head held him back. The paints and glues and resins had melted in the fire, and cooled in the following hours, sticking to his skin and hair. The pages twisted and tore as he freed himself, leaving coloured strips of vellum tangled into his beard and moustache. He combed his fingers through the knotted mess, but some fragments stayed put. A twist of paper, a painted arm itched at Jan's cheekbone, two pious fingers pointing into the depths of his nose. On his throat, another scrap, stuck with a clump of binder's glue, the screaming face of St Agatha, burning at the stake. The monks returned to their work, filling the hole they had been digging, concealing statuettes of Mary and carvings of the crucified Christ.

Jan lay in a shallow puddle of morning light, that dripped through the heavy canopy overhead and lit the remains of his book. As he turned from page to page, colours ran from the back and foreground, dissolving the saints and their persecutors into contradictory beasts, whose multiple heads bickered, and whose multiple limbs wrestled, but whose torsos and skeletons blended into one, and in many examples, melted further, souls indistinguishable from patches of weed, arrangements of architecture, hillsides and waterfalls, spotted with screaming mouths. Sentences ended mid-word, mid-letter. Binding thread unravelled in a loose tangle at the spine. Jan began to salvage what he could. He stripped the embossed leather covering and folded it to one side, he unpicked the binding thread and wound it round a twig, until he had a little reel, a bobbin. Loose pages caught in the wind, but were grabbed and bashfully returned by monks who lingered to watch his dissection, his ceremony. He sorted the back portions until he found ten or fifteen undamaged pages; these he took, rolled and stuffed into his satchel. The rest, a calendar of saints, a cycle of seasons, depictions of the kingdom of heaven, curiously overlaid with the kingdom of Scotland, and the tattered rags of a hundred more pages, soaked, melted, burnt and stinking of smoke, he pushed these into the loose dirt which the monks were trampling down. The last glint of their holy relics disappeared beneath the earth, and they spread pine needles back and forth, then brushed the whole clearing with a branch, obscuring the scarred earth. Then they took a small hatchet and cut a symbol into the bark of a silver birch that stood next to the hole. Then they stared at the trees, the hard ground, the bluish sky above, straining to commit to memory this particular patch in the endless mud and frost, these exact intervals in the unbroken cross-hatch of tree branches.

Quietly, they picked through the woodlands to a small abbey, hidden from sight of the town in a little valley. They were pursued, possibly surrounded, by odd clinks and strikes. Heavy thuds and crackles, blacksmithing noises, branches breaking, calls that could have been crows, rutting foxes, or women in pain.

'Come in,' one of the monks took Jan by his elbow and steered him through the cold corridors of the abbey, to a seat at a long bench where the six from the woods joined another ten who served them porridge in habitual silence. The six lowered their heads and hugged their bowls, while the ten fussed around in barely concealed panic. Their grand fire was lit, and when the fuel ran low, instead of leaving the abbey to collect more from their sheds, the monks broke spare stools and benches and threw them inside. That morning, they unpicked the stitching of their robes and coats, cut the material into the shape of breeks, shirts and jackets, copying from a template made of manuscript papers. The surfaces of these makeshift sewing patterns were covered in lines of delicate writing, decorative letters upstaged by hares, snails and weevils, leaping and crawling through thickets of language. When they held the paper template to their bodies, it was as though they were planning on becoming the books they copied, but as the template was laid aside and the rough calico of their robes was cut and stitched again, the templates were passed on and eventually trampled in their activity. In exchange for more porridge and a mug of weak beer, Jan offered his improvised bobbin of binding thread, saved from the spine of his golden book. As the afternoon neared, Jan could see his thread, spotted with flecks of paint, appearing in the crotch of a pair of breeks, in the armpit of a jacket.

The monks stoked their fire, sharpened their knives and stripped down to their waists. Their sagging stomachs, their pigeon chests exposed, they blushed red in the cold. The abbey lay still and quiet, but for the hush of scissors and knives cutting away their tufted tonsures. They rubbed animal fat on their heads and sharpened their knives again, and scraped away the very last of it. Then they washed their heads and laughed at one another, pointed out flat spots and scabs. Ran their hands over the hard bristles that remained. They dressed in the simple grey clothes they had made, and portioned out the alms and tributes, collected over the years and months previous, and they slipped away in twos and threes, each group in the opposite direction from the one before. They would forget how to read and write, they would learn how to talk. They would forget their God and adopt another, descend from their perch of duty and concentration and become sinners again. Some couldn't wait – they began their sinning at the doorway, or the first turn of the path, they clubbed their brother to steal their money, or their clothes, or only to settle an old score. Others despaired, and stayed behind. Sinned by staring at the dark woods and the crumbling abbey, and seeing no difference between them.

Jan sat among the last of them, the dottering old men who hadn't had much tonsured hair to cut away, whose coats and trousers held so loose on their bodies that they still looked like robes. In the kitchen, he ate from plates that would be left for ever unwashed, the pot of porridge which hadn't been soaked, the bread and meat which hadn't been covered, left for mice and flies. He filled his pockets, and wandered on from there. Ignoring the ancient monks who questioned him, he found a stack of blank paper, nib pens, paints and inks, filled a sack with a dozen colours and a heavy sheaf of parchment paper, and walked away unnoticed. As he left, stamping through the abbey garden, he spotted a crowd of black jackets, bleary-eyed, reeking of smoke, pamphlets sagging from their hat bands, collecting in the woods and paths around the abbey as it was slowly abandoned. The peasants who had cheerfully looted the Laird's grand manor house were standing in the shadows, waiting for something to happen. Jan found a lonely spot, a tangled hawthorn bush, and he threw away all of the paints, pens and papers that he had stolen. What use were they now? He returned to the heights of the hill, gazing down into the abbey, watching as the woods around it began to fill with the torches and voices of the crowd. From there, leaning against a tree trunk and chewing his tongue, he could watch what was about to happen.

CHAPTER THIRTEEN

In the evening hours, the night of his great miracle, Gillis had lain in his bed, bristling with energy, waiting for his phone to ring. It took some time, but by six or seven in the morning, there it went.

'You could have told me, you could have said,' Nichol broke immediately into jubilant monologue. 'My guys called me in a panic, thinking I'd be raging. They were all for having you arrested. They had a printout waiting for me.' Nichol laughed, he was holding the picture now. 'I said, *I know that face.*' Clipped from the CCTV footage, the saboteur, the thief. 'They thought you'd jammed something in the electrics, but I know, *I know.* And it hadn't even occurred to me! Didn't even think! Couldn't see my nose for my face or however you say it. The forest and the fucking trees! How did you – or why did you – think to go healing animals as well?' Nichol left a tiny pause in his speech. 'Well, anyway, *now* I'm a believer, now I'm in. Hundred per cent. Anything you want. After seeing that. Anything.'

'*Blessed are they,*' Gillis tried out a new tone, '*who believe without seeing.*'

'Absolutely! What're you after? A house? A motor? I could get you a boat? I could get you a diamond ring, I could kiss you, big man, I could.' He laughed as he paced about his office. The noise of crumpling paper was Nichol kissing the printout. 'You're a life-saver, you don't even know.' The money. The creditors. The health inspectors and lawyers. The pressure, the weight on his shoulders. And now. The lorries he could stuff full of fish, and the pockets he could stuff full of money. All the lies he had told – *everything's fine, everything's normal, everything's on the mend* – they were all, at once, coming true. And what could he give? How could he repay something like that?

'I didn't do it for you,' Gillis replied. 'Or to get anything. I was led to it. I was told. But you'll be busy now. With the fisheries, I mean.'

'I should think so,' Nichol said. 'We can expand everything, we can push our way out, right across Scotland into England, away into Europe. If disease isn't a problem? We can deepen the pools, we can fit thousands more fish in there, we can heap them up, we can feed them the cheap stuff, we can cut every corner—'

'Then you'll need help,' Gillis interrupted, 'with all the new business.'

'You wanting to be a fisherman, is that it?'

'Not me.'

A weighted silence grew, he could hear Nichol's breathing. Then the penny dropped and there was a jangling sound of laughter. 'You want me to hire her back, don't you?'

'Yes. I want you to give Rachel her job back.'

Even across the empty phone line, he could tell that Nichol was shaking his head. 'You're too nice, Gillis, you're too nice.'

With pious gestures at the furniture, Gillis denied it. Wasn't it just what anyone would do?

'Mind what we spoke about, you have to be a bit evil these days. You have to be a bit grim. . . But it's up to you.'

With contracts to renegotiate and new orders to fulfil, Nichol was suddenly absent from the kirk and the manse. Left alone, Gillis paced from day to day, room to room, reading from his Bible, striking poses with the severed hand. Imagining the hand raised in anger, the hand lowered in forgiveness, the hand pointing onward, into battle, into the glorious future. When, one evening, a knock on the door finally came, Gillis expected to see pilgrims, or militants, followers he hadn't yet accumulated, conspirators he had only imagined.

Instead, Rachel stood on the front step. 'I hear you're a miracle worker?' She let herself in. 'That's me back on the back shift. Next week I'll be on days.' She leant across and gripped his neck, pressed a kiss against his cheek. 'I could kiss you,' she said, all out of sequence. Her skin was scalding cold, and Gillis shivered involuntarily as the cold air found the impression she had left. They jostled around the corridor, and as Gillis moved to close the door, one arm trailed back and pulled Jamie across the threshold. With his head bobbing wearily, he tripped over the front step. He wore his pyjamas underneath a rain jacket, plastic camel in one hand, box of felt tips in the other.

'Shouldn't he be in bed?' Gillis asked.

'We've both been working, haven't we?' The boy ignored her. 'Couldn't get a sitter. Mother-in-law's through with me, or so she says. And Jamie was up anyway. . . you couldn't sleep, could you?' She unfastened her jacket and rolled it over her arm. 'I wanted to come yesterday, but we were so busy.' She tried to walk forward but Jamie was hiding his face and shoulders in her legs. 'Nichol told me everything.' She nudged the boy onward with her knees until he fell in line behind her, holding on to the hem of her black skirt.

'The miracle?'

She turned a set of wide eyes to the minister, 'Hmm? He told me you'd saved his life, or at least the fish's lives. They still look half-dead if you ask me, but he's confident – we've got orders lined up for weeks. He's got big plans, we're going to double sales, we're going to expand into the Scandinavian market. You know how he gets.'

'He didn't tell you everything then—' Gillis tried to recount the insects, the light, the angel, the severed hand. But she interrupted before he could get going.

'And we're OK for tomorrow?'

He smiled politely, not knowing what she meant. And went on recounting the flash of light, his run through the offices, the strength of his knee.

She was half-listening, or quarter-listening at least, as she settled Jamie into a chair at the kitchen table. 'Have you got any milk?' then crossed the room and flicked on the kettle, answering her own question by pulling a bottle from the fridge. She checked the smell and the expiry date and the smell again. 'It's fine,' she said. Jamie left it to curdle. The kettle clicked and Rachel busied herself with the mugs. She brought them to the table, and they stared at one another, both expecting the other to speak. 'And we're OK for tomorrow?' she asked again. 'The funeral. You didn't pick up when I called.'

'Tomorrow?' Gillis patted his pockets and scanned the countertops. The missing days and weeks must be lying around somewhere.

'Everything's OK?'

'It's good, it's golden, I've got it all planned.' He didn't. He didn't even tell her he was halfway out the door. On gardening leave or administrative leave or whatever they were calling it. This purgatory. But he assumed that the higher powers had something in mind. Throw over the tables of the money lenders. Lean against the pillars and destroy the temple. Flee to the sea, get eaten by a fish. It would work itself out.

'OK,' she closed one eye and squinted at him. Then flinched, startled by the clock mounted on the wall, ticking toward midnight. 'Is that right?' She double-checked her watch and phone. 'No. It's only eleven. You need to turn it back an hour.'

'Did the clocks change?'

'Maybe a month ago.'

Gillis stepped onto his chair and pulled the clock from the wall. Turned it over to find the mechanism, but failed to understand the simple switch and dial. He laid it face down.

'We should be in bed,' she prodded Jamie's jacket. 'Shouldn't we?' Her boy had uncapped a few of his pens, but didn't have any paper to draw on. 'Give us a few minutes to talk, and then we'll go.' She led him down from the table, pushed the felt tips into his hand and grabbed a sheaf of papers from the kitchen bunker. 'Here we go,' she said. 'These have some nice drawings on them already. Maybe you can colour them in?' She walked him through to the living room and pulled a thin blanket over the sofa. Laid the paper and pens on the coffee table and turned on the TV. They were showing a documentary about rice. They were growing it, cutting it, packaging it. She laid the remote on Jamie's legs, but he ignored it.

'You know how to work it, don't you? Beep, beep, beep,' she mimed with the buttons and when she got no response, touched the tip of her finger to his nose – he blinked at least.

Gillis wasn't listening, he was too busy attributing her presence to divine providence. The placement of every object was beginning to seem wilful, heavy with connotations that flew over his head. He imagined searchlights and tracer bullets scanning the Kirkmouth skyline, watching through infrared cameras, through rifle scopes, through drones and heat-seeking missiles. If the powers only knew. The forces of evil, the government killers and surveillance czars, the satanic military-industrio-pharmaceutico-psychological-operative types that you read about, if they even had an inkling. They'd drop an atomic bomb on bonnie Scotland just to stop him crossing his back garden.

But through in the darkened hallway, he could see the bright reflected silhouette of woman and child. He stared at that spark. Could always kindle it? Love the woman and raise the boy. Look after them, and be looked after by them. It was one or the other. The hills, the calling, the severed hand; or the house, the family and the job. In order to walk even two paces toward the living room, toward Rachel, he would have to throw his severed hand in the bin, deny and curse God, renounce the prophet's calling and leave Scotland to its own devices. It would muddle along like it always had. *Devil*, he said to himself. *Away and tempt someone else.* Hidden in the gloom, he watched her for a few moments longer. Then she left the living room, and he turned to meet her.

'Something seems different about you,' she squinted and examined him as she returned. Something around the eyes. There was no longer any sarcastic twist to the mouth, no defensive scowl, no stammer, no fidgeting.

'I've been working out,' he pointed to the rumpled shorts and socks heaped before the washing machine. 'I'm running again.'

She thought that was good. 'I would have liked it, I think. Being in England. Watching you win.'

He smiled. 'Waiting in the stands all day? I can't imagine it.'

'Used to do it.'

'You used to complain about it.'

'But I went. Whenever I didn't, I'd just spend the day wondering how you were getting on. But when I went, I got annoyed that I was just trailing around after you. I got annoyed either way. So I think it was better to be annoyed with other people than annoyed on my own.' There was an order of service on the table, and a bundle of handwritten notes. 'I had some ideas,' she said. 'But they don't really matter. I'm sure you'll do a good job.' She turned them over so the words were hidden. 'It went all right last time.'

'It's not very hard.' Perhaps for the first time, Gillis realized what could be done. With nothing but a pulpit and a captive audience.

'You look prouder,' she said.

'Something's pressing me. Into a new shape.' His hand gripped the empty air and formed a fist that he held in front of him. 'And it'll use me to change things. The world. Or Scotland at least. Or this bit of it. Even just this room. Me and you and the boy. It took me a while. To see that I need to let myself be used. It'll become clear. Here it is, the world'll just have to reconfigure around it. It's the wheel, the steam engine, the light bulb, and this,' he counted the world's accomplishments on one hand, the relic on the other. 'I didn't even need to be special, or do any training or pass any certificates or get anyone's approval or anything. But here it is, it's with me. I was chosen. Maybe it's more of an indictment of everyone else, than any kind of praise of me?'

She didn't know what he meant, but she assumed he was half-joking, half-bragging about his work, his ministerial calling. And he said it all with such confidence that she couldn't help but smile. 'It's good to see you have so much passion about something again,' she said, and a moment passed and neither knew what to say or how to avoid one another's eye.

'I'll have to check,' she stood. 'On Jamie.'

As she passed through the hallway, Gillis watched her catch herself in the mirror and briefly study her fringe, her forehead with its single wrinkle, a hatchet mark dividing her eyebrows. She dragged the back of her hand across her brow and went on, through to the living room. The TV was off. The room was still. Jamie had pulled the blankets across himself, and lay blinkered, face buried in the arm of the sofa.

'Asleep,' she whispered as she returned to the kitchen and sat. Her hair was laid across one shoulder, a spot of light lay in her clavicle. She leant back, drawing her hair together, pulling it all upwards and binding it at her crown. Elbows above her hands, armpits exposed, slightly blue as the hairs grew in.

Their knees were touching, and he raised his hand to graze across her shoulder and lift the thin strap of her vest under one finger.

'Maybe we shouldn't?' she muttered, before she leant forward.

Irritated by the barriers between them, they pulled at belt loops and sleeves, stood and pressed their hipbones painfully close, bashed teeth and lips and wondered again, should they? Then walked upstairs, lying to themselves, as if they would make a clearer decision up there. They avoided the lights, so their bodies remained empty outlines. He remembered her. She turned her back on him, and he pulled at her hair. She muttered nonsense and closed her eyes as he loomed over her. The light from the door cast a golden triangle across her body, a mole on her hip, a scar on her stomach. She pressed at him with her heels and took over with her fingers. After, as their heartbeats slowed and their skin grew cold again, she muttered, 'I can't keep doing this.'

They lay still, and Gillis was led from the bed toward a tribunal of some kind; he watched as a group of men were sentenced and punished, he looked on and did nothing, standing among a chattering crowd. But at his ankle, a little flower grew from the trampled dirt. Moved by the wind, it appeared behind his heel, and seemed to sprout a sister flower alongside itself. Soon, other shoots had appeared to the side of his toes, and they began to tangle, leaves interlacing, double-knotting. He tried to step back, but his shoe had been riddled with holes, the sole thickly woven with roots. He pulled, and grabbed onto the crowd behind him, tearing away the flowers and tangled stems; his leg jolted out and broke the image, and he stepped from the dream out of the bed. He must have dozed off for a few minutes. Stood naked and cold, he turned to see Rachel still lying in his bed. Her eyes were open, bright with light from downstairs. He walked to the bathroom to wash his face and drink from the tap. Pissed, conscious that Rachel was lying there, listening.

'Now that we're. . . whatever we are, I wanted to apologize,' he returned to the bedroom, pulling at his scrotum, one bollock was lying funny across the other. 'I keep thinking about me going to England and all that, not coming back.'

She sat up. 'Thought you were about to tell me you had an STI.'

His hand quickly flit away from his crotch. 'No. You can check if you want?'

'I believe you.' Her vest had been rolled into a belt at her waist, and she picked through it until she found the straps, hooked them over her shoulders and stretched the material until her breasts were covered again.

'Well, listen, I *am* sorry.' He sickened himself with excuses that drifted toward lies, which he tried to push back toward the truth, but failed mid-sentence and stopped. She didn't seem to be listening, but searched for her skirt and underwear on the floor. She found them and lay back beneath the covers, shuffling around as she dressed.

'Honestly? I don't think about it.'

'Not even a bit?'

'No. I used to, but I got married and had a kid. I wasn't just sitting dreaming about you. I was pregnant at the wedding, and I had a kid all the way through uni. When did I have time to think about *England and all that*?'

'I just wanted to say—'

'Why? Is that meant to be us now? Are we going to walk about town holding hands? Am I going to go stand behind a rope and cheer you on again? That's the only bit, actually, that I ever think about. Standing outside. Waiting in the car with your dad. I did other things with my life when you left. It might not matter, but I was, I actually was married. It doesn't mean much maybe, but it doesn't mean nothing.'

'I didn't say it was nothing.'

She nodded and cleared her throat. She wasn't angry, it was only talk, she was thinking out loud. 'Maybe it was a mistake. Everyone said I shouldn't, that we hardly knew each other. The girls said there was no rush. Now, it's like nothing happened.'

Gillis knew that if he moved or spoke, she would close up, hurry to her feet and leave the room, so he leant back against the wall and listened.

'See at the wedding?' she continued with one eye on him, ready to stop at the first sight of cant or pity. 'I didn't even know half his pals. He was on so many teams. We had all these midfielders and goalkeepers along. Eating and drinking. There was about two dozen ushers. He couldn't decide. They all had the same haircut, the same name, the same tattoos. Koi carp. Celtic crosses. And before the dinner, me and him were shaking everyone's hands, and by the time I was sitting down, my face was dripping wet with kisses. They kept missing my cheek and getting lips or neck, or the bottom of my ear, and they all wanted to say something really sincere. Take me to the side and tell me how Dougie had stood up for them, or pulled them out a hole or gone and got them when they were standing at the cliffs at night. They said things like, *I hope you're going to let him out every now and again.* Or like, *So you're making him an honest man?* With these sarcastic looks on their faces. I just thought, *Was he not honest before?*

'And none of them were supposed to have plus ones, but Douglas OK'd it last minute, so they brought these girls along. Just wee lassies really, they didn't know how to do their make-up yet. When everyone was dancing, I sat staring at their ankles. At these high heels they were wearing, thinking, *They'll break, they're all just going to start snapping. Everyone'll panic. The walls'll collapse.* But everything was fine.

'And they cheered us on when we left. Drove this ancient car, in a big circle, round from the front of the hotel, round to the back. He tried to carry me over the threshold, but the corridor was too tight. Almost put a hole in the wall. We never even had sex on the wedding night. It was too weird. The curtains and bedsheets and the pillows and the carpets were all covered in flowers and glitter, and little paper hearts. There was this massive bottle of champagne by the bed, with a white ribbon round it. I was thinking, *Did I choose any of this?* But I must have. . .'

She brought her knees up, and wound the blankets around them. Stared at the foot of the bed, the peeling wallpaper and the damp corner of the room. 'I probably did love him. But I had a baby, so I didn't have time to. And you end up thinking, *Am I happy? Is this it, am I happy?* So you're probably not. When you're hungry you know it. And when you're thirsty you know it. But not with happiness or love, you can't tell. You just have to decide. *OK, here I am, I'll be happy.*' She turned to Gillis, and he pushed himself away from the wall, into a quasi-military pose. 'Would you put some clothes on?'

'I didn't want to interrupt.'

His boxers and T-shirt had been caught in the outgoing ebb of blankets and duvet cover, then lost in the returning tide. He rifled through each level of his chest of drawers, until he found boxers mercifully free of holes and a T-shirt whose cracked white lettering read PARTICIPANT, above a cartoon of a clappered-out thistle wearing trainers. As he searched for a particular pair of jeans, Rachel spoke to the back of his head, to the late hour, and the empty room. She talked about Jamie, she'd known he was coming and then the wedding happened and then she had him and that was that. She wanted a girl. But a girl that was twenty or twenty-one. Someone to sit next to, watch TV with, buy things for, treat yourself with, get away for a holiday, just the two of them. Hadn't worked out that way. Douglas got really angry when she didn't get things right. He said he was more of a mother than her. But she learnt.

'People tell you it comes naturally, but it didn't. You have to work at everything, why would that be any different?'

'Wanting it's enough,' Gillis surprised himself as he interrupted. She looked at him as though he was able to continue. He tried. 'Wanting to be there's as good as being there. It's when you don't want to be there. That's where there's bother.'

'Well, that was part of the problem. I was there too much. . . Everyone said we needed to make time for ourselves. So we'd get my mum and dad to take the kid, and get dressed up as if we were going to go out. At first we made plans, but then we stopped, and we used to just drive back to the house. I'd sit there with my hair up, with a dress and my heels on. He'd be looking at his phone. We just ignored each other. Go and pick Jamie up later on, pretend we'd been out. *Oh, thanks so much, we had such a good time, the dinner was great, thanks,* when all we'd had was a packet of crisps and a bit of toast. Got so I liked it. It was a chance to be alone. Then toward the end, I was just always alone. He was out working every night. So he said, anyway. And I thought maybe there was another woman? But he always came back with his trousers covered in mud, and his jacket torn, stinking of fish. He'd just say, *They needed me.* Make his own dinner, fall asleep in the chair. Jamie'd be crying and I'd get up to settle him and see Douglas standing outside the room already, he'd see me, or see my shadow, and go back to his chair. Back to sleep. I never wanted to argue. So he said I was cold. But I didn't know how else to be. I tried to say things that cut through. Evil things. I'd lie and he'd just nod along. Not believing me. I'd say I'd been out meeting other guys. I'd name them. Give them jobs and addresses. He knew I was lying.

'Then there was police at the door, saying there'd been this accident and Douglas was drowned. I just kept thinking, *How do you drown in an office?* Like he'd got tangled in the dishwasher or flushed himself down the toilet. But he was out on the boats. Why was he wearing his suit still? It's like he was sitting there doing the accounts while the boys were hauling at the nets? He needed space. That's what Nichol told me. So he brought him out on the boat. He told me I didn't know what it got like. How dull it was. Sitting in an office every day. I could scream, honestly, I could bite someone.'

She pressed her back against the wall and strained her arms beneath the covers.

'The house is too clean now. It was terrible, the smell of all that fish, but I do, I actually miss it. His clothes were thick with it. He threw away good suits and expensive shirts. Something must have changed in how they did things. Because he used to be really clean. Wore aftershave. Brushed his teeth. Moisturized even. But then his breath, and his sweat was stinking. It just lingered in everything. And it's funny things, like when I come down in the morning, the TV used to be tuned to the football. And I'd watch the highlights before I put the cartoons on for Jamie. Now it's just wall-to-wall silliness. I'm living in a kid's book. We're getting lessons, we're counting things, we're being kind to people, learning to spell, putting out fires. All these dogs and cats with smiley faces. Jamie ignores them, he'll just sit and stare into space, but as soon as I change the channel to something grown-up, he whinges. You get him some pencils and paper and he'll put them back again. You give him your phone and he's not bothered. Even in the playpark, he'll just wander back and forth like he's scoping the place out.

'Douglas wanted to get him checked out. But he's fine. Douglas said it was getting to be deviant behaviour. Said he wouldn't be surprised if Jamie became a serial killer. It was a joke, but what kind of joke is that? Imagine your dad saying that. Whenever I think about him, I think, *What a prick*. I can look at a photo for hours. Think about all his failings. What he did to me. What he made me into. How boring I am, how it's his fault. I can think about it for hours. But it doesn't make a difference.'

Her eyes glossed over, her features changed, she hid, pressing knuckles into her skull. He stared down at her – it was as though she was holding two halves of her head together, and spots of water were dripping from the seam to the bedsheets.

'Can you not see I'm upset?' She spread a clear runnel of mucus from her nose along the back of her wrist. Gillis walked to the edge of the bed and lifted his arm, she ducked beneath it and pressed into his ribcage. Just then, as he'd been lying next to her, it could have been the early two thousands. He could have been nineteen, twenty. Now he felt older than ever, forty or fifty, one or two hundred, ancient and wise. He laid his palm on the top of her head, a sort of benediction.

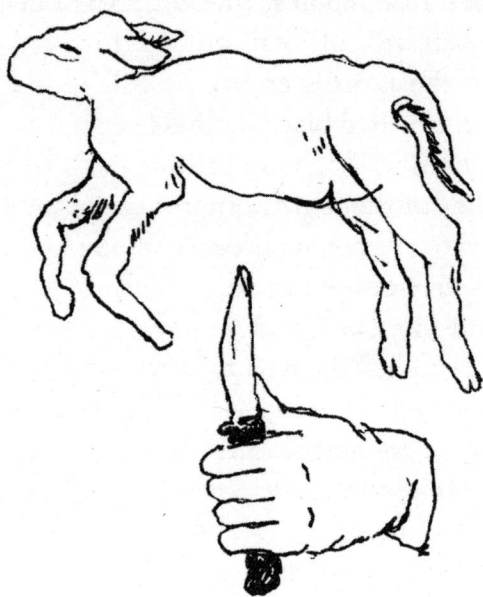

The abbey had burned, the last of the monks escaping under a hail of acorn husks, pine cones, shells and pebbles, thrown from the gathering crowd. Magistrates, officers and sheriffs had appeared, riding from the Laird's empty house. Feathery shirts bright white, brushed black jackets fastened to the neck, their broad hats holding new, pristine pamphlets. Freshly printed, a blow of the ram's horn from a distant leadership. The whole two or three hundred gathered there, took their various hats, from the most pert and upright to the most slouched and shapeless, and removed the old pamphlet, then carefully folded the new to sit straight and proclaim the latest message. It sounded very good when a sheriff stood on his horse and read to the crowd. And the old message, *Beggars Before Priests*, was dropped to the ground, and pulped into the grass.

They were joined by the local gentry, landowners who had contended for generations with the Laird and the Laird's father and grandfather for rights to the woodland and river, and had paid vast taxes to the abbey that surely warranted returning? As the magistrates read out charges of blasphemy and licence, the landowners made a diagram of the abbey's lands in the dirt. They divided the hillside from the valley, the woods from the river, and each took those corners of land that got the sun and shed rainfall and lay shielded from the harsher winds, leaving bogland and flood plain to fall into common use. All settled, the landowners conferred with the black jackets, pointing out their portions, then they climbed back on their horses, took their silver, brass and gold and returned to their grand estates, now a little grander.

The magistrates took turns shouting accusations. Racking their lungs, they described strange meetings and conferences, monks who sneaked around at night to meet emissaries of the Devil and the Pope, or to peep through the windows of young brides; the crowd had been held back to allow the landowners' servants into the empty building, who returned with silver candlesticks, communion plates, brass bells and a golden crucifix. Then it had been the turn of the merchants, running in to retrieve the painted table runners that draped the altar, wide sashes of velvet which hung over the chapel windows and the remaining barrels of communion wine. Then the yeomen, the richer peasants from the back hills, entered the abbey, to take the pews and the altar itself, the simple beds and three-legged stools from the monks' cells. Finally, when the abbey had been stripped of any value, the masters had pressed torches into the hands of the peasants. 'Burn it,' they had said, and the youngest boys ran toward the cloisters and threw their torches into the roofs of thatched buildings, and the billowing smoke charred the surface of the moon, scalding the eyes of the poorest men and women, who huddled close, waiting to see what would be left for them. Brother Malcolm, the very last of the monks, stood among the ash and smoke and shouted up to the tangled assemblies of the poor.

'The evening of the world approaches. Will you take in your washing? You won't have time to fold it. Will you light a fire? Another will be warmed by it. Where will you run? Every field will have a fence around it. Every flower will be loyal to some oncoming faction. Your cow will betray you. A cat will poison your children, and will brag about it! Where

will you sleep? The only common land that will be left is
the stinking hole beneath your outhouse. You will be forced
to live there and your children will sleep in the graveyard.
You fought for the apple, and they have given you the core!
Take the seeds inside and grow your own orchards! Sinners!
Repent!'

The roof beams burned through, and brickwork tumbled
into the foundations, and the monk was gone. They waited
all night. Some fell asleep in impious positions, heads resting
in the laps and breasts of strangers. Morning dew collected
on their clothes. What was left for the beggars? Embers
cooled and beggars tiptoed through them with scarves over
their mouths. But they walked home disappointed, to nurse
the burns and blisters on their fingers.

All that fury and panic and anger had been and gone, and the
weeks passed by to find Jan hobbling with a pebble in his shoe
along the big road that led south. But at some point, he must
have accidentally stopped, turned and walked the other way,
because the road seemed to lead him back to the same river.
He tried the hill paths, which the villagers had warned him
against. It was a place that God had only half-made. Sick of
His work, with Sunday to look forward to, He had thrown a
slop of clay and grit together, dragged His fingers through
it and set wild people in the nooks to scratch out their lives
in service to cows and sheep. Jan couldn't find the pebble; it
danced along his heel, but disappeared whenever the boot
was turned upside down. He sheltered by a rounded hillock
with a tree dying at its peak. A small cottage had its fire going
strong and the people inside knew nothing about the castle
or the abbey. Four families were collected in one room and
they ignored Jan, even as they set out a bed and passed him a

bowl of broth, thin as water, studded with notches of onion, like mile markers sinking into a moor. The men began to flit in and out, attending to a braying cow, who had been left the run of the house next door. She groaned in pain, and the children mimed pregnancy, bloating their cheeks and stuffing their stomachs, waddling back and forth, giving birth to handfuls of straw.

The men came to the fire to warm themselves, smeared in blood, mucus and shit, looking grave, then laughing. They tied a rope around the calf's legs and pulled it free. Its head slapped dumb against the mud. They took the dead calf and dragged it to a gibbet between the houses. The cow stamped and kicked. They hid the newborn from her view and slit its belly, pulled the organs out. Dogs nosed at the men's heels and were kicked back, they yelped and fled to shadow, but lingered as the work progressed. Driven manic by the stink of blood, they ate the mud where it had fallen, licked the grass on which it had spilt. Followed the trail back to the cow, who turned in circles and kicked at the walls of the house. The men took handfuls of hay and stuffed them deep into the carcass of the calf. They poked out its eyes and tongue, they cut the meat into portions for each family. Replaced the organs, veins and belly fat with hay, forced to the empty corners of the dead calf's body. Then they washed the blood from their arms and elbows, dipped themselves in the rain barrel, laughed and huddled by the fire. They carefully hemmed and sealed the belly. Then took the placenta, and the grease from the cow's womb, and smeared it over the head and neck of the dead calf, then dragged it across the floor, underneath the cow's nose. Forcing her to nuzzle the stuffed creature.

'Will she be fooled?' Jan asked.

'She'll know. But her milk won't.'

They watched as the cow tried to rouse the dead calf. With blankets draped over their shoulders, they kept their dogs back from the scraps.

Next morning, they milked the cow. Jan stared at the empty eyes of the tulchan created from her offspring. Watched as its best flesh was cooked and eaten, and the second flesh was salted and stored, the innards, cleaned and dried, blood congealed, boiled with oats, and hands stained red were held steady for dogs to lick clean.

In the following days, the families shared the calf, and ignored their fields and pens so they could watch the veal being dried above a great fire. Breathe the sweet air, full of iron and salt. Pinch pieces when no one was looking. Their stomachs complained against the over-rich meal. The cow was pushed back to the small stable at one side of the house, and the family moved in again, scraped their floor, burned the hay, repaired the holes and dents in their walls, and made their bed again. Though they tried to keep the calf's meat away from the cow, they ate a porridge warmed by its blood, and cooled by the mother's milk.

Later, they found the tulchan kicked to pieces. The woven knot of one eye had burst, and spilt its false stuffing. They cleaned and repaired it, poured sour milk over its head, smeared its legs with the mother's shit. They found it kicked into a corner of the stable again; the skin had lost its shape, the hay had emptied from the head and been forced into an obscene bulge in one leg. They shook the skin and brought fresh hay, rags of sackcloth, but the empty form lost all definition, and the cow's milk began to thin.

CHAPTER FOURTEEN

'Need to get a hold of myself. Getting too old to be carrying on like this.' Rachel straightened her skirt and played with the label on her jumper.

A shooting gallery of other men's faces passed through Gillis's mind. Fishmongers, fishermen, office managers, book-keepers, left backs, midfielders, weekend warriors, part-time dads, squaddies, permanent students. Each one with a different haircut, bearded or clean-shaven, moustachioed, uniformed, stinking of aftershave, bragging about their hobbies, fixing their cars, renting out flats, doling out financial advice, calling into radio stations, sticking to exercise plans, going for pro-motions, posing for photos, making time for their families, discovering new sides to themselves, learning new languages, seeking out new opportunities and looking on the bright side, men full of health and vitality. 'Carrying on like what?'

She ignored him. The clock had overcome the lean hours of evening, and the hands swung like sharpened sickle and scythe, harvesting the first minutes of the early hours. Rachel stamped down the stairs and along the hall, conquering territory, pulling wrinkles out of her tights as she went. 'I should go, I should have gone already,' she said.

'It's the middle of the night.'

She stopped and blew her fringe out of her eyes. 'But I really need to get Jamie back. We have to sleep before tomorrow.'

Gillis got out of her way. He retreated to a corner of the kitchen, found his shortbread tin and picked away with a thumbnail at the edges of the print, now so deeply scratched and eroded that in a bright light, it looked as though the castle was failing to defend itself from an artillery barrage.

'Don't you ever put the heating on? It's Baltic in here.' She quarrelled with her right shoe, pressing the heel back and forth until it gave in and sat straight. 'Hands are freezing,' she held up translucent fingers and pressed them into her neck to warm them. Head bowed, as though in prayer, 'I was here for a reason.' Checked her watch and looked out her bag. 'Is there anything I need to know, before tomorrow?'

'Tomorrow.' He was running out of time.

'My funeral,' she assumed he had forgotten again. 'The man I'm meant to be mourning.'

Gillis was about to confess, let her know that he was currently suspended. But paused. This was his chance. He could throw away all his notes and let the severed hand write a sermon. Speak to the assembled town. Tell them what it all meant. Where they were all going.

Last time, he hadn't known the game he was playing. He'd set out on an egg-and-spoon race, and found himself in a marathon. This time, without a doubt he'd figure it all out, just in time to pass the message on. He felt excited. 'OK, I'll do it.'

'You're already doing it, aren't you?'

'And I'm ready to do it. As in there's nothing more you need to know.'

She nodded and collected her jacket from the kitchen, confirmed her car keys were in the pocket, and paced quickly by the minister, stood on her tiptoes to kiss his cheek. 'I don't know,' she muttered, confused by her own gestures. She paced through to the living room, slowly opened the door and stared for a second at her boy, tangled in the blankets, surrounded by pens and pieces of paper. The TV was back on, still quietly broadcasting. She began to whisper. 'Wake up, wee one. Wake up.'

'Leave him, let him sleep,' Gillis pulled at her arm. 'You can stay here.' The three of them could stir the stale air, enliven the dead furniture. They could tidy the garden. Plant vegetables. Buy chickens. Get a few beehives. Dig a moat around the foot of the hill. Set up a telescope in the kirk spire. So he could spot his enemies. Pour boiling oil on them. Display their bodies on the cemetery gate.

'That's not a good idea.'

'It's as good an idea as any other.'

'I need my funeral outfit. Can't wear this.'

'It's black.'

She pointed out the pulled neck, and the streaked food stains.

'We're not burying him till twelve. We'll set an alarm.'

Rachel studied his eyes for a second, then sighed. 'Some widow I am.'

She quietly entered the living room and searched for the remote control. A young woman on the screen was gesturing toward an outline of Scotland. A storm which looked like a tuft of sheep's wool caught on barbed wire. Heavy rains predicted. A month or two's weather all coming at once. Rachel turned the TV off and tucked the blankets tighter about her son. She carefully closed the door and Gillis followed her to the kitchen. She took her car keys out of her pocket, and laid them in the middle of the table.

'Should we go back up then?' she pointed through the ceiling.

'You go,' Gillis's words echoed slightly. 'I'll be up in a bit. I need to finish a few things by tomorrow.'

'OK. I have to be asleep, though.'

'I'll be up soon.'

She shook her head. 'I really can't believe I'm doing this.'

Gillis sought out a cliché. 'Everyone mourns their own way.'

'It's OK,' she assured him. 'A bit of shame'll do me good.'

She slept in his bed, and he kept meaning to come up and sleep beside her, but the severed hand refused to help him. Although he knew that the hand probably couldn't hear him, he assumed that the heavenly powers which controlled it would be able to relay the message. He whispered his intentions, imagining a guardian angel standing behind him. *Give me words to say and I'll say them. Or I'll shout them. Everyone will be there, and I don't care how I look. I'll say anything, just give me the words.* He began to confuse his imagination with divine inspiration. Brainstorming, blue sky thinking, pop psychology, fortune telling. He opened the Bible at random pages, and tried to force the severed hand to point at words. Then he wrote the alphabet on a large piece of paper, and tried to corral the hand into speaking as a spirit might. It moved in many directions. A, O, G, D, Y, V, A, X, S, I, J, U, L, M, C, O, E, P, A, H. It didn't seem to mean anything.

The Ten Commandments had only taken a few hours to inscribe in stone. Why was this taking so long? The hours slipped by in twenty-minute portions. He shuffled his papers back and forth. Dozens of drawings and useless scribbles. Some of them seemed to be missing, but they all looked so similar, it was hard to tell. He turned them upside down. He laid them alongside one another. Animal stepping through frame. Cloud. Distorted body of a man, grown plantlike from the seed of his foot. Apples cut in half, revealing little faces. Aimless doodling, loops that looked like letters of an unknown language. None of it meant anything at all. He opened random pages of the Bible and read the first verses that his eye fell on. Types of bread, types of blemishes, mention of sackcloth and ashes. He turned from Psalms to Prophets to Proverbs, *Surely the churning of milk bringeth forth butter, and the wringing of the nose bringeth forth blood.* Then he split the book in half. *He fills His hands with lightning, and commands it to strike its mark. His thunder announces the coming storm, even the cattle make known its approach.* He sat for a moment, trying to force the message through the pulp of his brain. Nothing happened. And as morning approached, he grew more desperate.

'Have you been up all night?' Although he couldn't remember falling asleep, he recalled the furniture beginning to skew, leading to empty moments which could have concealed a few minutes or a few hours. Either way, all he had to show for his efforts was a kitchen full of smoke. Rachel opened the back door and fanned the air. Although on the way in she had skirted the papers which covered the floor, on the way back she trampled through them and narrowly avoided treading on the severed hand. It lay in the centre of the floor. It had stopped moving hours ago.

'I hate that thing,' she said, but otherwise ignored it.

Gillis crawled around beneath her, collecting all the papers together. The images were disconnected and illegible, no prediction had been made, no truth had been unveiled. 'I don't think I can do it,' he admitted. 'The funeral.'

She had left the room to wake her son.

He watched as the air cleared, and he took a cupful of ash and cigarette ends and threw them into the holes he had dug outside. Placed the stinking cup in the sink and tried to scrub the brown staining from his index finger. Then he wandered through to the living room where Rachel and her son sat together, folding the blanket and pulling cushions back to the sofa. On the coffee table, a colourful set of scribbles. A handspan of purple, a knot of blue, green and yellow, random spots of red. He stepped closer. Underneath all the colours, black doodling. Gillis howled and pulled all the drawings together. 'What have you done?' He turned from one page to the other. The severed hand's drawings had been coloured over. One, two, three, five, seven, nine of them, ruined. He turned on the overhead light and held the pages up to the bulb. The relic's linework was completely obscured by the colour.

The felt tips were scattered below the sofa. 'What did you do?' Gillis waved the papers before the boy.

'Don't speak to him like that.' Rachel pulled Jamie to her side.

Gillis flicked through the drawings again, throwing the worst of them to the floor. But one or two were still discernible; at some point, the felt tips had begun to run out, and fractions of the drawing were still legible.

'Does he know how to write?' There was lettering underneath one of the drawings, highlighted by pale yellow marks. 'Did you write this?' The boy was still silent. Face completely blank. 'Get him to tell me,' he ordered Rachel.

'This is what I told you – he doesn't speak.'

'Since when?'

She shrugged. It had been a long time.

'Tell him to speak.'

Obviously, she had tried that. It was the very first thing she had tried.

'Can he write?'

'Kind of. He writes little letters.'

'Ask him if he wrote this.'

'He definitely did the colouring,' she turned the ruined drawings over. The felt tips had soaked through to the back of the paper. The coffee table was stained with a half-dozen different colours. 'Maybe it'll come out.'

Gillis was leaning down to the boy. 'What does it mean? Did you write it?' The boy's eyes were empty and motiveless. It was like he was sleeping with his eyes open. Gillis held the drawing to the light again, and read the inscription that looped around the feet of a strange drawing. *May God end my misery and make of my ending a happy one.*

Rachel had set the table with a couple of bowls, and made a potful of stodgy porridge. Her own bowl sat thick and congealed, untouched. Jamie stared at his spoon, glued to the side of the bowl by a glob of starch.

'Is it still too hot?' She took the spoon and licked it. 'That's fine now. Eat up.' As Gillis sat down next to her boy, she pushed her bowl across the table to him. People were texting her. They were asking about times and places. 'I'll need to head home,' she looked cautiously at Gillis. 'If I go, get dressed. Get him dressed. . . We slept too long. It's ten. Twenty minutes to get back, hour to get dressed. Twenty to come back. Should be fine?'

'See if you can make sense of these.' Gillis laid a bundle of drawings across from the boy.

'He needs to eat,' Rachel pushed them away.

'How did he do it?' Gillis read and reread the lettering. 'How come I didn't see it?'

'He likes puzzles.' She didn't see why Gillis was interested. Kids' drawings were all alike. She normally threw Jamie's in the bin when he wasn't looking.

'Don't do that again,' he made her promise him. 'I'd like to see all his drawings. From now on. And if he says something, you need to tell me what it is.'

She tried to catch his eyes. 'Are you feeling OK?'

He was and he wasn't.

'Are you going to be all right? Should I call a doctor?'

Gillis claimed he would be fine, and followed her to the front door as she ran through an itinerary for the day. Certain people would arrive at certain times. They'd set up the hall, they'd bring food and drink, the coffin would arrive, the grave was already being dug. She pointed out of the kitchen window, where the elbow of a little tractor could be seen, and the movement of its hand as it scoured the earth. She crossed the threshold and stood on the frost-covered steps, looking the minister up and down. 'Will you be OK on your own?'

'You could leave him here,' Gillis pointed to the boy, who was leaning his head against her legs. 'We could do some drawings.'

'He's fine with me,' she said as they left.

Alone in the manse, Gillis tried to imagine a *good and happy ending*. He tried to write a little sermon, something to declare from the pulpit as the body was buried. Honoured to be using the same pen that the message had been transcribed with. *A good and happy ending*. He hadn't expected that. Films end in violence, books end in boredom. TV and the internet never end. Just go on and on and on. How does anyone's life end? In misery of one kind or another. Throughout the bundled papers, Gillis could see moments of the message appearing. Certain scribbles that looked like letters. Words and partial phrases hidden within drawings which had fuelled whole weeks of his life, now in context. Not much context, but enough to be getting on with. After copying the sentence into his notebook, he was stalled. Nothing else came to mind.

His phone had been buzzing, the screen had been lighting up, and Gillis avoided looking at it. Knowing that the bright colours and clean-lined graphics tended to dispel the kind of oversized, abstract thinking he was attempting. But the phone buzzed again, and for a moment, deciphering the drawings didn't seem as appealing as the incoming message.

What's this I'm hearing? the elder had texted. *Pls get in touch. Cheers, Ally x*

Several missed calls.

Please answer your phone. Cheers. Ally, x.

Mixed among them, a spate of text messages from his father.

Call me.

It's urgent.

Don't call me! They might be listening.

Hold on. I'm coming over.

'What have you done?' Gillis's dad pushed through the front door and gripped his son by the shoulders. He looked confused and aged beyond his years. Although he lived down in the village, a half-hour's walk or a five-minute drive, they mostly kept to themselves, politely ignoring one another until Christmas or a birthday brought them back together. The sight of him scared the minister. Had the man's hair ever stuck on end? Had he ever skipped a shower or a shave? Changes that were unnoticeable in most men were signs of a great, epochal shift in his father. A season passing, a sunset. Gillis staggered back and looked down at the untucked shirt. He could even smell alcohol from the man's pores, confused by a little toothpaste and aftershave.

'I had the police in my living room last night telling me you're running around with a *body part*. Is it true?'

Gillis squirmed away from him. 'Would you relax. It's fine, it's just a hand.'

'What do you mean, a hand?'

'A hand! You know,' he whirled his own around.

'But where did you get it?'

'I found it.'

'You found it? Jesus Christ. . . you need to put it back!' He muttered curses and blasphemies he hadn't used in twenty years. 'What have you done?' He looked afraid. Mind clearly racing, his eyes flicked back and forth as though reading words written over his son's face. Gillis tried to explain. How the ancient elm tree in the manse garden had been leaning toward the kirk, and the spire had started to crack. So they had to pull the tree out. And Gillis had fallen into the hole they'd left and found this hand. Which was strange enough, but the hand could actually move and it drew pictures as if it was trying to tell us all something, though it was anyone's guess what the images were meant to represent. 'Here, wait here,' he said, and grabbed the papers from the kitchen table, then brandished them at his father. He told him how recently, only last week, there had been a miracle. The flash of light, the angel, the insects and the fish.

'And look at this,' Gillis lifted his famous gammy leg, and swung it about, up and down and up and down, showing the range of movement, side to side, drawing little circles with his toe. 'It's the one I buggered years ago, remember? Could hardly walk for a while. Look at it now. . .' He repeated the motions, hands on his hips as he waggled the leg, smiling into the astonished mask his dad's face had frozen into.

'Why didn't you tell me. . .? We could have got you some help. . . Christ. . . What are we going to do?'

Gillis didn't have a clear idea. But he tried to explain Nichol's business plan. There was some scheme in place, a website, a club, a kind of therapy. It seemed small-minded now, irrelevant. There was no limit to what could happen. 'Now the miracles are important,' Gillis persisted. 'But the hand's here for a reason. It's trying to say something.'

The older man nodded like a dog struggling to swallow its dinner. 'We'll get this thing tidied away and we'll drive out to the Kirkmouth pier. Or we could burn it.' His dad stepped backward, trying to beckon him outside. 'We could go away up behind the industrial estates and set fire to it?' He stared into his son's eyes, searching for the last embers of the boy he had raised. He approached and spoke very clearly, 'Where's the rest of him?'

'Rest of who?'

'Whoever should be on the other end of this hand. What have you done with him?'

Gillis laughed, and a look of disgust crossed his dad's face. He swallowed it. 'People make mistakes and they need help. Maybe I've not been around enough, but I'm here now and I'm going to help. But I need you to tell me. . . Where's the rest of him? So we can get it all cleaned up and tidied away, then we'll talk about what to do. Your uncle John knows some guys in Canada. Maybe that's an option. We'll think about it.' His dad stared at him with such deep regret and determination to protect, that Gillis was briefly lost for words.

'Your granddad would've known what to do. . . He'd have a plan. But we'll do our best. . . You want to look it up on the phone, don't you? But that's how they catch them these days.' He looked up from his muttering and spoke in a voice that he hadn't used for decades. Fatherly and condescending. 'Are you ready? Get your jacket and get in the car, come on.'

Gillis obeyed on impulse, took a step forward and stopped. His dad was holding him by the arm.

'Look,' his dad continued, pulling him another step toward the door. 'Whatever happened between you and the other boy, whatever he did that made you do that, I'm glad that you finally stood up for yourself. I never saw it in you. You just daydreamt and laid about and folk trampled all over you. But there's a limit. A man's got to draw a line. Here and no further. And I just want to say. . . A lot of guys can't draw the line. Not saying it's right, but back years ago, you know, a man's pride and all that. Well. . . does a man not have pride any more?' He turned, his eyes glimmering with tears that wouldn't fall, and his fingers knotted into folds of Gillis's jumper. 'And think about William Wallace! He killed a guy for laughing at his trousers, and look at him. They had to cut him to pieces and scatter him all over the country. And even that only made him stronger. He didn't let that killing define him, did he? He got his head straight, and he moved on to other things. I'm getting myself in knots, I'm trying to say I'm proud of you, son. . . Now get your stuff and pack a bag, will you?'

Gillis ignored all the pride talk, the word was dusted down every year or two to be used against him. Bait for a trap. A drunken Christmas, a car ride back from a second-place finish, it was normally the precursor to a pep talk, pull socks up, get act together, pull head out of arse. Gillis didn't have the time to explain, or the heart to let him down again. Instead, he looked at his dad thoughtfully and said, 'They did cut him up, didn't they.'

'What?'

'Wallace. They cut him up.'

'You wouldn't get away with it now. They get you on the smallest traces.' They shouldn't really be hanging around, his dad said, they needed to start bleaching his floor and car, burning his clothes. 'What about Quebec? Or Catalonia? Some wee separatist place. They might like how you're Scottish and we could say you were an activist or it was a political killing kind of thing.'

Using one finger, Gillis's dad goaded his phone until it brought up flight details and train timetables. He wanted them to switch tickets, turn up for the wrong flight, get off a stop early and double-back. He watched telly. He knew how they operated. They have all kinds of methods now. 'Maybe we'll get two tickets, I could come along, just until you were on your feet. Maybe it'd look a bit less suspicious as well, like taking the old man on a holiday or something. I dunno.' He was suddenly embarrassed by the idea, the product of his first real drink in two decades, caught daydreaming by the cold, harled house, the drab wallpaper, the threads of the carpet, and his own son. 'Anyway, where is it then? I better see it.'

'What do you think of these?' Gillis ignored his dad's question and tried to hand him the bunch of drawings, but they spilt onto the floor. He retrieved the most important one. 'See the boy, he noticed something. See here, *May God*. Then here, *End. My Misery. . .*'

'We need to burn it, pal.'

'I'm trying to explain why I can't.'

'Come on and help me,' his dad ran to the bookcases and began to fill his arms.

Thick hardback books, thousand-page commentaries that dissected two or three verses of the Bible. Separate volumes of endnotes and indexes, broad ambitious histories of interpretation, all heaped in the garden. Flung into the hole beneath the elm tree, while Gillis looked on impassively from the flower beds. It didn't matter. Histories of the Church, biographies of its leaders, memoirs of political figures, speculative treatises on angels, anthologies of song. Men with comb-overs and moustaches, awkward beards, ill-fitting shirts, who scowled, or worse, sometimes *smiled*, from the inside cover and dust jacket. They asked questions that now seemed absurd. What would heaven look and smell like? How could a heavenly Kingdom start in the heart, and be expressed in the world? Their pages flushed translucent as Gillis's father squirted lighter fluid into the hole.

'We can't burn this.' Gillis tried to rescue the leather-bound volume his dad was carrying. It was a facsimile of an original King James Bible. Rough blackletter carved from wood, preserved for centuries. All *thy* and *thine*.

'Is it worth something?'

'It's a Bible.' Gillis pulled it from his dad's grip and flung it onto the grass.

'Would you *help* me out here, it needs to burn for a good long time.' Dad threw a dozen New Testaments on top, a Children's Bible, a biography of John Knox and several editions of *Pilgrim's Progress*. Ran back inside and returned dragging a great sack made from the blanket that draped the sofa, wrapped around a hundred or more of the non-religious books. Pulp sci-fi and cheap, battered editions of Shakespeare, Walter Scott and Robert Louis Stevenson. School prizes, Christmas presents, family heirlooms, the books were all flung together and soaked in butane.

'Lighter?' His dad ran from the garden to search the cutlery drawer. He returned with a long-handled gas igniter, tore a few pages from the front of a weathered copy of *Jane Eyre* and held them to the delicate flame. 'If we can get the fingerprints burnt off it and most of the blood boiled away, hopefully they won't be able to identify it. If the rest of the body's well hidden? Is it? Don't tell me. It's better I don't know.' The pages caught and he turned them over, coiling the flames around his hand. 'Where's the thing?' He dropped the burning paper amongst the books and stepped back as the lighter fluid caught in one great flame, surrounded by a tint of blueish smoke.

Gillis ignored him, kneeling in the grass with the ancient Bible opened before him.

'Where's the thing?' his dad asked.

'What?' He was studying the frontispiece which opened the book. An elaborate etching of two dozen men, stacked according to rank, draped in white robes, bearded, wielding pens and books. He had been examining the expression of their hands. Maybe a new book would be written. A second Revelation. A third Testament. A fifth Gospel. Beginning, what was it? *May God end and bring my ending to a happy one.* Something like that.

He started walking over to the manse carrying the Bible to his dinner table, while his dad went on and on, pressuring him to surrender the severed hand. They jostled one another through the hallway and stopped suddenly.

'All right, big chap?' A heavily bearded man in a black suit had opened the front door and poked his head into the living room. Sat on the sofa and looked around. 'Am I the first here, am I?' He took out his phone and answered a call, directing someone up the hill and into the kirk car park. 'Aye, aye, I can see yous now. I'm waving, look, naw, I'm in the wee house.'

Two more black-suited and bearded men, accompanied by their girlfriends, wiped their feet on the carpets and took up the rest of the living room. As other cars arrived and carefully parked end to end, blocking one another in, whole families pushed through to Gillis's front room.

'Are you meant to be working?' Gillis's dad was trembling.

'Do yous know there's a big fire out there?' A young guy in a grey suit looked around the room, trying to find the homeowner.

Gillis's dad explained. Recycling was a bloody scam. They preferred to burn it themselves. Better for the environment.

'Just as long as yous know.'

Gillis slid along the wall, skirting the incoming crowd; he walked into the manse garden, staring over at the kirk, then back at the elm and the hole it had left. The heaped books were furiously burning. Scorched pages, severed from the spine, rose with the smoke and drifted across the graveyard.

After the calf's meat had been salted, cured and stored, and the best cuts had been shared among them, the families began to notice their charity. Jan was in their way, sitting closer to the fire, further from the draughts, clutching the best blankets. His broth looked thicker, his slices of bread fuller, and when he followed them out to the fields to clear stones, he did nothing but check his nails, itch and fidget, worry over his torn boot heel and ask when they would eat again. Whatever black mood or sickness had affected the cow, travelled to her neighbour, and the milk began to dribble and spot from both their udders. The families' morning oats were cooked with spring water.

One morning, sensing their impatience, Jan woke early to help repair a cart, shouldered the weight of the axle, and watched as the work cut little notches into his knuckles. He collapsed and the cart collapsed over the wheel and the wheel sprung its spokes and bent out of shape. Back in the house, the children were peering into the stinking bundle which he had guarded so closely, secretly checking on it after every meal. In the middle of these rags, they found the very last, remnant pages of his golden book. The children had never seen a refined colour, strained from the world, a blue that wasn't in the sky, a red that wasn't blood, purples and yellows that weren't flowers. And the edges of gold crumbled onto their fingers. Their mother shouted and lashed with her ladle, spattering soup across the room, over the blankets and straw bedding still tangled along the floor.

Jan ate in the fields, and helped the men to right an upturned fence, then chased a few raggedy sheep down from the peaks of the surrounding hills. Unfortunately, he chased one off a hidden, little cliff. It broke its leg and the men made him carry it back. They returned as the sun was setting, hands trembling, fingernails cracked, thumb split and bleeding, clothes soaked through from the smurry rain, too tired to notice the deep quiet his presence brought to the women and children. He pulled his hands underneath his shirt and held them in his oxters, pressing some warmth back into them. Then he noticed the unfurled bundle, and the book pages laid out, demanding notice. Politely, the family ignored him as he rolled the pages, tied and covered them with the rags they had been kept in.

Through the night, the cow bellowed. The family led her into their home, stoked the fire and draped the trembling animal with heavy woollen jackets. They took the tulchan and stuffed it with new hay and clover, washed the staining from its hide, and inserted ash branches into each leg, so that the calf no longer flopped and scrunched, but held the vague shape of a lame newborn. The cow kicked a hole in the wall, and the bare remnants of the tulchan calf were torn open and trampled into the dirt floor. Next door, Jan pressed his face into the ground, trying to force sleep to overcome the brays and complaints of the suffering animal.

'Please,' the family asked him. 'Do something.' They pointed to the bundle of rags.

Jan found himself in the cow's house, with a dozen pairs of eyes watching through holes kicked in the loose stonework.

He tore a page from the book and walked toward her. Transfixed, the animal settled, staring at the shimmering gold as Jan shouted a prayer in polyglottal nonsense. His own Lowland language, mixed with Latin phrases from mass. Then he laid the paper over the cow's eyes and took one of the briquettes of pigment from his satchel. Spat into his hand and swirled his finger across the chalky surface until a lather of yellow paint built up on his first and second fingers. Then he lifted the page from the cow's head and smeared the paint down and across the forehead, making a pale cross; he muttered something holy and walked backward from the house, holding the page before him, rolled it away as he left the door. The cow turned in a circle, complained a little, but sat, and fell asleep.

Jan's head was propped with the best pillow, and his body covered by the best embroidered blanket. When he woke, he tasted fresh new milk, running thick and fat again. Sipping from his cup, he inspected the yellow cross with which he had blessed the cow, topped up the thin parts with his pigments and nailed that scrap of the book to the eaves of the house. The villagers pulled the tulchan calf from underneath the cow's feet. Split it by the belly, scrubbed its skin, scattered the chaff from its insides and waxed the hide. Draped it over Jan's shoulders, measuring him against the dead calf, and marked them both with chalk. They made a jacket. A speckled white stomach lay across his back, with a little collar made from an offcut ankle, and the legs of the calf were doubled over, so that Jan's left arm was covered in the front pair, and his right arm with the back. Parts of the tail were used to patch the elbows. They lined the jacket with coarse black sacking material and stuffed it with sheep's wool. They found five wooden buttons, and cut wide eyelets in the calfskin to house them. They presented the jacket to Jan, in thanks for his help. On his back, a wavering line of criss-crossing embroidery imitated an image from the book page, still fluttering from the eaves of the cow house, a red cross, capped and flanked with leaflike thorns.

Jan cleaned his boots, washed his clothes, cut a clean, straight line at the bottom of his beard and another in the hair above his forehead, a tufted fringe, daft enough to look tonsured. He asked these families to introduce him to anyone who he might help, anyone who might need a blessing in the old religion. They walked him to the next farm over, and waved from the limit of their land. In the empty stretch between crofts, he rehearsed his movements, licked his lips, stood straighter, and walked a little slower, as he had seen the priests doing when they swung their censers and approached the altar. Cheerily, he felt his stomach grumble, and raised two fingers to the sky, imitating the saints of his book, closed his eyes and paused in a spiritual gesture, watching through his eyelashes, as the workers in the distant fields spotted him. They drew close, they whispered, and agreed to shelter this holy man.

CHAPTER FIFTEEN

Incoherent phrases drifted upstairs from the collection of mourners who were jammed into the lower half of Gillis's house. He stared into the bathroom mirror as he buttoned his black shirt over the sheaf of drawings which he had managed to push into the waistband of his boxers. Pulled up his fly and tightened his trouser belt around them, then fitted his dog collar into the throat of his shirt. Looked out a comb and ran it under the hot tap. Tried to tame the night before and the morning after. Then he ran a shallow pool of warm water and stirred through a little dodd of soapsuds. He lowered the severed hand into the sink, touching it for the first time without cringing in fear. With a facecloth, he wiped down the palm and the fingers and each knuckle, though he avoided the raw stump at the wrist. The water tinted brown as the dirt and dried blood rose from the cracks in the skin. He pulled the plug and ran the tap until the skin looked clean. He rinsed the shortbread tin and dried it with his bath towel. Settled the severed hand in its housing and closed the lid. Lifted his jacket from the side of the bath and squirmed his arms through the sleeves.

Overlaying the noise of the mourners, his dad was trying to whisper through the door. 'Where are your papers? Your bank account and insurance stuff? Is it all in that yellow folder? We'll order our tickets in the car.'

Gillis tried to imagine a life in exile. He clothed himself in a white suit, yellowed with sweat and tobacco stains. He'd send handicrafts home. A patterned blanket for his mum, and a hat with tassels on it for Rachel. Hidden in the brim, directions to his hiding place. He imagined her travelling. Boat, then bus, then taxi cab. They could run a bar together. A Scottish place where they'd receive diplomats, ply them with roasted peanuts and imported lager, get the fuckers talking and sell the information. Open up a secret channel of communication between virtuous statelets. Survive the odd assassination attempt. Hold the severed hand over a world map and a copy of the *Financial Times*, make it reveal to the canny observer the hidden movements and gestures of that invisible hand which groped and pressured the world market. With these secrets revealed, Gillis could prevent capital flight, currency devaluation, and all the other mysterious terms he'd heard in passing and didn't understand.

Through the misted glass of the bathroom window, he could see the books burning, the stump of the elm tree and the squint spire of the kirk. *A good and happy ending.* First, he needed to see all of this through. He could take a holiday once he had worked out what the severed hand was for.

'You look strong, son, you look good.' His dad had been waiting on the balcony. He was impressed by the fine cut of Gillis's suit, the neat furrows of his hair. 'Grit your teeth. Keep the head. There's another minister arrived. We'll sneak out the back.' He had a rucksack choked with clothes, and a phone charger draped around his neck.

'They must be selling us in batches,' Fowler, the duplicate minister called his joke up the stairs, pointing to their black shirts and dog collars. They stared at one another as though from opposite ends of a telescope.

'We're going to clear out,' Dad pointed to his rucksack as they walked downstairs. 'Let you get on with it.' As they drew side by side, Dad turned to Fowler and asked, 'Maybe this is a strange question. But are there Churches of Scotland elsewhere in the world?'

Gillis retreated to the stairs and sat himself above eye level, so that none of the people pushing through the corridor were tempted to speak to him. *A good and happy ending.* He imagined himself at the pulpit. Delivering his message. Reading the sentence. Holding the severed hand before the crowd. And its purpose would become clear. Parting clouds, column of fire, pillar of smoke, Gillis would transcribe the ongoing message, condensed into a ten-point summary, suitable for a modern audience. He would use one of the big photocopiers in the library. Get someone to help him fold and staple a little booklet, illustrated with the severed hand's drawings. Rachel and Jamie could hand out copies of his revelation while he stood on a bench, or a wall, or a set of ladders, holding the severed hand above an enormous crowd. The spurned and hated of Kirkmouth and its regions. Maybe he'd walk at the head of a column of people?

He imagined that the manse was crowded with his followers. They could march on the capital, bringing chaos to A and B roads, collecting followers as they walked, the curious becoming the committed; growing in strength, they collect on Calton Hill, sleep in one another's arms. In the morning, heads and bodies are whirled together in knots of warm skin; cooled by morning mists, they light fires and study their booklets. And they would have no irritating questions or clarifications and no disagreements, but would see in what had been written a clear vision of the future. The great powers of this world would expect Gillis and his followers to march on the palace or parliament building. Squadrons of riot police would block their way, identification numbers torn off their uniforms. Scottish military units would be locked into their barracks, replaced with English squaddies. Tanks would roll down the Royal Mile as the severed hand's followers descended from the hill. Kitchen porters, waitresses, security staff and cleaners would leave their shift managers and irate customers behind. Dishes unwashed, buildings unlocked, vacuum cleaners still sooking, whisking dirt from the streets into the buildings, the offices, cafés, universities, libraries, all closed as the keyholders left or never showed. The depressed and bored, the restless and pitiable and fearful ones, all tied their shoelaces and followed his followers. A great swarming crowd, united in purpose, carrying him onward, holding the severed hand high above his head.

He would see others, caught in their own crowds, coming from the south and the west, holding strange objects above their heads. Battered rucksacks, brightly coloured Tupperware, an open violin case with a severed foot inside, a bag for tennis rackets that held a severed arm, crooked at the elbow, a fish tank which held a head. Descending the Royal Mile, collecting crowds that spilt from trains and buses, forced to stop as passengers climbed out of the windows and fell onto the tracks. Bodies were broken in the mass passivity, the great goal, the crowd pressed into police lines and pulled at their helmets and body armour until they were stripped and trampled, riot shields broken, truncheons, pepper sprays and guns dropped down the drain.

They'd climb Arthur's Seat and bring the body parts, cello case with torso, eyeballs in a clippy purse, knobbly knee wrapped up in a bedsheet; they'd press the bits together and they'd miraculously begin to stitch, glue and combine into the form of an ancient leader, a saint, or a king? Or a great thinker who could focus so intently on the impossible contradictions of world, nation and individual, until they broke completely, and shattered into a brand-new way of being. The daydream was a mess, and its parts were too loose to hold. Gillis pictured the great leader, recombined from a hundred separate body parts, kneeling on the ground and writing in the dirt, but what would happen after? Fuck knows. They'd throw the monster off Arthur's Seat and go home. The beast would need administrators and bureaucracies to implement its vision. The ones that already existed would do fine. They would implement the new rules in the accents of the old.

'Party's in here, is it?' Nichol pushed his way through the front door and tried to shout over the crowd. 'Folks, we're ready for you in the kirk. In the kirk!' There was no obvious leader of the group to bully or convince, so he pushed into the hall, forcing a domino effect on the tightly packed bodies that ended in a couple of young women being pushed into the kitchen to free up space. He spotted Gillis's knees and climbed the stairs. They were too narrow to sit side by side.

'Feeling OK?' With one knee raised four steps above the other, Nichol was straining his suit trousers to their limit.

Gillis surfaced from the remnants of his daydream. The downward trajectory of Western civilization seemed to be using his shoulders as ballast, the only steady point remaining, strong enough to tie the old ship to, burl the thing around, strain the hull and split the mast, but set forward again, facing into the howling gales. 'Fine, mate, totally fine.'

'Is that our pal there?' Nichol winked. The severed hand was sitting on the step behind Gillis, concealed in a thick supermarket bag, printed with a wavering Saltire. The minister clutched it to his chest.

'Folks!' Nichol turned from the stairs and bellowed toward the faces which pressed against the rails of the banister. 'Thanks for gathering here, thank you, everyone.' His voice boomed from the hall and silenced the living room, heads turned in the kitchen to shush one another. 'We're all set up next door, ready to go!' He chose a thin, nervous-looking man as his Judas goat, pushed him outside, then invited everyone else to join. The man had been well chosen, he turned in confusion and beckoned from the driveway for his wife to follow him. The wife brought her work pal and the work pal brought the man who was trying to chat her up, and so on until the hallway and the living room and kitchen were all drained of their occupants, asking one another as they left who had led them into the wrong house, and whose house it was anyway?

'Perfectly fine, perfectly fine, but we're all set up for you next door,' Nichol kept a monologue going which switched into little dialogues as grannies complained about their knees, and co-workers complained about their bladders, and tears were beginning to fall, and explanations were being demanded. Why were they burying poor Dougie again? Just when they thought they were over the worst of it. The grief, the grief came back. You never forget, it never goes away. But there's no sense crying, if you start you'll never stop. It's terrible to be old and for nobody to be wanting you.

The crowd was pooling in the car park, uncertain where to go, so Nichol began to use handshakes and backslaps as away's and come-bye's, ushering the flock to the front doors of the kirk. But they circled one another and the stale patterns of people confined in the manse opened out, and long-absent friends reconciled, and ex-girlfriends gave patient, almost kindly smiles, and the smokers and e-smokers took their opportunity.

So the manse was suddenly quiet. A brief moment of blessed silence, and even the furious winding of gears and pulleys within the workings of Gillis's brain paused for a moment, to enjoy the ticking of the clock, and the cold space between things, no longer occupied by dozens of strangers. Gillis walked downstairs and tucked his plastic bag underarm.

'Everyone away?' Fowler had hidden himself in the kitchen so he could look through his phone for ten minutes in peace. He looked up and down from his messages until catching sight of Gillis's expression. 'You know, I didn't want it like this. To. . . what's the word. . . *usurp* you. I'm just doing as I'm told.' He patted Gillis on the shoulder. 'We all get like this, pal. A little stressed.' He went on to recommend running. It had really helped Fowler to get out of himself. Return to the world. To nature. Get back amongst other people. It wasn't about competition. It was about the road underneath you. It was about one foot in front of the other. Take it real easy at first, he advised. Run between lamp posts. 'If you've never done it before, you have to build up the stamina.' Build up the strength in your legs. Bit at a time, it'll get easier. You'll be able to do five K. Then ten. Fowler had run a half-marathon, dressed in a silly costume. 'Can you guess what I was?' He had been a bumblebee. It was for charity. Just a laugh. Can't take yourself too seriously. His time was atrocious, but it wasn't about that. It was about camaraderie. He recommended yoga and good food. Little treats. A pick-me-up at the end of the day. Did he drink? Cut it out if he did. Did he smoke? Pack that in.

Gillis nodded along, 'Aye, aye, aye, listen, listen, I need to get up there and say a wee something. Just a word or two at the end. It's important.'

'What you want is a network,' Fowler wanted to stress this. 'Good people. Close friends. It's important to talk to other men. But it's also really important to talk to women.' Sometimes it's enough to just wake up in the morning. He should write lists. Tick things off. Get a good feeling of accomplishment. Write down stuff like brush teeth, make bed, wash dishes. Silly things like that. You can build up to the bigger stuff. Failing that? Maybe see a doctor. Speak to someone professional.

'Just five, ten minutes. It's just I have this thing.' He rustled at the bag, but Fowler laid his hand over the plastic, keeping the shortbread tin closed. 'You know I can't let you do that. I'll have to phone Edinburgh if you can't behave yourself.'

Gillis stared.

'Just let this one go. Take a rest. They might let you back on the admin side in a few months.'

Fowler excused himself and stood in the open doorway for a second, watching the car park and manse garden speckle with rain that grew heavier the longer he waited.

Mourners bottlenecked at the kirk entrance, each trying to politely cut the queue, but everyone needed to shake Rachel's hand and offer her their condolences, so they lined up beneath the small protection that the guttering offered. Fowler folded the back of his suit jacket over his head, and ran into the rain like a kid in high winds, hoping to take flight.

'He's already phoning folk,' Gillis's dad was crouching at the living room window, twitching at the curtains and trying to lip-read. 'I don't know who they're all phoning but they're all phoning folk.' He ran to meet Gillis in the hallway. 'They've got it in for you.' Passport, wallet, birth certificate, money. What else? Spare clothes, boxers and socks, what else? All in the rucksack. They were good to go. They'd have to make it quick.

'Are you listening?' Dad manoeuvred his head into Gillis's blurred line of sight. 'We can just about make the one o'clock train, get to Glasgow and out to the airport for three. Flight's at five. Get to London about six, half-six. If we can get that far without the police bothering us, we should be all right. You don't need to tell me all the gory details, but we'll talk about what happened. You'll get a job. I'll get a job too. I'll speak to your uncle, he'll know a guy who knows a guy. We'll do that. It's good! It's good. . . Remember that year we went to Gran Canaria? We could get a wee flat like that. Beer on the balcony. . . That was nice that year, wasn't it?'

Why does anyone travel? Gillis thought. *What's in another country? Sunlight. That's about it.* It didn't matter anyway, he knew that any attempt to escape from his destiny, whether it was a flight to Canada, or a train to Glasgow, or even just a step or two outside the bounds of the manse and kirk gardens, would be severely punished. The train would be derailed, the plane would crash, the boat would sink and he'd be swallowed by a giant fish, pulled back to his destiny. Dragged through the shallow waters of a lost tributary, cowering inside the fish's mouth, sparking matches, consulting the severed hand: *Go on*, it pointed, *keep going, work your way down the fish's gullet and into the stomach, go on further, make your way to the intestine.*

He was no longer standing in the manse, he was being retched and dragged back up the gullet of the great fish that had swallowed him, and he was being spat onto the shale and pebble of a fog-covered loch. His hands were not white-knuckle gripped onto a poly bag, they were scrabbling over rocks, flinging clumps of algae to one side, uncovering his shortbread tin and the severed hand inside. Glowing beatifically, the hand pointed further into the fog, uphill, through deep forest. A hidden place, slowly coming back to life after a hundred years of sleep. Sunlight purging the cold, as Gillis, prophet and hero, hobbled through thickets of heather and thistle, clambered up the roots of an ancient forest, timber last felled in 1915, for the Great War, and the time before that, 1815, the Napoleonic wars, and the time before that, 1715, to fight for the Old Pretender, and the time before that, 1615, cut to make crosses for the new national Kirk.

The minister climbed further uphill, amazed to see no tin cans or polythene bags mixed with the fern and moss, no planes overhead, no ships on the horizon, no electric cabling running through the trees. Grouse and capercaillie fleeing his feet, herds of deer barely flinching from him, he began to see stones set on their end, arranged in an uneven line, etched with letters that could have been yoga poses or martial art stances, gestures of resignation, hostility and arrogance. Consulting his shortbread tin, the severed hand pointed upward: *Follow the stones*, it seemed to say. Brute Druidic lettering gave way to looping crucifixes bound in poison ivy. The stones reached higher, and the forest grew sparse, the ground underfoot began to harden and as Gillis reached the summit he saw that a hundred different paths led from a hundred different shorelines, all to this apex. The severed hand pointed to a tall cairn of stacked rock, an ancient altar elevated high above the sleeping land below.

The great fog was clearing from the loch, and from the steps which led to the altar, the mighty rivers and waterfalls which contributed to the depthless water looked like streams of whisky. Spotted with boats and ships of all sizes, all heading toward the island, and the great hill and altar above them. A British clipper ship, three masts and nine sails, the crew outfitted in pantaloons and wigs. A long rowing boat, manned by the warrior caste of a tribe in search of their god, who had abandoned their idols and shrines. An aircraft carrier in the north spat fighter pilots and helicopters whose passengers were blindfolded and bounded at the ankles, submarines, whaling vessels and thousands of fishing trawlers, pleasure boats and canal barges approached, holidaying families hidden inside panicked. How had the quiet Leithside waters become this?

Gillis could see that every river and stream and leaking sink led here, there had never been a quiet stretch, or an empty afternoon, a sunny spell, or a cul-de-sac, all was connected. Coursing around their boats, hundreds of thousands of salmon, herring and bream, haddock and eel, shark and octopi, squid, calamari and kippers, king prawn and fried monkfish, breaded and battered cod, all drawn by impulse to this landscape outside of time, where Gillis climbed the cairn like a sort of podium, and the great crowds drawn there, called out of history to create a country, all waited for him to do something.

Now, at the very top of the world, the severed hand could no longer simply point onward. It pointed down to Gillis's feet, where a strange artefact lay to one side of the altar, speckled with lichen, a long curling ram's horn, the size of his arm. He scraped at the surface, and unveiled a gold mouthpiece at the sharpest end. All along the body of the instrument was inscribed with a series of letters and numbers, with dozens of little levers and buttons that adapted its form, so that in each opening and closing, the instrument spelt out a new word, and tallied a new number. So Gillis would climb onto the altar, and lick his lips and stretch his fingers and put the golden end into his mouth. But the mouthpiece just rasped and dribbled. The fog began to descend once more, and the ships and boats began to turn away from the mountaintop, the passengers blinked in confusion, losing the vision they had seen. The great fog would fall on the mountain, and it would sleep for another hundred years, until a new challenger climbed the altar and tried the ram's horn.

All seemed lost until Gillis lowered the strange instrument into the shortbread tin, and the severed hand climbed up and covered several more tone holes. Gillis licked his lips, and though he expected a silly toot or parp to ring across the valley, provoking nothing but a snigger from the retreating ships, the perfection of the instrument overrode the simplicity of the player, and the severed hand danced across the levels and keys, and these musical sequences were also words, an ancient language was being spoken as the golden clarinet or flute or trumpet, or whatever it was, was played, and the song, which began to sing itself, the words were. . . well, they didn't come to mind. But the fog parted and the ships returned, and the people began to ascend the mountain and shelter in timeless tranquillity. Cut trees to build houses and windmills and crofts. But now that the daydream had reached its height, the set-up needed a pay-off, and again, Gillis had no idea what to want or how to get it, and even this strangest wandering of his imagination could only deviate into silliness, sheltering in daft illusions. *What do you want?* he hissed at the severed hand.

'Passport, money, change of clothes, we're good to go, pal, this is it.' His dad held a backpack fit to burst, packed with essentials for a trip that Gillis would not make. 'We can't burn that thing with all these people around. We'll chuck it in the sea. We don't have time to fuck about.'

Dazzled, still tweedling on the ram's horn he had conjured, Gillis stared through the misted window where images of the fog-covered loch, the ascent to an ancient altar, and the atonal horn he had found and played, and called into existence a new king, or a new kingdom, all of it disappeared – replaced by the dull driveway of the manse and the kirk beyond, like the greasy thumbprints and scratches on a giant TV screen, only visible when the screen lies quiet.

'You're not going over there.' His dad attempted to assert some authority. 'We're going to stay here and calm down.'

'I'll be two minutes.' Gillis gripped his severed hand and climbed the stairs two at a time. 'Just getting changed,' he bellowed back to his father. From the bedroom he could see the burning books fizzling out as the rain doubled and doubled again. Movements of the wind were now visible as curved lines of rain whipped past the building. He opened the window and stood on his bed. If only that great elm hadn't been cut down, he could have climbed into its branches and safely descended. Instead, he squirmed his legs out and leapt, almost tearing his trousers on the window latch; he fell and doubled over and his ribs gripped his stomach, and his knees clashed with his jaw. Excruciating pain immediately rose from his bad leg, but he had no time to fix it with another miracle. He limped to the building and steadied himself on the harling. He had bitten his lip, and blood rose to cloud his eyes. He was laughing, amazed at his certainty. The eerie air, the yellowing cloud, the fire, the hymnbooks and Bible commentaries were hissing, a thin chemical smoke extracted from the leather-like binding, all mixed with steam, a cloud of incense. He spat a mix of blood and saliva into the mud, pushed through a gap in the hedges, and limped toward the funeral.

L ate winter morning, two months had passed and clouds shaped like anvils scaled the height of heaven, to soon be struck by thundering hammers, and spit sparks down to earth. Before the storms, it snowed and rained, or fell in uncertain expressions, neither one nor the other. The fishermen stayed on shore and the farmers cooped in with their cattle. Restless men ran back and forth, from shed to pigeon coop to barn, and stood in the awnings and eaves with their neighbours to judge the weather. By its smell it wouldn't last, by its looks, it would never end. Sea and river mouth too choppy, land too sodden, animals fed, sticks whittled, songs whistled and hummed, wife and husband fucked or fondled in boredom, they collected in an informal alehouse, and paid for their drink with armfuls of coppice branches that burned quick and sweet. Drinking thin beer throughout the afternoon, bodies packed tightly together, steam rising from wet garments, hazing the room, misting their belt buckles and the blades of their knifes. Several monks sat in disguise among them, defrocked, uncomfortable in jacket and breeks, soft little hats that shrouded their scalps, hiding the remnant of their tonsure, itching as new hair grew in. Each strand, heretical. They drank slowly, carefully, and paid with bright, clean coins, looted from the abbey's reserves.

'It's just like fox fur!' One of the monks was bent double, hat on the ground, head gripped in the armpit of a fisherman, who was running his fingers through the close haircut, and dragging the man around the room, offering the scalp to the children who sat among them.

'It's more like deer skin.'

The monk tried to dig in his heels and pull back, but the fisherman gripped tighter, and the features of the monk's face ran one into each other, wet lips into dripping nostrils, into salting eyelids; he tried to swing a punch, but only skinned his knuckles and loosened a few stones from the wall.

As the joke withered, the arm around his neck became an arm around his shoulders, consoling, kind, the fisherman straightened and laughed, backslapped, pressed a new mug into the monk's hand and poured more beer. Apprenticing themselves to the men here, the monks were now fishermen. The lone callus that used to lie on their middle fingers, shaped against the pressure of a pen, was now replicated on the underside of every knuckle, shaped against salt-saturated rope and wood prone to skelfing. Spilt beer stung in the blisters, but calmed the throat, and the monk laughed along and looked around as though realizing something, silenced the room with his confusion, ran his hand over his head and frowned, 'Wait, it's not hairy like a fox or a deer, it's hairy like a big bollock.' He hid among the laughter and the backslaps, shying from the glare of the older monks, the two who still prayed, even at sea, who still muttered to each other in Latin, who claimed to hear bells ringing, holy armies of heaven, angels that trudged through the peat, parting curtains of haar with their outstretched wings, holding great knives which they would use to cut heads from shoulders, and re-tonsure the scalps of repentant monks.

When the door knocked, the boisterous room was silent, suddenly face to face with a pillar of pure white, surrounded by feathers of snow. The monks, expecting their avenging angel, sneered in disappointment. Jan, apprentice painter, now wandering holy man, was frosted with sleet. He was greeted by a shuffling of the assembled drinkers. They asked him, 'Is it getting worse?'

Jan cracked the surface of his frozen calfskin to answer them, separating hem from button, collar from scarf and undershirt. The jacket was battered with a stick and hung over the fire, the old men made room for the drips, and a puddle that began to search across the floor. Jan perched on a tall stool in the corner, elevated above the benches on which the drinkers sat, and the floor where the women and children lay. As his jacket twisted on a hook, unwinding as it dried, it revealed its red threading, the looping cross stitched across the back. Shepherded by their mothers, more children found their way inside; one was pushed toward Jan to ask, 'Where have you travelled from?'

But Jan didn't answer.

Young girls arrived, and huddled into corners, held on to each other's sleeves and hid in shadow, preparing to giggle. And the boys climbed the scaffolding of the house, to perch on the eaves or dare their fingers into candle flames, or chase and grip the cat by the head, pressing down on its eyes until it hissed. Another asked, 'Where are you from?'

Jan didn't answer.

They brought him a blanket of yellowing sheep's wool so thickly felted that it barely folded around his shoulders, but lay like a kind of thatching, wicking the melting snow from his skin, shirt and hair. The woman who folded it around him asked, 'Who are you?'

But he didn't answer.

A little crowd had formed behind his back, and at the flashing sight of the white of his eye, the first mother asked, 'Will you please bless my little one, my only one.' She curtsied. The apprentice painter turned in his seat.

The room was bashful, and they looked up in fear as Jan
stood on the stool, and steadied himself by the rafters. His
bundle unfurled and he brought out his book, the charred
remains of it, and told its story. Brought here on a terrible
voyage, flung from the deck of a ship by Satan-worshipping
sailors, Jan, apprentice painter, had bravely leapt into the
waters, hoping to give his last breath to bring this book to
shore. Maybe a poor child would receive it and bring a great
blessing on their parents. Instead, like a fool, Jan, apprentice
painter, had tried to deliver the book to its rightful owner.
The Laird of all these parts and the parts beyond. But the
man had thrown the book to the ground. Wonderful pages
like this, spattered in mud and horse shit, wrinkled by rain
and river water. The book was even burned! Taken by
Godless rebels and burned in the midden of that Laird's
castle. And again, he, Jan, apprentice painter, who had
worked on the delicate images inside this wonderful book,
risked his life, hoping to give his last breath, to bring the
book to its true and only owners. As he finished his speech,
one he had given fifteen or twenty times – he had lost count,
refining it as he went – he knew to wait here, pause, and let
his audience look around themselves. Who could he mean?
Where would he go? If the Laird wasn't worthy, and the
priests weren't worthy?

'Friends. I mean you.' He took a pair of scissors from his
pocket, and began to cut a little strip from the edge of the
first tattered page. The young mother lifted her baby and
turned him in the light. 'His cheeks are red and his forehead
is red and his ears are red, and he coughs.'

Jan flicked through his book to find a page of painted
sky and cloud, he showed the mother the image, a spring
morning, the clear light of heaven beaming down to bring
up an ascending saint. He cut a thin strip. 'Blue and white, to

cool your baby's illness.' He tied the strip of paper around the baby's neck. 'Heaven help you,' he said, and made cruciform gestures.

'Thank you, thank you,' the mother held her baby closer as she left.

An old woman supported her husband, whose eyes searched the dark thicket of thatched grass overhead, and whose arm was twisted inward, fingers trying for the elbow. 'My man talks nonsense, his head is in one place, his body's in another. He thinks he's young and I'm his sister. When I wake at night, sometimes he's standing in the snow thinking the cold is the sun's warmth. Help me and bless him, God and Christ save us.'

Jan looked for a page of yellow and orange, but could only find the speckled yellowing green of a meadow where a saint lay appeasing a lion, sparrows and starlings resting on his outstretched arms.

'Green and yellow. Warming light of youth.' Jan cut a long, jagged strip and tied it over the man's eyes. His eyelashes flickered and the paper danced on the crook of his nose.

'He'll never keep it there.' The man's wife tried to stop his wandering toward the paper; his nose was crinkling, he was blowing upward with his bottom lip. His wife held his hand back. 'We'll need to tie him up.' The fishermen helped her. They found a thin rope, and struggled against the old man, until they managed to bind his wrists to his belt. Jan took an offcut of vellum, and tied it in a little bow around the ropes, to bless them. 'When will he be healed?' the wife asked.

'In a week.'

She thanked him, kissed his hands, kissed his cheek, and rummaged in her bag for a coin. 'I'll be back, I could give you a goose? Or a necklace?'

'The necklace.' Jan took it from her neck.

'Blasphemy!' One monk amid the others shouted over
the pious silence, but was elbowed back into his seat. Jan
burrowed his nose through the last of his book, selecting
carefully from the scant pages. Examining the complaints
shown to him – bared skin, odd lumps, swellings, bruises,
seepages of a hundred colours – and searched his book for
the opposite colour.

'Bless me in my illness, please.' A woman uncovered her
neck, down to the collarbone, a rich speckled purple; the
orange trousers of a painted merchant made a lovely contrast.

'Blasphemy.' Exasperated whispers came from the
defrocked monks as their little table was overshadowed by
queuing villagers, holding hens and cockerels, dogs with one
leg, babies with croup, old men riding piggyback on their
sons, young wives flung over the shoulder of embarrassed
husbands. Long strips of vellum were tied around barren
bellies, looped across painful hearts, rasping lungs, broken
and ill-set fingers, rotten toes, cankered gums, cauliflower
ears, and one young man, waiting till the very last, asked Jan
to see him in the very corner of the room, and showed him
a painful rash on his stomach.

'Is that all?' Jan asked.

'No.' The boy took out his prick, and turned it over; a
weird spot, an evil growth, festered there.

'God help you.' Jan found a rare strip of chipped golden
paint, looped and tied it around the man's member. And
wished that he could have helped, and that the colours could
do anything to affect the world. But the young man was in
tears as he thanked Jan and blessed him, and promised to
bring him a pair of good boots and a spare hammer he had,
now that his father had passed on. He was due to marry in a
month, and even the most innocent of brides would know
not to touch him there.

'When will it heal?' he asked. 'Will I be in time?'

'In a week.' Jan nodded along. 'A week from now.' They led him to a warm bed, hidden behind curtains, they gave him a folded scarf and a little brooch shaped like a leaping hare.

Jan turned toward the heaven he suspected was empty, and asked, 'Please, God, let me get a good week's head start on them.'

CHAPTER SIXTEEN

'Thanks for coming, thank you, thank you for coming,' Rachel was shaking hands at the entrance. By the touch of her hand, mourners assumed their roles. Some struggled to adapt, greeting her with a broad smile, spillover from conversations in the car park. They pooled around her, like water about a plughole, circulated one last time, saying hello to one last acquaintance, before they shook her hand and bowed beneath the doorway. Some bent in for a kiss on the cheek, others gripped her by the shoulders or waist. Men found their wives, bachelors walked in pairs.

Gillis came at the end, the knees of his trousers dirtied, ash settled in his hair. Rachel caught his sleeve. 'When were you going to tell me?'

Gillis couldn't respond, something was holding him deadly straight, tightening his muscles, gripping him by the throat.

She searched his face, but there was no response. 'You didn't think I needed to know? I'm in two minds to even let you in.' She got nothing from either sentence. 'Are you going to behave yourself?' She indicated the bright blue plastic bag, the cracked Saltire, and beneath it, the golden corners of his shortbread tin.

He struggled to nod.

Further inside, the mourners greeted the replacement minister. Gillis held back, innocently searching the kirk, ignoring his duplicate's joke, 'They must be selling us in batches.' Ignoring as Fowler tried to step forward, tried to ask him to leave. Then a kind of threat. A kind of muffled pleading, '. . .what with what they've all been through. . .' Gillis took a sudden turn into the side rooms as he heard his dad's voice behind him, greeting Rachel, apologizing, attempting to explain, 'I don't think my boy's very well.'

The side room was outlined with long tables joined one to the other, shields of tin foil arrayed like a medieval armoury. He passed a cluster of checkered trousers and white jackets, KPs from the hotel, arranging heaps of smoked and roasted salmon into sandwiches, across crackers and pastries, rolled around dollops of cream cheese. Nichol strode among them, swigging from a wine glass, chewing, trying little bits. 'How's this?' he called. 'How's this for a send-off?'

Gillis slipped further into the building, peeking into the vestibule. It was a chaotic tangle of colour. The little room had been filled with a great jumble of scaffolding, stacked plasterboard and reels of electric cabling. A dozen ceramic toilets, disconnected, all faced each other; in their midst, sitting alone on a computer chair, Jim Macintyre sat alone. 'Have you been tidied away too?' the man asked, and rose, tried to pick his way through the mess. He stumbled, and his pocket jangled, keys to a thousand forgotten doors, windows, lockups and garages long gone. Gillis ignored him and took a right turn into the hall, straight to the front of the assembled mourners. The organ was sitting to one side, its double keyboard stricken with red lights, humming its way through a preset hymnal function. Chattering mourners stilled some as Gillis strode across, unsure if he had the authority to begin proceedings.

He climbed the pulpit and stood for a second, feeling his inspiration gather. In the first row of seats, Jamie sat on his own. Legs jutting from the padded seat. His mother's empty jacket beside him. Drawings and felt tips draped over his legs. The coffin was there already. Mahogany and brass. White lilies. A picture of Douglas. Clean-shaven. Sober. Smiling slightly. Collar too tight. One head after another raised from the crowd, then turned to shush one another in deference to the minister. Gillis set the shortbread tin down on the lectern and surveyed his peaceful, attentive herd. He was ready. He wasn't perfect, but Moses had a stutter, didn't he? Bonnie Prince Charlie was an inbred weakling. Jonah was a coward. Rob Roy was a thief. John Knox had anger management issues. But they were taken and formed by the task in front of them. Made into men of purpose. Purpose and history. Column of fire, pillar of smoke.

He watched as Rachel caught sight of him and started hurrying down one side of the pews, with Fowler rushing down the other. His dad was still by the door, waving at him to get down, to run. But he wouldn't. He was going to open his mouth and speak. He was going to take the severed hand and raise it over the crowd, and bring it down like a gavel struck in terrible and irreversible judgement. He opened his mouth, but there was still nothing to say. He opened his mouth again, expecting God to take hold of his head, and wield him like a sword.

'Why?' Rachel whispered from the bottom of the pulpit, looking up at him with a mixture of fear and anger, 'are you doing this?'

'Because. . .' he started, but couldn't finish. His stomach ached, his throat was constricted in grief and embarrassment, as all momentum and energy was lost.

He didn't have a good answer.

'Please, Gillis. Come down,' Rachel offered her hand. He looked back out at the congregation, all waiting for him to begin. But he had nothing to give them. He took Rachel's hand, let himself be led from the pulpit, intending to turn back as soon as the words came to him.

He gripped his poly bag tighter. *A good and happy end, God end me and end a good and happy end, and God end.*

Fluorescent police uniforms appeared through the collection of mourners who circled at the doors. They were followed by a shirt and trousers. A pink tie. A rain jacket and a folder full of paper. A doctor.

In loud, rounded vowels, this doctor introduced himself as Brocklebank, seeming not to have noticed that he was entering a funeral, or blind to the convention of quiet. Sidekicked by stab vests, Brocklebank grasped at the poly bag and piloted Gillis up the aisle through the double doors, parting the crowd, turning them toward the side rooms.

'Let's just go in here, easy now, just for a little discussion,' said Brocklebank, calming the situation. But as soon as they entered the room, Gillis utilized the empty space and turned his body, pulling at the bag until it yawed and tore, the Saltire stretched and split into two useless, contending arrows, and the doctor tripped on his own feet and fell back into the catering table, an elbow stabbed into the sandwiches. Gillis scrambled across the floor to protect the severed hand.

'Mr Gillis, please,' Brocklebank clambered back to his feet. 'You're more than welcome to hold on to that. We're not here to take it away from you.'

The minister noticed a flanking manoeuvre in progress as the two policemen closed the doors at each side of the room and walked toward him, although both had their hands behind their backs and were smiling, almost whistling in mock innocence.

'Detective Cormack?' Gillis recognized the tall one who had spoken. 'Were you demoted?' The constable tried not to answer, but Gillis asked again.

'Yes.'

'Fail the exam?'

'I did, mate, aye.'

'Have you been sleeping at all, Mr Gillis?' The doctor touched him on the elbow, and guided him toward a couple of seats by the wall. He had some paperwork. An assessment. Was that OK? Could he answer a few questions? Had he been taking any medication? Was he currently on any illegal drugs? Was he seeing things?

'And what do you have here?' The doctor poked at Gillis's belly. He looked down. His shirt buttons had popped open, and the severed hand's drawings were spilling from the waistband of his trousers. The doctor pried one loose and examined it. A horse, sort of folded in half, drowning in a little river.

'I understand you're about to lose your job?' He set the drawing to one side.

Gillis nodded.

'And that your house is tied to the job, so you've also lost your accommodation?'

He nodded again.

'And the car's a company car, isn't it? So we'll be losing that too.' The doctor ticked and scribbled through the documents in front of him and turned them overleaf. 'I've been hearing a lot about your wonder-working what-would-we-call-it? Talisman? Fetish? Is this our man here?' He tapped the shortbread tin.

Gillis nodded, and the doctor waited patiently as the minister's arms relaxed and he placed the shortbread tin on the floor.

'Will we open it up? Have a looksee?'

Gillis eyed the police officers. They had blocked either exit.

'They're only here for legality,' Dr Brocklebank assured him. 'To make sure that you're well looked after.'

Gillis opened the tin, and watched the severed hand squirm, scratch index finger and thumb, turn, point at his forehead. The police officers leant in.

'OK, OK.' The doctor prodded at the severed hand's fingers with his biro. 'Have to say, it's looking healthy as these things go. My expertise is limited in these areas, and I'd have to defer to the judgement of. . . maybe a neurologist or a. . . a. . . a hand expert, I suppose. It's certainly fascinating!' He suddenly laughed and sat back from the shortbread tin. 'It's a real puzzler! I admit you've got me stumped here. It's been a long time since medical school, I'll tell you that.'

Cormack, the demoted detective, loomed over the tin. 'Christ, how's that moving?'

'Well, it can't be,' the doctor laughed.

'I can see it.'

'Would a real severed hand move?' The doctor stared at Cormack until he was forced to concede that no, it wouldn't. 'Well. . . follow the logic. . . if a real hand can't move, and that's moving, it can't be a real hand, can it?'

'I'm just saying I can see it moving.'

'Are you a doctor?' Brocklebank snapped. No, he wasn't. Was he some kind of specialist? Some kind of expert? So who was he to pronounce on it? Someone in Edinburgh would be able to say. And if not Edinburgh, London. And if not London, New York. And if not New York, then some university somewhere, some laboratory, some roomful of professors could say, one way or the other, what was going on here. 'And anyway,' Dr Brocklebank mastered his irritation by running his palms up and down the front of his trousers, then as he spoke, he opened his palms in prayerful gestures. 'This doesn't matter to the matter at hand, so to speak.'

Soon they had Gillis sitting up straight, breathing deeply and agreeing to things. Signing bits of paper. They located his dad and pressed him into the opposite corner, and he asked about visiting hours, sleeping arrangements and mealtimes. And what about post-treatment? Could Gillis's dad be relied on to put him up for a few weeks at least? Support him financially, until he was back on his feet. Ensure that he took whatever medications might be prescribed, repeat the mantras and ensure he ate well, got regular non-strenuous exercise and quit any smoking and drinking.

'Of course,' Dad tried to make some calculations in his head.

They took him to the hallway, past the mourners who filled the doorways, jostling for a view of the ongoing incident. Rachel was standing at the front, arms folded, hands gripping at her jacket. 'I'm sorry,' she said as Gillis passed with his escort. 'You started to scare me. Get some rest and I'll come and visit you.'

He thought she probably would, if only he said something, even something small, even just a yes or an OK, or a thank-you or a sorry, or if he took the risk and told her that he wanted to see her, that she brightened the room, just something, but he didn't, in case the words overwrote and confused the holy speech he had been waiting for. He pictured himself as a radio, tuned to one signal or another. Maybe he should open his mouth and refuse to close it until the words came. Wait as long as it took. Months, years, yawning at the world, waiting. But he didn't do that either.

She nodded toward the hall where the mourners were pretending not to be eavesdropping. 'Better get on with this. Second time lucky.'

The sun was concealed, draped in dark cloud. The police officers shied from the rain speckling their jackets, and Dr Brocklebank waited in the entrance of the kirk, one arm extended into the rain, trying to unlock his car from a great distance. It looked as though he was holding a TV remote, attempting to change the channel to something more interesting.

'Can I take this?' Cormack quietly slipped one hand onto the shortbread tin; his latex glove had torn across his thumb where the nail poked through.

Gillis tried to grip tighter. 'Why?' he asked.

'You should have shown us this weeks ago. None of this needed to happen.'

Whole weeks of his life, he'd hated every minute. But in hindsight, hadn't it been worthwhile? Hadn't it felt important? Grievous decisions to be made every morning. Now, if he handed the shortbread tin over to the police officers and psychiatrists, and the state that stood behind them, he would pass into obscurity. Having taken a wild, desperate shot for the goal, which by fluke and miracle cut through a tight defence, loomed and aligned on the target, only for a teammate to race across and tap the ball in, stealing all his glory. Or worse, maybe they were on the other side. Defenders and goalkeepers confusing him, calling for the ball as he ran toward goal. No, the glory would be his. *Lord, send me*, he would scream at the sky. *I'm open.*

He twisted and pulled his shoulders free, and Cormack stared at him in surprise. Then he stepped on the ugly black boot, forced the man backward and started to run, but Cormack grabbed at Gillis's shirt and the collar and sleeves suddenly tightened. Gillis retched as he was strangled. Outraged at the unsportsmanlike behaviour, he searched the empty kirkyard for referee or linesman.

The other officer arrived and soon he was held by both sides; stuck in the boundaries of his clothes, he wrestled back and forth in the give of his jacket and shirt.

'OK, OK,' Gillis admitted defeat and glared alternately at the two policemen. They wouldn't let go. They were trying to find their handcuffs, until Dr Brocklebank ran from the cover of the kirk and intervened. This was not an arrest. This man was not a criminal. 'We're all here to help, aren't we?' The doctor laid his hands on the policemen and they loosened their grip. 'Thank you.' He spoke in hushing, sympathizing tones.

Gillis wiggled his shoulders so his suit jacket straightened, stared at the hands which gripped his elbows until the officers let go. Stepped away from the slick trench of mud they had been digging as they fought.

'Are you going to calm down?' Cormack twisted the shortbread tin in a circle, and Gillis's fingers slipped reluctantly from the bag. The policeman handed the shortbread tin back to his colleague, who flung it to one side of the kirk entrance.

Brocklebank put his hand on Gillis's shoulder. 'We're just going for a walk. We're here to help you.'

Gillis closed his eyes and simpered, said a frail thank-you as he arranged his feet and then ducked and thrust himself between the scrummed bodies. Cutting his shoulder deep into the broad gut of Dr Brocklebank, and as the doctor fell Gillis nimbly picked out the spaces between the man's knees, and leapt over him, his back foot trailed terribly close to the man's face. Could have broken a cheekbone or nose, torn an earlobe or put out an eye, but he was clear and he saw the empty kirkyard open before him. He ran from grave to grave, zigzagging, focusing on his feet until the moss and grass

suddenly shifted to bright green plastic. Sheets of AstroTurf
arranged around a grim, open hole that loomed before him.
A pile of dirt beside it. Edges sheer, corners correct, in one
long blasphemous lunge, Gillis leapt over the empty grave.
Held back by professional decorum, the police officers
refused to jump the grave and were forced to loop around
the little orange digger, and the confused operator who sat
in the cabin with a racing paper over his knee. Gillis gained a
good ten metres in the diversion. Little tricks. That was how
to win. The limit of the kirkyard approached, leafless hedge
that delimited the boundaries of his game, whose rules he
still didn't know. He met the line and turned to circle the
building, where the gutters spilt into a permanent puddle,
where the bins were picked through by feral seagulls, where
scrap plasterboard and two-by-four lay in a heap, ridden with
nails and screws.

The noise of the pursuit brought the mourners from the
kirk, Fowler spluttering about the dignity of the dead, Rachel
marching ahead of them, high heels first scattering gravel
then sinking into turf. She left one shoe behind, and took
several disgusting steps in the soaking mud, until she stopped,
leant on a headstone and raised her bare foot. Turned back
and stared longingly at the abandoned heel.

The policemen's fluorescent jackets rounded the corner
and disappeared, and the crowd's attention turned to the
opposite side of the building, in expectation of the minister's
reappearance. They heard his footsteps.

'Here he is!' a man called. 'Here he comes,' they made
way for him, and Gillis searched the kirk entrance for the
discarded shortbread tin. It lay at the crowd's feet. He pushed
them aside and rose with the tin under his arm. He cleared
his way with a rugby player's stance, one hand extended, legs
powering behind.

'Here's the polis.' Some parted and some tried to lock shoulders after he passed, to protect him and prolong the fun, while others tried to block and push him away from the hall and the unattended coffin.

'That's enough.' A matronly figure had locked her arm through the handles of the double doors, seemingly willing for her wrist to be broken. Instead, Gillis leapt to one side, to a corner by the coat racks, unsnibbed the top and bottom latch of a hidden half-door which led into the condemned spire. The little crowd almost applauded at the unexpected turn.

'He's up there, he went in the wee door!'

'Belt up, ya grass.'

As the policemen pushed through the tight corridor, voices were raised in complaint. This was meant to be a bloody funeral. An old man claimed he had never seen the likes of it. A minister and a pair of polis running like Benny Hill round the graves. They should be ashamed of themselves.

'Can we clear a path here, folks,' Cormack tried to command the crowd, but his uniform and his belt full of gadgets all hung loose on his slim frame. Despite his height, his face looked boyish, and the crowd ignored him. His colleague was only five four, but had a good set of lungs and heavy stubble, and tattoos that couldn't be shown to children. The crowd backed up and the police made their way to the half-door and pressed through to the spiral staircase. Cormack ran up the first two steps, but his colleague pulled him back. 'Take it easy, mate, the silly cunt's backed himself into a corner,' the officer pointed up the spiral staircase. 'He's either falling off or he's coming back the way he came.'

Heads appeared in the doorway, the most curious and bold of the crowd followed the police officers and tried to ask questions.

Who was he? Why were they chasing him? And what was he running for?

'I think he thinks we think he killed somebody,' Cormack answered and rolled his eyes.

Jan was busy throughout the winter and into the spring. Blessings were needed now that the chapel was closed, and the priest had been punted from jail to the stocks, dressed in cabbage leaves and carrot peel, chased to the coast and overseas, and the monks were apprentice ploughmen or fishermen, their pained expressions wearing in like new leather, cracked in sore places, soon to be softened in use. And the black jackets had whitewashed an inner hall of the court, decorated with a single, unmanned cross, and on Sundays, they chased families down from the outer villages into the town. Black jackets came and went, alone, in twos, in groups of two dozen, moving from town to town on obscure business. Ringing the changes, closing the public houses, overturning beer into streams, chasing rumours around the hills. Someone was spotted dancing on the frozen river, and torches were carried back and forth, pursuing ghosts who mocked the Sabbath. Until a boy fell in, and drowned in darkness. They buried him, and the magistrate read from his Bible. This God spoke English.

The new ways were all very well, but blessings were still needed. On the cattle, on the fragile shoots of wheat and oats. On carrot leaves and turnips, on bairns just born and old folk bordering death. Jan obliged, he touched their aching heads, put his fingers in their mouths, in their ears, he closed over their eyes. Tied ribbons of vellum around their cancerous guts, their bedsores, broken bones, strained muscles, torn ligaments, knotted foreheads, broken ankles and unravelled belly buttons. Until his pages were almost gone, and he cut his strips thinner, shorter, he tied them tighter. To save material, he started to tie folk together. One little strip around two fingers. Hold it for a week and feel God's blessing, divided among you. His pocket jangled, and he slept long into the morning, warm beneath the best blankets, passed from house to house like a precious secret. Sometimes in the night, he rolled over to feel the sleek surface of warm skin that hushed and crept over him, smothered his words. But in the early morning, warm skin and smothering heat transformed into a farmer's daughter or a fisherman's wife, who wanted a whole figure cut from the book, a saint or an angel of their own, to nail on the apex of the roof and bring blessings for a whole lifetime. When Jan refused, they threatened to tell what he had done in the night. The very last remnants of his book grew holes as though moth grubs were chewing all day at every edge.

One morning, after he had squatted and splashed in a bucket of warm water, scraped dirt from the obscurest parts of himself, after he had eaten a good breakfast, searched out his shirt and jacket, drying out above the fire, snorted muck from his nose into the gutters, and finally pulled on his boots and waved goodbye to the families, without as much as a thank-you, his host and his family soured some on the deal they had made. Evening candlelight had danced across the colours of the tattered book, seeming to make the figures move, but in early afternoon, overcast and sunless, the faces disassembled into nothing but scratches of black chicken's feet, colours growing among them like moss and mould. The host looked at the empty pot and pan on his stovetop, scraped clean, and the hostess scratched at her itching crotch.

Jan, beard shaved and hair cut, at his next stop, rucksack weighted with a stoppered skin of sour ale, five or six smoked fish wrapped in oily rags, a half-loaf of bread and a thick blanket of yellowing sheep's wool that he struggled to fold or lash to the bag. He was beginning to meet old acquaintances, houses he had visited before.

'God's blessings?' he asked at their doorway. They'd point to a tassel of coloured paper, a little sad and worn-looking now, and point him on to another household. They no longer asked him to stay or collected the wider family, or spread out a meal for him. They gave him a rusk of bread, or a handful of raw peas or oats. They didn't want him sleeping in their stables; a man by the coast who'd been sheltering a monk, celebrating mass, was stripped and slapped raw before the courthouse. The monk was in jail. Jan found a nook of the abbey's ruins and made it his burrow. Bound in his felted blanket, he crawled beneath a toppled wall, whitewash flaking like autumnal leaves. His breath and his sweat filled and warmed the fireless hovel. From there, he trekked out to the fields and byways that surrounded the abbey, and called, 'A blessing? God's Gift to you!' Fluttered his pages in the wind. He pressed men in the fields back into belief, sent children running home, asking for food to pay for a bracelet of paper already dangling from their wrist.

'Careful,' some said. The magistrate, the black jackets, the protestor troops were garrisoned in the Laird's castle, and from there, they essayed into the regions, looking for trampled grass and cleared heather, signs of hidden sacraments, in search of the Devil and the fair folk that served him, who lived underground and worshipped weird images.

And his blessings began to fail. Cancers grew, pox of the skin spread, ankles broke again, scars deepened, animals trod on last legs, cuts on the feet led to mushrooming gangrene, pallors thinned, ribs showed, milk curdled, meat spoilt and the rain fell on and on, breaking the chew of the soil and floating roots to the surface, where they untangled and spoilt. A roof was blown off. Lightning struck a pine tree and left a strange inscription, written down the split trunk. A well shaft collapsed and a man's arm was broken in the repair. A boy went missing. The peat they cut burned over-rich and ran down the chimney. There were aches and pains. Boils in inconvenient places. Mothers found out secrets hidden years before, and in the open, before the neighbours, cursed and raged and denied their children. Milk was brought to the boil and burned. Sparks flew from the grate into the baby's cradle. The dog's tooth cracked and began to rot. The blacksmith lost a finger to his hammer and his fire burned in strange colours. The horses shied from their path, avoided their fields, desperate to shamble in the moorland, as if led by the halter, or ridden by an invisible rider. Fish were pulled from the silted bottom of the river, they spoke, they were Catholic fish, they demanded a return to the faith. A seagull appeared at a kitchen table and cawed as the family fled. Its call was a disgusting blasphemy, a word which should never be uttered. A cow fell in the river and lost her milk. The udders were cut and the cow was eaten. Stomachs struggled against the meat and that night, the darkness was spotted with candles laid in the grass while villagers retched and shat the cursed cow.

What use were all his blessings!

Jan began to see twists of his pages discarded on the road, trampled into the ditch.

'Keep your magic.' A woman in the field showed him the scabs that had appeared around her neck – burns, she said, brought there by a paper necklace, tied there a month ago, how could he not remember? After what they had done together?

As Jan walked back one evening, toward his nook in the ruins, having only sold the one piece of paper, a whole figure for a bite of a peasant's lunch, a stone fell to the ground next to him, then another fell short, but scrambled to his heel. Hidden in the rising wheat, someone shouted, 'Heretic!' Another stone sailed over the road. Then one struck the base of his skull. Terrible and sharp, rattling blood across the sky and the fields. A vision of the world burning. Jan closed his eyes and ran, holding the bleeding cut while more stones scattered around him.

'Magician!'

'Papist!' Insults called from the wheat, as if the stones themselves were shouting. Then they appeared. Boys holding sticks, one carrying a rock as big as his head. As Jan stepped onto the road, he tripped, and his stumbling broke their stalemate, and the boys ran toward him, his legs tangled in his satchel; his waist was pulled and a handful of his hair torn out as he fell into a melee of strikes, full of joy expressed against him, life and labour and strength of youth, enforced on him, pride of the community, heat of the blood, brothers and cousins that sang songs when they cut hay and threshed grain, but as they battered Jan, apprentice painter, they were silent.

They lifted him by the satchel and spilt its contents across the path. The book had been reduced to only a few pages, the most ornate, the ones he had been saving, hoping that the black jackets would be overrun by some foreign force, and the chapels redecorated, and maybe a cathedral or two commissioned – those pages would have been his portfolio. They were torn in pieces and scattered around him. Head plastered with algae, kicked into a ditch and rolled around until a little trumpet sounded, and the path was confused. The boys tried to scatter, but horses came among them and ornately dressed soldiers lifted Jan to his feet, and pulled weeds from his eyes. He was turned to face his attackers, held by their collars like a brace of pheasants.

'Who is he?' the soldiers asked the boys.

Their faces pressed together they answered in chorus, 'A magician, a fake priest.'

Asked to respond, Jan, apprentice painter, wilted and fell to the ground, into dreams undergirded by the taste of his blood.

CHAPTER SEVENTEEN

Running up the spiral staircase, Gillis focused on the steps in front of him, as though no obstacle, finish line or podium could intervene in his running, as though the prize, the crowd and every other competitor was irrelevant. All that mattered was the strength of his legs, the placement of his feet and the depth of his lungs. He leant to one side as he circled. Though he quickly discovered the limit of his escape route and stood on the very top step, a small platform at the top of the kirk spire. If only the staircase could have continued a little further. Up through the cloud, connect him to heaven, weave his way through commuting angels to file his complaints. But he was forced to stay put and stand on that top platform with nothing to seal the staircase which was already echoing with policemen's footsteps. He looked around. Nothing but a couple of empty whisky bottles. His lungs began to ache, lactic and stomach acids began to stir. He waited for the voices to quiet, and the footsteps to near. Listened for one voice to rise over the others and call out to him. It asked him to be reasonable, and a uniformed arm appeared. Cormack explained that he was going to come up, and they were going to talk. Gillis reached for the first whisky bottle and flung it into the brickwork above the stairs, spilling glass over the retreating policemen. Then the other. Angry howls echoed up from the stairs below and he heard his dad crying out, 'He's not dangerous, he's just scared!' Gillis scanned the room, but there was nothing else to throw.

He opened the shortbread tin and stared at the severed hand. *What now?* he demanded. *What do I do?*

The severed hand pointed vaguely toward the window, and Gillis scanned the skies for descending horsemen or veils between worlds being torn in two. Nothing on the horizon, nothing rising from the ground. Only Rachel, standing alone in the graveyard, back in both shoes, heels sunk into the moss and scant grass. She stared at an untidy heap of dirt, and the carefully cut grave.

He watched her turn and hold out her hand toward the building's entrance. Jamie walked to meet her. The boy was holding a sheaf of papers. His drawings mixed with the cryptic doodling of the severed hand. When the boy came near, she pulled the hood of his jacket over his head. A long, digestive rumble of thunder circled the kirk. He heard it move across the shadowed landscape, over the town that stretched below him. The fisheries and the empty fields, the high street that curled toward the empty harbour and shingle beach. The clouds lay so heavily that the sea met them in one continuous gradient. From there, the very highest point of Kirkmouth, staring down on the whole town, on the sea beyond it, he could raise the severed hand against the world, watch it take the shape of a fist, and bring that fist down, with overwhelming violence, scattering everything, to start over again.

In his distraction, the officers had regrouped and rounded the last few steps and now stood with their eyes at his ankle height, stepping quietly, trying not to breathe. Behind them the doctor, behind him the crowd, then a short spell in hospital and weekly check-ins with a support group, a bottomless supply of pills and rehabilitation techniques. Their boots scratched the shattered glass and Gillis turned, caught their eyes, pushed his shoulders through the metal framework of the window and stepped out. He felt his weight pitch backward and scrambled to grip the top of the window and a spar of scaffolding. The police officers were talking on their radio and shouting down the stairs while Gillis flung the shortbread tin onto the pitched roof and rushed to follow it as it skittered to the edge, jostled by the uneven tiling, but coming to rest on a jutting nail. He threw one leg onto the roof and it slipped. Tried again and committed this time, stabbed the toe of his shoe into a gap in the stonework and he was up. He scrambled over a layer of rotten leaves and moss. His face was wet, he dried it on his sleeve. Legs were trembling in fear. Rainwater spilt across every surface, and he steadied himself by lying flat. He reached for the shortbread tin and held it to his chest. The severed hand squirmed and pointed upward. Into the black cloud. Cormack's disembodied head appeared at his feet, slowly turned and tried to speak, but all was wind and rain, and beyond him, Rachel and Jamie stared from the empty grave. Gillis pressed into his heels and scaled the steep roof tiles.

The usual fog that hung over the town began to thicken, and the sweet, salted rot of fish coated his mouth as the wind changed. He coughed the smell into his elbow, and ignored all the shouting coming from his feet.

Jump, some were shouting. Others were giggling.

A loose spiral of seagulls ascended to heaven and returned with no message save an incoherent screech. On the horizon, blurred between cloud and sea, no drones and no missile strikes. The established powers seemed to suspect nothing. Why would the light of God's grace and truth have fallen here?

Rain and cloud and roof tile, moss and bird shit, he pushed himself to climb further. To the very peak of the spire and the upright cross.

A golden door might open? Something might be passed to him. Or he might be asked to return the hand to its original owner. The Archangel Michael, or the Pale Rider who announces the end of this world. Or maybe he would be welcomed inside, into the hallways of heaven. The waiting rooms. The conference centre. Might meet one of those terrible beings, the ones with eyes all over its wings and wings all over its eyes. Wheels spinning above and below. A sword for a tongue. He wished he had his Bible with him.

Gillis could slip in and out of these ideas, believing, then not believing, toggling between third and first person, staring down at the crown of his own head, embarrassed and self-conscious. Then back behind his own eyes, staring down at the shortbread tin held in front of him like a weapon.

'Go on, jump,' a man shouted up and was silenced by nervous laughter and an elbow to the ribs.

'See if he slips, you'll be sorry.'

Gillis stood, hands and legs all tangled in the cross. It came to his waist. It rocked a little in its housing. He could see down to them. They shielded their eyes from the falling rain and covered their mouths.

'Jump! Jump! Jump!' Gillis could see a bald man chanting and a woman chasing his mouth with her hand. He dodged her palms with the head movement of a boxer.

Gillis tried to ignore them all. He raised his arms, and the shortbread tin clinked as rain fell inside and soaked the severed hand.

Between his raised elbows, he saw a pulse of blue light down the hill. Curling through the thin woodland, a fire engine was being coaxed up the tight winding road toward the kirk car park, suddenly met with dozens of cars double-parked, and each driver and passenger standing, all staring in one direction. They began to point and shout, and elderly men folded their arms and competed to doubt. 'You'll never get through there.' Looking back and forth at the fire engine jostling, inching forward on clutch control, then over at the building, the scaffolding, the policemen who were shouting illegibly, the mad minister on top, holding something in the air. An engineer, a brickie and a paramedic filtered through the crowd to offer advice, while drivers jangled their keys and shouted at one another, trying to free up space for the fire engine to approach the building. They mounted the kerbs and flattened the last of the flowers.

'Watch these holes!' A lone fireman examined the remainder of the book burning. No one seemed to know who lit the fire or why it was there. Though some folks pointed to the man up there, the boy gripping the spire. Seemed like the kind of thing a guy like that might do. Car followed car onto the grass and drove slowly down the avenues of gravestones. 'On you come, bit more, bit more.' Bumpers rested against graves, wheelbase straddled *Mr and Mrs James McCann, 1876–1924 and 1882–1933*. The drivers read the inscriptions and gave guilty smiles to the crowd. They pulled in their wing mirrors, and the fire engine squeezed through to sit below the spire. People applauded.

Gillis tried to ignore the firemen as they scrambled their ladders and steadied their engine with struts that pressed heavily into the soil of the graves. He tried to concentrate on the elemental forms he was surrounded by. Cloud, wind, rain and perilous height all helped to convey a tone of timeless seriousness, and if it wasn't for the polyester blend of his jacket, and the brittle plastic of his wristwatch, he might have fully convinced himself that he was a prophet of God, having ascended Sinai to receive a few amendments and annotations to the Commandments and Gospels. Here to get the Lord's signature on a few documents. But the cheap fabrics and plastics could all be forgiven, forgotten and ignored, if not for the shortbread tin, that suddenly seemed tacky and inappropriate, disrespectful even. He wished he had stored the severed hand in a more serious material. But he had what he had and he lifted it up as though he was the pageboy at a wedding, or a crown bearer at a coronation.

'Easy, buddy, take it easy.' A yellow helmet and mustard-coloured jacket approached, encased in the caging of a cherry picker. The man yelled from far below the scaffolding. Then tried to argue strategy with the policemen who were leaning out of the windows below, insisting that they had everything under control.

Somewhere in the cloud, a curling staircase might be notched. Maybe the first step would descend to Gillis. Maybe it led toward a throne on which a forgotten king had been waiting. Gathering the parts of his body, pieces which had been scattered in a rancid ritual. Hung, drawn and quartered. Severed head dipped in tar, bowels pulled loose and fried in a skillet, limbs sent around the country to be displayed outside courthouses and jails as warning to the plebs. The great, good leader was reassembling himself from all corners of the country, and Gillis held the last part, the good hand. The one which held the pen, which would write the new covenant and draw a new flag, the one which would hold the sword, and etch a line in blood and earth along the border.

Or maybe there was nothing but rain, that once fallen would be slowly absorbed into mud, easily consumed and immediately forgotten. Replaced by another cloud, another rainfall. He felt embarrassed. Other prophets had been shy, but Gillis was keen to insinuate himself into history. He wanted to act. And he wanted to be seen acting. He wanted to scream at the crowd and be admired for it. To rebel, and to institutionalize his rebellion. Be thanked and congratulated as he upended all existing values. Be hung, drawn and quartered, but survive, retrieve his intestines from the fire burning in front of him and shove them to one side as he gave exclusive interviews, photoshoots of his flattering scars. He wanted to be drawn, painted, carved into stone and cast in bronze, commemorated in song. In a time and place when no one remembered how to draw, or paint, or sculpt, or sing songs. He held the shortbread tin higher, and ignored the shouts coming from the crowd below him, and the fearful instructions coming from the policemen who were trying to summon the courage to climb the scaffolding. He listened to nothing but the building pressure in his own head.

'Easy, pal, are you listening? What I'm going to do is I'm going to. . .' The fireman tried to shout over the wind. He explained that he would open the door of the cherry picker and step onto the scaffolding. Then he would climb to the guttering and onto the roof tiles. He wanted Gillis to hold on where he was. Grip the cross as tight as possible. The man had a carabiner clip in one hand, and a length of rope in the other. But the fireman's first step onto the scaffolding was stopped by a great throat-clearing grumble of thunder that echoed from the back of Kirkmouth. The crowd below were quiet, shielding their eyes from pellets of rain; a spirit had passed over them. Then a flash in the corner of the eye as lightning struck somewhere.

The fireman scrambled back to his cherry picker and called to Gillis. Explaining his regulations. The great risk of pushing an iron cage into the sky in a thunderstorm. Gillis ignored the man's pleas and thrust the severed hand higher, lifted the good leg onto the crossbar of the steel crucifix. They shouted at him, they told him not to, but he bounced from the bad leg and stood there for a second, as high as he could go, as close to heaven as he could get.

raped over a horse, and carried back to the town he had fled from, Jan, once an apprentice painter, now more like a magician, or a wandering healer, a liar either way, soon stood outside the Laird's castle. He had watched its looting, and now he was witness to its revival. The troops that had captured him wore long blue coats that were split up to the waist, so they sat well on either side of their horses. The men looked different from the black jackets, their backs were straighter, their stride was longer, their arms and legs were sinewy and thin. Their strength came from training, not from the fields. Jan was led into a small room lined with ornate woodworking, stained black by threads of smoke tapering from candles which lined the walls. An enormous table separated Jan from a pale interrogator. On the tabletop lay the remnant of his beautiful golden book. The scraps he hadn't had time to sell. A rats' nest of thread, and a handful of tufted paper. The largest scrap flickered in a cold breeze that came through the smashed window. It was St Peter, legless, armless, a holy torso that guarded heaven, and on the other side, a field of flowers that grew from his back. Two paintbrushes lay beside a bradawl and knife, half a carrot, a button, an apple, trodden on. On the other side of the desk, a man draped in a silk gown smiled, exposing a long gap in the bottom row of teeth that his tongue played through. The man examined his fingernails, then combed them back through long, carefully tended hair, that dripped wet at the ends, causing the embroidered silk on his shoulders to darken.

'Are you a pine, magician? Or are you an elm?'

Jan didn't understand the question.

The man had a little plate with the remainder of a meal scattered across it, and as he spoke, he licked his thumb to collect spots of oil, sugar and salt, then dipped his fingers in a cup of water, from which a curl of steam arose. It sat on a little metallic scaffold, suspended over a candle.

'A pine, as you know, will grow a long and straight trunk at the expense of its branches. It reaches upward and sheds its seasons and its years by its needles. Whether we're in spring or autumn, the pine is green. It chooses to grow tightly, along with its kin. So tight, in fact, that they will block any sunlight from the forest floor. Don't they? And their shed needles brown, but refuse to rot. They dry slowly. They work back to the roots of the pine, and rot at the very base, to ensure that their deaths nourish only their own. That's the pine.' The man dried his fingers on the silks and took his cup from its scaffold, swirled the water and drank. Smacked his lips and sighed. 'Or are you like the elm? It grows alone. Even avoids its own kind. Is diminished by another's proximity. Grows wayward, wherever winds press, or rains coerce. And allows even its strongest boughs and branches to imitate the perverse burrowing that goes on beneath the skirts of the earth.' The man enjoyed his words, enjoyed the last of his dinner and enjoyed a lingering look around the room. A coloured glass window, shattered, the heavy oak table, one side eaten by fire, a red cloth draped across the burn, thick, soft candles that melted and merged into the cloth.

'Proddy or Pape?'

Jan didn't know how to answer.

'We've heard about dead calves and poisoned children, ill omens. A strange-shaped moon. And we've been finding these.' He opened a drawer of the enormous table and freed a tangle of paper dollies, crosses, bangles of vellum, painted necklaces and charms, and threw them into the opened wings of the golden book. The man pulled a thick velvet robe from the back of a chair, trimmed with geometric latticework. He looked priestly. Over his head, a golden crucifix pinned the shadows in place. On the table, among the cutlery, manuscripts copied, not printed. Monk's vellum, not paper. The guards wore red leather jerkins under their jackets, metal helmets in place of black hats. There were no leaflets folded and held in the hat band.

'We heard about a country blessing. We were told it was blasphemy. We had other things to worry about. Protestors to chase. Black-jacketed men to find. We have them penned. And we'll shear and geld them soon. And just as we decide to finally go and find you, to taste this blessing ourselves, you fell into a ditch, didn't you?' He sipped at his cup. 'We know that a stream can separate from the river, can't it? And run to the foothills until its water begins to taste mud and take on a strange colour, but it's still river water all the same, it fell from the same mountain and it'll go to the same sea.' The man clutched at the middle of his robes, pulling them from his ankles as he walked around the table. He leant across the tangle of Jan's possessions, flung the carrot and apple to the corner of the room, where a dog suddenly formed from the shadows. 'Collect all these other things.'

Jan pulled together the nest of binding thread, the feathered bunches of torn paper and followed the man, flanked by silent guards, down the dark corridors of the vast house. The delicate tapestries had been rehung, despite the holes burned or torn into them. The house was being scrubbed and washed, waxed and varnished, restitched and resewn.

The man spoke over his shoulder as he walked. 'These black jackets arrive like locusts and strip the harvest of a hundred years, then leave. Forcing us who care and tend for the fields to sow our seeds again and wait for the reaping.'

They walked to the very end of the house, where the robed man chapped on a locked door. A latch unbolted and they entered. The room was empty, save for an odd hillock made of rugs and blankets, capped with dozens of jackets and shirts of different colours. An enormous fire flicked sparks onto the floorboards, emanating so much heat and light that Jan's face felt dry and tight as he entered. Slashed canvases and bedsheets had been stuffed into the splintered frames of broken windows, but the empty corners whistled. The remaining glass was wet on both sides. As they approached the fire, they could see that beneath the great heap of fabric lay a head.

'We found him for you. . .' The man in silk waded through the shallows of the piled fabric, to touch the head. It stirred and met them with a child's awakening smile, plastered to the crooked profile, bulbous nose, empty gaze and overbite of the rightful Laird. Sweating and coughing.

'Green can be symbolic of rejuvenation,' Jan said. On the bedding before him, stretched out as though expecting to be eaten, the Laird's bare leg, its flesh multicoloured, rotten and infected.

'Scratched by a loose nail in the carriage they took him away in. Isn't that right?'

The Laird nodded.

'And these black spots,' Jan pointed along the shin. 'Again, the earth is black, and seeds grow in darkness. As an illuminator, I'd be happy to have a leg like this.' Jan pointed to parts beyond the wound where dark purple bruises had seeped inward to the bone.

'This is a great healer we've brought to you,' the man in silk robes shouted over Jan's head to the Laird, 'who raised a stillborn calf back to its feet. And freed the tongue of a mute child. The crops he has blessed have begun to flower already!' The robed man kicked at Jan's foot, and the painter nodded along; sorting through the tormented scraps of his book, turning whirls of thread through his hands like unravelled knitting, he clutched at a knot of tangled paper, until he found some plausible remnants of a saint. He looked up for approval, but the robed priest's lips were sealed shut. Jan asked for a knife, and began to cut the paper, outlining the head and shoulders of the saint, torso turned to ash. Found a pair of legs on the reverse and folded the two pieces so they hung together. Then an angel that gripped a trumpet, whistling into oblivion, gave up its arm and the tattered paper saint was complete. Jan carefully laid it across the Laird's bare chest, where stumps of his ribcage shifted below the skin. The nobleman drew a laboured breath, and the head of the paper saint lifted, its expression very doubtful. The silk robes were joined by velvets, thin leathers and felts, soft suede boots padded from the outer corridors to stand just out of Jan's sight. On the outskirts of his vision, they whispered. Priests and deacons, captains and knights of useless patches of field and coast, merchants, the vengeful establishment of those parts and the parts next to them. Back with a dying man at their helm. Whose restoration implied their victory over cousins and errant brothers, usurping heirs and upstart rivals who had assembled under the banner of the black jacket. They watched as Jan pretended to pray. They whispered that this was peasant magic. The sorcerer, apparently, had made a mute calf speak again. The Laird's eyes were watering. Using words from his own language, Jan pretended to pray in a magical tongue, repeating the name of herbs and trees, rabbits, deer, carrot stew, soured milk, swollen oats, wild raspberries, chopped liver, blood mixed into gravy, ham hock, roast tatties, lentils boiled to green paste, mixed with chopped garlic leaves, salmon, bound in a wet paste of herbs, buried beneath a fire and dug back up, scorched in the coals. His stomach rumbled as he cut pieces of vellum and tied them around the Laird's wrists, and crossed himself over and over again, crossed the Laird, until he lost track of his movements and began to draw odd letters, squares, meaningless symbols, lightning bolts; his mind wandered, mouth muttered and slurred as he pretended to pray into the dark night.

Even by pale candlelight, Jan could see the Laird's body changing by the hour. The swollen yellow skin, the greenish knee, the wound below, spotted black, like a tree dotted with hardening wasp galls. Blood began to rust in the sheets as the body lost its limits, blushing purple as the blood congealed in the trough of veins, collected at the elbow, heel and ear, and abandoned the toes, fingers and face. The hands began to look like parsnips, the toes, a cluster of green potatoes, while the face changed expression, moving from pain to surprise, to eager anticipation. An idiot's joy, the blackened teeth were pressed apart by a swollen tongue tinted blue, the eyebrows arched back from the eyes, stretching skin until it folded. The Laird was dead. He looked like he was biting his tongue, and desperately holding back laughter.

CHAPTER EIGHTEEN

Something would happen. Gillis tottered and wobbled, balancing on the metal cross, the crowd below gasped and screamed as he dropped one leg to the roof tiles and jumped back up, pushing his shortbread tin into the wind and cloud. Something had to happen.

'He's wanting attention, and we're giving him it.' An old biddy tried to drag people from the crowd, but they ignored her, hands gripping their mouths, eyes fixed on the spire. The firemen were arguing with the police.

A good and happy ending. Engine noises, whirling lights, something had to happen. The clouds were holding back, the storm was gathering, the surface of the world was wearing thin, and everything which lies hidden behind all routine would be forced to reveal itself. The icons were about to be broken, the images were about to be burned and Gillis would take the very first step. He raised his hands even higher, and forgot about his feet. He expected to be taken and raised and wielded like a weapon, his skull used to smash the fractured kirk and pursue the people.

The wind pushed at his shoulders as though holding him back from a fight, but nothing spoke from inside the wind. Down to one side, the remains of his books lay in ash. Nothing spoke from the embers. A crow struggled against the wind and rested for a moment on the guttering below him. He expected it to turn into a devil, tempt him with worldly riches and fame, a do-over, a re-run. Not go to England, not kick rival in arse, not fuck the leg, not walk away from Rachel. And then what? He'd have to go back further. Away into childhood. Become someone else. And why not, if the Devil could get him a do-over, surely he could get him substituted too. The crow limped twice and leapt from the edge, blown back the way it came.

Didn't you need this? He held the severed hand to the sky. *Was I meant to find it?* He wanted to ask. *Am I here by mistake?*

And then, finally.

An answer.

The sky flinched and split with white static that he couldn't see. It broke above him, and raced toward earth, through cloud and rain; a great connection finally made, a tiny little line, a spark between the heavens and earth, found the young minister, metallic conductor swinging around his head. As Gillis fell, his feet tangled through the cross, and he clattered onto the roof tiles, his teeth rattled, his bones began to glow, and the slate, then stone, then earth absorbed a great fork of lightning that leapt from the centre of the storm. An enormous pain, a single brilliant syllable spoken by every part of his body. Affirmation in every hair, sprung outward from its follicle. Every existing connection of his brain, lit all at once, every memory activated, every idea, every moment, linked into one substance, kindling for the fire in his body. Every muscle strained to capacity, in the very fullness of possible strength. Eyes as wide as they would go, eyebrows at their apex, as if the holes in his skin might slip and expose yellowed bone. That bright and violent unity once spoken, went silent, and his body fell into darkness, and his thoughts were finally quiet.

But his ankle hurt. He couldn't lift his head to look at it. He was upside down, staring into clouds only confused by the steel cross, its arms buckled by his fall. His trouser leg was tangled in the lead flashing which sealed the roof tiles. A long crack of pain ran down his body, twisting across his kneecap and into the small of his back as he squirmed to tear his suit trousers free. He turned in panic and pushed himself around until he could grip something solid. He grabbed onto a jut of scaffolding and searched around the spire. The shortbread tin was missing. He looked into the sky. Had it been taken to heaven? He stared at the chaotic forms of clouds overhead, but nothing remained. He felt a great joy in his heart, and a painful cold across his body. Had he succeeded, had he delivered the hand back where it belonged, in heaven?

He turned to the scaffolding and groaned. No. It had fallen to the back of the building and was stuck in a buckled corner of the gutter, and as he leant over to retrieve it from the dreck which pooled there, he spotted, three storeys below, the shortbread tin and its lid, two golden rectangles in the grey and green. He pushed the severed hand and the muck that came with it into the pocket of his jacket and cleared his throat. There was no one below him, and it looked as though the fire engine had been abandoned, the cherry picker was empty, and the graves on that side of the building were quiet. He sprawled across the steeple and crawled back to the apex; the crowd were collected by the front of the building. A whirl of panicked screaming, the police and firemen were pushing through it all. Something must have happened. Gillis sat alone on the top of the spire. Strange to be ignored. He patted the severed hand in his pocket and opened some shirt buttons to touch the drawings he had stuffed down the waist of his trousers. Nothing was a dream. Everything was real. There was more thunder. He watched the edges of the crowd, several people on their phones, trying to describe their location. An ambulance fought through the woods, up the whirling driveway, into the wake of the fire engine. Gillis carefully lowered himself to the scaffolding and climbed back inside the building.

'This is your chance, ya dafty.' Gillis had only managed to sit down and indulge in one melancholic sigh before his dad had climbed the spiral staircase and pulled him to his feet. 'Here we are, here we go, one step at a time,' the two slipped and stumbled down the narrow stairs, shoulders scuffing brickwork as they unwound the great screw, the heightening tension as Gillis had reached the summit and apex of all these past months, one man alone, standing on the tiniest platform, finally facing heaven, about to ask the biggest question, all undone in two minutes. His dad hushed him as they tiptoed down the kirk hallway and through the hall. Douglas still lay there. The room brightly lit, completely empty, his coffin unaccompanied, the body waiting to be buried. They ran through, Dad pushing Gillis in front of him.

'Is it on you?' At the fire exit, Gillis's dad searched his pockets, pulling clumps of leaves and moss from the jacket until he discovered the pale fingers of the severed hand. He stuffed it back in and pulled the jacket from Gillis's shoulders, twisting it into a knot around the severed hand. 'We'll get it in that grave.'

The crowd was collected tightly together, and a sickening noise rose from its middle. A kind of animalistic groan which they were desperate to stop. They pulled the perpetrator out of the circle, and led her to a gravestone. 'Breathe in, one, two, three. And out.' It was a panic attack, they said. 'Breathe in, one, two, three, let's all do it together, out, one, two, three.' A knot of people surrounded the woman and closed their eyes in order to breathe in harmony.

People were shouting instructions to one another. 'Give him some space, please, folks,' Nichol was taking charge, trying to press the crowd away from its centre, but some horrific sight kept drawing them back to the middle. They would walk away, repeating blasphemies until they became prayers, *oh God, oh Christ, oh Jesus fucking Christ,* only to approach again from the opposite side, needing news and updates.

'What's happening?'

'Is he OK?'

'What are they doing?' The paramedics were flitting back and forth from their van with drugs and syringes and machines that came in their own box. Morbid curiosity blended with a solemn vigil that kept all eyes in the centre. The empty grave was unattended, even the gravedigger had abandoned his post. He was circling the very outside of the crowd, waving his head in sorrow and muttering, 'He's fucked, the wee man's absolutely fucked.'

'How can you talk like that?' a woman told him off.

'It's not like I think it's a good thing,' he waved his racing paper at her and they argued until others hushed them. It was no time for that kind of thing.

Gillis's dad held him by the shirtsleeve and pulled him away, circling round the back of the little orange digger whose motor was still running, and quickly chipped the balled jacket and the severed hand into the bottom, then pushed his foot deep into the loose soil and dragged it over the crisp edge of the grave. Wet black mud covered the jacket and if the fingers of the severed hand could have been seen, they were clutching at nothing, waving, or grasping, or asking for a pen. One last image to relay. *A good and happy ending.* Was this it? Gillis looked around him. Pulled his hand back through his hair and wiped the rain out of his eyes.

'Did we do it?' Gillis asked his dad.

'What? Do what?' Dad trod into the heaped soil again and flung more clods of dirt down until the jacket had disappeared.

'Was that it?' Gillis asked.

'That was it son, come on.' The car was boxed in on each side, and it looked freshly scraped on one corner. 'Who's the bastard who. . .' Dad struggled to swallow the loss, wouldn't matter when they were on the run. Rust would set in long after the resolution of this debacle. But still, it was the principle of the thing. He couldn't even get his front door to open wide enough for his belly to squeeze through. 'What kind of idiot parks that close?' But the motors were three deep, and there was no chance of getting out until the whole crowd had disappeared. None the less, he went swaggering into the crowd asking after the owner of a red Peugeot and a black Beamer, some flash fucker was triple-parked.

The crowd angrily hushed the pair of them, parting for a stretcher to be pulled from the ambulance. The paramedics disappeared beneath the assembled shoulders, and when they stood again, they raised the stretcher easily. Exhausted sighs and downward-spiralling whistles, sobs and complaints and fists shaken at heaven. A tiny body lay on the stretcher. Jamie, his black suit destroyed, now twists of burnt fabric, his skin smouldering. They carried him into the van and whirled the lights. Rachel stottered through the crowd like an exhausted long-distance champion, her arms being held and her legs being supported by the people around her. They reached out as she passed, like fans clutching for their part of a great victory. She climbed three steps into the ambulance and turned around to look at the crowd, ready for a bottle of champagne and an armful of flowers. They pushed her inside and there was some argument over who could take second and third place. The judges deliberated and controversially decided on Nichol, alongside the mother-in-law.

'I think I got hit too.' Gillis tried to pull at the paramedic as she passed him, collecting gear scattered over the ground, but the young woman quickly turned and shook her uniform out of his clutches. She looked him over, turned his hands back and forth, looked into his pupils.

'You seem fine,' she said.

'Maybe it scuffed me, but hit him proper.'

'You'd know about it,' she reassured him.

They slammed the doors closed, retreated between the graves and backed slowly downhill, ushered by several helpful mourners.

'A little further,' they said. 'On you come.'

After the ambulance had pulled out onto the main road, sounded its alarm and whirled its lights, eyes began to turn from the woodlands downhill and return to the spire, the fire engine, and the sodden smoke coming from the pyre of books. Eventually, they found Gillis standing among them, easy to spot with that little white ticket sitting over his Adam's apple. After a few minutes of uneasy silence, the questions started.

The Laird was dead. Jan's magic had failed. The gold paint looked false against greening skin. When the priests arrived, they screamed in outrage. A great man had died with a wizard by his side, a beggar, a foreign trinket-pedlar. The magistrates and military officers quickly abandoned the body and disappeared to spar in the rooms adjacent. Lower Lairds, who owned mounds of rotten brick plonked on infertile land, jostled against nephews and cousins of the Laird, who made uncertain claims based on barely sketched family trees, saplings which they held at arms' length, avoiding scrutiny until their men arrived with their swords.

Jan was marched through corridors, he would be the last stinking peasant to walk through those rooms for hundreds and hundreds of years. Expecting to be thrown into a cell, or a hole in the ground, he was confused when a grand doorway opened for him, a door ornately carved with looping vines of ivy. It was the grand hall, its flagstone floor covered in straw, and in one corner, two dozen men in black jackets stabled there. Imprisoned and miserable, they barely looked up as Jan entered. Their faces were blotched with cuts and bruises, they were lying down, or sitting with their heads propped against the wall, dreaming of Protestant heaven.

Over the next days of imprisonment, the scorched earth where the books and paintings had burned were filled with the cutting and planing of joists and planks of timber. A sweet and springlike smell drifted from the courtyard. Watching from the high windows of the grand hall, the imprisoned black jackets thought that gallows were being built. They were wrong. Holes were dug, and the timbers were half-buried to stand upright. Dried reeds were cut from the riverside and brought by the wagonload. Bound in sheaves, they were stored alongside the prisoners.

'They're going to set us on fire,' one of the men was panicking.

The black jackets denied it, comforted and silenced him.

'They're going to set us on fire.'

They denied and silenced and prayed.

'They're going to set us on fire.'

They cradled him in their arms as they denied it all again.

'Yes, they will.' Brother Malcolm had been imprisoned within the imprisonment. Enemy of both sides, ranter and blasphemer, he was tied up in a far corner of the hall. He had worked the gag out of his mouth by wriggling his tongue and grousing his lips. 'And they will burn me too. Do you doubt their sin? Errant brothers, think of the locks of your hair as a wick, and your body as a candle being lit in heaven, and imagine the Lord carrying His lantern down to earth, intending to fight the shadows which have stricken this nation. In the hundreds of years that will pass as He walks the long path to us, what will He find on His arrival? Friends, it will be a world stricken with illumination. Where no beastie or devil can hide. Every child, born like kindling, will burn when embraced by its mother and father, because each of them will be a burning torch, and their house will be built from smouldering embers. And their words will be air for that fire. Because your bodies will light fires which cannot go out, the Lord will pass unnoticed, just as one log cannot be discerned from another when flung into the grate of a fire, He will carry His lantern beyond this world. Repent, disgrace yourself, refuse to burn. The world must remain dark.'

The guards forced sackcloth back into his mouth and bound his head with twine.

The black jackets sang Psalms as they were bound to a rope and dragged from the hall. Jan tried to protest, he was only an apprentice painter! They were led through a loud, berating crowd, marbled with soldiers, priests and men loyal to the dead Laird. Four great staves had been driven into the ground, and surrounded by fresh, dry timber and bundled reeds. The magistrates spoke terrifying sentences over the black jackets, demanding their repentance. They refused and sang louder. The pyres were lit.

A priest climbed the newly built stage and screamed a history of defamation, brought up the Devil, mentioned certain animals, cats and owls, lately spotted walking in troupes behind these men. He held up the very last fragments of Jan's magical book.

'These glimpses of heaven were created in the low and desperate countries, by the finest illuminators, whose fingers and eyes are blessed by God, who are mercilessly persecuted for following true religion and pursuing their only calling. Our blessed Laird ordered this book to be created to open windows and let in cooling breezes from heavenly fields. To display in our chapel.' The priest held out the pages. 'Truly precious, bought with your taxes, burnt and torn by the heretics stabled here. Stolen and hawked by a thief here with them. People, what is your judgement?' He climbed down from his scaffold and walked among the first of the crowd. Showing them the contrasting pages. 'Compare, please, to

this,' and the priest showed a crumpled pamphlet, pulled
from a hat brim, which had lived through a long campaign
across the country. Soaked and frozen and singed in the fires
of several chapels and abbeys. The blotted black ink portrayed
the whore of Babylon squatting above a hole; underneath
her splayed crotch, a hoard of animals dressed in bishop's
robes and kingly garments, these were her children and her
incestuous suitors. On the other hand, the pale, thin body
of a virgin, skin blushing rose, offended by the sinner's gaze,
draped in silk, expressed in whispering yellow, cut with ochre
and scarlet daggers that were breaching and destroying her
body. 'Tell me which of these brings the new world closer?'
He held the images to the peasant crowd, and they squinted
and frowned, puzzling over what lay before them.

'Which?' he demanded. But the more they looked, the
more the virgin looked whorish and the whore looked
virginal. The coloured image was stained black with soot,
and the black print was peppered with so many stains that it
seemed finely, if eccentrically, illuminated.

The first of the prisoners was taken from the group, and
his right hand was tied to an iron ring on the end of a long
pike. He was brought toward the flames. They read out
charges of heresy and blasphemy, which the prisoner denied.
Then the pike was pushed into the centre of the fire and the
prisoner screamed. The magistrate tapped the pike with a
loose reed, and it was pulled from the fire. The restless crowd
pushed forward to look at the wound. Embers clung to the
man's skin. They laughed in disgust at the crackling noise
that the skin was making.

'Do you repent? Do you renounce?'

The prisoner refused and his hand was pushed deeper into
the fire. His legs collapsed, and the hand was returned to him
ruined, a charred lump of black flesh. The rope which had

tied him in place twisted loose and the man folded around his dead hand.

'Do you repent?'

'No.'

The black jackets shouted encouragements and sang together when the soldiers came by. Several volunteered to go next. The ground was slick with piss, and their legs were trembling, but they marched out and refused to repent, so their hands or feet were burned, and they refused again, so a group of four were tied to the trunk of a birch tree. Smouldering reeds were stacked in thick bundles that reached their chests. The crowd, who had laughed and taunted, were now silent, except for a slight crinkling noise. A pail of boiled eggs was being passed throughout the crowd, and like speckles of the first snow, or cherry blossoms in spring, eggshell littered the dark mud.

'Save yourself and repent!' a peasant yelled through spattered yolk. The bottom stack of reeds was smeared with paraffin oil, and a taper was brought to the edge. The men were asked again, *Renounce your heresy*. They refused and the pyre was lit. A sulphurous spirit of grey smoke began to move throughout the crowd. From their bindings, the four black jackets preached, staring deep into the eyes of the crowd and demanding that they search their conscience. Eggshell clung to the people's beards, rainwater fell on their bald patches, filthy puddles leaked into their clogs, crotches, arses and armpits itched with ticks and fleas, bellies were half-empty, arms and legs stripped to sinew by grappling with the earth. Terrified that these endless rains would rot or flood the crops, the men looked back at the preachers in sympathetic confusion.

The women, swollen with children, nipples scarred by teeth marks, hands stained black by the dark soil and scarred white with scouring lye, fingers with knuckles missing, notches cut from their thumbs and big toes, marks of the sickle and scythe, children at their feet and in their arms, moving around the world like severed limbs that refused to reattach, they looked at the martyrs in baffled empathy. But they liked their Psalm singing, and they enjoyed the tears that were falling from their own eyes and the eyes of their friends and the softness they were allowed to show one another. Pity for the damned, in their defiance of the Church and the Laird and magistrates. They clutched the rabbit fur and stoat skin that wound around their necks, and stole the very last grasp of warmth from these creatures to kindle their own. Where had it gone? Would it ever return? They saw the men burning and mourned for themselves.

Jan tried to scrape at the earth, tried to press himself to the back of the group, but as the prisoners sang and prayed and demanded bravery from one another, they pushed Jan to the front with fly elbows and knees. The guards bound his hands to a long iron pike and marched him toward the pyre.

'I repent,' he said immediately.

Maybe the guard couldn't hear, the leather flaps of his helmet muffled his ears.

'I repent,' he said to the first priest he passed. The man was staring at the harsh beauty of the pyre, and he frowned and turned his face away from Jan.

'I repent.' The row of soldiers stared at the crowd, the crowd stared at the men still burning, now angular and dead. The head priest, his white silks charred yellow by the smoke, demanded in ornate language that Jan repent.

'I do, I repent.'

But the pike was forced into the reeds anyway. He fell around on the ground, kicking at the flames that scurried over his body. He writhed and shouted, 'I repent! I repent! I repent!'

Pressed his shoulder and cheek into the ground, took to his knees, then held up his hand. Blanched, weeping red and yellow, it looked as though it had been painted by a child. 'I repent,' he told the soldier, 'I repent, I repent,' he told the priest and magistrate. The Psalm singing stopped, the black jackets were embarrassed. And the screaming and crying crowd began to sniffle and wipe noses across their sleeves. Jan stared into the crowd, looking for a sympathetic face, but they shied and demurred, mute until he caught the eyes of an old man, stooped and wizened. The man's face was gurning, eyebrows bowed in comic pity, mouth upturned and toothless, he whined in a weaselling voice, 'Ooooh. . . I repent.'

CHAPTER NINETEEN

A week passed in someone else's clothes. Someone else's bed. Grey joggers, black jumper, oversized slippers. A room to himself. A door that didn't lock. A cabinet to keep his things in. Gillis had to speak to people. Had to explain. Did his best to keep the lies consistent. Ate cereal, sandwiches, pie and beans, tomato pasta. Hospital food. Grey coffee.

The high-vis jackets, the lanyards and latex gloves, had all been reassuring. They wipe clean. They smell of disinfectant. Gillis was held in a world of impersonal plastic, pastel-coloured walls and flowery bedding, that suspended time and space; his mind had been dooked in bubbly dishwater and scrubbed, then sat to one side to drip dry.

There was something tempting in the free meals, the starched white hospital sheets and the unlimited attention of medical professionals. No obligation to wear trousers or tie his shoelaces.

In one black evening, Gillis succumbed to the temptation, and wondered if he had been learning about himself. Important things which other people could learn from. Maybe he could go on telly to talk about them, and be paid a lot of money. He could speak consoling words to the nation. He could become a relatable figure. *I thought I was a prophet of God*, he could say. And allow them to laugh. *I thought the nation could be saved from itself. And it was all up to me.* They'd nod. Been there. Done that. He could spend all of his money on clothes. Haircuts. Interesting socks and boldly patterned ties. House with a garden. That would be something.

He received visits.

'You should have told me,' his dad sat on the end of his bed. 'Made a fool of myself, trying to take the blame. Almost got myself arrested.'

Gillis had been claiming that the severed hand was made of plastic. A joke shop prop, bought to provoke conversation. 'Thought I could force them to believe. Drum up some customers for the kirk.' Then he'd laugh, and pretend that the delusions were melting away.

'Get your things together,' his dad was clean-shaven, well dressed, off the sick and back at work.

They gave him a black bin bag, and he filled it with the clothes they had loaned him, and the paintings they had helped him make. One, a lazy sketch of the industrial estates which backed the hospital, and two, a bright portrait, cheerful propaganda he had made to show his healing process. Nice smile, red lips, pink cheeks. In the background, his childhood home. 'I want to look after little Gillis,' he spoke through gritted teeth. 'It's time to begin to heal. My trauma.'

He had filled the journal they were encouraging him to keep with the plotlines of films and novels. 'I'm not ready to share just yet,' he held it close to his chest.

The nurses came in to change the bedsheets, and asked to look through his bin bag. They took a draughts board and a pack of felt tips. 'These are for sharing.' They let him keep the jumper and joggers, but they wanted the slippers back. 'And you're forgetting this.'

The black suit he had arrived in. Washed, pressed and folded at the bottom of his cabinet, no sign of the mud and moss that had plastered him when he arrived. The only remnant of his ordeal, the trouser cuffs, torn, snagged on the iron crucifix. He pushed it all into the bin.

'Keep hold of that, son,' his dad said, fishing it back out again. 'You'll need it for job interviews.'

'Everything's still here.' His dad pointed to a shelf full of trophies, and a rat's nest of medals sitting on the desk. There were boxes stacked on a single bed, posters on the wall which had turned yellow. Running magazines stacked in a corner. Spiked trainers festering in the cupboard. His dad invited him to watch TV, invited him to boil the kettle and make himself a sandwich. Reminded him how to use the shower, how to use the washing machine. How to rinse and separate the recycling. It had been years since they had lived together, and the rooms all seemed like foreign territory.

'I'll get a job,' he promised.

'No need, no need for now.'

Gillis asked around in the library and sports centre. But you needed an HND for both of those. He asked in the warehouses, but they wanted a forklift licence. He asked in the garden centre and the discount furniture outlet.

'We're all full, mate, you've just missed the Christmas intake.'

Same story in the post office.

'What skills do you have?' they asked him at the job centre. Former athlete, former minister. Degree in Divinity.

'What's that?' they asked. He struggled to explain.

'But what would it get you a job doing?'

He wasn't sure.

The customer service desk at the big supermarket seemed to be staffed by children. They took his CV, and then seemed to drop it into a bin. They denied it when Gillis confronted them.

Soon, his only options would be the fishmongers, the fish farms and smokeries, or the Nicholson Hotel.

It takes twenty minutes to do anything, Gillis thought. Ten minutes to square up to it, five minutes to do it, five minutes to wind down. Then you've got ten minutes to wind yourself back up, ready for the next thing. Smaller and smaller tasks revealed the twenty minutes hidden inside them. Waking up, sitting up, going for a piss, walking downstairs, turning on the telly, focusing your eyes on the screen, where does the day go? He had to push breakfast and lunch together. Printed out a few CVs and trotted back through town. Past the petrol station and car garage.

'Finish your apprenticeship? No? Did you do one?'

Gillis tried to ask how old you had to be for the cut-off, but they thought he was kidding. 'Thought you might need a guy to go fetch spanners or something, cheers anyway.' Gillis stuck his thumb in the air as he walked away. Twenty minutes for the embarrassment to dull down. Twenty minutes to nip into a corner shop and buy a packet of crisps. Twenty minutes to eat them, twenty minutes to fold the packet and tie it in a bow. Twenty minutes to find a bin.

Twenty minutes staring in the window of a letting agent's.

Comfortable two-bed detached house in startling location.

It was the manse. Twenty minutes became forty, became fifty, then lost all boundaries as the sun fell, and in darkness he climbed back up the hill to his peaceful congregation. Stone dykes and trees stripped bare of their leaves. Sheep and cows and the empty manse which he circled slowly, staring into each window, almost expecting to see himself, stumbling inside with a muddy shovel, terrified on that first encounter with the severed hand, begging it to stop existing. But there was nothing there. The carpets had been replaced, and the furniture was all stacked in one room, ready for the skip.

All of the holes he had dug in the garden had been filled in, and half a dozen offcuts of AstroTurf had been trampled end to end, barely disguising the muck beneath. And the heaving great stump of the elm tree, resistant to tow trucks and tractors, chainsaws, axes and diggers, had somehow been lifted and flung upside down into a distant corner of the garden. Its roots lay across the hedges like the arms of a prize fighter finally defeated, confused and tangled in the ropes. Gillis squeezed through the hedge, staring upward. The kirk lay even further askew, all pinned and held in place by sturdy brackets of scaffolding that now encased the whole building. Broad sheets of blue tarp rippled lazily in the wind, and beneath them, a terrible fracture in the brickwork led to a true split. The sandstone had crumbled and fresh-looking pieces lay on the ground. He couldn't see the cross he had held on to, or the slates he had slipped across. And he couldn't find a statue or a plaque or a tour guide who could tell him that Gillis, the young minister, had here, on this very spot, confronted his destiny and thrust a sacred, severed hand up to heaven and in return, been struck by lightning.

No one believed him. Not even Nichol, who denied it all, and distanced himself. And when the wind turned westerly and reeked, it seemed that even the miracles had come unstuck and lost faith in themselves. They all thought he was glory-hunting. But he'd been specially selected, mandated and chosen. Protected by hidden powers. Struck, or at least scuffed, by a bolt of lightning. Gillis listened as an imagined tour guide continued. *Some say that the severed hand was taken up to heaven. Where it remains to this day, waiting for the moment that a true prophet, a greater man than our minister, a man who can run a four-minute mile, and hold down a decent job, whose salary increases with inflation, and who at a critical moment of his life chooses not to kick an English boy up the arse, will return and climb the spiral staircase and reach into that cloud.*

And then what? Gillis pushed the tarpaulin aside and circled the building. Although it was dark, the kirkyard looked different. As if some other part of the world had been stitched onto Kirkmouth, and here's where the seam showed. There was an empty space where the dead should have been. The headstones were all gone and the dirt that remained was a mess of tyre tracks.

Others say that the severed hand was flung into an empty grave. Gillis walked onto the churned and settled soil. He tried to remember where the grave had been, walked to the fencing that limited the kirkyard and took long strides back and forth, measuring according to his memory.

'Here-ish,' he dug his heel into the earth. 'Or here.' He tried to scrape a cross there with his fingers, but the soil was partly frozen. He looked around for a stone or a stick.

And here, the tour guide pointed to a hidden corner of the kirkyard. *Several enormous stacks of rectangular rock.* Every gravestone had been wrenched from its place and layered into an enormous drystone dyke. Many of the gravestones lay broken, their names and dates confused.

'He actually did it.' Gillis's voice sounded strange. No one was there to hear it except him.

'You could walk out a job on the Friday, straight into another on the Monday,' as his dad checked the progress of a tray of oven chips, anecdotes from all throughout his working life mingled into a feeling that things were getting worse, and were only trending downward.

'I'd get you a job in my place, but. . .' His dad gave an apologetic eye roll, and Gillis made understanding noises. There's a limit.

Gillis finished laying a checkered tablecloth and two plates, can of Best split between them, cutlery flung in the middle. They were trying to avoid the TV. You can watch too much of that thing.

'You'll be needing this.' As Gillis took his seat, his dad placed a heavy envelope on the empty plate before him. It was around a handspan wide. Gillis turned it over, it weighed the same as his shortbread tin.

'You didn't?'

His dad smiled, 'It was no trouble.'

There was nothing sacred inside. Instead, a white box with a sleek pull tab on one end. Stiff plastic and cardboard delicately unfurled to reveal a stern, shiny black rectangle. Gillis peeled a layer of plastic from the screen.

'For a new way of life,' his dad patted his shoulder. 'Isn't that right?'

They went through the menus together. Setting up contacts, downloading apps.

'You can do all kinds of things.'

They placed a bet on that evening's football. They set the alarm clock and put their birthdays in the calendar. His dad made him stand against the kitchen wall, and subjected him to the cold glare of the internal camera. With these pictures, he finally joined social media.

'If you don't have one, folk'll think, *Why doesn't he have one?*' They uploaded images of Gillis with his extended family. Pictures of him on the bottom tier of a podium, grimacing, splattered with mud. They added his uncle and his dad's friends. It felt like they were getting their stories straight. Giving him an alibi for some future accusation.

'Do you not have anyone you want to add?' His dad pointed to a rounded box at the top of the screen. 'You just have to type their name in there.'

Gillis could only think of one person.

Thanks for all of your lovely comments, Rachel had posted several updates. A link to a newspaper article. *This explains everything better than I can.* Boy hit by lightning. Critical condition. Turning a corner. On the mend. Thoughts and prayers. Who was to blame? And what could we learn?

The comments below the article prayed that Jamie would recover quickly. Or that his family would find the strength to cope with his inevitable death. Further down, they began to doubt the story. Why would a bolt of lightning avoid the highest possible point? This, commenters claimed, was *physically* impossible. As in, according to *actual physics*. A church steeple with scaffolding, surrounded by trees, and below that, dozens of metal cars and a small crowd of adults; even the gravestones were taller than the boy who was hit. He must have been standing next to something. Holding a big lump of metal maybe. But the news report said otherwise. Rachel was quoted, saying she had never let go of the boy's hand. But seemingly, the lightning had spared her. Again, this was *physically* impossible.

Not trying to be nasty but the boy's mum literally must be lying. Definitely lying because that couldn't happen.

Luckily, the article said, emergency services were already in attendance, due to an ongoing, unrelated incident.

'Unrelated to what?' Gillis pointed out his appearance in the story.

His dad craned his head backward, then searched the table for his glasses. 'Papers don't report on suicides, really. In case it gives anyone the idea.' He trailed off. Then suddenly touched Gillis on his inner elbow. 'Not that you were trying to do a suicide. But you know what I mean.'

Gillis didn't know. And didn't want to ask.

'You should really go and visit,' his dad advised him.

'I wouldn't know what to say.'

A disappointed crowd, denied its tears, laughed as Jan was led away from the burning pyres and his confession was taken by a pair of priests, who pretended to rejoice at the return of a repentant sinner, while they stared over his shoulder at the black jackets who had refused. The priests incanted ornate language over Jan's wounds. They forced his hands together into prayerful submission, and the skin cracked and bled, the burns began to reveal their anger. He recanted and renounced and was paraded in front of the black jackets as an example.

'Why not repent, all of you? Save yourselves from the pyre.'

The prisoners stared with contempt. Behind him, the martyrs slumped and fell silent, their bodies impassive to the flames. Jan was held above the crowd.

'They are rejoicing in heaven,' his captors shouted, 'at the saving of one sinner.'

The crowd tried to cheer, but they saw men who weren't on fire every day. Their attention turned back to the flames.

Jan staggered toward his freedom, falling into a darkness within. They pursued him with slaps to the cheek, with water and shaken shoulders, to route him from where he had hidden, but his eyes wouldn't open. They dipped his tortured hand in cool rainwater and swabbed it with rags. They bound the weeping wounds into a tightened gall. His escape continued, beyond his body. They folded a blanket and laid it beneath his head. His eyelids flickered back and forth, he saw angels struggling to master their instruments, he saw a crowd of people, swarming toward the gates, flinching from the awkward music. By the gate, a saint was taking the names of all new entrants and writing them in the vast book of life.

'I can write myself,' Jan said with pride; taking the thin wooden pen from the saint's hand, he searched for a pot of ink, but found that the reed had splintered and was stuck in his finger. Blood leaked from the cut through the hollow reed, and dripped from the notched end. His knuckles spread as the reed began to swell and grow. A fresh green shoot appeared at the top of the pen, and sprouted a leaf. Tender roots reached from the heel of his hand and crawled across the surface of the book. New shoots and branches of the reed sprouted through his wrist and the flesh, the book, the ink and the pen were suddenly all one. He fell backward in panic, and pulled the book of life from the golden table. Pursued by saints and angels, he pushed his way through crowds waiting to be inducted into heaven, drowned men, murdered women, disease-addled children. He flung himself beyond and fell through the cloud, tumbling through white and grey and darker grey and black, and suddenly, Jan felt a torrent of cold raindrops, pursued by thunder and lighting, and he rolled through a pillar of smoke that was rising from a small town square where a crowd was dispersing. Pyres with a dozen men bound to them, their bodies now nothing but grease and charcoal. The crowd stared at their feet and covered their heads with scarves and hats against the rain. Unnoticed, Jan fell from heaven, and crashed through the roof of a tavern to land. A terrible fall broken by his own body.

Shackled to the world again, the shadows by his side forced him to drink and sip at thin broth. He had a stomach, and a throat and a pair of lips. His hand was bound in rags. The air was thick with smoke and the men who appeared in the room looked exhausted, their eyes white spots lost in copper and bronzed skin. Rain dripped between the rooms, finding weak spots in the thatching overhead. Outside, the burning reeds hissed against falling rain, until what remained was neither fire nor water, but sludge or ash, and the bones that lingered would be buried in a common grave.

His wound wouldn't heal. Jan had been taken to the edge of town and pointed northward. He sat beneath an oak tree and fell asleep. Since the burning of his hand, he couldn't keep his eyes open. Weak and dizzy spells confused him. Dream images bled from the red interior of his eyelids across the world. On waking again, into the depth of the afternoon, he untied his bandages and let the cold air calm his pain. The hand was yellowish, swollen and soft. He woke steeped in rainwater. A young woman stared at him. She was holding a crooked branch, herding her cows across the grass.

Her family rented a gnarled patch of land from the Laird of Hamilton, now dead; they didn't know who to pay their taxes to. They had seen columns of fire, but hadn't known that the abbey and all of its treasures had been looted and burnt, or that the Laird's house had been ransacked, the Laird murdered by a skelf in his leg, and the Protestant rioters rounded up and martyred. They reacted to the news with smirks of disbelief, then slow nods of disinterest, as though Jan was describing a long battle between gulls and geese.

'I tripped over a cat. Fell into a fire,' Jan tried to explain his wounds. They didn't care. They left the hand in warm water until the black scabs softened, then worked into them with the point of a knife, trying to pull dirt from the wound. The skin wrinkled, and a red swelling spread beyond his wrist. They wrapped the hand in clean linen.

Next morning, Jan wanted to help with their work, so stalked the middens for hen's eggs. Collected five, cradled in the tail of his shirt. But on finding the sixth, he stood too quickly, and a wash of sedimentary blood swamped his eyes. They found him with eggs burst all across his belly. They unwrapped his bandaging. Red and blue lacework of veins pressed through the skin. There was a shade of green behind the yellow.

'Could be symbolic of new life?' Jan said to the family. They went to fetch their neighbour. A tall man with shoulders so broad that they bowed. He had worked as a tanner for many years, and his arms were stained ochre in uneven patches to the armpits, worn back to scarred pink at the elbows and fingertips. He normally helped them to slaughter cattle. The tanner took Jan's rotten arm and turned it back and forth. Then he laid his forefinger across the wrist, as if to chop.

They wound a thin leather belt a handspan down from the elbow and tightened it with a stick until Jan's skin tangled painfully into the winding. Then they tied the strapping in place and waited until the blood drained from the gory hand. They forced Jan to drink more and more beer, so his head swam and his stomach churned. Then they laid him on his front and the young woman sat on his back. His dead arm was raised to a block behind him, stained with the blood of a chicken lately killed. The tanner sharpened his hatchet.

The hand came off in one cut, and the stump was quickly staunched and bound with packed wool, and the tourniquet tightened and all kept in place with strips of an old shirt, wound one on top of the other. Jan howled and cursed, and the hand was thrown into a bucket.

The room smelled of rusting iron, and dogs bayed at the door and scratched at the hard mud underneath, attempting to burrow through. In the morning, let inside, they ran to the chopping block and licked the ground beneath.

When the tanner took the severed hand out to bury, he saw it move. A finger seemed to point at him. He quickly threw sods of dirt over the hole and denied his eyes. The ground was heavily trodden in the spring. The young woman was married to Jan. When they danced, she held her new husband by the right hand and the left elbow.

Beneath them, the severed hand tried to move toward the face it used to have. Tried to find its eyes and nose, its mouth, where the screaming and crying should be coming from. But heavy weights lay on every joint and knuckle. Cold clay soil, tight and firmly packed. The hand tried to push or pull itself up, or press against the ground and raise the old shoulders and head, but nothing moved. There was no sight or sound, but the nerve endings still flickered and sensed the old body, and images were trapped in the severed hand, memory of movements, touches, sensations and feelings.

A long time later, the clay was broken by movement overhead, the soil was being tilled, the back field where the severed hand lay was being brought back into production. How many years had passed? Recursions of the same dreams, slowly losing details, as an abandoned house loses its fittings, then its floorboards and windows and soon the slates or the thatch, and eventually all that remains are the foundation stones, buried too deep to warrant lifting. Cold currents of water broke through the clay and by stretching a thumb forward, pressing into softened soil, the severed hand began to move. Wrist scalding with memories of the dull axe, the execution. By minute movements, the hand clasped at these memories, back and forth, slowly carving out a hovel, where it could turn from side to side, and collect water that dripped into its palm. And by the freezing and evaporation of that

water, measure seasons passing by, winters and summers
going and gone. The hand pared back its fingernails by
scratching against the clay, etching as it went, drawing figures
and writing words, finding stones and painful gravel that
blocked its expression and its passage upward. It bled into
the clay, and its blood was miraculously restored.

Then the long, long years of burial, as the ground grew
heavier. When the plough passed over, the severed hand
cowered from the tremors. Expanses of time like bodies
of water, still on their surface, but woven in contradicting
currents, fast eddies and drowning pools. The immediate
impression, of weight and water, encounter with stone, cold
skin of worms passing by, quick hours of battle, brushed by
some warm creature. The severed hand longed for the body
it once had, for its twin, its other dumber hand. The one that
couldn't draw, that could only hold down the page. Together,
they could have held that being down, gripped the head and
destroyed the body, worn the fur and eaten the flesh.

Body parts were a battalion, teeth held above arms, tall
legs, tender toes, feet for stamping. Exhausted and cold, the
hand imagined lungs that gripped cold air, sweat stinging
eyes that drank darkness, and a mouth, a jaw and a set of
teeth, taught to be gentle and caring by the soft tongue that
yelped when bitten, all held in a bag, a taut sack of skin.
All of these battling creatures, lashed together, how had it
ever worked? The warm being lay dead beside the severed
hand, and its blood slowly cooled as the hand burrowed out
of the tunnels the creature had made and hid there as eras
passed overhead and the only notice came by an elm's roots,
that very slowly spindled downward and cradled the severed
hand. It meant to move away, out of the grip, but didn't,
and thicker roots entangled with thin and soon the elm
was a world for the severed hand to move through, shifting

patiently through the centuries, drifting in the slow erosion of the earth.

Enlisted in battles of beetles versus ants, driven into a nest like an elephant let loose in Rome. Taken into warm companionship by a hare, whose babies had been eaten in a night of dark sacrifice by an old farm dog whose instincts had suddenly surfaced, and who returned to the elm tree some nights to gloat, or atone for the guilt it almost felt, and the severed hand was pulled into the hare's warren and cared for. With thumbnail and fingernail, the severed hand, languageless, remembered and traced images, sacred things from its book. Until the grand elm threatened a great lump of stone, and was dismembered and split, cut at the head, torso, then knees and roots wrenched loose, and rain fell on the severed hand again. So it mimed, and pointed and twisted around. Moved in idiotic repetition of old gestures, like a dreaming dog, leg twitching in anticipation of rolling fields of grass long since gone. Lit by no light, and breathed upon by no wind, encountering no image and no inner tide, circled by no moon and no sun. The severed hand reached out as though to grasp for something, desperate to cover the mouth it no longer had, and stop the ears it couldn't find, and close the eyes it didn't have.

CHAPTER TWENTY

None of the bundled flowers seemed big enough, so Gillis had bought two of the largest, unfurled the plastic wrapping and tried to bunch them together. Now no longer conical, the plastic and paper had torn and slipped around until it barely held its shape. In the jostling of the short car journey to the hospital, the elastic bands which bound the stalks together had snapped, and flowers were beginning to slip from both ends of the wrapping. The colours and heights of the flowers clashed and here Gillis discovered that floristry, yet another skill which he had assumed more or less didn't exist, actually *was* real and made some kind of difference.

'First hour's free. Is it? Or is the first hour a pound, and a pound every hour after that?' Gillis's dad didn't have his glasses, and couldn't make out the signage for the hospital car park.

Visiting hours were just starting, and the foyer was busy with confused family members trying to follow signs and coloured lines from the floors to the walls, to distant corridors and far-flung wards. Gillis hid in the little newsagent and gift shop which sat on the bottom floor. Flicked through a running magazine until he had calmed down. He found a comic to give to Jamie, and borrowed some sellotape from the cashier. They tried to repair his bouquet.

'I'd get a new one, mate,' the cashier tried to help. Pointed him across the way, to a competing gift shop which sold that kind of thing. Gillis wasn't listening. There was a greenfly crawling over his hand.

The blue line took him down a corridor and out of the main building, under a canopy which sheltered a half-dozen abandoned wheelchairs. There was a man with bright yellow skin standing outside Dermatology in his dressing gown, talking to his ex-wife on the phone. Asking her to bring his daughter along to see him. 'I know she hates the skin thing,' he said. 'D'you think I like looking at it?'

The children's ward was decorated with a weird bestiary of monkeys and snakes, giraffes and elephants all wearing odd and ill-fitting pieces of clothing. Multiple bowler hats, colourful jackets, braces and bow ties, they were eating big dinners and riding bikes, but something in the way that the eyes had been drawn made their mischief come across more like panic. But they were colourful and they were smiling.

'Here to see What's-his-name. . .' As he faced the nurses' station his mind went blank. 'Him that got hit by lightning.'

'I take it you're not family.'

While one nurse sighed and walked away from her seat at the computer, the other explained the rules. Safeguarding and all that. 'You could be anybody.'

But Gillis was no longer just anybody. He had a profile on social media, and he tried to show her it. But her colleague soon returned, and in her wake, Rachel in her work clothes. Black skirt and black top and black shoes, hair pinned up at her crown. She lifted her hand in greeting, then lowered her head as she walked the length of the ward.

'Yeah, I know him.' She thanked the nurses and took Gillis by the elbow. Walked him away from the children's ward, to a big window which overlooked the car park. He could see his dad's motor; the door was open, and his dad was swinging his arms around. Berating a parking attendant and trying to show him the chit in his hand.

'These are for you.' Pieces of the fresh sellotape had unfurled due to the watery stalks, and ended up stuck to his jacket. She took the bouquet in hand and he stepped back to untangle himself. 'Just to say sorry for everything. Who would have thought that what happened would have happened?'

'Nobody's blaming you.'

That stopped Gillis short. Hadn't it been his great confrontation? The end of his story. Hadn't a sacred hand been pointing at him the whole time? 'Well, I would blame me.'

She looked confused. 'Why?'

'That lightning bolt was probably meant for me. But it must have missed. But then you think. . . why would God miss? And then you have to think, maybe I should just stop trying to work it out. Let what happened happen. The whole scheme's sort of. . . written in the sky or something.'

'I'd keep that kind of talk to yourself.' She buried her head in the flowers and drew in a deep breath. Sighed and drew in another. When she surfaced, she had a few greenflies on her jacket and one crawling through her hair.

'They're real,' Gillis insisted. He had taken a seat next to Jamie's bed, and Rachel was cramming his flowers into the neck of a glass jug which had a remnant of orange diluting juice at the bottom. At a small sink between the beds, she struggled to fold the flowers and crook the jug beneath the tap.

'I know, I just can't smell them.' She tried again. The flowers seemed to have no scent.

'Maybe they take the smell out, for allergic people.'

Rachel doubted that.

'See what the minister brought you?' She set the flowers on the bedside cabinet and returned to the imprint she had left on one side of the bedsheets. Jamie was jammed on the other side with felt tips scattered across his knees, a sketchbook folded over, dozens of colourful drawings hidden inside.

'There's this as well.' The comic had been wrinkled by the watery flowers, and now that Gillis looked at the boy, he suspected it was too young for him. Jamie seemed worn beyond his years.

'He won't say *thank you*, but if he could, he would say thank you.'

'You're welcome.' Gillis tried to catch the boy's eyes, but they were fixed on the papers he was grinding a pen through.

'I saw the kirkyard. It was all empty. Did you manage to finish the. . . the thingwy?' He didn't want to say *funeral*, or mention Douglas, the body, or the coffin. He had often imagined the crowd traipsing home.

'The what?'

'You know, your function? In the hall. The kirk hall.'

Rachel covered Jamie's ears and tried to whisper. 'They've got him in a freezer. They're not charging us. Seeing as the circumstances. . .' She trailed off, and began to comb the boy's hair with her fingers. 'I think we'll end up cremating him again.'

The cards which surrounded the bed all said, *To a Brave Boy, For Our Little Hero, To a Special Fighter.*

'Everyone says it was a miracle, don't they?' She tried to turn the boy's head toward her. 'Know how I know it wasn't one?' She pushed Jamie to sit forward, and pulled at his armpits until he raised his hands. Then she lifted his jumper. A rootlike pattern had been burnt into his skin. She traced across his back and up to his neck. 'It sort of pours out of his head. Into his hand.' She pulled back his left cuff. The scarring travelled down his inside elbow, splayed across the wrist and over the back of his thumb, into his forefinger.

'That's his drawing hand,' Gillis noticed.

'It's all he wants to do now.' She tugged at his jumper and obediently, Jamie sat himself back and pulled his legs to his chest. He hid his sheaf of papers behind his knees and Gillis reached forward, trying to tilt the papers down. Hoping to see what was drawn there. But the boy dug his feet into the bed, and gripped the paper until it tore a little. A furious expression distorted his face, eyebrows and mouth steeply crooked as though all of his features were being pulled toward a point in the middle of his forehead.

'He's not wanting to show you,' Rachel laid a protective hand over the boy. 'He keeps them to himself. Don't you?' She turned to point at the drawer of his cabinet, where dozens of pages were sticking out from the top. 'He used to be a scribbler, really. But I think with everything that's happened, something's inspired him.'

Jamie tried to worm under the blankets, but Gillis, seeing Rachel's back turned, tried for the paper again, and this time managed to grip the top and wrench the drawing from the boy's hand. Jamie's head pulled up and he stared at Gillis.

On the paper, an image of a man drowning, with a smaller man standing on the eyeball.

'Oh, he's showing you after all, that's good.' Rachel sounded a little surprised as she turned back to them and leant across to look at the drawing. 'His skills are really coming on.'

'Is he copying something?'

'He just comes out with things.' Rachel coaxed the papers from her son and began to sift them from hand to hand, laying the best ones on the bed. Leaves and fruits and animals, hands open and closed and bodies twisted into hierarchies, sovereign blotches reining over a sea of dashed lines, levelled and inverted on the page next to it. Faces that appeared only to contort into seascapes or scraps of nonsense, bundled kindling for a future fire. Gillis tried to use his new-fangled phone to take a picture, but the intuitive design wasn't intuitive enough, the icons and colours baffled him and his thumb refused to swipe the screen correctly. He lost himself in the wrong app, and Rachel pulled all the drawings back together in a bundle and returned them to her son.

'I just chuck them,' she admitted. 'He makes too many to keep up. All my cupboards are covered already.'

'You have to save them,' Gillis said. 'It's important.'

'Why?'

Gillis still didn't have an answer to that question. 'He'll want the memories, when he's older.'

The boy's eyes had been fixed on Gillis's head, and when Rachel rose to speak to the nurse, Gillis met them and in silence they stared at one another. There was something lacking in the boy, his gaze wasn't hostile or friendly, it wasn't warm or cold, wasn't curious or incurious, it was just a stare. Gillis remembered his own boyhood. They thought he was very serious. They wanted him to smile. They asked, *Where's the old Gillis gone?* At some point, he had been very cheerful. Before language. Before solid food. He stared at Jamie and began to compare himself. The boy had so many advantages. He had the early biography of a saint or a prophet. Or if things went badly, an artist, or killer. The wee man had his life before him. Twenty-odd years to develop, already set apart by his scarring, already excused from daily life by his injuries. Already undertaking a strange vow of silence. Already stricken with a father whose body could not be buried or burnt. But which returned and returned, over and over again. For the first time, Gillis supposed that the lightning strike had been correct. Heaven's mandate had passed to the boy.

He turned away from the empty eyes and focused on the linoleum floor. The greenish curtains that concealed the other patients. The bristling strip lights. He felt that all this time he had been entered in the wrong category, running right from the starting gun in the wrong direction and now, having covered a marathon or two, was left hoping that some dutiful official could find him and point him in the right direction. Not knowing if he was winning or losing or even competing in anything, the memory of the starting pistol had grown distant, the hope of a finish line was swiftly diminishing. Gillis, always second or third, had begun to strain to place fifth, lag to sixth and seventh, and suspected that eventually, when all the scores were finally tallied, he would come in dead last.

A rattling trolley was beginning to round the wards, a brace of student doctors following a man around Gillis's age.

'You know they specialize,' Rachel returned from the nurses' station with a fresh jug of diluting juice, 'really early on. Children are practically a separate species to regular people.'

'Is that right? Funny how they all become human. . . isn't it?' He was staring at the boy. 'No one thinks to go and be something else.'

She rolled her eyes, exasperated by whatever he was trying to say. 'Look, Gillis. Thanks for coming and I'm sorry I didn't get a chance to visit you when you were in. . . you know, in hospital. . . but the doctor's making his rounds now, so. . .'

'Oh, you want me to leave. Yes, absolutely.' Gillis stood and patted the boy vaguely on the head, then followed Rachel away from Jamie's bed. He stole some glances at her as they walked side by side to the doors of the ward. 'What's your weekend like?' he suddenly asked.

Rachel stopped. She looked at him intently. 'Sorry to be blunt,' she said. 'But is that it over? You're not going to scale the building? You're not going to run off with someone's leg?'

He couldn't promise anything. So didn't. 'We could go somewhere.'

'The cinema?' The way she said it, made it sound ridiculous. 'Bowling? Eating dinner.'

'What's wrong with that? That's what people do.'

'And we're people, are we?'

'We're people.'

'You're a person?' she squinted at him. There was a question behind the question, and a question behind that.

'I'm a person.'

She looked at his shoes, his trousers, his belt buckle, his shirt and jacket, his clean-shaven jaw, the nick on his cheek and the greenfly crawling through his hair. She reached out and brushed it away. 'Maybe,' is all she finally said, before she left and went back to her son.

He turned as he reached the very end of the corridor. Rachel, in the distance, framed by the bright window, and the boy at his drawings, producing untidy mysteries that would no doubt be thrown in the bin. He walked quicker and quicker down the linoleum, following the blue line back through a covered walkway, picking through abandoned wheelchairs, almost jogging past the gift shop, through the foyer, slowing for the sliding doors, until he hit the cold air; and following a sudden instinct, immediately turned a sharp right, away from the car park. Away from the car idling in the distance, and the life that backed it up. His childhood bedroom and the struggle to find work, and the effort it took to seem serious and sensible and iron his shirt every morning and wash his clothes every week.

Round the back of the hospital, great bucket bins and loading docks for deliveries, chain-link fences and barbed wire and streams of plastic tangled with blue paper towel, all abandoned in the mess, and a hole in the fencing where someone could fit if they really wanted to. Then pine trees and waist-high grass and thistle. The distant hills of Kirkmouth. He could have run out to them and strained himself to the very limit, digging, scraping with his fingernails until he found the severed hand and brought it to that good and happy ending which had once been demanded. But he was standing still. And he turned back to face the car park.

There was nowhere to go. And nothing to be done. It was better to go back and sit in the passenger seat. Travel home and revise his CV. Learn to talk intelligently about his experiences. Explain away his years working for the Church. Find gainful employment, and work toward a decent salary. Enough to rent a little flat. Look into assuming some responsibility. Have a little family. Eventually. A wife and child. What would make a happier ending than a marriage? He pushed back through the fence. That's how things end. Marriages. Deaths.

He would let himself be photographed and filmed and described online by people he loved. He would sit quietly in the background of a family. Behave himself. Re-train. Save his money. Buy flowers and birthday cards. Say *thank you* for things. Go and visit his mother. Get himself back in the good books.

He pushed his hands into his armpits and stamped back and forth. He would marry Rachel. Or he would try to anyway, if she'd have him. Maybe he'd adopt the boy. And not that he wasn't nice, but he would have to learn to be nice. And not that he wasn't kind, but he would have to learn to be kinder. And not that he wasn't patient, but he would have to strain his patience to breaking point. He realized, maybe for the first time, that he would turn thirty-five soon, and then forty and forty-five, and fifty and fifty-five, on and on until he would keel over and die, and he had to not care. Go grey, then bald, then wither. Go the distance in the good fight, run the good race. Work himself to gristle. That would be something. A good and normal life.

But now that he'd imagined it, he felt as though he was holding it in his hands, and it might be pawned or traded or sold for something better. He thought again of the boy, and his strange drawings. He could be good for him. He could guide him. Make something of him. An example. A terror. A plague on this country. Speak until he could speak. There's greater compassion, Gillis thought. There's greater kindness. There's a greater kind of sacrifice. Like every former champion, he'd become a coach or a manager. Was the cruelty of a trainer really any kind of cruelty at all? If it made something important. He'd research, he'd formulate strategies, he'd think things through.

If he couldn't be King David, he could be Samuel. If he couldn't be Moses, he would be Aaron. If he couldn't win then he'd find a way of winning while losing. He'd find a way to cheat. He would guide them. They wouldn't dig up the severed hand. They'd wait. They'd watch the sky, they'd watch the TV and newspapers. They'd pay attention to their dreams. A signal would come. They'd go in the middle of the night. Gillis would know what to do. They'd have worked it all out. He knew it. He just had to wait. Something would happen.

ACKNOWLEDGEMENTS

Without the guidance of my friend Nicholas Stewart this book couldn't have been written. And without the help of Calum Barnes it never would have been published.

Thanks to Camilla Grudova, Ian Macbeth, Neil Scott and James Roxburgh, all of whom read earlier, longer versions, and Mary Chamberlain, who copy-edited this one.